Nominations due: August 25, 2025
http://bit.ly/SohoPressIN

Nominations due: October 1, 2025
http://bit.ly/SohoPressLR

MW01200436

THE RED SCARE MURDERS

CON LEHANE

SOHO CRIME

Published in 2025 by
Soho Press, Inc.
227 W 17th Street
New York, NY 10011
www.sohopress.com

Library of Congress Cataloging-in-Publication Data

TK

ISBN 978-1-64129-720-2
eISBN 978-1-64129-721-9
Interior design by Janine Agro, Soho Press, Inc.

Printed in the United States of America

10 9 8 7 6 5 4 3 2 1

EU Responsible Person (for authorities only)
eucomply OÜ
Pärnu mnt 139b-14
11317 Tallinn, Estonia
hello@eucompliancepartner.com
www.eucompliancepartner.com

Dedi TK

CHAPTER ONE

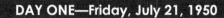

MIDAFTERNOON

You know what a witch hunt is? It's when a big lie declaring someone anathema to the prevailing orthodoxy gets a head of steam—think back to Salem, Massachusetts, 250 years ago and the prevailing orthodoxy then, Calvinism. In a nutshell, Calvinists believed all humans, except for them, were depraved sinners. A guy in the neighborhood would see someone—a woman—not following the orthodoxy. She might have walked differently; she might have dressed differently; she might have talked differently. First one person noticed; then, someone backed him up. Next thing, the church sexton said he saw her riding by on a broom.

Pretty soon, everyone agreed that—say her name was Sadie—everyone agreed, knew for a fact, that Sadie was a witch. Some of the accusers might have believed they saw what they said they saw; other accusers decided it must be true because folks said it was true; the rest of the folks went along because Sadie being a witch was now part of the orthodoxy. So the whole town got together and stoned Sadie to death.

And pity the poor bastard, too, who dared to question the orthodoxy. "Maybe it wasn't a witch you saw, Sam," the guy might have said. "The moonlight can play tricks on you. You see a weather vane silhouetted against the moon and it looks like someone flying by on a broom . . ."

"Don't listen to that son of a bitch," the keepers of the orthodoxy would have said. "He's one of 'em, too. Hang the bastard along with the rest."

Well, that was what was going on around me—had been going on since soon after we came home from the war. It wasn't witches run afoul of the orthodoxy this time. It was Communists—and anyone who looked like a Communist or might be friends with a Communist or might have a friend who had a friend who might be a Communist. Anti-Communism was the new orthodoxy, spearheaded by J. Edgar Hoover, Joe McCarthy, the House Un-American Activities Committee, and their fellow travelers.

I was thinking about these goings on because I'd gotten a call from Larry Dennis that morning. He'd been calling me every other day—each time more desperate—since about a month ago, when a pamphlet from a right-wing scandal sheet hit the street. *Red Channels: The Report of Communist Influence in Radio and Television* named him and 150 other poor souls in the radio and TV business as Communists. Larry, whom I'd known from my Hollywood days and who'd been an actor on a radio comedy show here in New York since the war ended, was fired a week after the report came out.

The first time he called he wanted me to tell him it was okay to name names. Before I could tell him anything, he said, "I can't give them any fucking names . . . I don't know who's a Communist and who isn't. I never paid attention to that shit. Trotskyites, Shachtmanites, Browderites, Communists, Socialists, who cares? I wanted to stop the Fascists in Spain. That made me a Communist?"

What he wanted me to do the next time he called, since I was a private eye, was track down some Reds the witch hunters didn't know about, so he could give the FBI a couple of names to prove he was loyal. "I'll give them the names, sign the fucking loyalty oath. I don't care if I can't live with myself; my kids gotta eat; they gotta have a roof over their heads."

Since I nixed that, his latest plan was for me to find Party members who were informers so he could turn them in. That way he could prove he was loyal and he wouldn't hurt anyone except for double-crossing rats.

When I told him I didn't know any, he said it was okay; he couldn't afford to pay me anyway. I knew he didn't call about hiring me for any job. His life had gone down the drain because he'd run afoul of the orthodoxy. He was bewildered and scared and needed someone to talk to who understood. That was me.

This morning he'd called to tell me he'd been fired again, this time from a job as a waiter in a joint the network crowd frequented. "The owner got a message from the purity police at the network that if he continued to employ a Communist, freedom-loving Americans would boycott the place. The owner took pity on me—I got kids to feed—so he's letting me work in the back of the house as a dishwasher. Minimum wage. No tips. Last month, I was making three hundred bucks a week. Now I'm making thirty." He screamed like a mad man. "I can't take it, Mick. What am I gonna do? . . . Mick, can I give them your name?"

"Sure," I said. "What else can they do to me?"

This was the state of things—the country awash in patriotic jingoism like The Red Menace, Better Dead than Red, America: Love It or Leave It . . . and a guy who only wanted to make people laugh and to feed his kids was coming apart at the seams, losing his grip over whether he should ruin some innocent people's lives so he could try to salvage his own— when the phone rang.

"Mick Mulligan, private eye," I said.

"I have a job for you," Duke Rogowski, president of the United Taxi and Limousine Drivers, said in return. "Be at my office in an hour."

Duke wasn't as big a deal labor leader as he thought he was. He wasn't John L. Lewis or Sidney Hillman. He wasn't even Mike Quill or Joe Curran, and certainly not Harry Bridges. But he liked to act like a commander of the working class and give orders.

"I'll take a look at my calendar," I said.

Duke chuckled and hung up.

Fuck him. He knew damn well I didn't have anything on my calendar.

I chucked the newspaper I'd been reading into the waste basket. I'd already worked my way through the *Daily News* and the *Daily Worker* as I did most days and was glancing through the *World-Telegram* when Duke's call interrupted me.

The news of the day, as it was on most days that summer, consisted of stories about the Korean War, the Atomic Bomb—should the US use it in Korea, as some bright-eyed proponents of mass murder would have it? Was the Soviet Union going to drop one on us if we didn't drop one on them first?—the perfidy of the Red Army in Eastern Europe, Russian spies in the US, Communist traitors, striking workers, and rising prices.

The orthodoxy, including the newspapers, by and large, supported the Korean War, were willing to give serious thought to dropping the A-bomb on North Korea or Russia, were outraged by the Red Army enslaving the nations of Eastern Europe, foursquare in favor of the Marshall Plan, and on the lookout for Reds under every bed.

On this particular day, the papers complained about Harry Bridges, head of the west coast longshoremen's union. The defenders of freedom were out to get Bridges because J. Edgar Hoover said he was a Communist. Bridges said he wasn't a Communist. He liked the Soviet Union, opposed the Korean War, and didn't throw the Commies out of the union when the CIO told him to. He walked like a Red and quacked like a Red, so for the newspapers he was a Red.

Interestingly enough, this was the reasoning—I went to meetings with Communists, I ate lunch with Communists, I agreed with Communists on certain things—that got me fired from my job as a cartoonist (we liked to call ourselves animators) at the Disney studio, won me a place on the Hollywood blacklist, and brought me back to New York City, where I hung out my shingle as a private investigator.

Well, bygones were bygones and the news of the day didn't care what I thought of it, so, weathering the hot and muggy afternoon, I hoofed it down to Duke's office. Mine was on Ninth Avenue at Forty-Ninth Street above a floor-tile shop. To be honest, it was more of a storage space than a real office, but it had its own door from the street, a plate glass window in front, and a window in back big enough that a small dog might fit through.

As I was leaving, my landlord stopped me. Herb was a former college professor who ran afoul of the thought police and now laid tile for a living in the new apartment buildings being built on the east side.

"Two men wearing suits came by looking for you yesterday. They didn't say who they were but you can be sure they were the you-know-whos looking for you to rat on someone. I told them you were in church. I imagine they'll be back."

"Fuck 'em." Usually, the FBI agents would whisper in the landlord's ear that he has a Red for a tenant hoping he'd evict you. Since Herb and I were of the same ilk, they didn't try it with him.

On my walk downtown, I stopped at the newsstand at Thirty-Fourth Street. Irv, the newsie, was a vet who got the stand from the city by virtue of leaving most of his right leg behind in the war. He carried the *Daily Worker*, so I threw him a couple of nickels twice a day. I got Stalin's view of the world in the morning from the *Daily Worker* and William Randolph Hearst's recap in the evening from the *Journal-American*.

The taxi drivers' union hall on Twenty-Third Street was across from the Chelsea Hotel above a greengrocer. On this lazy, late afternoon, the curb in front was lined with cabs, mostly Checkers and a few DeSotos. A sign above the door next to the grocery read, THE AMALGAMATED UNION OF TAXI, LIVERY, LIMOUSINE DRIVERS, AND ALLIED WORKERS, LOCAL 1299.

The lengthy moniker was more a wish than a reality. The AUTLD wasn't fully a union yet because they hadn't won recognition from the fleet owners. The most interesting piece of the name, though, was "Amalgamated," which meant Local 1299 was put together by combining a few other unions into one larger and, they hoped, more powerful entity. Therein, as they say, lay the rub.

Labor unions had tried more than once since the '30s to organize cab drivers and struck out each time. Hackies were a maverick breed: stubborn and cynical, mistrustful of everyone including each other; they were also angry—always and at everyone. I was reminded of this by the two drivers blowing their horns and leaning out their windows cursing at each other while they tried to get into the same parking spot in front of the union hall.

As I started up the stairs, a couple of drivers came trudging down. Their grim expressions and hollow stares put me in mind of a pair of worn-out, angry, and depressed GIs coming in after a night on patrol. Maybe these guys remembered battles that lay behind them; more likely they were gearing up for the one that lay in front of them. Duke was drawing up plans for a citywide cab strike to win recognition for the union. The last time the cabbies struck, it was war on the streets and sidewalks of New York.

The door to Duke's office was open and he sat behind his scarred wooden desk. Behind him, two tall, skinny loft-type windows looked down at Twenty-Third Street and across at the red bricks and black railings of the Chelsea Hotel. The union's two vice presidents—who'd come on as part of the package with two of the unions amalgamated into Local 1299—sat glowering at Duke. They headed up two factions: Sol Rosen from the Communists; Vincent Forlini from the Mob. There was a chair for me.

"Grab a beer out of the icebox, one for me too," Duke bellowed loud enough I could have heard him back in my office. "It's Friday afternoon."

Duke was a bombastic, bear-like guy and had a voice that went with his build. He'd been anointed to keep the warring factions of the amalgamated union from each other's throats. The first time I'd met him, the man introducing us said, "Duke, I don't think you know Mick Mulligan." "Of course, I do," said Duke, reaching out with his outfielder's-mitt-size hand to pump mine. "How you been, pal?" And then onto the next guy. I'd never seen Duke before in my life.

I grabbed the beers, opened them with the church key hanging on a string next to the icebox, and handed Duke his. The two VPs—one tall and slim, the other short and dumpy, both in shirtsleeves, ties loosened, top shirt buttons undone— weren't invited to join us.

Duke glanced at the VPs before focusing on me. "Gil said you could take a look at Harold's case and maybe come up with something to get him off. His bozo lawyer screwed up the trial. Anybody with half a brain knows Harold was framed." He paused to glance at each of us again, one at a time. The dumpy guy made a noise like he might say something until Duke glared him into silence.

I however did say something—blurted out something would be more like it. "You want me to take on Harold's case now!? I might come up with something!? Two weeks, Duke! Two fucking weeks! What am I supposed to come up with in two fucking weeks? You and Gil are both nuts."

The Gil in question was Gil Silver, the hotshot criminal

lawyer I did most of my work for, who also took on civil liberties cases when he was of a mind to.

I put my beer can on the floor next to me, took out a smoke and lit it. No one spoke. Harold Williams's trial had ended nearly a year before—and Duke waited until now to call me? My guess was the pressure on him to do something got too heavy, so now he wanted to look like he was taking Harold's case seriously.

He knew I needed the work. He also knew that no business and not many unions in the city would touch a Red-baited cartoonist-turned-private eye with a ten-foot pole, so he'd offer me a job no PI in his right mind would take.

Ignoring my outburst, he spoke calmly; his eyes narrowed a bit but weren't red and raging. He was noted for bellowing at his adversaries and stomping in or out of places when he needed to. But he was always under control.

"No one said it would be easy . . . You got a working stiff charged with killing his boss. Somebody got to pay for that. A Negro charged with killing a white man. Some places he'd a been lynched by now. Next, everybody knows he's a card-carrying Communist." Duke held up three fingers. "That's three strikes already. Only thing he's missing is being a faggot."

The Harold we were talking about, a rank-and-file leader of the union's organizing campaign, was at the moment sitting on death row in Sing Sing. He might or might not have been railroaded on a murder charge. The Commies said he had been. They'd thrown up picket lines and held protest rallies during his trial, but not so many as they might have. This was because every Red and fellow traveler in town had been busy picketing the federal courthouse in Foley Square where the leadership of the CP was on trial, charged with advocating the violent overthrow of the government.

At the time, like everyone else, I didn't pay as much attention as I might have to his trial. I was at the Foley Square courthouse as part of Gil Silver's legal team, though all I did was draw cartoons of the proceedings that I gave to the *Daily Worker.*

To make its case against the Reds, the prosecutors in what was known as the Smith Act trial brought in a parade of stooges and finks who told the jury what the prosecutors wanted them to hear. The Commies' defense was simple enough: They claimed they didn't advocate the violent overthrow of the government. Yet to get this simple idea across they spent ten months explaining in painfully exacting detail to the judge and jury the basic tenets of Marxism-Leninism.

The—not surprisingly—unsympathetic judge ruled the Reds out of order just about every time one of them opened his mouth, charged them with contempt of court on a daily basis, and at one point jailed a couple of the defendants for the duration of the trial. When it came to the verdict, the judge threw the whole passel of would-be revolutionaries, including their lawyers, into the slammer. The Party leaders got five years. The lawyers—except for Gil, who had washed his hands of the whole affair and left by the side door before the fireworks began—got six months for contempt.

Meanwhile, in a courthouse not far away, a cabbie named Harold Williams had been convicted of first-degree murder and sentenced to death. The facts of Harold's case were these. Irwin Johnson, the owner of the cab company where Harold worked, had been killed in the cab company offices above the taxi garage. His body was discovered by an office boy arriving early for work on a Monday morning nearly a year and a half ago. The medical examiner estimated the victim had been dead since the previous Friday night. A few hours after the body was found, an anonymous caller phoned the cops and gave them the medallion number of a taxicab and said that in the trunk they'd find evidence connected to Johnson's murder.

When the cops pulled the cab over, they found Johnson's wallet and watch plus a hundred something dollars in cash—and a gun—where the caller said it would be, in the trunk of the cab Harold was driving. A month before the murder, he'd led a wildcat strike against the cab company, causing, a number of people said, bad blood between him and Johnson.

It might be Harold didn't kill his boss, and maybe with time and luck I could prove he hadn't. The problem for me—and a worse problem for Harold—was that he was scheduled to die in the electric chair on August 4 at 10:00 P.M.; this gave me fifteen days, counting this one that was mostly over, to prove he didn't do it.

I could think of a hundred reasons not to take the case. Choosing a Communist accused of anything for my first client wasn't going to win me any new business. If I did what I set out to do and got him off, what did I accomplish in the eyes of the world? I put a godless Communist back on the street. If, on the other hand, I failed to prove him innocent, he'd die in the electric chair. How would I feel if that were the fruits of my labor?

Injustice was everywhere; I could take my pick. It didn't have to be this one. But I'd learned at my pop's knee that the working man got the short end of the stick at every turn.

The old man fought for people the rest of society thought weren't worth caring about. I wouldn't say everything about him rubbed off on me, but enough had.

Harold needed help, and it wasn't likely anyone else would step up. Duke was asking me to try to set things right and he'd pay me to do it. Even if I didn't trust Duke's motives—as far as I could see, he was hiring me to get the Reds off his back—I knew when I got through arguing with myself I'd take the job.

"I'm sure you had your reasons, Duke. But I wish you hadn't waited so long."

He directed a reproachful glance at the VPs, who shifted uneasily and shot withering glances at each other. "We had disagreements about what to do before I talked to Gil."

"You got anything to help me get started, something new the cops don't know about? Somebody wants to talk now didn't want to talk before?"

Duke shook his head. A big guy with a big head, he was leaning on his arms on his desk, so when he lifted his head and ponderously moved it from side to side, it was like watching a bull rolling his neck before he charged at you. "That's why we're hiring you. You're the private eye."

I turned to the two VPs, who regarded me blankly. "Two weeks. He goes to the chair in two weeks. You got anything to . . . ?" They looked at the ceiling. Duke's roar rattled the window panes behind him. "You tied up with other work? You got clients lined up out the door? I'm giving you a fucking job. What're you complaining about?"

I clammed up. I didn't like being bullied any more than the next guy, but I'd been knocked on my ass enough times recently for my pride to take a back seat when I might at other times had stood up. "Thirty dollars a day plus expenses. A week's expenses in advance."

The two vice presidents stood, nodded as if they'd done something useful, and left without a word. Duke went to a safe next to the small refrigerator that held the beer and bent to work the combination. When he stood, he handed me two twenties and a ten, then went to his desk. He wrote something down and handed me the piece of paper.

"This is Harold's mother's address. Go talk to her as soon as you can. She's been on my ass for months. Right after the trial, she started, like a bulldog. Now it's every other day she calls. And she ain't got a phone; she calls from the candy store down the street. God knows what she'd do if she had a phone. Tell her you're working for me and you'll get Harold off." He lowered his voice as if to speak confidentially. "If I was you, I wouldn't give her your phone number."

Before he said anything else—if he was going to—the office door opened and an attractive woman walked in. She didn't actually walk in; she swept in like she might be entering a grand ballroom instead of a seedy office. Wearing a tailored, off-white linen suit you'd see in Saks Fifth Avenue's window and a white pillbox hat, she wasn't so much haughty as aloof; not rude but focused, I told myself so as not to take offense at her ignoring me.

She looked past me like I might be part of the furniture. "Let's go," she said to Duke. "We're late."

Duke remembered his manners. "Cynthia, Mick Mulligan. Mick, my wife Cynthia." When she gave me the once-over, I felt like the hired help. A bit beyond the first blush of youth, she was the sort of dame you'd see at Club 21 on the arm of a banker. Not the wife you'd expect for a lunch-box sort of guy like Duke. Not someone who'd have any interest in meeting a down-on-his-luck shamus, either, though she didn't make up her mind about me right off once she looked at me. What might have given her pause was my suit.

"You're not a cab driver, Mr. Mulligan. What business are you in?" Her dazzling green eyes engaged mine.

"I like to think I'm a finder of lost souls," I told her.

A slight lift of her eyebrow. "Is that why you're meeting with my husband?"

"You'll have to ask him. My business relationships are confidential."

"How mysterious." Her smile was tight lipped. "I'll make Duke tell me all about you." She turned to her husband. "We should go."

Duke walked with me to the door. "Check with me in a couple of days." The last thing I caught was a glance from Cynthia that suggested she might not be through with me.

As I was leaving, Sol Rosen, the Commie VP, stuck his head out of the office next to Duke's and gestured for me to come in. I did and he closed the door behind me, putting his hand lightly on my shoulder to direct me to a chair in front of his desk. He stood straight and had a courteous, almost courtly, manner.

"There's a fellow who works out of Harold's garage," he said when he'd taken a seat behind his desk. "Frank DeMarco. He's the lead organizer for Manhattan and Queens. Talk to him."

"Anything else you can tell me?"

Rosen appraised me. His gaze was piercing, yet his manner was reassuring; like a doctor whose confidence made you feel you'd be all better soon. "I want to talk to Gil Silver before I decide what I should tell you."

"You can ask me about me." I met his gaze, hoping mine was as piercing; I didn't like people treating me like I was the kid and Gil the grown-up.

He chuckled; it was disarming, like the pat on the shoulder. "We'll have lunch after I talk with Gil." His expression became more intense. "One thing I'll tell you: Watch out for Forlini; he didn't want us to reopen Harold's case."

I thanked Sol Rosen for his concern about my welfare, recollecting as I did that he was no pushover himself, having fought in Spain and then in the Pacific during WWII, having come of age in steel mills before leading striking packinghouse workers in battles against the bosses, scabs, and the Chicago police in the thirties.

Standing in front of the greengrocer's getting my bearings, as they say, I watched Duke and his wife walk toward Seventh Avenue. Duke looked to be half a step off the pace, hurrying as if he might get left behind if he didn't.

While I watched them, Vincent Forlini sidled up beside me. "I saw you was talking to Rosen. Listen to him and he'll lead you off a cliff." He lowered his voice. "What'd he tell you?"

"He gave me a contact at the garage where Harold worked." I shifted to a more balanced stance and took my hands out of my pockets as you do when you sense the guy you're talking to might be trouble.

"He say anything about me?" Forlini spoke softly; you might think giving a few words of friendly advice. Yet his tone had an edge to it like a muted growl.

"He said I should be nice to you."

"Bullshit." Forlini moved closer to me, too close. "Let me tell you somethin'. The jig killed the guy. That's it. The Reds …" I could feel his hot breath on my neck. "You know Rosen's a Red, right? The Commies got Duke to hire you because they're sucking up to the niggers. That's all. Williams was a Red, so they gotta do somethin' or the coloreds'll figure out the Commies are full of shit. Which they are. Full of shit."

"Thanks for the tip." I don't suppose my tone came across as warm and cuddly either. Men like Forlini reminded me of punks I came across in the army. With most guys, when you got stuck on KP, you felt a kind of kinship, solidarity—the job stinks; we're in this together. You shared a smoke if you had one. Guys like Forlini came with a chip on their shoulder, sizing you up to see if they could get over on you.

He read my tone and his eyes went dark. "If you're smart, you go through the motions and make a few bucks for yourself. Somethin' comes up, bring it to me. I got a lot of connections. Ask your boss." He was referring to Gil, and I didn't like that he called him my boss. I'm my boss. I do work for Gil; I don't work for him.

I watched Forlini lumber off toward Eighth Avenue. He shot his cuffs a couple of times, yet because he was short and dumpy and walked like a goon, he came off like a guy wearing someone else's expensive suit.

Too many hoods like Forlini had wormed their way into the labor movement in the city—on the docks, in the trucking industry, in the garment district, in the hotels and restaurants. They'd muscled into the company board rooms also. But you didn't hear about that.

Forlini used to run what purported to be a union—Local

5—that had a few sweetheart contracts with small taxi garages, the contracts serving to funnel graft money to the Mob. When the amalgamation took place, Duke brought Forlini in because he didn't want to fight the Mob for the Local 5 garages. He made a similar deal with Sol Rosen for the garages the Commies had organized; that's how he got his two VPs.

No one had told me Forlini or his pals killed Irwin Johnson and framed Harold Williams, and I wasn't saying even to myself that they had. It was something I'd look into. Meanwhile, I had to start somewhere.

A few cabs nestled against the curb at the makeshift stand in front of the union hall and three or four of their drivers had gathered around the front fender of a DeSoto arguing about whether Stan Musial should have gotten the National League MVP the year before instead of Jackie Robinson. I lit a smoke and joined them, offering the pack around.

To get my feet wet, I asked the guy taking Robinson's side about Harold Williams. He didn't have much to say except it was a rotten shame Harold getting the chair for killing Irwin Johnson when what he should get was a medal. On the more helpful side, he told me about a Negro driver who was a friend of Harold's. This friend, he said, usually started his shift in the taxi line in front of Grand Central Station about this time. Since I now had expense money, I took a cab uptown. The DeSoto whizzed me up Eighth Avenue to Forty-Second Street and across to Park Avenue in style. The back seat was about the size of my apartment in Sunnyside.

CHAPTER TWO

LATE AFTERNOON

I picketed a section of sidewalk between Grand Central and the Commodore Hotel and waited. When a Checker driven by a Negro slid up to the curb at the end of the cab line, I climbed into the back seat. This alarmed the driver, who told me I needed to get the first cab in line. He didn't relax when I told him I only wanted to talk to him. The reason for his concern became clear when I saw three or four white cab drivers at the front of the line begin a menacing march toward us. I opened the cab door and got out.

"You need to get the taxi in the front of the line, buddy. Didn't the driver tell you that?" The spokesman for the group had a cigarette hanging from his lip, wore a scally cap, and needed a shave.

I braced myself. My nose had already been broken more than once, so it began twitching as if it sensed danger on its own. "I wanted to ask the gentleman a question. I wasn't going anywhere."

"Gentleman. You hear that, Mike?" Mike was a skinnier and less truculent version of himself, with soft timid eyes. The third man, whose eyes were not at all timid, was as big as the first two put together. Neither of the sidekicks spoke but something dawned on the truculent one. "Whatcha want to ask him?" He nodded toward the cab.

I didn't answer. I suppose I could've told him it was none of his business. But he knew that. That was why he asked, like poking me with a stick.

"You from the union?"

He'd keep pushing until I reacted, so I did. "Someone put you in charge of the hack stand here?"

Scally Cap took a moment to digest this before telling his pals, "I bet this guy's a Commie from the union."

"Jesus," I said when I should've bitten my tongue. "How's a smart guy like you, knows all the answers, end up driving a hack? You'd think you'd be a bank president or somethin'."

"He *is* a fucking Commie!" The should-be bank president balled his fist by his pants pocket and swung from the hip.

He telegraphed the punch, so I got my arm under it as it came toward me and it glanced off the side of my head. I moved to his right side—I'm left-handed—but didn't throw my punch, even though the side of his face was open.

That's why I was an easy mark as a kid, too. I didn't like to hit people, not even jerks like him. I'd boxed some at the PAL club and was okay in style and speed and footwork and all that. The problem was it made me sick—the crunch of crushed cartilage—when I hit someone with a solid punch, not a character trait they looked for in the Golden Gloves.

What I learned—the hard way, as my pop used to say—was taking a punch didn't make you tough. What made you tough was being able to hurt someone without pity or remorse. In this, I came up short. Another of my shortcomings was thinking about things instead of doing them. While I deliberated over whether I should smack the jerk who swung on me, the big guy beside him lowered his shoulder and charged like a moose, driving me into the side of the cab.

Scally Cap then managed to get in a punch—not a great one, but it landed on my forehead and the force bounced the back of my head off the cab's roof. The thump brought tears to my eyes and knocked my hat off. The big guy took that opportunity to land a short compact right hook beneath my rib cage that pumped the air right out of me. I went down like a sack of wet laundry, sunk between the curb and the gutter, landing on my hat.

A police whistle and a shout sent my pals scurrying back toward the front of the cab line, where they blended in with the other drivers who'd headed down to watch the fight— more accurately, the massacre. The cop helped me up and asked me what happened.

I thought the proper question was "Are you okay?" so I answered that one. "I'm okay," I said.

"What happened?" he tried again.

"I tripped."

He handed me my squashed hat. His ruddy face and bluest of blue eyes reflected a kind of world-weary understanding. "Those clowns who ran, I suppose they were helping you up."

"Something like that." His brogue reminded me of my father's. "Cork?" "Kerry," he said. "You're all right now, are you?" He didn't wait for an answer. "Suppose you go on your way while I'm still here, so you don't trip over them fellas again."

I saw my chance. "How about this cab?"

Casting a hard stare toward the front of the cab line, he

reached for the door handle, opened the door and closed it behind me, went out into the street, stopped the traffic, and waved the Checker away from the curb. The cabbie, who unlike me would have to face those thugs again, sat hunched over his steering wheel. He neither flipped the meter nor asked where I wanted to go. Instead, he turned into Vander-bilt Avenue alongside the terminal, drove a block or two, pulled up in front of the Roosevelt Hotel, and told me to get out.

When I told him I wanted to ask about Harold Williams, he turned to look at me. "I know Harold. What about him?"

"My name is Mick Mulligan. I'm a private investigator. What about Harold is he's going to die in two weeks if I can't prove he didn't kill his boss."

The driver assessed me with large sad brown eyes. He spoke slowly. "Harold didn't kill nobody."

"How do you know?"

"I know Harold my whole life. We were boys together. You ask anyone about Harold. He don't have a mean bone in his body. What they're doing to him is a terrible thing."

The driver, whose name was Sam Jones, didn't have much to tell me that was helpful, beyond that I should talk to Har-old's mother who lived in Bedford-Stuyvesant, which I already planned to do. Harold's father had passed.

I told Sam I was sorry if my run-in with the shanty Irish would make trouble for him. He wasn't worried. They kept their distance. He kept his. When I asked about the union, he said he hadn't made up his mind. He had a wife and kids and needed to work.

"When I said that to Harold, he told me, 'A lot of men got

wives and kids; that's why we be doin' this.'" Sam glanced at me through the rearview mirror. "I don't know about no Communist stuff. That's somethin' Harold did. We got enough troubles just gettin' by. I asked him, 'Why you wanna bring more trouble by doin' crazy white folks stuff?'" He caught himself. "I don't mean nothin' by that. Them Communists ain't near as bad as the Man say they are. That Ben Davis, why they do that to him? And why they do that to Harold for? Harold only been tryin' to help us workin' folks."

We chatted for a couple of more minutes about Harold, during which time Sam got curious about what I was up to. "I didn't know there was any such thing as a private eye," he said with an easy laugh. "I thought that was somethin' they made up for the movies."

I felt I'd gone up a peg or two in his estimation. "In real life it's not as exciting as in the movies," I told him—modestly, I hope.

This didn't dissuade him. "You one of them fellas who go out and catch the real crook and save the guy the cops thought done it?" Sam, who'd been meeting my gaze every now and again through the rearview mirror, turned all the way around to face me. "That's what Harold needs. Someone else killed Mr. Johnson. Harold didn't kill no one." After a moment's thought, he said, "Maybe it was them Communists he got himself mixed up with killed the boss."

"Maybe it was those guys back there I had a run in with." He wasn't the only one who could do maybes.

"I wouldn't put it past 'em. They some mean mothers."

The sun hadn't fully declined into the New Jersey hills yet, so I took a gamble and asked Sam if he'd drive me out to

Harold's mother's in Bedford-Stuyvesant, after a quick stop at my office.

My suit was crumpled and grimy from the gutter and stained from sweat, my hat misshapen. I changed into a sport shirt and a pair of slacks in my office, rolled up my suit, dropped it and my hat off at the Chinese laundry at the end of the block, and headed for Brooklyn with Sam. On the drive, he told me a couple of things I found interesting but doubted would be any help in proving Harold hadn't murdered his boss.

"His daddy was a union man with the tenant farmers back in North Carolina years ago," Sam said. "He got burned out of his house for his trouble. Not that his house was all that much to begin with. We all lived in shacks and our daddies turned over most of what they grew to the white folks they rented from."

That Harold's father had been part of Southern Tenant Farmers Union might explain why Harold himself was a union man; it also might explain why he was a Communist, since the Reds were a big part of organizing poor farmers in the south in the thirties. Something else Sam told me led me to believe Harold wasn't simply a blind follower of the godless Communists. Harold was religious. They saw each other every Sunday at the Cornerstone Baptist Church.

When Sam slowed down in front of a flat-faced four-story brownstone building on Lewis Avenue, we caused a delay in a stickball game that a passel of ragamuffins—none of them past nine or ten—were playing in the middle of the street. As soon as we parked, they went back to the game, giving us only a quick once-over, except for the outfielder, the smallest kid in the game, who watched us intently until the smack of the bat against the spaldeen sent him streaking to cut off the ball.

Still sitting in Sam's back seat, I made a quick cartoon drawing in my small notebook, an outline of a sketch: four or five kids in the field, a small group around home plate. I looked about us for a moment, taking in the neighborhood—a line of stoops across the street where a number of faces in varying shades of brown and black watched us curiously; a group of snappily dressed young men lounged in front of a liquor store—a picture I'd also try to remember for the sketch.

I paid Sam the three bucks we'd agreed on for the fare and made ready to haul myself out of the cab. Cocking his head, he asked if I wanted him to wait. "It's a hike to the subway and not easy to hail a cab in this neighborhood."

I was surprised he asked. I hadn't really thought about how I was going to get home. "Keep the meter running," I said.

The outer door of the Williamses' building wasn't locked and the inside door was ajar, so I checked the mailboxes and climbed a set of worn marble stairs and knocked on the door of Apartment 3A. The woman who opened the door wore a faded but neatly pressed flowery house dress. Her face was broad and pleasant but at the moment marred by irritation.

"I seen you out the window," she said. "Good thing you have that cab waiting on you." She looked me over like she would the Fuller Brush man. "Because you won't be spendin' long here."

"Mrs. Williams? My name is Mick Mulligan," I said. "I'm a private detective. I'm here to help your son."

I'd swear she looked at me with sympathy. "That's what they all say, them that got him in trouble in the first place.

Harold's a country boy. He don't know city ways. He didn't have no business getting mixed up with no Communists." Resignation and sadness colored her words. "It's his daddy's fault. He be like that, too. Thinkin' he could stand up to the Man, and always the Man knockin' him back down . . . You with that union?"

"The union hired me to look into your son's case." I tried to make this sound more consequential than it was.

In the quiet seconds after I said this the door from the hallway opened and the wide-eyed urchin from the stickball game inched his way in. He stared at me like he'd discovered a zebra in his kitchen.

"What you doin' in here, Franklin?" Mrs. Williams scowled at him but the lilt of love in her voice gave her away.

"I want a drink of water." He didn't take his eyes off me, even as he walked to the counter for a glass and then to the sink for water. He drank the water watching me as I watched him.

"This here's Harold's son," she said to me. "Say good day to the gentleman, Franklin."

"Hello," the boy said without moving.

Mrs. Williams didn't say anything else. I guessed she wanted to get rid of the boy before discussing his father, so I didn't say anything to him beyond hello.

When he had disappeared into the back of the house, I said, sounding as sincere as a bible salesman, "The union believes your son wasn't given a fair trial. I hope to find evidence that might have been overlooked or hidden, or to dig up a witness who didn't come forward at the time. If I can do this we might get your son a new trial."

Her eyes glazed over as she recognized a know-it-all who didn't know anything. I switched gears.

"Can you tell me anything about your son that might help me prove he isn't a murderer?" I was supposed to be the one with a plan, not her, and here I was right off the bat showing my hand, a busted flush.

She saw beyond me down the hallway into the past. "Harold was always a gentle boy despite his size . . . always wanting to please. When you'd have to warm his bottom like you do with all kids, he'd be so hurt, not from the pain but from him being sorry he'd done something that made you spank him, you'd wish you'd never done it." Her dark eyes were liquid pools. "That boy ain't no murderer. I told the judge and jury. They watched me blank as walls." After a moment, she said, "You might as well sit down."

I sat down in a long-serving cloth armchair; she sat across from me on a matching couch. The living room was tiny, the furniture and rug faded by time, but clean and tidy. She relaxed and let herself talk.

Hattie Williams raised six children, Harold the youngest. Their father died when Harold was ten. Hattie came north soon afterward, taking Harold and his two sisters who were closest in age to him. The others, old enough to fend for themselves, stayed on in North Carolina. One of Harold's sisters who came north was a bookkeeper now, the other a hairdresser in a beauty parlor in downtown Brooklyn.

Harold met a girl and married, too young, just out of high school. Not long after Franklin was born, the girl left and went back down south. Harold and his son had lived with Hattie since then. I asked about Harold's friends in the neighborhood; they might know him in a different way than the union folks and Reds in Manhattan.

Mrs. Williams said she didn't know anything about Bed-Stuy Communists and didn't want to know anything about them. She did give me a couple of names of friends Harold grew up with but told me most had drifted off after the war. Harold worked long hours driving his cab to provide for his son and spent the rest of his time on union work.

After a moment of silence, she said, "Now will you tell me . . . What are you gonna do about gettin' Harold free?" She spoke out of frustration, her tone was bitter, yet I heard a note of hope trying to sneak through her ingrained suspicion that I, like the others, would be talk but not action.

"I don't know yet," I admitted. "I'm just getting started. First thing I wanted was to let you know I'd taken the case, and ask if you had something in mind that should be being done that wasn't being done—and to tell you you could call me anytime night or day if you thought of anything I should know." So much for Duke's warning.

"Can't that union do somethin'? They supposed to take care of their people. Can't they talk to the mayor or the governor? Why don't they put on big protests and parades like them folks been doin' for that boy down south who got accused of killin' someone?"

I didn't want to argue with her about who did what. But I didn't want her to get the wrong idea either. "Other folks do the protesting," I said. "My job is to show the cops and the court that Harold didn't kill his boss. I need to find some facts everyone else overlooked."

"How you gonna do that?"

How *was* I going to do that? I had no idea. I didn't blame her for the skepticism; I shared it. I waited for her to lambast me for wasting her time when I had no idea what to do to save her son.

She surprised me. "I shouldn't be so harsh," she said quietly. "You're tryin' to help. I just hope to God you know what to do." There was a softness to her heavyset frame that extended to her manner of being. Kindness that came naturally to her outweighed her frustration. "I been tryin' and tryin' and ain't got nowhere . . ." Her eyes moistened and she turned away from me.

I was quiet for a moment while I thought about what I should tell her and how to say it. The truth was the protest movement would have better luck drumming up support for an axe murderer. I didn't want to tell her how long the odds against Harold were. I had two weeks, and it wasn't like I had a staff of operatives waiting at my beck-and-call. Yet I wanted to give it to her straight.

"Look, ma'am. I'm going to do my best. I'll work day and night. I don't know the facts yet. But I'll find them. If there's a witness on the face of the earth who knows something that will help Harold, I'll find them." I looked into her dark, sorrowful eyes. "The truth is—and I hate to say this—the prospects are bleak. I'll know more in a few days when I've read the trial transcript and talked to a few people. I'll tell you what I know then. But I don't want to give you false hope."

What I didn't want to do—what I wanted to kick myself down the tenement stairs for doing—was say this in earshot of Franklin, who eavesdropped from the doorway behind me.

After a ringing silence of despair, Mrs. Williams tried

for solace. "The Lord is my shepherd," she said. "I shall not want . . ."

I let her finish her prayer, then asked her for one last favor. She called Dr. Carter, the man leading the campaign in Brooklyn to free Harold, a physician and a board member of the Civil Rights Congress. He said he'd meet me in his office, which was in his home also in Bed-Stuy, in thirty minutes. I gave Harold's mother my office and home phone numbers.

When I got downstairs to Sam's waiting cab, my heart dropped. Franklin was waiting, straight as a soldier. He held my gaze as long as he could, but young Negro boys were taught not to look a white man in the eye, so he was looking at his feet when he asked, "Are you going to help my dad?"

I was glad he had dropped his gaze because I wasn't able to look him in the eye. I pictured Duke's bull head and wanted to smack him for getting me into this.

"I'm going to try my best."

"They're lying." Franklin spoke more forcefully than I'd expect from a boy so young. "My daddy told me don't believe he wasn't for America. He was just as American as they are. When I wanted to fight boys who said my daddy was a traitor, he told me to let them be. 'They don't know no better,' he said. 'Everybody lying to them, so they think Communists are bad. But Communists are workers like them.' My daddy always says we have to talk, not fight. He wouldn't hurt nobody. So why they say he kill that man?"

How was I supposed to answer that? "I don't know, Franklin. I'm going to try to find out."

Even a child—this child—heard the emptiness in my

words. "Are you goin' to see my daddy?" His voice was as quiet as a breeze.

"As soon as I can."

"Say 'hey' to him for me." His voice broke. "He don't want me to come to see him in the prison. He don't want . . ." Franklin bent and twisted away from me, waving his hand in a gesture he might have hoped would explain his anguish.

"I'll tell your dad 'hey,'" I said to his back, barely getting it out before choking on the words myself.

CHAPTER THREE

EVENING

Dr. Carter met me at the basement door of a brownstone building in the middle of a block of such buildings. This time I remembered my new business card and handed him one. It read Mick Mulligan, Private Investigator. In the upper left corner it had the scales of justice; in the upper right corner, a small American flag. The flag might as well have been a hammer and sickle because the Red-baiting usually preceded my arrival anywhere. The good doctor either hadn't gotten the news or didn't care.

I told him I'd been hired by the cab drivers' union to take a fresh look at Harold's case, and that the union had hired Gil Silver to work on the appeal, assuming the doc would know of Gil and this would give me an entry. I asked what the Civil Rights Congress had in mind to help Harold.

His expression hardened, an intimidating mannerism I suspected he'd taken up to stake out his ground as a Negro professional in hostile territory. "The usual things but in a half-hearted way."

The CRC—whose leadership and membership included both Communists and non-Communists—did what you'd expect a civil rights congress to do, and in doing it pissed off J. Edgar Hoover, Joe McCarthy, HUAC, and the rest of the witch hunters enough that they designated the organization a Communist-front. That Mortimer Carter, MD, a second-generation general practice physician in Bed-Stuy was part of the Congress's non-Communist contingent was clear a few moments into our conversation.

Carter took for granted I knew what the usual things were, which I did—rallies, vigils, demonstrations, petitions, delegations of dignitaries to demand audiences with the governor, and such, while the legal arm of the Congress tried various maneuvers in the courts.

"The Party has paid shockingly little attention to Harold's case, Mr. Mulligan." His tone suggested this might have been my fault. "They were wrapped up in their own trial obviously. But they also know they can more easily get support—and contributions—from liberals and progressives for fights in the Jim Crow South than they can for injustice in their own back yard."

He watched to see how this sat with me and then went on. "The South is a moral lightening rod for liberals. Segregation is codified by law; the terror and brutality is out in the open. Moral outrage is harder to come by in New York where discrimination is *de facto* rather than *de jure*. As segregated as it is, the city doesn't have the Jim Crow laws, or the lynchings, poll taxes, and all-white juries, the South is so proud to live by."

The good doctor's knowing Gil didn't boost my standing any. "Silver's a good lawyer. He's worked with the Congress. But he follows the Party line, too."

I knew from experience Gil didn't follow anybody's line but I let it go; I hadn't stopped by to change the doctor's mind about anything; I wanted information. "The legal stuff I leave to the lawyers, and the political stuff I leave to the agitators. My job is to find evidence that Harold didn't kill his boss."

I went over what I knew about the rival factions in the cab drivers union and Duke's unholy alliance with Vincent Forlini. "Gangsters kill people when they have a reason. I don't know that they had a reason to kill Irwin Johnson."

"Have you considered the Party?"

That sprung my eyes open. "The Party murdered Irwin Johnson?"

He watched my reaction calmly. "The Communist Party is a mess. Everyone suspects that everyone else is a stool pigeon." He spoke carefully, as you might do with someone you didn't know or trust.

The office was on the lower level of the brownstone; I guessed he lived in the upper levels. You entered from the vestibule into a small waiting room, next came the examining room, beyond that his office, with glass-fronted bookcases holding medical texts, the desk he sat behind, and a couple of leather arm chairs, one of which I sat in. You'd have to say he'd done pretty well for himself.

"Why would the Reds kill Johnson? Why would they let one of their guys take the rap?"

Dr. Carter again measured his words. "Some of the Party organizers in the taxi union suspected Harold was an informer."

He got me again. The accusation surprised me but I wasn't shocked. It was possible, though not probable. I wanted to see how far the doc would go with it. "Maybe he was."

The doctor's expression became a question mark. "Are you in the Party?"

It wasn't an are-you-now-or-have-you-ever-been question, so I told him I wasn't. Maybe he believed me; maybe he didn't. A lot of folks for various reasons wouldn't own up to being a Communist. This created a problem for the Party; they lied about who was in the Party and who wasn't. So the accusation that "Communists lied" held water.

The Reds had reason enough for secrecy, even before the Red Scare. Except for a short time during the war, when the US was pals with the Soviet Union in order to defeat Hitler, it was dangerous to be a Communist in the United States. You could lose your job, not get hired in the first place; if you were a foreign national you could get run out of the country. And there was always a good chance of getting bushwhacked by vigilante groups rounded up by the bosses to terrorize the radicals, like the American Legion rejects who attacked the Paul Robeson concert up in Peekskill.

The doctor sat straight, his shoulders back. Like the few doctors I've run across, he expected to be listened to. "Most white people are prejudiced, some more than others. For more than a few, prejudice is hatred. We could walk down Bedford Avenue and I could show you hate in the eyes of men we pass, something you might not recognize if you hadn't experienced it.

"Some of the cab drivers have that kind of hatred; a few men like that were recruited into the union drive, some into the Party. Communists believe they can overcome race hatred with education about class solidarity. Maybe someday they will. But I've seen that icy stare of hate directed at me from Communists . . . Not often, but often enough."

We were quiet for a moment. Again, I felt like he blamed

me for something, but that feeling might have come from me, not him.

After a moment I said, "For the sake of argument, let's say that the Party would frame a guy they consider an informer. My thinking is they'd make sure they were right before they did it, but I'll let that go for the moment. I have a harder time thinking the Party killed Irwin Johnson. Why would they? J. Edgar Hoover and Joe McCarthy notwithstanding, the Reds aren't engaged in armed struggle against the bosses just yet."

Dr. Carter weighed his answer. "I'm not saying the Party made a decision to kill the man. An overzealous hothead might have—someone new to the Party, a potential recruit, or an organizer who lacked discipline. The Party protected their man and framed Harold, whom they believed expendable if not a class enemy."

"What makes you think the Party suspected Harold was an informer?"

"He told me."

Carter came across as frank to the point of bluntness. Given his line of work, I'd expect him to be a careful thinker— to have done a little digging into Harold's standing in the Party before throwing around accusations—and he had.

"We of course discussed Harold's defense at board meetings of the Congress. At one meeting, I asked point blank if anyone in the Party suspected him of being an informer. The Party leaders on the board denied it, saying they were doing everything they could for him. I knew the second part to be untrue, which led me to have doubts about the first part. Later, I spoke with one of the leading comrades in the Congress whom I trusted. He didn't believe the Party had framed

Harold or had anything to do with killing the cab company boss. He said he'd look into it. He's a straight shooter, so I think he'd do what he said."

Carter didn't have anything else to tell me that would help with my investigation. Nor did he have any proof that the CP had murdered Irwin Johnson or framed Harold.

"The trial was a travesty." He said this emphatically.

"Why? Why do you say it was a travesty?" I hoped he had something I could hang my hat on.

He spoke deliberately, if not pontifically. "We're told that a man is innocent until proven guilty. Harold was judged guilty from the moment the police arrested him. What does a reasonable man conclude from that?"

Not that I'm so reasonable, but I concluded Carter hadn't answered my question.

He gave me the name of the leading comrade he'd talked with about Harold and told me he could be found at the CP section office in Harlem. Interestingly, I recognized the name. I remembered Victor Young from back in the radical thirties, when I was in high school.

As I was leaving, Carter ushered me to the door and became almost apologetic. "I appreciate what you're doing. I do, despite my skepticism." His tone was comforting, like he might reassure a patient. "I want you to succeed. I'll help if I can."

Sam had driven me to the doc's brownstone from Harold's mother's apartment and was waiting for me once more. We'd gone a few blocks down Eastern Parkway when I noticed his eyes in his rearview mirror, wide with worry. He caught my quizzical expression.

"A cop car's following me. He's waiting for me to do something so he can give me a ticket."

"What if you don't do anything wrong?"

"You always do something. Maybe I didn't signal coming out of Bedford Avenue. I might not make a full stop at a stop sign, might do five miles an hour over the speed limit."

Sure enough the flashing lights went on behind us; a toot from the siren and Sam pulled over.

"Jones, is it?" the cop said, holding Sam's hack license but looking at me. "And who are you?"

I reacted from instinct. "What's that got to do with anything?" I should have just answered the question, but I've never liked cops throwing their weight around. The neighborhood I grew up in was in what you might call a "Cheese it—the cops!" sort of territory.

"I asked you who you are."

"I'm a passenger in a taxi minding my own business." In the rearview mirror, I caught a glimpse of Sam's grim expression.

"You're having this man," the cop allowed himself a quick glance at Sam, "drive you around a colored neighborhood. That looks suspicious."

"Suspicious of what?"

He wasn't going to say what the real answer was—that something was wrong with a white man consorting with Negroes. "Suppose you get out of the car, so I can search you?"

"Suppose I don't?"

The officer turned from the cab and went back to his car where he presumably radioed for backup. While he was gone, Sam turned a pleading glance toward me. "You'd better do what he tells you. The cops in this district don't take no lip. They want everybody in his own place . . ."

The cop in question was back before Sam could say more. "When a police officer asks for identification, you're required to comply. You could save yourself trouble by not being a wise guy."

This reminded me of the friendly advice from the HUAC committee staffers who told me I would be doing myself a favor if I cooperated by naming names. I asked the cop if I was under arrest.

He had to think that over. "You're under suspicion."

"A white man visiting a Negro is cause for suspicion?"

"You visited more than one Negro. Maybe you're buying drugs."

"Do you have reason to believe Dr. Carter is selling drugs?"

"He might be. He might be a Communist."

I knew we'd get around to someone being a Communist sooner or later.

Another police cruiser pulled up and a sergeant hauled himself out of it, beckoning to the cop who pulled us over. They conferred alongside the sergeant's car before he lumbered over to the cab. A big man, tall, broad, and thick, with a ruddy Irishman's mug, he put his hand on the roof of the cab and bent far enough so he was eye-to-eye with Sam.

"You failed to make a full stop at the sign and you didn't signal a turn. Lucky for you, the officer wants to give you a break." He didn't so much as glance at me, yet I knew he was talking for my benefit. "We'll let you go with a warning. Now turn off your meter, collect your fare, and hit the road."

Sam face registered such confusion and alarm I thought

he'd explode. "I've got a passenger," he croaked. He cleared his throat and was about to try again when I interrupted him.

"You want me to get out here?" I asked the sergeant. He wrinkled his brow and glanced around—but not at me—as if he might have heard something. I leaned toward the front seat. "I'm getting out," I told Sam.

Sam's expression was pained.

"It's okay. You don't need to get fined a half day's pay because I don't like getting pushed around." I gave him a sawbuck, opened the door, and got out.

Sam pointed in front of him. "The subway's a few blocks that way."

I stood not far from the sergeant as we—together, in a manner of speaking—watched the cab drive off. The sergeant still didn't look at me. "Take a hike." As I started off dutifully toward Grand Army Plaza, he said to my back. "A lucky day for you, too. In the old days we woulda worked you over."

The afternoon had been hot, and it was cooling off as darkness set in, so I didn't mind the walk. Eastern Parkway was wide and the apartment buildings on either side stately. Grand Army Plaza, with the Brooklyn Library on one side and the majestic stone arch honoring the "Defenders of the Union" at the entrance to Prospect Park on another, was worth a trip out to Brooklyn to behold, though I wondered if Lincoln and Grant atop their horses might not have been frowning.

The IRT rides back to Manhattan and then to Sunnyside were uneventful, except that waiting for the Flushing Line train at Times Square I realized I hadn't eaten anything since that morning. When I got off the train, I stopped at the

Greek's on Queens Boulevard for the blue plate special, which happened to be meatloaf. The menu didn't specify what kind of meat the loaf was made from and I didn't ask. When I got to my apartment, I called my answering service and was told Gil Silver wanted me to call.

He said he'd arranged a legal visit for me to meet my client the following morning at Sing Sing, that he'd get me a copy of the trial transcript, and that the homicide detective in charge of the Johnson murder investigation was named Len Volpe, and I should talk to him.

Still feeling a bit bruised from my recent encounter in Brooklyn, I told him, "Cops don't like me much."

"They don't like me much either. Lenny slipped through the cracks. He was born in Italy; he doesn't think like American cops. He's a nose-to-the-grindstone guy who works on Saturday when he's on a case, which I happen to know he is. I'll tell him you'll be by after your visit upstate. The Eighteenth Precinct on Fifty-Fourth Street."

After the call, I lay down on the bed for a couple of minutes to think things through, woke up a few hours later and took my shoes off.

CHAPTER FOUR

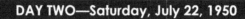

MORNING

I didn't need an alarm to wake up the next morning at 6:00, and I was at Grand Central in time to catch the 7:29 train to Ossining.

On the ride up, I drew a sketch of the stickball game I'd seen the evening before. It was on my mind because Harold's son, Franklin, had popped up in my dream. He didn't have anything to say, only watched me from an asphalt outfield with an expectant expression that felt like an accusation while I sat in a cab that didn't have a driver.

I thought about Harold, too. I had no idea what kind of man he'd be. Tall or short, husky or thin, shy or brazen. I had a longtime sympathy for the plight of Black folks, going back to lessons I learned from my pop. What he'd said was, "When it's the poor that's fighting the rich for what little they can get, a man needs to take their side whoever they may be."

He'd told me this one day as we stood on the sidewalk on Third Avenue near 149th Street in the Bronx, not far from our apartment, and watched marshals evict a family, hauling their furniture and belongings out of the apartment building and piling it all onto the sidewalk. Not more than a few minutes after they left we watched a group of husky Negro men and a few not so husky white men move the furniture and belongings from the sidewalk back into the apartment. Pop parked me on the stoop in front of the building and helped.

I learned later it was the Communists who led the movement against evictions in Harlem and the Bronx. I never heard Pop say a word against the Reds, but if he'd ever been tempted to join I never heard that either. He was a Catholic—no meat on Friday, kneeling by the bed for a minute or two for prayers at night, Mass on Sunday and holy days. But my mother was a veritable saint—fasting and the rosary during Lent, first in line for any novena that came to the parish, the women's sodality, setting up the altar on Sunday, Benediction on Friday, Confession on Saturday, her son an altar boy the day he turned seven, no two ways about it. The thought of her husband joining up with the godless Communists was unimaginable. That didn't stop him from knowing whose side the Reds were on.

As the train rattled its way north, I dozed off, and woke as the train cut through Sing Sing—right through the middle of the place, the grey walls of the prison buildings on either side of the tracks. I thought about jail cells and death as the train slowed down for its stop in Ossining.

Because I was on a legal visit, I skipped the frustrating rigmarole most visitors went through to spend an hour with their loved ones. Harold met me in space set aside for lawyers to meet with their clients, an antiseptic room you might say because of its blandness, but you wouldn't say this because of its cleanliness.

Harold's face was broad, as were his shoulders. His whole body was broad, his skin a dull charcoal, his hair black, cut short but still curly; his eyes deeply brown and smoky. He wore his prison garb and his troubles with an easy grace. He sat down across from me and folded his thick workingman's hands on the table.

I told him who I was and why I was there. His eyes didn't light up with hope and gratitude, but I did detect a speck of interest. Despite his surroundings and impending doom, he gave off a kind of positive energy, an optimism I'd noticed before in Communists.

"Mick Mulligan? That's Irish, right?"

I nodded. He gave no indication whether he approved or disapproved.

"My mother told me on the phone last night Duke hired somebody to get to the bottom of things." He sized me up, as if he wasn't so sure I was the somebody to do it.

I didn't blame him; I wasn't sure myself. The guy's life was on the line—his life in my hands. I remembered Franklin's tears. I told him I'd talked to Mortimer Carter and was going to talk to Victor Young as soon as I could get to it. He brightened a bit when I mentioned Victor.

"You know the Civil Rights Congress folks are working on my case," he said. "They know about these things. They don't let them crackers down South get away with railroading Negroes. They get the whole country riled up."

I didn't want to tell him it didn't look like there'd be much riling up on his account, so I said, "The Civil Rights Congress does what it does. What I do is different. Can you tell me anything that will help me get you out of here?"

His brow wrinkled and he looked puzzled.

I took a deep breath. "I know you've done this a hundred times. But I need you to tell me everything that happened around the time of the murder. Where you were, who you were with, who you might have seen or talked to even in passing."

"I told the lawyer all that." He shook his head. "It didn't do no good." His tone was flat, no indignation. "I was playing cards. Later I went to a Party meeting. The lawyer told the jury that. He said bringing in any witnesses wouldn't be no help. The jury wouldn't believe no Communists, no matter what they said. And the guys I played cards with . . ." He sighed. "Them guys? They jive. You know? They don't want nothin' to do with Mr. Charlie. And if they did say somethin', they know damn well Mr. Charlie ain't gonna believe 'em either."

He told me to ask Sol Rosen about the Party club meeting and gave me the name of the joint with the backroom poker game. He also gave me the names of the poker players he remembered from that evening, too—Mad Dog, Slasher, and Smokin' Joe. I could see where those monikers might raise an eyebrow or two when called to the witness stand. Slasher I'd be inclined to skip entirely no matter what he had to say.

When Harold told me about work the evening of the murder, he got off track, telling me about his fares that afternoon and evening. Not what I was interested in but I let him talk so he'd relax and possibly remember more than he otherwise would about who he saw at the garage at the end of his shift.

But he didn't get to it. "I dropped off that lady at Seventh Avenue and Twenty-Seventh Street, drove back to the garage, cashed out, and walked uptown to the poker game at The Pink Lady."

So much for easing him into things. "Who was in the garage when you parked the cab?"

He shook his head.

I tried to keep my voice even, my tone easy. "You get used to people being around, so you don't always notice them. If you try to recall that evening and only that evening, keep picturing it, you might remember someone. A driver might have cashed out before you or after you. Who'd you cash out with?"

"Fat Tony, the dispatcher."

"You sure it was him?"

"It was him. Tony's always there. It's like he's part of the furniture."

"Anyone else? Someone walking by?"

He tried. The best he could come up with was one of the drivers was talking to Tony but left before he got over to cash out. "The garage door was open. People walked by on the sidewalk."

"Did you notice anyone unusual?"

He shook his head. "My memory's fuzzy on that evening." He rubbed his thick hands together. "I didn't pay attention. I never knew it would be a big deal."

"No other drivers?"

He hesitated. "A couple of night drivers I didn't know real well were starting as I was finishing. I thought I saw Frank. I told my lawyer that. Frank told him he didn't remember seeing me that night."

"Frank DeMarco?" The guy Rosen told me about, the lead organizer for the union drive; this stopped me in my tracks. Harold's comrade might have been at the garage and hadn't come forward? Remembering what Dr. Carter said about the Party and the murder, I asked, "You think you saw him?"

Harold shook his head. "Naw. If it was Frank, he'd have stopped to talk for a minute. He always did. Maybe it was one of the night guys I thought was him." He sounded apologetic. "It was the end of a tough day at work. I wanted to get shut of the cab and the garage."

I didn't want to get on his nerves by pressing the point, so I switched gears. "Why didn't the dispatcher testify at your trial? He would've seen anyone else who was in the garage."

Harold's expression was unreadable—inscrutable. "The lawyer asked him, too. Tony said he didn't remember. Tony's good at not remembering."

"So Frank DeMarco, the organizer, and the dispatcher, Fat Tony, might have been at the garage that night?"

"I misremembered about Frank."

I let that go. I could talk to Frank DeMarco about what he remembered or didn't remember. I treaded softly bringing up Carter's accusation. But there was no easy way of telling Harold someone said he was a snitch.

By the movement of his face, a tightening of his jaw muscles, a furrowing of his brow, I saw he was stung by the charge. He shook his head. "No reason for anyone to think that."

"Dr. Carter said you told him."

Harold nodded for a moment before he said, "I might have told him that one time, but it was a passing thing that got straightened out."

"If DeMarco thought you were an informer—"

Irritation flashed in Harold's eyes. "Frank never said that. Just some guys talkin'. I told Frank when I heard it. He said pay it no mind; he'd straighten it out, and he did. I never heard nothin' like that again."

"Dr. Carter said the Party doesn't trust you." If he didn't exactly say this, it was what he meant.

Harold's face muscles tightened even more; but he spoke softly. "Mortimer's a good man. He's headin' up my defense committee. But Mortimer don't always see straight when it comes to the Party. The Man got him believing the crazy stuff the newspapers and the government says about us. The Man ain't no fool. He know once the working class comes to understand the class struggle he be done for, so he do all he can to stop us. Got Dr. Carter sowing doubts. Got you tryin' to turn me against Frank. You damn right someone's lyin' about me. But it ain't the Party and it ain't Frank."

My bad-mouthing the Party didn't go over well, so Harold wanted to make sure I knew where he stood. "There ain't no Civil Rights Congress without the Party. They's who sent a delegation to the governor for me. The governor ain't met with them yet. But when folks get riled up enough he will. The Congress got lawyers be taking the case to the high court." He paused and softened his tone. "I 'preciate your help, too, but I don't know what you can do they ain't doin.'"

I wished what he said were true, that he didn't need me, that a delegation from his defense committee would prevail upon Governor Dewey to commute his sentence. Maybe that would happen and maybe pigs would fly. "Do you know who Vincent Forlini is?"

"Yeh. I know. A stooge for the bosses."

"Might Forlini's guys in the garage have killed Johnson and hung the rap on you?"

Harold struck a thoughtful pose. "The guys in the garage, they're not gangsters; they workin' men like me that got steered wrong. They said they were the anti-Communists. I told 'em we weren't building no union for Communists. We were building a union for cab drivers. I ain't enemies with any man who drives a cab in New York City."

I had one more thing to talk about that I hated like hell to do, but I'd promised I would. "I met your son last night . . ."

Whatever was holding Harold up until that moment gave out on him. Misery displaced the proud and defiant demeanor he'd carried himself with since I'd sat down with him as the realization hit him that in two weeks he could be dead, never on this earth to see his son again.

"I'm sorry." My voice was a whisper. "He wanted me to say 'hey' from him."

Tears filled Harold's eyes. "I don't want him to see me like this. For the boy to see his father caged up like an animal, dressed like a fool . . ." He brushed his hand against the front of his prison garb. "I been tryin' to write him a letter he could read when he got older . . . He needs to know I ain't no criminal. If I'm gonna die, he needs to know his daddy died a fighter for justice. Those judges and politicians, they the murderers."

Once he began talking about his son, it was as if his true self began to come through. Or it might have been, as sometimes happens when a person is overcome with sorrow or grief, he needed to say what he had to say and I happened to be there.

"I ain't so good at writing, so you can tell him this. I ain't no murderer. I ain't no criminal. If we lose and I'm put to death, I want him to know I gave up everything dear to me—even him—fighting against injustice."

He leaned forward and squinted at me. "I don't know why I said all that. It just come out . . . Just that you saw Franklin yesterday, I feel like you carrying something of him with you, and maybe you can carry somethin' of me back to him."

Talking to Harold hadn't gotten me any new information. But it got me to know him a bit. He was a man of convictions, no denying that. Though some of what he was convinced of might be built on shaky ground, the convictions were all about making a better world.

Sometimes a person strikes you as genuine. I have to say not many people have struck me this way—my time in Hollywood might have skewed my view—but Harold did. Still, first impressions often proved to be wrong. Take my ex-wife's vow to love, honor, and such things till death do us part.

For his own self-preservation, Harold had every reason to encourage me to set my sights on the gangsters in the union. But he didn't. This gave me pause for couple of reasons. For one, it made me think I might have bet on the wrong horse. Gangsters and Communists are easy fall guys when you're looking for a culprit. Harold didn't say this, yet he got me to thinking. Irwin Johnson could have been murdered for any number of reasons besides running afoul of one of the battling factions of the taxi union.

CHAPTER FIVE

EARLY AFTERNOON

I got back to my office around 2:30. Whether I had a reason to or not, and most of the time I didn't, I went to the office every day except Sunday unless I was wearing out my shoe leather on a case. I did this because it made me feel like I had a job. A profession, I used to say, until Gil told me I didn't have a profession—I had a job—and knocked me off my high horse.

My office consisted of a battered wooden desk with a rickety swivel chair behind it that I sat in and two wooden chairs—refugees from a Depression-era bank failure—in front of the desk that clients, when I could drum some up, would sit in. The office also housed a metal file cabinet about four feet tall, a coat rack that was sightly taller, a fluorescent light in the ceiling, and a standing lamp behind my desk. The only thing on my desk was a framed picture of me with my daughter Rebecca on my knee. We both look happy—happy and oblivious.

The standing lamp was there because Gil insisted I needed incandescent light in the office. Without it, he said, the flickering of the fluorescent would ruin my eyes. Gil had quite a few ideas he never backed up. Still, he gave me the lamp so I used it.

I started a file on Harold's case and picked up my tool kit—one of which tools I should have had on me when I ran into the shanty Irish the evening before. The file cabinet, much like Mother Hubbard's cupboard, was bare, only a couple of folders sagging in the top drawer. I made a few notes on my first day-and-a-half on the job—I considered skipping the embarrassing encounter at the cabstand, but, because you never know what might be important, I included it—and stuck the file in the cabinet.

In my albeit brief time as a PI, I've learned I work best by following my nose and letting it lead me where it thinks best. In Harold's case, time was short, the odds were long, and the stakes were high, so I needed to get a move on. Despite this, I wasn't going to make a plan; I didn't trust them. I saw what happened to plans during the war: Something always went wrong.

The thing to do was to figure out which way to point my nose. More than a year had passed since Irwin Johnson's murder. Witnesses would have moved on. Memories would have faded. Physical evidence would be long trodden under. Despite these flies in the ointment, I intended to reconstruct the circumstances surrounding the murder to my satisfaction from whatever bits and pieces of recollections, details, particulars, facts, and figures I could dig up.

The circumstances might have been as the judge and jury were told. But they might not have been. I'd have been happier if my visit to Harold had supplied me with a few leads—a couple of reliable witnesses to vouch for his whereabouts far from the murder scene; an overlooked suspect or two with reason a-plenty to kill Johnson.

What Harold told me of these things added up to not much. But he had given me a couple of things to look into, including two of his fellow workers: Frank DeMarco, the guy Rosen had told me about, and Fat Tony the dispatcher, whose last name I didn't know. One or both of them were in the taxi garage the night of the murder and either failed to mention it or lied about it. In addition, I had the homicide detective who conducted the investigation into Johnson's murder on my list for the day.

The Forty-Second Street Library takes up two blocks on Fifth Avenue between Fortieth and Forty-Second Street. Out front, two lions stand guard on either side of the stone steps that lead up to the front door. Behind the library, Bryant Park stretches to Sixth Avenue. The library is in its own way as imposing as a cathedral. It's free and open to the public, and I've discovered librarians are the folks you turn to when you want to find out something.

I walked the four long blocks over to the library and found my way to the periodical room on the first floor. The librarian I talked to was polite and efficient although she stiffened a bit when I told her I wanted to look up a murder.

Despite her disapproval, she brought me the newspapers she said would be most helpful: the *Herald Tribune, Journal-American,* the *Daily News,* and the *Daily Mirror* from the first few days of April 1949, when Irwin Johnson was murdered, and early October 1949, when the trial took place and Harold was convicted and sentenced to death. The newspapers came in bound leather volumes and took a while to go through. After a couple of hours, I hadn't come up with much.

The murder made a big splash the day after Irwin Johnson's body was found. The *News* photog got a shot of his body covered with a sheet lying in a drab hallway and another shot of a tall, grim-faced detective standing in front of the taxi garage on West Fifty-First Street. A small fuzzy snapshot of Johnson in happier days was tucked into a corner above the photo of the body. A couple of the papers noted he was the scion of a prominent New York family listed on the social register. They also mentioned he left behind a wife.

Another spate of stories appeared a day later after the cops picked up Harold. The scandal sheets made a big deal over his being a Communist, with one of the *Daily Mirror* columnists reminding readers he'd warned them Communism would turn American working men into murderers.

Nothing then until August, when the papers covered Harold's sentencing, a bigger deal than most because he was sent to the chair. The *News* printed a photo of Johnson's widow alongside the story. She was dressed all in black including a black veil that obscured most of her features but not enough to disguise the fact she was quite a looker.

When I left the library, the afternoon was warm but not as muggy as the day before. I stood on the steps between the marble lions and watched the sunlight bouncing off the brick and limestone buildings across the street and the cars streaming down Fifth Avenue, most of them cabs.

A summer Saturday in the city. The Yankees were at home against the St. Louis Browns. A kid named Ned Garver pitching for the Browns was at the moment the best pitcher in the league on the worst team. Whitey Ford, an up-and-comer himself, was pitching for the Yankees.

I could be at the Shamrock Tavern in Sunnyside drinking beer and watching the last few innings of the game, listening to Mel Allen on TV; I might even be in the bleachers at the stadium. The truth was I would have felt pretty empty no matter where I was. At least when I was on the job I had something to think about instead of revisiting for the millionth time what my life had been before the witch hunters came after me and the bottom fell out of it.

I hiked uptown and then back across town to Hell's Kitchen. Sol Rosen had given me an address but not a phone number for Frank DeMarco. He lived in a railroad flat on Fifty-Fifth Street between Tenth and Eleventh Avenues.

Any complaint I had about the four-flight hike up to the apartment, or the hallway reeking of cooking smells and diaper pails, died in my throat when the door opened. I beheld a beguiling pair of brown eyes, flashing with a kind of bubbly cheerfulness you'd not expect to find on the top floor of a worn, sagging tenement in Hell's Kitchen.

"Hello?"

Her expression was shy and bold, charming and watchful. I appreciate pretty women as much as the next guy, but I don't go nuts over them. At least I didn't until this vision opened the tenement apartment door. I couldn't stop looking at her. She wasn't gorgeous, not glamorous like my former wife; not a Hollywood beauty. What she had was unadorned prettiness, sparkling eyes and a pink tint to her cheeks, the city version of the farmer's daughter. I stared at her until her smooth brow wrinkled into a frown.

"Yes?" she said.

"I'm looking for Frank DeMarco." I blurted this out loud

enough for her to take a step back and hold up her hands to ward me off. The sound bounced off the kitchen walls as if I'd used a megaphone.

As she turned away, I panicked and reached for her hand but caught myself before I grabbed her. "Who are you?" I bellowed this too but not quite as loud this time. It was a stupid thing to say. I said it because I was hoping she wasn't Frank DeMarco's girlfriend or, worse, his wife.

Her eyes flashed but then her smile went wider. "I'm Elena. Who are you?"

"Mick Mulligan." And then. "Really nice day." This was the only thing I could think of to say? I felt like an idiot. At least my voice was at normal volume this time.

Her smile crumbled as she waved behind her at the kitchen's dull grey walls, the sagging ceiling, the battered stove, the awkward leaning icebox. "Thanks for letting me know. You can never tell what kind of day it is living in this rat trap." Her eyes caught up with mine again. "Why're you looking at me like that?"

I said the first thing I thought of. "Because you're so pretty."

She laughed, the light dancing in her eyes. "A sweet talker, eh? Oh boy!" She twirled like a debutante at a ball though this belle wore a plaid shirt and overalls and was barefoot. "I'll get Frank."

The beguiling eyes flashed at me once more over her shoulder as she waltzed across the sloping kitchen. Once she was out of my sight I pulled myself together. A bit dazed, I blinked a few times until I could see straight, something you might do if you'd been hit on the back of the head with a two-by-four.

In a moment she was back, nodding for me to follow. She walked a step in front of me through two spotless worn linoleum-floored bedrooms, each room housing two beds and one with a small crib tucked into a corner. The beds were neatly made, everything put away. She led me toward the parlor at the front of the apartment, talking to me over her shoulder. "You're not from the Party, are you?" Her tone was light-hearted.

The nonchalance of her question surprised me. Most people didn't mention the CP these days unless they were under oath at a Congressional hearing. How did she know I wasn't from the Party and how'd she know I'd know what Party she was talking about?

"I'm not," I said.

"No sweet talkers in the Party." Her eyes sparkled. She was younger than I'd first thought, a girl who knew she was pretty and thought it was fun.

CHAPTER SIX

EARLY AFTERNOON

Frank DeMarco sat at a small desk with his back to me. Piled high on either side of him were pamphlets, newspapers, stacks of leaflets, all of it wobbling precariously while he pecked at a portable Royal typewriter. He continued to peck for a minute or so before he turned. His dark eyes, brown like Elena's, were intense behind horn-rimmed glasses; his black hair, curly and unruly, gave him a startled look. Otherwise, his expression was open and friendly where I'd expected it to be guarded like that of other Reds I knew. He resembled Elena in some vague way, darkly handsome in his own right.

"What's up?"

"Mick Mulligan, private eye," I said handing him my card. I told him what I was investigating and that Sol Rosen said I should talk to him.

He brightened. "You know Sol?"

"I talked to him yesterday."

"He's an amazing guy." Frank went on to tell me about his heroics. I listened politely. By the time he'd gotten to the Abraham Lincoln Brigade, I'd had enough. Yet the brightness in DeMarco's eyes stopped me from making a wise guy remark. The shine in his eyes came from belief—the kind of we-shall-overcome belief I'd once had. Who was I to stomp on his dream of a better world?

Nonetheless, I cleared my throat to try to rein him in.

He got in one more shot. "He's the nicest guy you'd ever want to meet."

His glow faded when I didn't agree. Rosen seemed nice enough. But so do swindlers seem nice enough.

After a moment, Frank remembered why I was there. "I don't know what I can tell you that would help. It's a shame. I've been hoping something would happen to change things. But it doesn't look good. We've protested, we got thousands of petitions signed. We're holding vigils and rallies at the prison." He lowered his voice. "Have you found out something new? Are they reopening the case? It's pretty late in the game."

He didn't need to tell me. I knew how late in the game it was.

"I'm the only one reopening it," I said. "Even if you've told others, even if you think what you know isn't important, can you tell me what happened in the days or weeks leading up to the murder? Anything about Harold Williams or Irwin Johnson?" I hoped he might bring up on his own how he saw Harold in the garage the night of the murder. I hoped he might tell me about a few other drivers who were likely to have killed the boss.

Frank shook his head. "I told Harold's lawyer what I knew. Harold was a proud man. Johnson pushed him again and again."

"What do you mean by push?"

He didn't come up with any examples. "It wasn't any one thing. Johnson had an attitude. He looked down on workers, especially Negroes."

"Arguments? Fights? Other drivers Johnson had trouble with? What about the gangsters?"

He didn't show any surprise when I mentioned gangsters, but didn't say anything about them either. I asked about the organizing drive, and he went over the organizing campaign pretty thoroughly. The Party targeted the taxi industry as ready for unionization. The drivers worked long hours, most of them twelve-hour days, six days a week, and had a lot of gripes; the main one that they were being short-changed by the fleet owners who wouldn't raise their commission rate.

The Party's industrial section sent Frank and a handful of comrades to get jobs as hack drivers and colonize the largest garages. Sol Rosen had been put in charge of the operation. The organizers worked underground, picking out drivers who were open to forming a union and whom the other cabbies would listen to, holding secret meetings away from the garages.

Frank and his comrades trained each new recruit, assigning them tasks, encouraging them to bring one or two trusted fellow workers to a meeting. They then tasked those new recruits with bringing one or two more trusted pals to the next meeting, and so on until they had a cadre of on-the-job organizers in garages throughout the city. Harold was one of the first men Frank recruited to the campaign and the first Negro.

The union committee grew slowly—meetings of garages across the city in all of the boroughs, each meeting larger than the one that preceded it—for six months or so until more than half of the fleet drivers had signed with the union and they were strong enough to go public. Once they were out in the open, they began to pull in the rest of the drivers who began to believe the union had a chance of winning.

"Groups of workers break down like that," Frank said. "Some are leaders; others will take a chance and join up early in the drive; the last bunch wait to see which way the wind is blowing—who's most likely to win, the union or the boss—before signing on.

"Forlini and his crew showed up not long after we came out in the open." Frank's expression turned sour. "We were rolling. Everyone was talking union. Drivers were coming to us to sign up; we didn't have to go looking for them. And then these bums show up, telling us they're from Local 5 and we're working together . . . You knew by looking at them, their patent leather shoes, tailored suits, skinny ties, bulges under their armpits, who they were.

"We coulda built a progressive union. We didn't need the Local 5 hoods, but they had a few garages under sweetheart deals and Duke wanted any garages he could get. The Party decided we shouldn't fight him. We shouldn't split the drivers into competing unions. Sol said the Party had organized competing unions back in the twenties and that had been a mistake.

"He said we'd get the union built and then push out the hoods. So what we got was two factions, ours and Forlini's. We're supposed to get along, but we're fighting with each other for members, even though we're the same union."

This factionalism wouldn't make sense to most people. But workers, with everything in common and power to win better pay and working conditions if they stuck together, have seldom been able to figure out how to do it. The Socialists and the Communists were so busy fighting each other in the Weimar Republic that Hitler and the Nazis walked in and took over. Back in the robber baron days in the US, after he crushed the Knights of Labor strike, the railroad boss Jay Gould had told the world, "I can always hire one half the working class to kill the other half."

My father was one of the organizers of the United Subway Bus and Trolley Workers in the thirties. He and other exiles from the IRA who'd been run out of Ireland after the partition built the union with a lot of help from the Communists, so militant trade unionism was my heritage. This wasn't the case with all of my fellow workers.

"I visited the prison and talked to Harold this morning." I watched for Frank's reaction. But there wasn't one. "He said he saw you at the garage the night of the murder." I waited again. This, of course, wasn't what Harold said; you might argue it was the opposite of what he said. I didn't know why I tried to trick Frank. A second before I did it, I didn't know I would.

If he was surprised, he didn't show it. He spoke earnestly, his tone as sincere as a priest in the pulpit. "He's wrong. I didn't see him that night. I thought about lying and saying I did. I didn't because I figured I'd trip myself up if someone pressed me on it; I'm not a good liar."

There was no reason to press DeMarco. He might be lying; he might be telling the truth. I was inclined to believe him. Harold believed him and Harold had a lot more reason than I did to want a witness to have seen him leave the garage.

"It's not only whether you saw Harold that night. It would be important if you saw anyone else, the real killer for instance."

Frank's expression was solemn behind his horn-rimmed glasses.

I asked if he knew of any trouble between Forlini or any of Forlini's men and Johnson. I guess I was still hoping to find an opening to pin something on the gangsters.

"If you ask me," he said, "Johnson would rather have Forlini's brand of unionism, where the boss pays off the union boss and the workers get screwed, instead of our militant rank-and-file union."

I moved on. "Any trouble between Sol Rosen and Johnson?"

"Sol?" His shock may have been faked but he reacted like I'd accused Mother Cabrini of running a whore house.

It seemed like a reasonable question to me. "Johnson was fighting the union. What did Sol think about him?"

"Sol didn't care what Johnson thought. We were organizing the workers. He cared what they thought. Tougher bosses than Johnson tried to beat the union and ended up signing a contract. Henry Ford swore he'd shut down all of his plants before he'd go union. His workers built the UAW and shoved a contract down his throat."

Frank's you-gotta-go-down-and-join-the-union pitch was as automatic as a flinch, as was his defense of Sol Rosen. I asked him if he and Harold were friends, another reasonable enough question, I thought.

But his face went blank and he stammered. "We were comrades . . . We worked together. We did things together . . . You could say in the Party everyone's friends."

"Have you visited him in prison?"

His friendly mug iced over. "No."

I waited.

He bobbed and weaved, as if clearing his head from a hard punch. "We demonstrated at the courthouse. We protested at the sentencing and got cleared from the courtroom . . . We got petitions signed to bring to the governor. We hold vigils at the prison."

This was the same canned answer he'd already given. He recognized this, so he avoided looking at me and studied his hands; then he got interested in some papers on his desk. A child could tell he was embarrassed.

"I'd expect more from the Party."

"We did what we could. We haven't given up." He'd felt the rebuke in my tone, so he kept talking. His answer wasn't good enough, so he kept trying for a better one, telling me what I already knew about the loyalty oaths, the purges, the Smith Act trial, the Party leaders jailed or underground.

"What about everyone else?" he asked. "What about the liberals or the rest of the labor movement? What are they doing?"

"Maybe they're waiting for the Party to take the lead."

He grabbed on to this. "That's what should happen, but the liberals give us the cold shoulder these days. The Red-baiting makes it harder, more like impossible, to build coalitions."

A good point.

He looked at me curiously. "Were you in?"

I'd been asked that before. Since I walked like a duck and quacked like a duck, a lot of people assumed . . . In high school, I'd flirted with the YCL. When I was growing up, if you did anything progressive, you did it with Communists. They were good organizers. They were around everything progressive happening in the city and mostly on the right side of issues. They had good parties.

When I went to work in Hollywood, the Screen Cartoon-ists Guild, like many of the Hollywood unions before the war, was led by Reds. Aside from putting their foot in their mouths with their foreign policy shifts, they were reasonable to work with, and they were militant trade unionists. I spent five weeks on a picket line at Disney Studios six months or so before I was drafted.

I told Frank, "The leaders of that strike were Reds. They were stand-up guys. I don't see them deserting one of their comrades."

He walked over to look out of the small window in the back wall of the parlor; I guessed to gather his thoughts. From where I sat, I could see what he saw: blank brick walls and the dilapidated wooden back porch hanging off the tenement behind his. When he came back to his desk, he pushed aside stacks of leaflets, copies of the *Daily Worker*, *Political Affairs*, *Masses and Mainstream*, clearing out a space so he could lean on his elbows. If he searched through back issues of *Masses and Mainstream* and the *Daily Worker*, he'd find political cartoons of mine.

He took whatever it was he'd been working on out of the typewriter and put it in the desk drawer. When he opened the top drawer, I caught a glimpse of a small revolver.

"Why the gun?" I asked when he turned to face me. The small caliber handgun wouldn't be the weapon you'd want for overthrowing the government, but it wasn't a toy. I didn't necessarily connect it to the murder of Irwin Johnson either. But I'd keep it in mind.

It didn't bother him that I'd seen the gun. "We're dealing with some rough characters like we were just talking about. I got a wife and kid. Who else is going to protect me?" His face reflected the resolve I'd seen in other guys like him who'd signed on to build a new world and a better life for workers. Their vision had flaws but I didn't make fun of those who believed in it.

"Maybe you were in; maybe you weren't," he said in a quiet moment. "Maybe you dropped out. I ain't asking. It's not easy. You sacrifice. You're committed, but you're still you. You have a family, mother, sister, brother. Sometimes what the Party asks is too much. Harold was a good Communist. He said he didn't kill Johnson. We take him at his word."

I'd been sitting on a straight-backed chair from which I'd moved a stack of Party literature. I stood and retrieved the stuff I'd put on the floor and put it back on the chair. Frank didn't sound convinced Harold hadn't killed his boss, and I wondered why. I hoped it wasn't because he knew something he wasn't telling me.

CHAPTER SEVEN

MIDAFTERNOON

As I was passing through the kitchen on my way out, Elena looked up from washing dishes. "I'll walk out with you," she said. "When my brother meets with his comrades, I have to leave. They have big secrets, like which subway stop they'll hand out the *Daily Worker* at."

She'd said her "brother." My heart leapt.

I'd stayed away from women since my wife left. I didn't feel right getting involved with anyone because I felt I had a part missing. My motor wasn't running right; it was tough getting it started and tough to keep running if I did get it started.

More than once during the war I'd thought that the worst thing that could happen would happen. I was going to die. Once Rebecca was born and I had a wife and daughter I worried that something even worse might happen—that circumstances would become such that I would be forced to leave and wouldn't have them anymore—and then it did happen. So I kept feeling like I still had a wife and baby daughter waiting for me at home when I finished work. It was a feeling like Irv the vet who ran the newsstand told me he had. He still felt his leg that wasn't there anymore.

• • •

Elena wanted to walk out with me. That was a surprise. I would've been sorry to leave and never see her again, but that's what I expected would happen. Now my thoughts were blurred.

"I'll be ready in a jiffy." She dashed into the bedroom I'd walked through and came back in a flash with her hair brushed, more color in her face, a wisp of red on her lips, and sneakers on her feet. I followed her down the four flights of stairs, which she seemed hardly to notice. When we reached the sidewalk, she stopped for a moment.

"You were talking to Frank about Mr. Johnson's murder." Her expression was serious, the girlish flirtation replaced by a no-nonsense expression.

I told her what I'd told her brother, that I was a private investigator trying to prove that Harold had been wrongly convicted.

"I thought that was all over. It happened so long ago. And it's so close to—" The darkness in her eyes said the rest.

I wished people would stop reminding me of that.

"Did Frank tell you I worked for Mr. Johnson?"

Bam. That's what you got when you didn't do your homework. A private eye won't last long in the business when a witness he didn't know was a witness asked the important questions instead of him asking them. "No. I should've known that."

She took my elbow and propelled me toward the river a couple of long blocks west. We found a bench in DeWitt Clinton Park on a tree-lined walk next to a wrought iron fence where we had a view of the Hudson, the cliffs of Jersey on the far side of the river, and a giant ocean liner with a red and black smokestack berthed a few blocks down river. The scent of salt air drifted in on the breeze from the river.

As we sat down, she squinted at me. With her eyes half-closed and her brow wrinkled, she reminded me of a cartoon schoolgirl doing arithmetic. "I know what a private investigator is." She waited as if I should be impressed by this. "I listen to *Philip Marlowe*."

"I'm not as tough or handsome as Philip Marlowe."

She looked me up and down and lowered her eyelashes. "You'll do."

I probably beamed. "Do you mind if I ask you about Mr. Johnson?"

A frown brought wrinkles back to her forehead. "I shouldn't say I worked for him. I wasn't his secretary or anything. I work in the office. There are six of us. His private secretary, Mrs. Simpkins, Alice Simpkins, would know about him."

I wrote down the name. "I'll talk to Mrs. Simpkins. But I'm sure you had some impression of the man. What was he like?"

"He was handsome," she said quickly. "He could be nice when he wanted to. He could also be scary."

"Scary?"

"You had a feeling you wouldn't want to get in his way when he wanted something." She said this with what sounded like grudging admiration.

I got the picture. Like a lot of girls who worked in offices, she was more impressed by guys who wore a suit and carried a briefcase to work than she was by guys wearing overalls and carrying a lunchbox.

As charming and pretty as she was, Elena might well be

one of those office girls who hoped to parlay their good looks and clean fingernails into a house with a picket fence in Westchester with one of those men in suits. Yet something about her told me she knew better. Maybe it was her brother's influence, more likely her own brains. I sensed she was smart enough to get herself out of the hellhole she was born into using devices other than a swishing behind.

"Did you like him?"

She looked at me blankly. "No."

"Why?"

She took a moment to answer. "He was mean."

"To you?"

She hesitated. ". . . To lots of people."

"Could he have done something to create an enemy, to make someone hate him enough to kill him?"

Without batting an eye she said, "He could certainly do that. Make someone hate him."

I waited for her to say more, but she wandered off into her own thoughts. I prodded her. "Why would someone hate him?"

Either my question or her answer angered her. "Rich people think they're almighty." She glared at me. Maybe she was closer in spirit to her brother than I'd thought. "He was mean to the girls in the office, treating them like they're stupid. He'd yell at the drivers and the dispatchers. Men in suits would come to talk to him and he'd yell at them, too. They'd have mad faces when they left."

That was that on Mr. Johnson. She didn't have much to tell me about Harold either. She only knew him to say hello. There were only a few negro drivers at Johnson Transportation and she wasn't prejudiced. She tried to be pleasant to everyone. "Besides, Harold was more of a gentleman than the other hackies. They gamble, they fight, they talk dirty, they cheat their fares, they cheat one another, they cheat the company."

"Some of them are family men," I said.

"Yeah, and some of them are pimps."

"Your brother's a cab driver."

She considered this. "Not really. The Party sent him to organize the union. When he gets that done, they'll send him somewhere else. They want him to go to Russia to study."

"Oh?"

She dismissed the idea with a toss of her hair. "He has a wife and baby. He can't go running off to Russia."

That hit home. For a moment, I pictured Rebecca and couldn't think of anything else. When I came around, Elena was studying my face, as if she saw the sadness I felt.

"Driving a cab's a tough life," I said, dropping in another one of my conversational gems.

"And look at my life." Anger tightened her face and made her body rigid, not a momentary flash of irritation but bitter anger she should have been too young for. "When I was sixteen, I quit school and went to work in a stitching shop. Ma made me. I was good in school. I coulda gone to City College. One of my teachers told me I could. But no. Frank was the one supposed to stay in school. He was the boy and needed an education. So he went to City College and became a Communist. She's not too happy about that. What did a girl need college for? Marry a drunk, have babies, spend her life bent over a sewing machine." She stopped. Her pretty brown eyes settled into mine. "Do you have a wife?"

"No." That was the truth and not the truth. I tore my gaze away from hers.

"Men lie about that."

"I was married. My wife left me a couple of years ago. We're divorced."

"Why?" No pussyfooting around for Elena; she went for the throat. "Were you mean to her?"

"No. We were different. I lost my job and couldn't find work. When the going gets tough, differences between a couple become more important." What happened, I finally got around to telling Elena, was I got named. That meant the blacklist, and that meant no work for me in Hollywood. Our life went downhill fast. When Deborah married me, I'd had a good income and, with some help from her folks and the GI Bill, we bought a house in Malibu. A couple of years later, she left me behind in a run-down motel in Westwood, took our daughter, and went home to mom and pop in Beverly Hills.

Elena understood my dilemma differently. "It's hard to be married when you don't get paid enough to live on. Like for Frank and his wife. Karen don't complain, but I know she doesn't want to be living with Ma and me. She tries to get along, but Ma treats her like a servant girl." Elena smiled for the first time in a while. She lowered her lashes over her eyes. "I take Ma and the baby out sometimes, so Frank and Karen can have a chance to screw."

I wasn't sure what to say after that, so I didn't say anything.

She bowed her head demurely and folded her hands in her lap. After a moment, she perked up. "I'm sorry about your divorce and all. But your wife wasn't a very good wife if she'd leave when the going got hard. A good wife stands by her husband." Elena said this with an emphasis that made clear *she* would not be the kind of wife who left her husband when things got tough.

Of course what happened with Deborah was more complicated than that. I hadn't figured it all out for myself yet, so there was no way I could explain it to Elena.

After a moment, she brightened again. "What does a guy like you do for fun?"

The question caught me in the gut. What did I do for fun? Nothing. Drank dime beers and watched the ballgame—and walked. I wandered the city, wore out the soles of my shoes, and sat on park benches when I was tired and drew sketches. I liked jazz. Once in a blue moon, I'd go to one of the clubs on Fifty-Second Street. A couple of times, Gil took me along when he went up to Harlem, to Small's Paradise or The Savoy. Mostly, I couldn't handle the nightlife if I wanted to make a living in the daytime.

When I told her I liked jazz, she turned up her nose, so I added, "Sometimes, I go to the ballpark, to the stadium."

Her face lit up. "Yankee Stadium? I'd love to go to Yankee Stadium." She wasn't being coy; she was excited. "I want to see Joe DiMaggio."

I said maybe I'd take her one day and tried to sound like a guy who spent big on casual dates, not a guy a payday or two from the soup kitchen. Attempting to get back to business, I asked her who was running the company since Irwin Johnson's death.

"Mr. Johnson's wife and some man are in charge now," she said. "The man is creepy, and I don't think Mrs. Johnson likes me."

I asked her if she could introduce me to Irwin Johnson's private secretary.

"My introducing you wouldn't help," she said. "Mrs. Simpkins don't like me neither."

We sat for a moment watching the river. Elena crossed her legs and leaned back on the bench to let the sun touch her face. Her long eyelashes fluttered as she spoke. "It's beautiful here, peaceful, too nice of a day to talk about bad things." After a moment, she said wistfully, "I wonder if I'll ever sail away on a ship." Her eyes popped open. "Did you ever sail away on a ship?"

"A troop ship."

She turned up her nose. "Talk to me for a little while. I don't want to go back in yet. Tell me about your private eye adventures."

I was a little surprised but mostly glad she didn't ask about the war. I didn't want to talk about it. I didn't much want to talk about my private eye adventures either. The guy I trained with did mostly divorce work, insurance fraud, some criminal work for Gil. I took over the criminal work when I got my license. That work was mostly interviewing witnesses. No gunfights, car chases, or damsels in distress. The hot item in the gumshoe trade these days was background checks. For obvious reasons, I didn't do those.

From somewhere down the river, an ocean liner's horn blasted a long deep-throated howl that meant it was leaving the dock. I didn't tell Elena any private eyes stories but I did tell her a couple of Hollywood stories. She wasn't much interested in the Disney films I worked on without getting any credits. She did like that I met Elizabeth Taylor at a party.

She liked even better that Cary Grant gave my wife and me a lift in his limo one rainy night.

"I'd give anything to be in Hollywood," she said.

"Pretty much, that's what Hollywood would want from you."

It was peaceful sitting by the river. I felt contentment I hadn't felt in a long while, in large part because I was sitting beside Elena. I thought I might put my arm around her, and she might not have minded if I did. I didn't because I wasn't sure I knew why I'd be doing it.

The peaceful river in front of me and pretty Elena beside me notwithstanding, I knew I shouldn't be sitting in the park when I needed to be looking for whoever killed Irwin Johnson if Harold Williams didn't, so reluctantly I stood.

A few minutes later, I walked Elena back to her building and we stood facing each other for a long moment, she on the second step of the stoop, me on the sidewalk. She wanted to say something and so did I. But neither of us did.

CHAPTER EIGHT

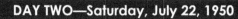

LATE AFTERNOON

The Eighteenth Precinct was a couple of blocks away, so I walked over to try to catch the homicide detective Gil wanted me to talk to. The building, harmless looking enough except for the police cars scattered on the block around it, gave me the shivers. I didn't want to go in because I was afraid they wouldn't let me out. I'd started running from cops when I was in grade school and nothing much had happened since then to change my approach.

The sergeant at the desk didn't look up, even after I'd stood in front of him for longer than seemed polite. When I asked to see Detective Len Volpe, the sergeant gave no indication he'd heard me, so I waited a bit longer, took a couple of steps back and asked again in a much louder voice. He flinched but gave no other indication that he cared if I stayed, left, or fell over dead. After a moment, a man who might be described as tall, dark, and handsome stuck his head out from a hallway behind the precinct desk and hollered, "Who's looking for Volpe?"

I waved. Already put out by the desk sergeant's welcome, I was ready to battle with Volpe. He gestured that I should come toward him and smiled. The smile knocked me off my perch for the moment. I think I smiled in return; not something I did often. His wasn't a salesman's smile and he wasn't a glad-hander. The toughness was there in his dark eyes when he asked, "What can I do for you?"

"Mick Mulligan, I'm a private investigator." I held out my hand. "Gil Silver said I should ask you about the Harold Williams case."

"You work for Gil?"

"Yes and no."

His expression darkened to tell me without words he wasn't going to play games.

"I do a lot of work for him. On this, he's not my client."

"Client?"

I shrugged. "He's not paying me. Someone else is."

"Do you mind telling me who?"

I didn't want to play cute, since I wanted information, so I told him. "The cab drivers' union. Duke Rogowski."

He led me down a hallway to a bare-bones room with a metal table and wooden chairs. It wasn't my idea of an office. Then again, my office wasn't my idea of an office either. We sat down and he looked at me straight, his eyes as hard as coal. "What exactly am I supposed to tell you? You think we did something wrong?"

Volpe was no kid. I felt like a jerk telling this guy who investigated murders for a living that I hoped to prove him wrong about Harold. "Look, I'm not trying to second-guess you . . ." I stumbled over the words because this was exactly what I was doing—second-guessing him.

He waved me off. "I don't take pleasure in sending a man to his death. My job is to collect evidence and give it to the prosecutor. Williams didn't admit to anything. He turned down a plea deal that would have saved him from the chair. A jury decided he was guilty, not me."

Volpe was polite with a kind of old-world charm, not the bluster or bullying I usually got from cops. I caught the Italian accent at the edges of his voice and remembered Gil told me he was born in Italy.

I told him what I knew about the case. "The cops got a tip and found a gun and Irwin Johnson's wallet and cash in Harold's cab. Some drivers testified Harold and Johnson didn't like each other. Anything I might want to know that wasn't in the papers? Witnesses? Fingerprints?"

"That's pretty much it," he said. "Once the DA's office issued a complaint, we worked with them gathering evidence to support the indictment. An office boy found the body in the hallway near a back door that leads to the garage. Two bullet wounds to the chest. The way it looked he was shot in a room off the hallway, a kind of break room, and staggered out. The crime scene guys dusted the entire upstairs and didn't find any prints that didn't belong there. No prints on the gun we found in the cab, though we're pretty sure it was the murder weapon."

"Why there? What was Johnson doing in the office after hours? How would Harold know he'd be there alone?"

Volpe shrugged. "You might ask about any murder why did it happen exactly at the moment it happened and why in the place where it happened. For a lot of them I couldn't give you an answer. Williams said he wasn't there and didn't do it. We couldn't ask Johnson. No one we questioned could answer either of those questions. It's likely no one ever will." Something like good-natured humor cracked his stoic expression. "Unless you can find an answer."

I stayed the course. "Was anyone besides the murderer at the scene when the murder took place?"

Volpe weighed his answer. "We found no reason to think anyone else was there." He pursed his lips—or he might have smiled again but I didn't think so. "That's not the same as saying no one else was there. But again the two people we know were there—"

"Only one you know for sure was there." I said this without thinking—never a good idea in my business—but he didn't disagree. He didn't agree either. I pushed my luck. "What about the person who tipped off the police?"

This got a reaction. He leaned toward me so abruptly I jumped. "You're right. I wanted to find out what she knew, too. She called from a phone booth. We never got to talk to her. We looked for her. She didn't show up for the trial. The prosecutor said he'd be okay without her. She'd provided the medallion number of the cab. The patrol officers testified as to the evidence they found. The gun was pretty damning. Williams had no explanation for how it got there. Still, I'd like to have asked the caller how she came to know what was in the trunk."

"You think she saw what happened?"

He shrugged one shoulder. "She might be a good citizen who saw him put the stuff in the cab. On the other hand, someone might have told her what to say."

"The real killer?"

His frown or maybe a scowl told me he didn't think much of my supposition. "That's possible. It could also be Williams told her, not knowing she'd blab. What I thought at the time—and still do unless you come up with something better—is someone knew what happened and had it in for Harold. Wanted to make sure he didn't get away with it."

"Or wanted him to take the rap whether he killed Johnson or not."

I'd pushed my luck as far as it would go even though I'd have bet Volpe had doubts, too. Whether he did or not, with a snort and a deeper scowl he made clear he'd had enough of this.

"We can speculate all day. Williams was convicted. His lawyer raised a bunch of these might-have-beens that didn't sway the jury."

I waited a moment and started down another track. "Did anything else not add up? Anything you might have wanted to look into you didn't?"

He sat back in his chair and kind of physically absorbed the question. If I was a judge of character—a risky endeavor at best—I'd say he was trying to be helpful. "Witnesses put Williams in the garage that evening, though earlier. Witnesses attested to bad blood between Williams and Johnson over union issues. Witnesses named Williams as a Communist. And the murder weapon was in his possession." Volpe took note of my expression. "Okay, more or less in his possession." He took out a pack of cigarettes and offered me one. We both lit up and watched the smoke rise for a minute.

"Williams couldn't account for his whereabouts at the time of the murder. He had a story but nothing we could verify. I might have looked into that more. Still, his lawyer should have done that and probably did. He never came up with an alibi witness."

I added up what I'd just heard. "Harold had an alibi no one

verified. A witness with important testimony never showed up. This doesn't sound like an airtight case to me."

He didn't agree or disagree.

"What about a known organized crime figure involved with the taxi union? Did anyone wonder where he was at the time of the murder?"

Volpe didn't get angry, defensive, or argumentative, yet he wasn't about to apologize either. "The case against Williams had holes. But it wasn't a railroad job. If we'd found anything implicating someone else, we'd have followed it up." He put out his cigarette and pushed an ashtray across the desk to me.

I stubbed out my butt. "Vincent Forlini, a union vice president, is an associate of Big Al Lucania."

Volpe scrutinized me for a moment and I guess made a judgment in my favor. "Big Al has something to say about a number of unions and a number of businesses. Whatever anyone says about him, he doesn't get his hands dirty. If you ask him, he's a respected businessman. You're more likely to find him at dinner with the mayor than in one of his betting parlors. He might be shaking down half the businessmen at the mayor's dinner but no one will mention it."

I knew most of this but I listened without interrupting.

"Being a known confederate of a crime figure isn't a crime. We didn't find anything linking anyone besides Williams to the murder." He sat back in his chair, bracing his hands behind his head. "I don't have a problem with you taking a fresh look. If we got the wrong man, I hope you prove us wrong before it's too late." He met my gaze with something like sympathy. "I'll tell you again. The case against Williams wasn't ironclad but a lot of cases aren't. Nothing pointed to anyone else."

This time I took out my pack of Luckies and offered him one. He took it, leaned forward for a light, and sat back and exhaled.

"You have your work cut out for you if Big Al is your suspect. A couple of years back, a restaurant supply company owner was murdered after he tried to stand up to a protection racket. The mobsters harassed all of the company owners in the industry—with strikes, fires, broken windows, hijacked trucks; the big thing was the strikes—until the owners joined the employer association. Once they signed up their labor troubles stopped. A lieutenant of Big Al's ran the employers association. Another lieutenant ran the union local.

"The one owner who wouldn't go along filed a criminal complaint and named names. The organized crime unit charged one of Big Al's lieutenants with extortion. Before they could bring the guy in, the complaining owner disappeared. Not long after, his body turned up in a freezer delivered to a restaurant in Queens. From then on, nobody knew nothing. The rest of the owners joined the association and swore on their mothers' eyes they'd never been threatened."

I thanked Volpe for his cautionary tale. I kinda liked him. He might have held back some things or he might not have. Gil would tell me I didn't ask the right questions. Maybe so, but on this one Gil didn't know the right questions either.

When I left the precinct, I walked over to the Johnson Transportation garage on Fifty-First Street. It was a nice day, not quite as hot as the day before and quieter because the stitching shops weren't running on Saturday and the trucks were parked. The garment workers and truck drivers were union. The cabs were running, though, most of the drivers coming up on sixty or seventy hours for the week. The cab drivers weren't union.

I didn't know what I might find at the garage. I didn't know what I was looking for. What I found was a crusty guy, wearing a ratty suit that I'd bet hadn't been cleaned or pressed since before the war, sitting at a desk in a glassed-in cubicle next to the garage door. The makeshift office reeked of cigar smoke; years of it coated the glass walls.

The guy at the desk chewed on the nub of a dead stogie; a large brown glass ashtray overflowing with ashes and cigar stubs sat on the desk surrounded by a half dozen empty De Nobili cigar packs. The guy lifted his bushy eyebrows to tell me he knew I was there, but this didn't take him away from whatever he was doing with a stub of a pencil on some sheets of paper on his desk. I moved closer to take a peek over his shoulder. He was working on a scratch sheet, doping out the trotters at Roosevelt that night.

"Stanley Dancer driving?" I asked.

Bending closer to the paper for a moment, he worked out something before he glanced up. "The second and the sixth race. You bet the driver?"

"I'm told with trotters you do well to bet on the driver."

Like a normal New Yorker, I rooted for a baseball team and bet the numbers and the ponies with my neighborhood bookie. When I was flush after the war, I'd go to Hollywood Park and bet on the thoroughbreds. Since I came back to New York, I mostly bet on harness racing. I like to watch standard-bred trotters and pacers, too, but didn't get to the track so much anymore.

My advice had some merit. Harness racing is more

predictable than the thoroughbreds. The same horses run more frequently, the distance is pretty much the same for all races, and the drivers have more control over what happens in a race.

This makes a good driver important. It also makes the races easier to fix, and makes it harder to find a winner at good odds. Most horse players lose more than they win no matter what they bet on, so they don't have much confidence in their judgment, and being unsure of their picks, as well they should be, will take advice from any bum off the street.

The dispatcher went back to his scratch sheets for a moment. "I dunno." He glanced up, a more serious take this time. "So what do you bother me about? I ain't buying anything if you're selling. Boss don't allow it." His eyes went wider. "Wait a minute. You ain't from the union? Cause if you are—" He reached under his desk and came up with a baseball bat.

I saw that coming. "I'm not from the union," I said before he could straighten up. "My name is Mick Mulligan. I'm a private detective."

"Really?"

I showed him my license. He took it from me and examined it like a jeweler counting carats. "Wow! I never saw one of these. You like Philip Marlowe, the private eye on the radio?"

This was twice in the same day me and Marlowe in the same breath. Maybe I was starting to look my part. "I want to ask you about your boss's murder."

"Why's that and where you been?"

I told him I was working on behalf of Harold Williams, leaving out Duke and the union so he didn't go for the baseball bat again.

"I'm Tony." He looked at his hand, up at me, back at his hand, and decided against a handshake. "They call me Fat Tony. But I prefer Tony."

I kept my hand to myself also. "Was Mr. Johnson a good boss?"

"I never had a good boss. You got a good boss?"

"I don't have a boss."

"Lucky for you. Johnson was like all the bosses: Squeeze a nickel till the buffalo shits."

I smiled. Whatever the rest of America might think of the class struggle, it was alive and well in Hell's Kitchen. "Did you know Harold?"

Tony took the cigar nub from his mouth and waved it at me. "Of course I knew Harold. He was okay for a colored guy. The boss didn't like him 'cause he was union and made trouble with the colored drivers. Me, I don't like unions. My brother was in the cooks' union. They didn't do shit. They're all crooks. Harold was okay though. He didn't take it personal you disagreed with him." He put the battered stub back in his mouth and spoke around it. "What makes you think Harold didn't kill Mr. Johnson?"

"What makes you think he did?"

Tony's answer came quicker than I expected. "What makes you think I do?"

He had me there. Despite the shabby suit, the Racing Form, and the city-streets diction, Fat Tony was nobody's fool.

"You don't believe what you read in the papers?"

"Any one of twenty guys coulda put somethin' in the trunk of that cab."

"There's a woman involved."

"Ain't there always?"

Fat Tony's intelligence was clearly underutilized running a taxi garage. "Someone called in a tip to the cops that they should search the cab. The caller was a woman."

"You ain't gonna find her here. No women in the garage. The office girls go in and out of the office from the door near Eleventh Avenue. They don't come down here for nothin'. Them with their high heel shoes and nylon stockings think they're too good for hackies." He took the mangled cigar out of his mouth, looked at it, put it back in his mouth, and chomped on it.

"Harold told me you were in the garage the night of the murder. Can you tell me who else was here that night?"

A dark cloud descended over Fat Tony; he paled slightly as if he might be getting ill. He removed the cigar butt, took a deep breath, and looked at the ceiling. After a moment, he turned his vacant glance on me. "Like I told them lawyers, I don't remember who was here. I didn't remember if I was here. It was the same as any other nights. A bunch of drivers come in; a bunch of drivers go out. I don't remember who's who."

He might be telling the truth. He might be lying. Arguing with him wouldn't change anything, so I moved on. "Did any of the drivers have it in for Harold . . . maybe because of the union?"

Tony squinted to consider this. "There's two sides in the union fought wit' each other. Harold was on one side. The other side might not have liked him so much."

"Any beefs?"

"Someone's cab might get a flat or a smashed windshield. Some guys got fake fares to somewhere out in Brooklyn and got smacked around out there in Canarsie or Sheepshead Bay. No one said Harold did any of that. The colored drivers kept to themselves.

"Except one time, they, the coloreds, thought they got a raw deal on which cabs they got. They put up a stink. Milled around outside the garage until Mr. Johnson went and talked to them. He met with Harold and another guy and they worked somethin' out."

"Who was the other guy?"

"Another union guy, a white guy, Frank something."

"DeMarco?"

"Right. They say he's a Red. Anyway, the colored guys went back to work. Mr. Johnson said everyone should have the same shot at a cab, no favorites. Me, I don't play favorites. Some of the dispatchers, maybe they did. They'd get a couple of bucks, a box of cigars from the drivers. Me, I mind my own business."

"Did Johnson have any silent partners?"

He lowered his voice. "That's not something I'd know about."

"The widow, does she have partners?"

Tony clamped down tighter on the cigar. He chose his words carefully. "You'd have to ask Mrs. Johnson about that."

"Did she come to the garage before her husband's death?"

"She never came to the garage. As far as I know she never went to the office. No one knew Johnson had a wife. Now, she comes here in the office, even in the garage. Acting like she owns the place." He wrinkled his brow and cocked his head. "Which I guess she does."

If you can't get in the front door, you try the back door. I tried again. "With someone?"

Tony took the stogie out of his mouth and dropped the mangled plug of tobacco into the ashtray. "With a guy you don't want to run up against." He lowered his voice and his eyelashes. "Her adviser, she says. You know any advisers what walk around with two bodyguards?"

CHAPTER NINE

Irwin Johnson was still in the phone book despite his untimely demise. Tony let me use the office phone to call the widow, which I did knowing it was unlikely she'd be home on Saturday evening, and even more unlikely she'd be willing to talk to me. A maid answered; more precisely, a woman with an Irish brogue whom I assumed to be the maid answered.

"Whom might I say is calling?" The sound of her voice reminded me of my mother. She had the same decisiveness as my mother also. When I said I was a vacuum cleaner salesman, she hung up.

Fat Tony recommended a driver Artie Kaplow, who was leaving the garage to start his shift, to take me to the Johnson home in Riverdale, in the far northwest of the Bronx along the Hudson. I'd been to Riverdale a couple of times on cases looking for deadbeats. Otherwise, there was no reason for anybody who didn't live there to go there, though it was a pleasant place, like a gigantic park with houses—big houses— and postwar high-rise apartment buildings looming among the trees and rock formations of Lower Paleozoic Fordham gneiss.

I was surprised I remembered Lower Paleozoic Fordham

gneiss. I did because of Mr. Weiss, my geography teacher junior year at DeWitt Clinton High School. My mother had been big on education. Unlike my father, a farm boy and veteran of the West Cork Brigade of the IRA, she'd been educated in the north of Ireland under the British and believed herself something of an aristocrat, living in a Bronx tenement and working as a washerwoman notwithstanding. When it came to education there was no two ways about it, so as a kid, while I wasn't so good on behavior, I got good grades.

The thing about Mr. Weiss was that he loved rocks more than anything, probably more than he loved his wife. When a teacher loved his subject and taught about it with bubbling enthusiasm, it rubbed off on a student if he paid attention, which I did out of fear of running afoul of my mother. Running afoul of my mother meant no movies on Saturday, barely short of a death sentence.

Riding up the Henry Hudson Parkway in the cab that afternoon, watching the river, I thought about rock formations and Mr. Weiss because I'd remembered he'd been a Communist in those days, and I remembered reading in the *Journal-American* when I first got back to the city from LA that he'd been fired along with a passel of other New York City teachers because they wouldn't sign an oath swearing that they weren't now and never had been Communists.

His firing made me wonder, because there hadn't been so much wrong with being a Communist back in the thirties, or at least it wasn't illegal; same during the war, when the US had been allied with the Soviet Union. So something Mr. Weiss had done that hadn't been wrong at the time he was

doing it had now become wrong in retrospect. Was he supposed to decide today to not have done it years ago?

The sun was low in the sky above the palisades on the
Jersey side as I considered how I would approach the widow.
I didn't know why I had to rush off to the Bronx to see her
right that minute. She might have gone out. She might refuse
to talk to me. The trip could be a waste of time and money.

One not-so-good thing about me is I tend to do something
as soon as I think of it, often to my regret. On the other hand,
the afternoon was shot anyway, the clock was ticking on
Harold, and I needed to do something. I thought I might ask
Artie Kaplow if he knew Harold, but Artie had a forbidding
manner behind the wheel so I held back, leaving him to his
murderous commentary about the other drivers on the Henry
Hudson Parkway.

By the time we began the climb from the parkway into the
hills of Riverdale, I'd decided I'd be straightforward with Mrs.
Johnson. Why wouldn't she be helpful if I told her the truth?
Wouldn't she want her husband's murderer brought to justice
and an innocent man freed? Of course if she was the murderer,
she wouldn't.

Twenty minutes later, I rang the doorbell of a stately stone
house that fronted on a bluestone driveway which Artie's
Checker cab now graced. I'd given him an extra fin to wait
for me. Behind the house, a manicured lawn drifted toward a
cliff that overlooked the river. It was hard to believe I was in
the city.

"Hello," I said to the not-quite-young woman who opened
the door. She looked like she stepped off the stage of the
Copacabana. Her blond hair tied back, her dark eyebrows

arched over her blue eyes, a low-cut halter top draped over her breasts and open in a large V between them, she was stunning. My gaze traveled from her eyes to her breasts and back to her eyes and back to her breasts. When my gaze dropped to her tight-fitting white shorts that at first I thought were her underpants, I took a breath and stepped back.

She watched my unraveling with an amused expression, taking the trouble to switch her weight from her right hip to her left hip and back again. A bump and grind that would've been worth the price of admission to the Copa. Yet something in her face was almost childlike, even with a wrinkle here and there. With a tiny mouth and nose, pale unblemished skin, and long flickering eyelashes, she looked bashful.

"You surprised me," she said.

"You can say that again." I swallowed, or perhaps I gulped. "Am I interrupting something?"

"No. I've come from the pool." She gestured to her voluptuous body.

"You dress nicely."

"Thank you." Her lashes lowered over her peepers. "You're a kind man," she said when she lifted them.

This took me aback. "Why would you think that?"

"Your eyes." She let go of the door. "People try to take advantage of you when you're a widow." Her gaze was steady. She wasn't looking for sympathy.

"I'm sorry about your loss, Mrs. Johnson. I'm sure it's been hard for you."

"You don't know the half of it. Since Irwin's death, I think I've met every swindler in New York." She glanced at me curiously. "You're not a swindler, are you?"

"To tell you the truth, I'm a private detective."

"Just as bad." A flicker of amusement crossed her face. She didn't bring up Philip Marlowe.

I told her I needed to ask her some questions related to her husband's murder. "A man's going to die in the electric chair. He might not be the killer."

I couldn't read her expression. Maybe skepticism. Maybe impatience. "He had a trial. They found him guilty. How's it you know better?" When I started to answer, she interrupted me. "You can come in." I followed her swiveling hips toward the interior of the house. "I hired a private detective to follow my husband," she said over her shoulder.

When we were seated on white couches facing each other across a gray-and-black patterned carpet, she said, "Irwin bought him off. I should have known. Everyone's for sale." She caught my reaction. "You're not for sale, Mr. . . . ? I didn't catch your name."

"Mulligan. Mick Mulligan. And no, I'm not for sale."

"You haven't been offered enough."

Actually, I hadn't been offered anything, but I didn't see any reason to mention that. "Why did you hire a private detective?"

"I was tired of Irwin cheating on me. I wanted to burn him in a divorce."

"You knew he was having an affair?"

She made a gesture with her eyes, not exactly rolling them but similar, that suggested she forgave my innocence. "My husband was a playboy before he married me, and after. He was wealthy, family wealth handed down to him. He'd always had more money than he could spend and would continue to have more money than he could spend if he drove the taxi company into the ground, which he would have done if not for me. Because of this, I wanted the company in a divorce settlement."

Well, there was a motive for you. I didn't say anything.

We were on the same wavelength. "Now I get the company as his widow instead of as a wronged-woman divorcée. Poor Irwin got a raw deal."

"Getting murdered is pretty much a raw deal, I'd say."

"Don't get me wrong. Irwin's death horrified me. He was spoiled. He was—I don't know how to say it—he thought himself more important than anyone else. He was self-centered, selfish. But he didn't deserve to die like that. In his own way, he was good to me. I live well." She gestured at her surroundings. "This, my bank account, my business, all of this as long as I kept a blind eye to his dalliances. I got tired of charades, tired of him. Still, he didn't deserve to die."

"Business?"

"Yes. I run a small business, a catering service. I plan parties—elegant affairs—for women in Irwin's social circle who don't have the class or taste to do it for themselves—dinners, engagement parties, bridal showers, anniversaries, intimate gatherings. Irwin had the connections and the money to get started. The event-planning business made money. Irwin realized I was smarter than he thought I was."

"Did you love him?"

She took a moment. "Ah, love!" She smiled at me like a grown woman noticing some sweetness in a child. "Irwin loved himself. Anyone else's love was superfluous. He wouldn't know what to do with it." Her smile would be condescending if I didn't believe it was genuine. "You're a nice man. You'll fall in love or you're in love now. With men like Irwin and the women they take on—like me—it's a transaction. We each get something out of it, but not love. Not that anyone admits this is how it is.

"I grew up with unhappiness. Pa gets drunk and slaps your ma. Everybody's crying and complaining. Everyone's unhappy. You go to school and try to be good. You dream. But you get beaten down like your ma, like everyone around you. And then you get a little older and you learn you have something men want." She crossed and recrossed her shapely slim legs, not brazenly, perhaps unconsciously, as if to call my attention to what that something was.

"Call it, for the sake of decency, beauty. Men call you pretty. They say nice things to you. At first, it's the awkward boys in the neighborhood who don't know any more than you do what they want or how to get it. They kiss you; they fondle you. They want more. But you know—because it's a sin and because your ma warned you that you'll end up like her—there's nothing in it for you.

"Then you're lucky; you have some talent as well as looks. For me, I could dance. An agent found me. I danced in a line at a nightclub. There, you meet men who do know what they want and how to get it. So a man takes you in a chauffeured car to a champagne dinner. He puts you up for a night in a hotel room with carpets you sink into up to your ankles and a bed as big as the living room at home and as soft as you imagine a cloud would be."

She watched me for a moment. "Am I boring you? Do people often invite you in and tell you their life stories?"

Actually, people a lot of times did tell me things, I guess because I cared to hear what they wanted to tell me. "Not usually," I said not entirely truthfully.

"Well, you get the picture. The poor girl gets whisked away, like the dairy maid in the fairy tale gets whisked away by the charming prince, to a life of luxury. The charming prince—a wealthy man in my version of the story—gets what he wants." She lowered her eyelashes. "I was flattered that a man who could afford to buy anything he wanted wanted me . . ." She smiled, not shyly and not out of embarrassment, and batted her eyelashes. "Wanted to buy me."

She waited, I thought for me to approve of what she'd done or to forgive her for it. Maybe neither. When she'd waited long enough, she said, "I don't know why I told you that. I don't want you to think I'm terrible. If I didn't love my late husband, I didn't hate him."

What she didn't want me to think was that she murdered him was my guess. "His getting himself knocked off was a break for you, saved you getting a messy divorce."

She was neither shocked nor insulted. "No. Irwin would have paid for a divorce if I caught him with his pants down. Men like him are accustomed to paying to make things go away." The twinkle left her eyes. "Despite your kindly nature, I'd expect you to be a man a woman wouldn't want to cross."

"You put a lot of faith in your impressions."

"A girl must make quick decisions about men." A light went on behind her eyes. "That's why you're here. You're a private eye looking for a killer. That's—" The light got brighter. "Oh my God, you think I killed him." Her surprise was so genuine it was almost funny.

She took a cigarette from a shiny box that might have been onyx next to a silver lighter on the coffee table in front of her. "Help yourself." I took one, a Fatima, king size, cork tip. I preferred Luckies, but Fatima fit the surroundings. When she leaned toward me with the silver table lighter, the halter top gaped open. Noticing my eyes brighten, she caught herself and reached to close the gap. This time when her eyelashes drifted over the blue eyes she blushed.

We got the cigarette lit and both of us sat back. She narrowed her eyes like a good poker player, no mirror to her soul. "Why do you think the taxi driver didn't kill Irwin? If he didn't, one of those other drivers did."

"Why would one of the drivers kill him?"

"Because they're greedy. Greedy lowlifes."

Her take on the cab drivers matched Elena DeMarco's, not so different than how most New Yorkers viewed the poor bastards. Driving a hack was a tough job, twelve hours a day, six days a week, a rat race, full of stress and frustration, not much reward. I didn't like Mrs. Pampered knocking the guys whose labor paid for her mansion on the hill, her sparkling jewelry, her silk underwear and satin sheets.

"Be hard to run a cab company without them," I said in as reasonable a tone as I could manage. "They've got a right to join together and get what's coming to them."

The atmosphere in the room grew chilly. Her babyface didn't change, her eyes were just as blue, the eyelashes just as feathery, but the ice in the depths of the blue was like that in a debt collector's eyes. That the drivers were trying to unionize was Exhibit A in her argument they were greedy.

"The company owners earned their wealth," she told me.

"Why should they let bums who don't know how to do anything but drive a cab take it away? Over my dead body."

The dead body in question was actually her husband's, but I didn't say this. Neither did I say her husband earned his money by being born. What I said was "A lot of bosses in the city negotiate with their workers. They still make money."

"If the owners talk to anyone it will be through The New York Taxi Cab Owners Association. We've engaged a labor-management consultant."

I saw what was coming. "Not Big Al Lucania, by any chance?"

She stiffened. A blow torch wouldn't melt her stare. "Mr. Lucania has been advising me since my husband's death."

"From what I hear, Big Al mostly helps himself. The owners' association is how the owners pay him for having the unions he controls keep workers in their place."

"What's wrong with that?"

Such a pretty face with such a black heart. Still, it wasn't for me to give civics lessons, so I moved on. "Does Big Al have an interest in Johnson Transportation?"

The confidence drained from her expression. I expected she'd tell me it was none of my business but she surprised me. "The company is privately owned; a couple of Irwin's cousins have stock but never did anything but collect dividends. Mr. Lucania, it appears, invested in a subsidiary of the company."

"Appears?"

She leaned back on the couch and crossed her arms. "I discovered after Irwin's death he had a bank account I didn't know about. The bookkeeper and the accountant didn't know about it either." She rounded her lips and blew a smoke ring.

"Mr. Lucania and Irwin created a subsidiary for livery service with Wall Street financial companies and banks.

"Johnson Transportation drivers did the work but the payments went to a different bank account. . . . It's nothing shady if that's what you think." She took another cigarette from the onyx box on the glass table and lit it with the silver lighter before she noticed she had a lit cigarette in the ash tray.

Nothing shady? "Shady" was the first thing that came to mind. In one way, Eva Johnson was guileless. She didn't have to answer my questions, but she did. On the other hand, she was partners of some sort with Big Al. Hidden bank accounts, partners with a gangster—she was either naive or a double crosser and perhaps a murderer.

You wouldn't put it past her that she might prevail upon Big Al to use his good offices to speed up the process of Irwin handing over the cab company. It could also be that Eva's late husband was foolish enough to get in Big Al's way, something she had nothing to do with. Lots of things were possible.

Eva stubbed out both cigarettes and stood, interrupting my reverie. "If you're finished with your questioning, I have things to do." I was getting on her nerves, so it was time to leave. I asked her for names of her late husband's friends, business associates, and relatives. She claimed not to know his friends or business associates, named a couple of cousins who lived in Westchester, and told me the name of the private detective she'd hired, Walter Bauer. I didn't know him—private eyes weren't much for solidarity—but I thought I'd look him up one day soon.

CHAPTER TEN

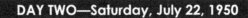

EVENING

When I left Eva Johnson, I noticed another cab, a DeSoto, parked on the bluestone driveway behind Artie's Checker. What's more, Artie and the driver from the other cab were grappling with one another, the other driver at the moment holding Artie in a headlock. After my encounter with the thugs the day before, I began carrying a sap—one of the tools of the trade—so I used it in this instance to persuade the interloper to let up on my driver.

I didn't hit him especially hard but I caught his ear, which got a yelp out of him as he jumped back from Artie to tend to it. As he did, Artie gave him something else to worry about with a right cross to the jaw, right on the button. That didn't seem fair, so I waved the sap at Artie letting him know I'd give him a whack if he didn't stop. He did and stood in front of me red-faced and panting.

When he stopped puffing, he picked up his cap, and we stood over the man on the ground, whom Artie said was Mike Sheehan. Mr. Sheehan bore a striking resemblance to the quiet thug from my encounter in front of Grand Central the night before.

The beef came about, said Artie, because Sheehan got too big for his britches. Sheehan's side of the story when he felt up to talking—sitting on the ground, leaning back against the red fender of his DeSoto rubbing his jaw and gingerly touching his ear—was that as Mrs. Johnson's chauffeur he was obliged to protect her, and how was he to know what a guy was up to who had no business parked in her driveway and wouldn't say why he was there.

After getting back behind the wheel, Artie tucked away the paperback he'd been reading while he was waiting. The book he put into the glove box was *Never Come Morning*. The sultry woman on the cover had brown hair and wore a tight-fitting orange dress; her expression, filled with terror yet at the same time seductive, reminded me of Eva Johnson.

"How's the book?"

"Reading's good for the idle time. I picked up the habit in the army."

Turned out Artie was more willing to chat on this leg of the trip. He had known Harold Williams, he said, and liked him. He knew Frank DeMarco, too, but wasn't so sure about him. "They say he's a Red. Frank's an okay guy. But if you listen to Senator McCarthy, he says the Reds are trying to take over the country for the Russians."

"I don't listen to Senator McCarthy," I told him.

"A lot of people do." Artie had a good deal to say about Joe McCarthy.

"I'm not a fan of the man myself," I told him when he'd finished. For reasons I wasn't sure of—maybe because it's a long way from the North Bronx to Sunnyside—I told him about my run-in with the witch hunters. He thought it was a shame I was blacklisted. But he wasn't going to agree with me that the witch hunters were the real anti-Americans. He wasn't vehement about it. "It's hard to know what to think," he said. "The guys I know, they like Joe McCarthy."

Artie was of the breed of worker the Communists couldn't get through to because he believed in the American Way—despite his particular American Dream putting him behind the wheel of a Checker twelve hours a day, with no health insurance, pension, or guarantee that he'd make enough for lunch at a greasy spoon on some days.

He was for the union but had no interest in upending the order of things to create a workers' state. If you asked him—which I didn't—he'd say life was what it was, and it wasn't up to him to change things. What he did say, without my asking, was that Mr. Johnson did the best he could by his workers, loaning money to a number of drivers when they fell upon hard times.

Johnson loaning his workers money struck a chord—more like a gong. He might have loaned his own money, or since he was in cahoots with Big Al, he might have been a middleman for a loan sharking racket. Big Al sat atop pretty much all of the city's rackets, loan sharking included. "What kind of interest did Mr. Johnson charge for his loans?" I asked. The going rate for the loan sharks was six for five.

"I wouldn't know about that. It was done private and personal. Guys could go to Mr. Johnson when they were in a jam. He was square with them." Artie checked on me through his rearview mirror. "They say Harold was a Communist, too. You wouldn't know it. You never knew what he was thinking. Negroes are like that. You don't know what they're thinking."

Artie, like most white American workers, didn't know what to make of Black folks. Guys like him were puzzled more than angry about Jackie Robinson. They didn't expect him to be as good as he was. Quite a few would have preferred he stay in the Negro Leagues. Others didn't want to admit he was better than most major leaguers.

White workers for the most part believed Negroes were supposed to get the short end of the stick; that was their lot in life, the minor leaguers to white guys' big leagues. Joe Louis was a great fighter, these guys said, because his head was thicker than a white guy's head so he could take punches better. This didn't explain how he came to punch so hard and so quickly. But it wasn't like they thought very deeply about their belief.

Negroes were okay, most of them would say, as long as they stayed in their place. That place was somewhere other than white neighborhoods and white workplaces. Most of the AFL craft unions had exclusionary policies and were lily white. The CIO wasn't exclusionary; it believed all industrial workers belonged in the same unions and acted on this belief. That didn't stop white CIO workers from every now and then going on strike against and occasionally rioting against their fellow workers who happened to be Negro.

Artie and I were at odds on how we saw many things in life, and he was smart enough to recognize this after our brief exchange of views. Yet when he pulled up in front of my apartment building, he told me I could call him whenever I needed a lift. He gave me his home phone number and instructions on how I could track him down through the taxi dispatcher.

Despite our differences in outlook, he knew, as I did, we had a connection, bound together simply because we both worked for a living and both believed every workingman was owed a square deal and a helping hand when he needed one, something the Communists, but not Artie, would call class solidarity.

CHAPTER ELEVEN

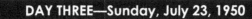

MORNING

I went to the nine o'clock Mass at St. Teresa's, a storefront on Skillman Avenue—a sort of branch office to the main church out Queens Boulevard in Woodside. The Diocese of Brooklyn was raising money so the Sunnyside Catholics could have a church of their own. It hadn't got there yet. But it would. The diocese stood second to no one in shaking down its followers.

Sunnyside was an unusual neighborhood, though I suppose all neighborhoods are unique. Sunnyside's uniqueness had to do with garden apartments—hundreds of them—and not for rich people. Sunnyside Gardens was built in the 1920s specifically for workers and that's who lived in them, a lot of Irish, for one. A bunch of Italians also lived in Sunnyside Gardens; they were Catholics, like the Irish, though I didn't know where they went to church.

Quite a few Jews lived in Sunnyside Gardens, as well. They, of course, weren't Catholic, and went to a synagogue on Forty-Second Street near Forty-Fifth Avenue. As far as I could tell, everyone got along—in Irish bars, Jewish delis, and Italian spaghetti joints—and used the Chinese laundry. Folks who looked like Harold Williams were as scarce as hen's teeth.

On Sunday morning if you happened to be around

Skillman Avenue and Forty-Fourth Street you might think you were in Dublin. I was raised Catholic, stopped going to church for a while, went to Mass such as it was in the army. I started it up when I got back to New York since this was the thing to do on Sunday morning in Sunnyside.

After I got home with the *Sunday News* and was reading the comics, Larry Dennis, my pal the recently blacklisted comedian, called again. Usually, Larry was excitable and jittery, like a chipmunk; that he was all-in-a-dither you could usually tell even over the phone. This time was different; he was somber, funereal. He sounded distant, as if he didn't remember we were friends, as if I were someone he was asking directions from.

He wanted me to recommend a lawyer.

I tried to lighten things up. "You need a lawyer? Are you getting sued or suing?"

Nothing doing. "I got big problems, Mick . . . Big problems. The guy they arrested? That atom bomb spy Rosenberg? I knew him. We were friends at City College, good friends. He tried to get me to join the Party. For years, he kept trying."

"That was a long time ago—"

"They don't forget. They'll ask if I knew he was a Communist. Of course, I knew. He wanted me to join. I'm all over his address book."

"But you didn't join."

Larry was quiet for a few seconds but only a few seconds. "This isn't just about being a Communist. It's worse. It's about being a spy for the Russians. They'll crucify me. They'll say I'm a spy, too."

"Take it easy." I could feel him shaking through the phone.

What secrets was he going to give the Russians? He made his living—or used to, at any rate—spouting lines someone else had written. What was he going to do, hand over secret jokes to the Russians?

"I'm at the end of my rope, Mick. Yesterday, the boss told me some guys from the studio saw me going into the kitchen. They complained I was still working there. The boss sounded like he's having second thoughts. He don't need no trouble, he says." A loud sigh from Larry. "Me, I don't have anything but troubles. The bastards from the FBI come and talk to him. That'll be it. The sons-of-bitches won't even let me work as a dishwasher.

"You know what I'm looking for . . . one of us. A lawyer who'll answer some questions for me. I gotta be able to trust he won't blab to anyone about what I ask him." He paused for a long moment. "Someone like you who won't rat no matter what it costs him."

I told him lawyers had what was called attorney-client privilege. "It's like the priest has the seal of confession. With this lawyer, they could rip his tongue out before he'd give up anything." I gave him Gil's phone number.

Larry didn't have anything else to say—not even thanks— so I wished him luck with whatever he was up to, and he hung up. Little did I know.

A half hour later, while I was scrambling a couple of eggs, Gil Silver called. "Where've you been?" he said. No Hello.

"I've been to church. Now I'm cooking breakfast."

Gil grumbled. He didn't believe in church. I don't think he believed in breakfast either.

I started in on him before he could get to me. "Do you know a Dr. Mortimer Carter?"

"I do."

"What can you tell me about him?"

Irritation seeped into Gil's voice. He didn't like talking about things he didn't bring up. "What do you want me to tell you about him?"

I went over what Carter said about the CP framing Harold Williams. "Were any of witnesses against Harold Party members?"

"Read the transcript."

My scrambled eggs were burning so I got irritated myself. "For a reputedly wise man, you're not much help."

Gil harrumphed. "An element of wisdom is knowing what you don't know."

"I burned my eggs for this? . . . The CP framing Harold— would you look into that?"

I started to tell him the rest of what I'd been doing but he stopped me. He didn't like talking business on the phone; he said his phones were tapped. So he told me to meet him at the Lexington Candy Shop, a luncheonette near his apartment on the Upper East Side. We'd met there a few times before, so I figured by now the FBI had that joint bugged, too. But I didn't say this. Instead, I dumped the last of my burnt scrambled eggs into the garbage can.

Sunday was the day for my weekly call to my daughter. If I'd stayed in LA, I would've had a three-hour *supervised* visit with her. The supervision was because my ex-wife's shyster lawyer convinced the senile divorce court judge that the Communist plan for world domination—which I promoted—called for the destruction of the nuclear family.

I approached the phone calls with both joy and dread; joy

because I heard Rebecca's voice and with luck her giggle; dread because she was two years old, so how could I tell her anything she'd understand? How could I tell her I wanted to be with her more than anything?

This call, like the others, lasted two or three minutes and left me staring at the wall, my eyes blurred, telling myself I should go back to LA and wash dishes. If Larry Dennis could wash dishes, why couldn't I?

Gil wore a pinstripe suit to the lunch joint. Despite everyone in the place wearing their Sunday best, he stood out among the after-church, East Side, late-breakfast crowd like the Lord of the Manor paying a visit to the serfs. His manner would suggest he was oblivious to the side glances from booths and tables, though knowing him—and I knew him better than he thought I did—he was aware of them. He expected he was the star of the show wherever he went and most of the time he was.

Before he'd gotten himself settled, I told him Larry Dennis was going to call him.

"He already did. I saw him this morning."

I looked at Gil curiously. It had been only a couple of hours since I'd given Larry his number.

"He called this morning from a phone booth across from my apartment building."

"So you talked to him?" This was my backdoor approach to finding out what Larry needed so desperately to talk to a lawyer about. I should have known better.

"We talked."

"I'm worried about him," I said.

"You should be." His glance was meaningful, though I didn't know what it meant. Whatever Larry's problem was, Gil wasn't going to talk about it. He asked about my visit with Harold, so I told him.

"I hope you've got a profound legal theory to get the poor guy off because I don't know what the hell I'm supposed to do in two lousy weeks."

He showed mild interest in me while he took a napkin from the dispenser and tucked it into his shirt front to serve as a bib. As a trial lawyer he had lots of mannerisms that seemed inconsequential but served his purpose of momentarily knocking you off your game.

His bib ritual was to make me wonder if I'd said the wrong thing already, so I stammered. "I'm not sure I should have taken the case. I don't have the experience." I told him about my latest encounters in addition to Harold, his mother, and Dr. Carter—Frank De Marco, Lenny Volpe, Eva Johnson. I left out Elena and the Irish hooligans.

When I finished, he didn't have anything to say, so I kept going. "There may be lots of reasons why the trial wasn't fair. That doesn't mean Harold didn't kill the guy. Maybe he had a good reason . . . Do you know that he's innocent?"

Gil had finished his tucking and regarded me calmly. "I know from the transcript he wasn't proven guilty beyond a reasonable doubt. The prosecutor reminded the jury that Communists were murderers. Harold was a Communist. Therefore, Harold was a murderer. I'm sorry to say I doubt an appeals court would find anything wrong with that argument."

"There's the gun," I said.

He shrugged and then gestured to the counter guy, whom

he called Ed, and asked for a chocolate malted. He was wearing a pinstriped suit and a bib—and drinking a malted. I ordered another cup of coffee.

"Harold Williams is innocent?"

"I wouldn't have told Duke to hire you if I thought he'd be wasting his money." Instead of looking at me, Gil took in his surroundings. Nearly all of the booths were occupied, most by couples, some by families with a kid or two or three. But the row of stools along the marble soda fountain counter was empty.

"My first job when I was a kid was in a drugstore behind a counter like that." He nodded toward the soda fountain. "You had to work your way up from being a sweeper or a delivery boy to become a soda jerk . . . To correct a misunderstanding, the term derived from the action of pulling the lever that squirted the soda into the glass, a jerking motion. It wasn't meant to characterize the intelligence of the fountain attendant.

"This was during Prohibition. The druggist I worked for sold what was called medicinal liquor—Old Forester bourbon from Kentucky—which was legal to wealthy customers, the respectable people in town, who had prescriptions for the alcohol to cure various maladies. Around the holidays, the local gentry, the police chief, judges, town councilmen all came down with the grippe, bronchitis, pharyngitis, and other ailments."

I didn't ask him the point of this recollection. I knew he had one. Starting back in our army days when I was his legal clerk, Gil, believing he needed to widen my understanding of how the world worked, would pass along his recollections and observations he felt would enlighten me.

When I didn't ask about the larger meaning of his having been a soda jerk and assistant bootlegger, he said, "Scare tactics convinced a jury if they failed to convict they'd be aiding and abetting Stalin's crusade to destroy the American way of life."

He looked up from his malted, his wire rimmed glasses magnifying his soulless grey eyes so I felt like I was looking into the abyss. "Is being a Negro and a Communist enough evidence to sentence a man to death?" He waved my answer away, if in fact I planned to answer. "You can be sure it is. Pointing out a few discrepancies in the facts won't change anything. You need to find the killer."

I did a double take. "Right. Hand over the killer. Got it. Why didn't I think of that?" My coffee had gotten cold, so I put the cup down without drinking from it.

Gil ignored my sarcasm but showed some interest in my battle with the coffee cup. "You can't afford to waste time."

"You're telling me?"

He winced at the volume of my raised voice.

I didn't care. "Why did Duke wait until the guy was about to be strapped into the chair to give me the case?"

Gil took his time answering, as he always did. His answers, he believed, had consequence, unlike the trivial utterances of the rest of us. "Duke walks a thin line. As you've discovered through your own painful experience, one hitches one's wagon to anything having to do with Communism at one's peril. Harold's death sentence is collateral damage in the world-wide struggle for supremacy between capitalism and communism. Duke's trying his best not to be part of the collateral damage himself."

The answer was too grandiose for my money; I was more of a meat-and-potatoes guy. Yet I knew sometime down the road, maybe a week or two, maybe months or longer, I'd come across one of those details or particulars I was looking for, put two and two together, and remember what he'd told me and it would make sense.

Gil sipped his malted through a straw, his expression like that of a kid on one of those fountain stools. I took a slug of my cold coffee and regretted it. I had another question but should have known better; I'd already asked one question that got his nose out of joint. I mentioned Vincent Forlini's prominent role in the union and told him about Eva Johnson's chummy relationship with Big Al Lucania. "Any possibility Johnson got himself on Big Al's bad side?"

He snarled. "How the hell would I know?" He stirred his malted with his straw, whirring it around like he was using an egg beater. When he'd calmed down, he drilled me with his witness-liquefying stare. "I have no interest in the business activities of my clients. I thought you understood that." He took off his glasses and his eyes returned to human size, albeit with an unnerving intensity. "If a defendant can't be shown beyond a reasonable doubt to have violated a law, he's innocent. That's all—"

I stopped him before he could get started on how his providing legal representation to reputed gangsters didn't make him a gangster, any more than representing Reds made him a Communist. I knew what he was going to say and didn't need to hear it again. He sometimes forgot he was no longer an officer and I was no longer a corporal.

The extravagant legal fees the mobsters paid him for

keeping them on the street enabled Gil to live high off the hog. The times I'd been with him on one of his Mob cases, when the mobsters began to talk business we got up and left the room. As for the Commies, they didn't want him around when they talked business because half of them were secret members using phony names.

"So you don't know. I get it. By the way, Forlini said I should ask you about his connections. Since you obviously don't know about his business interests, I'm asking if you were to take a wild guess, who would you guess he listens to?"

He removed the napkin he'd tucked under his chin and brushed at his tie. Not a spot. He folded the paper napkin, placed it on the table, and inspected me. If I didn't know better I'd have thought I detected a hint of concern. Despite his protestations, he knew a lot more about what went on with the gangsters—and the Reds, and the politicians, and the wheelers and dealers on Wall Street—than he owned up to.

He handed me a folder he'd brought with him—the transcript of Harold's trial—and made ready to leave. "Al Lucania has an interest in the taxi industry." He put a dollar on the table to cover my coffee and the malted and a good tip. "He'd not have much regard for Forlini, who's an old-school punk from the shoot 'em up days before Big Al took the reins. He's not Al's guy; but he's under Al's umbrella."

"Can you set up a visit with Big Al?"

An unusually long silence before he said, "I could, but I won't. What would you talk about?"

"Who murdered Irwin Johnson."

He might have smiled. "You and a battery of gumshoes like you couldn't pin a murder on Aloysius. If he had anything to do with it, he'd be three or four levels removed. When you get to level three, let me know; I'll set up a meet."

It didn't do any good to argue, especially as I hadn't yet made it to level one.

Gil could call the head of the Communist Party. He could call Big Al. He could call the mayor. Probably he could call the president. They'd all take the call because Gil was judicious as to when he stuck his nose into something. He didn't ask favors. If he called you, you owed him or you'd get something out of it. He wouldn't make any calls for me because I didn't have anything to offer anyone.

Since that was all I was going to get about Big Al for now, I moved on. "While we're at it, Sol Rosen intends to ask you about me. Maybe you can tell both him and Forlini I'm a good guy with a delicate constitution, and you'd be really mad if anything bad happened to me."

Gil had a better opinion of Rosen than he did of Forlini. The gist of it I already knew—and if I'd forgotten anything had been reminded of by Frank DeMarco. "I'll tell Sol you're competent."

That was Gil. "Thanks. You don't want to go overboard with praise." Oh well. I had promises to keep . . . and miles to go. "One more thing . . ."

He waited.

"Johnson was killed on a Friday night. His body wasn't found until Monday. Nobody missed him? He'd been in an empty office in an unused section of the building. What was he doing at the garage, much less in an abandoned office on a Friday night? Volpe didn't have an answer."

"You'd wonder, wouldn't you?"

"Was he up to anything shady?"

Gil took a moment. "That's why I knew you'd make a good private eye, Mick; you think the worst of people."

He stood to leave. The buzz of conversation around us stopped so everyone could watch him stand, straighten his tie, and dust off his lapels. Somehow he stayed rail thin despite drinking malteds on Sunday morning. He reminded me of a taut-muscled greyhound about to spring from the gate. The last thing he said was, "You need to have a positive attitude, Mick. Believe you can do it. I believe in you."

"You believe I can do it. Clear Harold Williams?" My chest began to expand.

"I didn't say that." He furrowed his brow. "If anyone can, you can."

"What if I can't? . . . He has a kid, you know."

CHAPTER TWELVE

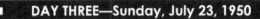

EARLY AFTERNOON

I walked over a couple of blocks and sat on a bench on the outskirts of Central Park near the art museum and spent the next hour or so reading the transcript, glancing up now and again at a parade of couples with baby carriages or strollers and little kids on roller skates heading into the park, remembering Rebecca twisting around in her stroller to smile at me. Some days, I felt more alone than others.

I'd seen enough trial transcripts to not be surprised by incomplete answers, garbled syntax, and stupid questions attorneys asked followed by unrelated stupid answers from the witnesses.

I wrote down the names of the cabbies who described the bad blood between Harold and Irwin Johnson. That bad-blood testimony was a key piece of evidence, though there was also the police report on what they found in Harold's cab—the gun being the star exhibit—and testimony from a CP turncoat who explained, with death-defying leaps of logic, the connection between Marxist ideology and murdering your boss.

How Johnson's possessions got into Harold's cab became a major point of contention, with the defense attorney arguing anyone with access to the garage could have put Johnson's belongings and the gun in there. To rebut this claim, the prosecutor asked one of the cabbies if Harold had been in a position at any time to put Johnson's possessions in the trunk of the cab. The driver said he didn't know.

The prosecutor pressed him. "You saw Mr. Williams near the back of his cab on more than one occasion?" "Yes." "Could he have opened the trunk and put something inside?" "He could have." "The defendant could easily have placed the items belonging to Mr. Johnson in the taxi's trunk," the prosecutor concluded and the driver agreed.

Harold's lawyer did point out that no one actually saw Harold put anything in his trunk. A point that didn't carry much weight with the jury. Both the drivers struck me as uncomfortable in their roles, what Gil would call reluctant witnesses. I didn't get the sense that either of them had it in for Harold.

Harold's court-appointed lawyer also elicited from him— what Harold himself had told me—that on the night of the murder after he'd finished his shift he stopped at a bar in San Juan Hill and sat in on a backroom poker game for a couple of hours. The attorney didn't produce any witnesses to back up Harold's story. The backroom gamblers who could have vouched for Harold's whereabouts might have made a difference but it was doubtful. Even if they'd been willing to testify—a long shot for openers—their testimony wouldn't carry the same weight as if Harold had been at, say, a Rotary Club meeting.

The attorney did call three character witnesses—a minister, a former cab company supervisor, and a former teacher. Gil had scribbled a big NO in the margin next to this. Even

I knew calling character witnesses was a mistake because that opened the way for the prosecutor to call his own character witness, the snitch, who this time testified that he was present at meetings of a Communist Party club that Harold attended regularly.

In addition to the bullshit about Marxists murdering their bosses, the fink managed to get in that the program of the Communist Party included taking up arms against the US government and that Harold and his comrades took orders directly from Stalin. You'd think the idea that Harold got a phone call from the Kremlin telling him to murder his boss would be too much for anyone with half a brain to swallow. But the jury swallowed it.

As I read, I noted that no one saw anything incriminating or otherwise on the night of the murder. This got me to wondering again if someone had seen something that night but never came forward—maybe saw someone in the garage who didn't belong there. Vincent Forlini might have stopped by, for instance. No one at the trial had asked where *he* was that night.

Finding this missing witness, if there was one, wouldn't be easy. Most cabbies in the big city minded their own business. "Don't see nothin. Don't say nothin." This would be especially true if they happened to see something carried out by those known to provide cement shoes and river dunking for folks who see somethin' and say somethin'.

I wondered for a moment if this reticence might apply to Frank DeMarco. Probably not, but it was something to keep in mind. Frank would also be the person to ask if it would be worth my while talking to the cabbies who testified at the trial. I wished I'd known to ask him about them yesterday; I didn't especially want to trek over to Hell's Kitchen on the chance he'd be home. But if I wanted to talk to him that was what I'd have to do because I'd forgotten to get his phone number. The walk from the Upper East Side in the midday heat wasn't a gambol on the greensward. And it would all be for nothing if he wasn't home. But this was what I'd do.

Sometimes I don't tell myself everything going on in my head at a given moment. In this instance what I didn't tell myself was that I had the glimmer of a hope that if I visited the DeMarco apartment this sunny Sunday afternoon I might catch another glimpse of Frank's sister Elena of the flashing dark eyes.

A picture of her pretty face had drifted across my mind's eye any number of times in the twenty-four hours or so since I'd first met her. It hung in front of me like a carrot in front of a mule as I walked the long blocks to the DeMarco apartment. When I pictured her face, I saw something within her expression that was deadly serious, as if she didn't have patience for frivolity though she sparkled with vivacity. It was that seriousness that bespoke intelligence beneath the coyness that kept me thinking about her.

After I'd knocked a second time, fate smiled and Elena opened the door. She wore a bathrobe and her hair was rolled up in curlers. She stared at me blankly for a moment and then with a sly smile, her dark eyes sparkling with mischief, said, "A gentleman caller shouldn't take a lady by surprise." Her scrubbed face had a pink freshness; her lips without lipstick were plum colored. She'd that moment gotten out of the bathtub, I realized. I felt the warmth floating from the robe and imagined the pink flush of her body beneath.

She might have sensed what I was thinking because she turned slightly and pulled her bathrobe tighter, her smile shy. "You can come in. I'm the only one here and I need a minute to get dressed. You go on back to the parlor."

I told her I was looking for Frank, letting her know by my tone I was on the job, not about to be sidetracked.

She pouted. "He'll be back soon. Don't you want to wait with me?"

"I'll wait," I said gruffly.

She laughed. Our eyes met and held for a moment. She deposited me in the parlor, closed the connecting door, was dressed and back in the parlor with her hair still in curlers by the time I'd cleared myself a place to sit amid Frank's propaganda.

"I brought you a glass of lemonade." She wore a yellow dress that I guess you'd call a sundress; it was quite modest, buttoned up to her throat, with a full skirt. The scent of roses drifted around her. She'd touched her lips with pale red lipstick; she was barefoot and altogether fetching. "I wasn't thinking you'd rushed back to see me." She batted her eyelashes. "But a girl can hope."

"Are you about to go out? Am I holding you up?"

She smiled in a way that let me know she knew I hoped she wasn't.

"I'm going to the movies with my friend Doris. I'll throw her over if you want to take me dancing." She laughed as I stammered, the laugh lighthearted. "What are you investigating today?"

I told her what I was up to. Surprising myself, I wanted her to know what I was thinking. Mostly, I didn't talk about my work, partly because a lot of it was confidential, partly because I didn't want to jinx it, partly because I didn't have anyone to talk to. It was a bad idea anyway. Talking about what you're doing has a way of taking over and keeping you from doing it. For a long time after that day, I'd wonder why it was different with Elena, why I wanted to tell her things I didn't tell anyone else.

"Witnesses don't always come forward," I told her, "especially if stepping forward might reveal mischief of their own."

Elena twitched her nose and wrinkled her brow. "That could be any of the cab drivers, couldn't it?"

Thinking of Artie and Sam Jones, I said, "Not all of them. You're not too fond of your fellow workers, I guess."

"Why should I be. You should hear how they talk to me and to the other girls when we walk by the garage and they're standing outside." She made a face like a grade school girl in high dudgeon. "Because you dress nice and . . ." Here she lowered her gaze demurely. "And might be pretty, they want to make you out to be cheap. Like they need to bring you down to their level. Why can't they act like gentlemen . . ." Her temper got the best of her again. "Even though they're not."

I wasn't going to argue with her. She had a right to her pride, even if she put too much faith in courtly manners. I moved on and asked if she knew who Vincent Forlini was.

"I've heard Frank talk about him. He's a gangster who has something to do with the union."

"Did he ever come to the office to talk to Irwin Johnson?"

She shook her head. "I wouldn't know; I don't know what he looks like."

"His name never came up?"

"Only from what Frank said about him."

We talked for a few minutes, mostly me asking questions and her answering, until she jumped up and said, "I have to stir the sauce."

While she was in the kitchen I talked to myself—about her. She couldn't be more than nineteen or twenty. She'd told me she'd dropped out of high school at sixteen to work in a stitching shop and then went to secretarial school at night, learned typing and stenography, and became an office girl. When she came back from the kitchen, I asked if she liked her job now.

"Office work is better than getting your hands mangled in a sewing machine," she said. Being an office girl had its problems, too. "Men gawk at you or think they can put their paws on you . . . I shouldn't say this kind of stuff to a man. Girls know all about it. You don't tell men." She looked down at her hands. "You're different. You're easy to talk to. I knew you'd be nice. I knew you'd—" She stopped. "Are you still in love with your wife . . . your ex-wife?"

I didn't expect the question and took a moment to catch up with the answer. "I told you we're divorced."

"Would you get back together if she wanted to?"

This one didn't have an easy answer either. "I don't expect she'd want to. Things got nasty during the divorce. She made it so I couldn't see my daughter. That's hard to forgive." I didn't tell Elena anything more about Rebecca. I couldn't bring myself to talk about her. If I did, I'd start bawling. And that would be a hell of a thing.

Elena nodded solemnly. "I don't wanna have a baby, not in this world."

"The world might get better."

She laughed. The laugh had a bitter echo. "You've been listening to Frank."

I didn't like the sullen Elena so I asked, "Where is he?"

"Are you tired of me?" she snapped. Her quick temper was another reminder that I wasn't dealing with a child. Childhood in the slums doesn't last long. Girls of the tenements lose those rose-colored glasses pretty young.

I wanted to reach out and comfort her. Her body had gone rigid with her anger and I wanted the softness again. "I'm not tired of you at all. Don't be sore. I've got a job to do."

"How's Frank gonna help you?"

"He can tell me about the drivers who testified at Harold's trial, tell me if there were other drivers who should have testified."

For a moment she was quiet. I thought she was still angry. When she did turn to me, she spoke calmly. "I don't see how you're going to find out anything to change what happened, not after all this time."

"The truth is," I told her, "no one tried very hard to find out what really happened the first time around. Maybe I'll find out something. Maybe I won't." A picture of Harold's wide-eyed, pleading son flashed across my memory. "I gotta try."

After a moment she said, "I can help you." She waited for my reaction. "I could check the log sheets and tell you which drivers checked in the night of the murder. I can ask questions." The bitterness was gone. She bubbled with life. "It would be fun snooping around." Her expression was earnest but playful. "I can be your assistant."

She was hard to turn down. "I can't afford an assistant."

"You don't have to pay me."

"Do you talk to the drivers?"

"If I want, they'll talk to me."

Why not? The drivers would talk to her and she might find out something. I told her to ask questions but not to push it, to let the men talk.

"What would I ask them?"

"You want to get them talking, have a conversation. You might say, 'On some Friday nights I would've been in the office but I left early that night' or something like that. A driver might say, 'Well I was there that night,' or something like that, 'and I didn't see Harold Williams,' or 'I saw Jake' or whatever."

"Who's Jake?"

"No one. It's an example. I made it up."

She rolled her eyes. "Okay. You can take me to dinner Wednesday night, and I'll tell you what I found out." She added quickly, "It doesn't have to be expensive."

When I said okay, she smiled broadly and then began digging under her brother's stacks of Communist propaganda and yellowing *Daily Workers* to free a record player. She put on the Andrews Sisters, then Patti Page. She started dancing along to the "Tennessee Waltz," and held out her hand to me. I'd touched her shoulder and taken her hand when we heard the apartment door open. I let go of her and sat back down.

"Chicken." She laughed.

Frank, and his wife carrying their baby, came into the sitting room. He took the baby and stared at me like I'd broken into the place. His wife—her name was Karen I remembered—smiled and held out her hand. "You're the private eye,

I bet." She shot a quick girlish glance at Elena. "She doesn't stop talking about you."

Elena began a protest but stopped, blushing.

Karen was cheerful like Elena, dark-haired, pretty, vivacious. Yet marriage and motherhood had tarnished her youth, given her the beginnings of a careworn look, circles under her eyes, something between worry and apprehension lurking behind the brightness in them.

"We were in Queens," she said, "at a wildcat strike in Long Island City. Frank's going back after dinner. Would you like to stay? We're having pasta and sauce, Frank's mama's fabulous meatballs, and some really good bread. There's plenty."

Frank made a sour face but she didn't bother to check with him.

"Where's Ma?" Elena asked, taking the baby, who reached for her.

"She's back from the novena, talking to Mrs. Genovese on the stoop."

Frank's reaction had made me uncomfortable. I spent enough time where I wasn't wanted during working hours, so I tried to avoid it on social occasions. "I should go," I said. "I have some questions for Frank, but I don't want to interfere with dinner."

"I am in a rush—" Frank said.

Elena touched my arm. "Don't pay attention to Frank. He doesn't talk to us at dinner anyway." She turned on her brother. "Don't be a crumb, Frank. I'm allowed a guest."

He looked like he wanted to punch her but manners and family tradition caught up with him. "Sorry," he said to me. "The strike's a big problem. We just got the union in there.

They walked out on their own. Forlini's got Duke thinking because the strike wasn't authorized he's got to stop it. Now I heard Forlini's planning to help the boss bust up the picket line." He put his arm around his wife. "Sure, you're welcome to dinner. Please stay. We'll have a glass of wine."

The Sunday dinner was pleasant. When Mrs. DeMarco arrived, she got flustered because she hadn't expected company. She yelled at Elena for not telling her I would be there—ignoring Elena's plea that she had no idea I was coming—and then yelled at her for not stirring the sauce. She yelled at Frank because he planned to rush out and couldn't stay with his family for Sunday dinner.

To me, she spoke politely and apologetically, as if I'd been offended. Her family had no manners, she said. I should forget about them, have some antipasto and a glass of wine, relax and take my time with dinner because eating too fast was terrible for my digestion.

The spaghetti and meatballs were delicious, so I was of a good mind to take her advice. Frank calmed down and grew more expansive as he ate and after he drank a glass of wine. "It's a small garage," he said to me, though everyone listened. "We got the boss to recognize the union by holding a rally and marching into his office.

"Negotiations won't go anywhere until we get more of the garages organized. The drivers got ahead of themselves." He pounded himself lightly in the chest, a mea culpa gesture. "I shoulda saw it coming. Yesterday, the boss fired one of the guys, so they all walked out. Now they have a list of demands. They think being mad will win a strike."

I remembered the Disney strike before the war. "We

thought it would last a day or two. It went on for five weeks. By then we thought it'd never end."

Frank glanced up from his spaghetti. "I forgot. You've been on a picket line."

"More than one."

His face lit up. "You could help. These guys have never been on strike. They don't know what they're doin'. The boss'll bring in scabs; Forlini will get muscle from the gangster locals on the docks. I'm going back tonight because I think they'll try to take the cabs out through the picket line. If they get the cabs out of the garage, the strike's over. The drivers'll be picketing an empty building."

CHAPTER THIRTEEN

EVENING

A wildcat strike wasn't what I had in mind for Sunday night; I usually listened to Jack Benny. But Long Island City was on my way home, so I said I'd stop off and picket for an hour or so. Frank and I left before dessert and didn't talk much on the walk over to Times Square, nor did we talk on the subway ride to the other side of the East River. When we got off the train, I asked if he'd lined up any help besides me. He told me the party was sending a few guys and some of the unions would also.

The garage, a one-story brick building with two wooden rolling doors facing the street, was in a semi-residential neighborhood of two-story attached houses and one-story cinder block garages and warehouses a few blocks from Queens Boulevard. When we were about a half block from the garage, someone came running toward Frank, and behind him two more guys. They turned out to be Frank's comrades who told us three or four cars full of rough looking goons had been circling the block.

"Scabs," the first arrival said. "They're getting ready to go in. Should we call the cops?"

Frank chuckled. "The cops'll help them go in and get the cabs. They ain't gonna help us."

"We got to keep them out, Frank," said one of the comrades, a broad-faced, broad-shouldered, salt-of-the-earth type who looked like he was born to the picket line.

"They'll have clubs," the other comrade, a thin, wiry guy with big round glasses, said. This one wore a suit and hat and looked like he should be behind a desk with an adding machine instead of on a picket line.

The drivers with makeshift signs—ON STRIKE! UNFAIR!—walked in a ragged circle in front of the garage. The few-and-far-between streetlights gave the picket line an eerie dull orange glow. The air was electric. Alongside the garage was a lot closed in by eight-foot metal fencing where a dozen or so cabs were parked.

On my first impression, Frank came across as quiet and unassuming, confident in his unorthodox beliefs, otherwise unremarkable. On the street, he was different, sure of himself, inspiring confidence. I'd swear he grew a couple of inches taller as he walked toward the picket line. The drivers who'd been milling about rudderless stopped to watch him.

No one cheered, no shouting; the change took place beneath the surface. Before, they were aimless, desultory; now they had a leader, so they pulled together and looked to be more of a force. Frank gave orders. He'd worked out a strategy with his comrades and the few other men who'd shown up from the transport workers and the electrical workers unions, men who'd been through battles on the picket line before.

He kept his voice low but his tone was decisive. The two comrades got their orders and headed off. Frank turned to me. "In those barrels in the alley alongside the building across the street are a bunch of batons. The guys on the picket line think we got them to make picket signs. You, Mike, and Larry hand them out. Some guys may be scared to take one. Tell them they need to hold 'em. If someone objects, you got to shut them up. Send them home. We don't have time to debate."

Frank showed no inclination to debate with me either, so I did what I was told. Mike and Larry, guys from the transport workers union, knew the drill. There were twenty or so cab drivers in front of the garage. Four or five of them took the clubs eagerly, two of them too eagerly for my money, both thick-necked and thick-armed guys, brutality narrowing their eyes. Others took the batons, searching my face for an explanation, for reassurance I couldn't give them. These guys were family men; they'd rather give you a hand up than smash you down. They'd never whacked another man with a club, and some of them wouldn't do it when the battle came.

While the transport workers and I armed the picketers, one of the cars circling the block slowed at the curb in front of us. My heart stopped. I waited for the doors to open and the goons to jump out, but the car moved on. The next car slowed, too, but sped up again. A hush fell over the men in front of the garage; everyone stopped walking. Then came a collective gasp, followed by a roar. One of the cabs in the lot alongside the garage had rolled into the metal fence and burst into flame.

The men from the picket line first rushed toward the fire. Mike, Larry, and Frank held them back, steadying the picket line and getting it moving again. Faces appeared in the small windows at the top of the garage doors. Two men ran out the side door into the yard, took a look, and ran back inside.

The small door in the front of the garage opened, but closed quickly when one of the strikers whacked it with a club. During the hubbub, a couple of the men from Frank's small platoon came out of the darkness dragging six-foot-long lengths of chain and chained the handles of the garage doors closed.

The two comrades, who'd disappeared early on and who I now realized had torched the cab, reappeared as if they'd dropped out of the sky. They had more lengths of chain and chained the metal gates of the yard closed. All of this happened in the matter of minutes, if it took that long. I don't think I took a breath the whole time.

Seconds later—or maybe it all happened at once—one of the circling cars, a black sedan, pulled up to the curb and men carrying clubs jumped out. Behind them, another black sedan pulled up and more men with clubs piled out. They waded in, but expecting to club and not be clubbed in return, they hesitated after their first couple of swings when they caught on that the strikers were clubbing back at them.

The fight didn't last long. It was loud and disorderly. A couple of the strikers went down. Others were bleeding but still swinging. A couple of thugs got hammered pretty good and went down; one of them looked like my pal with the scally cap from my Grand Central fracas. A couple of their fellow thugs dragged those that fell back to the cars. I didn't swing my baton at anyone, though I did ward off one of the goons, whacking the guy's club aside a couple of times, and then poking him in the chest like I was one of the Three Musketeers in a sword fight.

The would-be strikebreakers, facing men armed with

batons when they expected to club their way through a peaceful picket line, turned tail. The men from the third car never got out. Sirens wailed in the distance as the attackers drove off. My pals from the transport workers union retrieved the batons and got them back into the barrels before the police arrived. The fire in the cab was pretty much out by the time the firetrucks got there.

The first cops on the scene attended to the picketers on the ground bleeding from their heads; one of the others called an ambulance from the cruiser. The next cop car to arrive brought a sergeant. He gave the picket line the once-over and went inside the garage. In the next few minutes, three more police cruisers pulled up and reinforcements climbed out of the back seats. Soon there were eight or nine cops lined up on the curb, holding nightsticks and looking menacingly at the picketers.

After a few minutes, the sergeant came out and studied us for a moment and then hollered, "Who's in charge here?"

The picket line kept up a slow trudge. No one answered.

"I'll haul in the lot of you, I will," he shouted. The phalanx of cops brandished their nightsticks.

Frank stepped forward. He waved his arm in an arc, taking in the picket line. "It's a wildcat strike; no one's in charge."

"You'll do. What was the fight about?"

"They were strikebreakers. We explained the situation. They left."

I was close enough to see the glimmer of a smile in the sergeant's eyes. "And the cab caught fire? How'd that happen?"

Frank shrugged.

The cop looked at me. "You're awful interested. You know how the cab caught fire?"

"Spontaneous combustion?" I guessed.

The smile left his eyes. "I'm gonna leave some men here. There won't be no more shenanigans tonight. If men come here and want to work, you're gonna let them go through. You got that?"

Frank took another shot. "Why don't you tell the boss to talk to us?"

The sergeant nodded. "I thought so." He nodded toward me. "Outsiders. You're the union guys, right?"

"Hey, Tom," one of the drivers called to the sergeant. "These guys came to help us. You know Friedrich." He nodded toward the garage. "Friedrich's the troublemaker. Why're you on his side?"

The sergeant looked sheepish. "I ain't on no one's side. I'm doing my job, Sam. The law's the law."

The talk went back and forth. A couple of the drivers knew the sergeant; others knew a couple of the cops. It became a gabfest with Frank and me spectators, the upshot being the sergeant went back inside to talk to the boss.

When he came out, he told Frank to go in. The guys on the picket line chose three drivers to go with him. The men left behind were excited. They told one another that the boss couldn't hold out, that he'd have to cave, each one spoke with more certainty than the last. But they didn't believe it any more than I did. They were whistling past the graveyard. What they knew and I knew was the next time the scabs came, there'd be more of them, they'd be better armed, and they'd get in.

An hour passed. The excitement wore off as the men trudged back and forth like old dray horses. When the garage door opened and Frank and the committee came out, every-one rushed toward them. Frank led the group away from the building.

What they got out of the talks, Frank told them, was the drivers could go back to work. The guy who was fired could go back too. They'd get none of their other demands. "Some-times you gotta take what you can get and live to fight another day," he said. "We're not strong enough yet to take on the cab bosses. But we will be."

The drivers had a lot of questions. Frank hung on and answered them. I told him I'd catch up with him tomorrow and left. He nodded without really hearing what I said.

CHAPTER FOURTEEN

MORNING

My answering service called me promptly at 9:00 to tell me I'd had three calls already that morning. "One of them sounds urgent," the operator told me and gave me a phone number in Brooklyn. The others were from Larry Dennis and Sol Rosen. I called the Brooklyn number first, pretty sure I knew who I was calling but with no idea why.

A hysterical Hattie Williams answered before the first ring had finished. She'd been waiting next to the pay phone in the candy store. Before I said a word, she poured out tears and words, lamentations, wails, and weeping, questions, demands, and entreaties, all in a prodigious rush of sound such that I could barely decipher what had happened and what she wanted from me.

When I got her to calm down and put some spaces between her words, I learned that Franklin had taken some money from an old suitcase, where his father had been tucking away a few dollars each week for the boy to go to college one day, and headed off to Ossining to visit his dad.

This news got me to the border of hysteria myself. Sing Sing wasn't far from Peekskill, where a vigilante mob had tried to lynch Paul Robeson not long before. It wasn't the backroads of Mississippi or Alabama where any Negro kid might be fair game. But the hatred and the meanness—and support for the Ku Klux Klan—along the backroads of upstate New York wasn't anything to sneeze at.

"Franklin left a note that said if he went to the prison, the guards would have to let him in and his dad would have to talk to him." She said this hopefully, believing perhaps that the guards would let him visit his dad, or if not that they'd hold onto him until someone came to get him.

She was likely wrong on both counts. The boy's chances wandering around Northern Westchester County were about the same as a pet rabbit loose in the woods. Once someone discovered the dad he was searching for was a Communist and a convicted murderer, God himself might not be able to save the boy.

This wasn't part of my job description: Saving Harold Williams from the electric chair didn't require rescuing his child from whatever mayhem he got himself into. But there was no denying Hattie Williams's entreaties to save her grandson. She was prepared to go herself, hoping I might give her a lift—or as she put it, "carry her upstate to the prison," which I understood to be Southern for provide her transportation.

I told her no need for her to come along; I'd take care of it, saying this offhandedly to suggest that such an effort—tracking down a lost Negro boy in a KKK infested countryside—was all in a day's work for me. It took a bit to calm her down and get her off the phone. I did this by giving her a handful of assurances that I'd have the boy home by evening, sounding so confident by the time I finished that I almost believed myself.

Fortunately, before I headed out for the train for what would be an hours-long trip to Ossining, I remembered Artie's offer to lend a hand when I needed one. He'd told me he worked Sundays and took Monday off, so I called at the home phone number he'd given me. He was asleep but his wife said she'd wake him since I was a friend. This was stretching the truth but I let it go.

Artie didn't seem pleased or irritated by my request, taking it in stride, as a kind of Call of Duty, and told me he'd pick me up in front of my building in forty-five minutes. A man true to his word—a minute or two after 9:45, I heard the tap of a horn and took a gander out my window at the roof of a checker.

"The boy got an early start," I told him when I got in the cab.

"Kids do the damndest things," Artie said. "My kid is eleven and he thought he could drive the cab. He drove it right through the hedge into the neighbor's yard. He ran her into a tree or he'd still be going."

We zipped through the Queens-Midtown Tunnel, crossed Manhattan, and headed north on the West Side Highway, and the Henry Hudson Parkway through Riverdale—where I took a moment to wonder what Eva Johnson might be up to—and then north into the unknown.

Artie was quiet, not interrupting my thinking or planning. Not that he would have interrupted much if he had butted in. I watched the trees and the bushes and the few cars heading south on the other side of Route 9. How do you find a city kid in the country?

Franklin would have taken the train from Grand Central and might have noticed that the train had passed through

Sing Sing on its way to the Ossining station. Then again, he might not have noticed. If he did notice, he'd know he could walk there when he got off the train. Not a block or two but not more than a mile. Nothing for a kid.

Our first stop would be the prison gate to ask a guard if anyone might have seen a boy and see what that got us.

What it got us was nothing. For the length of a football field, a twenty-foot-high wall of granite block, built by prisoners with their own hands a century ago, proclaimed silently: "He who enters will have a helluva time getting out again." In the entrance designated for visitors, a couple of human sentries, with facades no less forbidding than the wall's, listened to my concerns with as much interest as the toll collector we passed on the Henry Hudson Parkway Bridge.

The guard I talked to hadn't seen a kid and kids ain't allowed in to visit without an adult. That the kid was lost, had come from the city on his own without an adult, that his grandmother was worried sick about him, didn't raise an eyebrow. "We ain't gonna let him in here. If he's a runaway call the cops. Some people don't know how to take care of their kids shouldn't have them."

I wasn't going to argue with a man obviously so knowledgeable about child rearing. He most likely spent his quiet time in the guard booth reading Dr. Spock. So instead of telling him what an ass he was, I tried an end around. "Have you been at this desk all morning? Maybe one of the other guards saw him. Would you ask?"

"The kid ain't been here." He said this as flat and tonelessly as he'd said everything else. "If he'd come here, any guard woulda sent him away."

"Will you hang on to him if he shows up?"

He had to look at his partner for an answer to this one. The partner lowered his eyebrows over his eyes and furtively shook his head—once to the left, once to the right.

"We can't be responsible for no runaway. If we see him we'll call the cops."

I thought of a dozen names to call the jerk, but I put a clamp on my temper. "Thanks for nothing," was all I said.

He raised his gaze to meet mine. If I relied solely on the expression in his eyes, I'd say he'd been dead for some time.

Back in the cab, I consulted with Artie. You had to believe Franklin arrived in Ossining an hour or two before we did, giving him plenty of time to have gotten to the prison. Since he hadn't gotten there—assuming the guard was telling the truth—it was likely he'd been intercepted along the way. The odds were the interceptors would be the police.

A little boy lost should certainly seek out a police officer. This would be the right decision, I believed, for just about any kid anywhere. If there was an exception, my guess it would be for a Negro kid in this neck of the woods looking for his father who happened to be a Communist biding his time in Sing Sing until he would be strapped into the electric chair.

Nonetheless, we headed into the village to look for the police station. We needn't have bothered. As we passed through a residential neighborhood of quiet streets, tall trees, and modest houses with small back yards, a section of town as quiet as a graveyard, the police found us.

A Ford cruiser tapped its siren behind us. As Artie pulled to the curb, I noticed two and then three police cars nearby, and a number of cops stealthily creeping around in the small yards of the modest houses. I wondered for a moment if there'd been a prison escape.

The cop who approached Artie's driver's side window was young, fresh-faced, well-built, and smiling in such a way as you'd believe he did that, smiled, most of the time. "Good day, sir," he said to Artie. He looked over the Checker approvingly. "I've only ever seen a couple of these up here. Taking someone to visit at Sing Sing?" He glanced at me, still smiling.

I was about to tell him, but Artie beat me to the punch. "We're looking for a young Negro kid." He tried to describe Franklin and didn't do a very good job of it, so I helped him out.

"Closer to four feet tall than to five, skin the color of a Hershey bar, slim, arms and legs no thicker than your nightstick, large brown eyes, opened extra-wide at the moment, I'd guess, in terror. The kid's ten years old and thought he could visit his dad in prison."

"That's the kid we're looking for." He reflexively glanced at his fellow workers scouring the neighborhood.

The lightbulb went on. I told myself it couldn't be, and then I knew it was. I gestured to the police activity around us. "Is that what this dragnet is for?"

The young cop blanched. He didn't have to answer.

I was apoplectic. "You gotta be nuts with this god damn pincer operation! He's not a criminal. He's a kid who misses his dad."

He cringed and took a step back. I realized how loudly I was shouting at him. Artie was cringing, too.

The cop got a hold of himself and pulled himself up to his full height, which was a good six feet or better, puffed out his chest, and put his hand on the grip of his gun. "Criminal trespass, attempted breaking and entering . . ."

"Breaking and entering?" I tried to keep my voice from rising again. "Breaking and entering where? What? He's ten years old."

"A woman saw him in her yard, getting ready to break into her garage. She called to him and he made a menacing gesture and ran." He spoke like he was reading from an APB.

I pictured Franklin playing stickball in Bed-Stuy, the smallest kid on the street, as thin as a rake. The cop I'd been shouting at could pick him up with one hand, yet a dozen or more armed men were hunting him down.

"You gotta stop this," I said as if I were in charge. The Paul Bunyan–size cop outside the cab window snapped to attention like I might be. I pushed my advantage. "I'm a private detective hired to find the boy." I held out my license.

Some men are conditioned to take orders no matter who gives them.

"You have to talk to the chief about that."

Since I was on a roll, I said with authority, "Please go get him, officer, so we can straighten this out." I'd been ordered around enough in the army to know how to give one.

"Yes, sir." He started to walk away, hesitated after a few steps, began to turn back, changed his mind, shrugged his shoulders, and kept going.

The chief was what you might expect a small-town police chief to be, if you had any idea what a small-town police chief might be like. He wore his uniform stiffly like a newly commissioned second lieutenant, as if it were a clanging suit of armor that might topple him over at any moment. Yet the

chief was no spring chicken. His dark eyes held the unforgiv-
ing glare of veteran cops everywhere.

"Would you mind getting out of the car?" was the first thing
he said. "Not you," was the second thing he said, this to Artie.

I got out of the car.

"Are you carrying a weapon?"

I had a sap but I said no anyway.

"Lean against the car." He planned on patting me down.

I stood my ground. "Does this come under the heading of
professional courtesy?"

He pondered that, so I held out my license and he pondered that.

While he pondered, I told him I was working on a case
and had done nothing illegal, so he and his police force had
no business interfering in my investigation. My thinking was
he hadn't had much experience with private eyes so he wasn't
sure where I stood on the crime-fighter pecking order.

The chief turned back to me, his expression softer now,
slightly bewildered. "What are you investigating?"

I took advantage of his uncertainty and, as Gil would say,
created a narrative of the facts that laid out the story the way
I wanted it understood—though I might have dressed it up
a bit. "That's confidential," I told him and paused dramatically.
"I'll level with you. I'm searching for a missing boy. I'm not
going to go into the facts of the case." Again I paused, this
time to rub my chin and squint for a moment. "Since it looks
like you're looking for the same boy, I'll tell you this much.
He's a Negro boy, ten years old. His name is Franklin Delano
Williams. Do those first two names ring a bell?" I didn't give
him a chance to answer. "That's right. 'Franklin Delano' is

most of the time followed by Roosevelt, the late president—
who as you know had a home not so far from here. The boy
was named after him . . . after the husband of the woman his
mother worked for."

I threw in a long pause here—something else I learned
from Gil; silence often works better than words. "I don't want
to start making phone calls and pulling strings. But I'll tell
you this. There will be hell to pay if anything happens to that
boy. You can't go hunting him down just because some Nervous Nellie saw a Black boy in her neighborhood and had a
fit. You need to call off your manhunt. If you want your men
to look for Franklin, I'd appreciate the help. But they better
do it offering hot dogs, soda pop, and ice cream, not with clubs
and dogs and guns."

The chief thought this over. He had a few questions about
why the boy was missing, where he was from, and such, but I
told him all those things were confidential. He didn't know
if he should believe me, but up against a situation he'd never
come across before he chose caution. After a few moments'
thought, he called off his troops.

"He's your case, you find him . . . and you better do it
quick and get him and you out of here. If I find out what
you're telling me is hogwash, I'll throw you and the kid in
the hoosegow."

During the entire exchange, Artie had sat stiffly in the
driver's seat of the cab, his hands at 9:00 and 3:00 on steering
wheel. I don't think he'd have moved if the chief and I had
started exchanging gunfire. He gave no indication of having
heard anything we said but we were only a couple of feet from
the cab and his window was open.

"We gotta find that boy—and fast," I said as I got in the cab. "I'd say we have less than an hour before the chief finds out he's been hoodwinked and the entire police force and half the townsfolk—with pitchforks and torches—come after us."

"I didn't know Harold's mother worked for Mrs. Roosevelt," he said as he pulled away. We'd only gone a block or so before he reconsidered. "She didn't. Did she?" He eyed me through the rearview mirror with disapproval.

Artie drove slowly up one street and down the next with me hanging out the back windows, first on one side of the boxy Checker cab, then on the other side, searching driveways, backyards, every once in a while hollering out Franklin's name down the tree-lined streets. I'm sure we made quite a sight. Women wheeling baby carriages, the Borden's milkman, and the Dugan's bread truck driver stopped to stare. A couple of youngsters tagging along behind their mother stopped and waved. Maybe they thought we were part of a parade. I was too busy searching for Franklin to wave back.

Birds chirped, kids squealed from a backyard somewhere, a delivery truck rumbled by now and again, but the relative quiet made me feel as if something wasn't right. Missing was the rumble and the roar of the city that became part of you when you lived there long enough. You didn't so much hear it as feel it, energy, like a giant furnace or generator had become part of you, or you it. I wondered if Franklin felt like that, like something that kept him going, went missing.

We drove by a kind of small farmyard, incongruous in the neighborhood, a ramshackle house with a couple of even more tumbledown outbuildings, a large apple tree with green apples in the middle of a circular dirt driveway, chickens meandering around the yard. I wondered what Franklin would think of the place. Probably the only place he'd ever seen a whole chicken was hanging by its feet without its feathers in a butcher shop. A woman—the farmer's wife?—came out of the house, started to cross the yard but stopped to stare when she caught sight of the Checker. Something about her face, her composed expression—interest without judgment—struck me, so I asked Artie to stop.

I got out of the cab rather than bellowing from the window and told her I was looking for a lost boy.

"A Negro boy?" she asked.

"Named Franklin."

"And who are you?"

"Mick Mulligan." I showed her my license and said I was helping out his grandmother. "His dad's in prison," I told her. "He missed him terribly and thought if he came up, the guards would let him in and he could see his dad."

"What a brave little man." She gazed off into the distance. and her face became careworn, wrinkling and aging before my eyes, as she watched whatever it was she saw in her memory.

"I lost a son in the war," she said.

"I'm sorry," I said. I don't think she heard.

"The boy is inside finishing his lunch. He was so hungry I doubt he's looked up to see you're here." She turned toward the house. "A piece of pie and then you can take him away." She glanced at Artie, who watched us from the cab. "Would you and your friend like some lunch? I bet you're famished, too."

I sneaked a quick glance over each shoulder like a skittish shoplifter before saying, "I'm afraid we don't have time." I didn't want to tell her the police might be after us any minute. I didn't know what this woman—whose name I didn't even know—would do once she learned our runaway child was the son of a Communist and convicted murderer. I kind of hoped she'd continue to do what she was doing.

Sure enough, before Franklin had finished his slice of apple pie while I anxiously watched from the doorway, a two-tone, brown and white police cruiser nosed its way around a corner a couple of streets down. Whoever was driving didn't see the Checker and turned down a side street. That was a break, but not much. The cruiser I saw wouldn't be the only one looking for us.

Trying not to let either Franklin or his benefactor see the panic I felt, I said: "Time to finish up, Franklin. We have to get going. Your grandmother's waiting."

He'd recognized me as soon as I appeared in the farmhouse doorway and understood why I was there before I told him. The good thing about my mentioning his grandmother sent me was he immediately accepted that as her emissary I spoke with her authority.

He gobbled up the last of the pie, thanked the woman— whose name I never did get—politely and profusely. He called her "ma'am" so I did too, thanking her as profusely and politely as he did while I hustled him toward the cab. I was diving into the back seat after shoving him in before me when I caught sight of a cop car turning the corner a block away.

Artie had caught sight of it too and turned his worried gaze on me in the rearview mirror.

"Time for talk is over," I said. "Step on it."

He slammed the noble Checker into gear, popped the clutch, and floored it. Once the staid old girl got the bit between her teeth she took off like a sports car, taking to the wide-open spaces of the countryside like an old milk wagon horse free of its harness.

Franklin and I were pushed back against the back seat, both of us wide-eyed, Franklin's grin almost as wide as Artie's.

"You okay?" I asked Artie.

He laughed—maybe not like a madman but close—twisting the steering wheel, kicking the old boat into third gear. "I can run circles around these hicks."

When he hit third gear, I'd swear we left the ground. Franklin and I hung onto the armrests on the doors and swayed with the cab. I didn't want to bother Artie with small talk since I really wanted him to concentrate on keeping us on the hard surface, so I took a quick glance out the rear window. A cop car was following us and another one behind that. I expected the cop on the passenger's side to hang out of the window with his gun and take pot shots at us like in a James Cagney movie. But no one was shooting.

The bucolic countryside flashed by the cab on either side. I had no idea how fast or where we were going. Artie, however, had a plan, turning left here and right there, wandering through the country roads, surprising me by heading in the opposite direction than I expected, north rather than south toward the city.

He had the look about him of a man who had things under control, leading me to wonder if he might not have been a getaway driver for the mob at some point. Maybe we were headed for Canada like the bootleggers once did to get away from the feds.

After we more or less settled onto something resembling a highway the cop cars behind us tangled up in some traffic, he told me, "I drove a Dugan's bread truck up in this neck of the woods for a year or so when I got fed up with driving a hack right after the war, so I know my way around. I'm betting getting away is more important to us than catching us is to them."

Artie's plan was to stay on the road we were on until we reached a town named Bedford. From there, it wasn't far to the Connecticut border. His thinking was the cops following us would drop off in Bedford, or if not in Bedford, certainly by the time we crossed the state line because they'd be in some other police department's jurisdiction.

He was right. The cops tagged along for a couple of miles but were gone by the time we got to the town of Bedford. We crossed the border into Connecticut there and found the Merritt Parkway a few miles down in Stamford.

Franklin and I hadn't talked at all during the chase, outside of my asking if he was okay. I think he was concentrating on keeping hold of his ham sandwich and apple pie. Once we were on the Merritt I told him he could relax; we were in the clear.

"Do you think my grandmother will be mad?" He looked like he was asking the judge how many years was he going to get.

"You bet your ass she'll be mad," I told him. The poor kid looked so morose imagining his fate I tried to brighten him up. "I'll put in a good word for you . . . I'll tell her you came peaceably."

He cocked his head, looking perplexed. His grandmother's response to misbehavior and disobedience was no joking matter. He wanted to know if I was mad at him. I told him I wasn't.

"So you're still going to get my daddy out of prison?"

This tugged at my heart and my conscience. I told him I would, not saying what was truth, that I'd try my best but my saving his dad from the chair wasn't something the smart money was betting on.

"Are you going to tell him?" He said this with hopeless resignation.

"You think he'd be mad?"

Franklin hung his head. When he glanced up at me after a moment, his eyes had reddened and tears dotted his cheeks. "I missed him too much ..." He tried to say more but couldn't get it out.

I patted his curly head and put my arm around him. "Your dad might say he was mad. What you did was dangerous for a boy your age. But underneath he'd be proud of how brave you were."

He hung his head again but this time leaned over and rested it against me.

The truth was his grandmother was so happy to find him alive and in one piece, she couldn't get mad at him. After hugging him until he must have felt like a squashed bug, she pulled a bowl of cold fried chicken from the icebox and some corn bread from the bread box, sent me downstairs to get Artie, who'd once more chosen to wait for me, and sat us all down at the kitchen table. Clearly, the thing to do with a runaway boy was to feed him—in Bedford-Stuyvesant as well as Ossining.

She offered to pay me. I told her no. But she insisted, so I said I'd send her a bill, which wasn't true but quieted her down. Artie lived in Brooklyn, so I told him to go home; I could take the subway back to Queens. He wouldn't hear of it and drove me home. I gave him a double sawbuck for the day's work. He said it was too much, so I told him the dough was from my expense account, which might have been true.

CHAPTER FIFTEEN

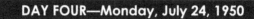

AFTERNOON

It was still fairly early in the day, and I was already beat; I'd had enough of the world and its troubles for one day. Unfortunately the world and its troubles were far from done with me. What I'd planned to do before young Franklin Williams threw a monkey wrench into the works was track down Sam Jones—I'd been spending a lot of time in cabs since I'd taken on this job—and ask him to help me check out Harold's alibi.

I remembered he hung out in the taxi line in front of Grand Central, so I went there and waited hoping to see him. This worked out better than it had the first time. For one thing, Scally Cap and his pals weren't around. The line was short and this time when Sam pulled up I waited for him to get to the front of the line. It was busy, a lot of folks waiting for cabs, so I had to elbow my way past a couple of dowagers, earning me a few "the nerve ofs" and "some gentlemans" hurled after me.

Sam didn't recognize me right off but remembered before I reminded him. I wouldn't say he welcomed me like an old friend. But he didn't throw me out of the cab either. I told him I'd been to see Harold at Sing Sing and needed his help to find a couple of people. I told him who I was looking for and that they frequented joints in San Juan Hill, The Pink Lady being one of them.

His eyes got large. "Why you want to go there?"

San Juan Hill was Harlem before Harlem was Harlem and was still the home to a handful of bebop joints, jazz clubs, pool halls, ordinary gin mills, and related businesses. Some folks say San Juan Hill was the birthplace of jazz; others say it was where the Charleston was invented. At one time it was called the worst slum in the city. Most of the uptown part of the neighborhood between Sixty-First and Sixty-Fifth Street was demolished after the war to make room for the Amsterdam Houses and the rest was slated to go soon, as part of urban renewal. Meanwhile Mad Dog, Slasher, and Smokin' Joe were skulking about somewhere within its environs.

Sam turned to face me, leaving the cab to find its own way uptown for the moment. "That Pink Lady's not a place you oughta be goin' to." He groped for the words. "It ain't like them places up in Harlem white folks go to . . . And them men you talkin' about, you don't want nothin' to do with 'em. I don't know what Harold be doin' with them."

"Playing cards."

"He should know better." Sam turned back to the road.

Despite his misgivings, he drove me to the Pink Lady. Double parking in front, he told me to stay in the cab and went in. He didn't find the men I was looking for, so he spent the next half hour taking me to a half dozen dimly lit or not-lit-at-all basement establishments on and off Amsterdam Avenue, joints I'd think twice about entering even if they had a WELCOME sign above the door, which they didn't.

In the couple of places I did venture into on my own, all

eyes turned when I came through the door and the folks I encountered listened like I spoke a foreign language. Sam reported back from the places he checked out that he'd been told no one had seen the cats I was looking for in months.

"Likely, that ain't the truth," he said when I threw in the towel. "But you ain't gonna find them fellas unless they want to be found."

"What about money?"

He nodded. "Money'd help."

For the moment, I put Mad Dog, Slasher, and Smokin' Joe on the back burner. If it turned out I needed them, I could track them down later. I had Sam drive me over to the Johnson Transportation garage.

On the way, we passed throngs of homeward-bound workers—longshoremen, garment workers, furriers, textile jobbers, machinists, office clerks, secretaries—trudging east from the shops, warehouses, and docks on the far west side. Who knew where they all went after work? Somehow the city absorbed them, clearing the streets of the city's workforce before darkness fell.

It was a bit after 5:30. Frank wouldn't be back to the garage until 6:30 or 7:00. While I waited, I thought I might try again to get Fat Tony to talk about the night of the murder. In the back of my mind also, I knew 5:30 was quitting time for office workers and I might run into the beguiling Elena DeMarco.

Fat Tony, chewing on his cigar and barking at the drivers as they turned in their trip sheets and cash or picked up their keys and trip sheets for the evening, raised an eyebrow to let me know he saw me but that was it. He was too busy to talk.

I went and stood on the sidewalk at the corner of the garage nearest the entrance to the cab company office, smoking a cigarette and watching the parade of weary workers.

And then, there she was, in a plain green dress with what I understood to be an A-line skirt and shoes that looked like black leather slippers. She wore the stone face that pretty women took on to keep from being pestered by men on the street. I had to call her name twice before she turned toward me. Her blank cold expression didn't change when she recognized me.

"What're you doing here?" The question was more a challenge than a greeting.

Surprised, I didn't say anything.

"I haven't talked to anyone yet." Her voice had a hard edge.

I tried to sound engaging enough for both of us. "I didn't expect you had. I stopped by to see Frank but he isn't back yet and Fat Tony is too busy to talk, so I was standing here hoping I'd see you."

She walked toward me, a half smile forming on her lips. "You're just saying that. Why do you want to see Frank and Tony?"

"I have a couple of questions I didn't get around to asking Frank yet. Tony, I thought I'd see if his memory improved since the last time I talked to him . . . And, like I said, I was hoping I'd see you."

"Liar." She said this with a cute smile. "I thought I was the one talking to the drivers."

"You are. But I'm not turning the entire case over to you . . . I do have something to ask you about. Someone told me the Party might have let Harold take the rap for Johnson's murder because they suspected he was a stool pigeon. Did you ever hear anything like that?"

She waved the idea away. "People always accuse Communists of something. What Communists do is go to classes to learn about Marx and Lenin and go to boring meetings where someone drones on about how great the Soviet Union is. When they aren't doing that, they're handing out pamphlets that read like they've been translated from the Russian . . . You really were waiting for me?"

I told her I was.

She put her arm through mine, her eyes dancing. "Frank won't be back to the garage for an hour. Come, buy me a cocktail . . . and tell me more lies about how your heart went pitter-patter when you spied me coming down the street."

We walked to a small lounge on Ninth Avenue, more genteel than you'd expect in the neighborhood, not the place for a shot and a beer. I had a beer anyway. Elena ordered a Seven and Seven. Seated across from each other, at a small table with a white tablecloth next to a window facing the street, we talked. I told her about my adventure tracking down Harold's son in the wilds of Westchester. I tried to make light of it, but she burst into tears before I got to the funny part. I stopped and let her cry for a minute.

After a moment, she said, "The poor poor boy. His daddy's going to die." She dried her red and swollen eyes with a napkin. "Now I look a mess."

"You look fine." I reached across the table and patted her hand. "I'm sorry I made you cry."

"I didn't know he had a child." She took a swallow of her drink and braced herself. "Can we not talk about that now?

Can we talk about something else? . . . Tell me about your dumb ex-wife and why she left you."

I told her a little bit about Deborah. Not much. I didn't really want to talk about her or our life together, and I sensed Elena didn't really want to hear about her, only that Deborah was gone and wasn't coming back. That was probably true. Yet my one-time wife wasn't so easily dismissed. Maybe someday I'd figure out how something you thought was firmly settled in place disintegrates, and I would tell Elena about it.

Elena didn't seem to mind my half-assed answer, so I asked why she didn't have a boyfriend.

"I'm going to start over with you." She folded her hands on the table. "Before, I went out with boys. Some of them were quite handsome. But they were grabby and could never think of anything to talk about. Then I saw a couple of older men and they were creeps. They thought I was dumb." She stared into space for a moment, her expression darkening. Her liveliness and brightness were gone as she remembered something, or maybe it was someone.

After another moment, the brightness came back. "You're different. You make me feel pretty without acting smutty about it, and you don't think I'm dumb." She looked at me over the top of her highball glass. "I like your smile; it's cute. But mostly I like that you're nice."

Probably, I was nicer to her than I was to most people; I wasn't used to this kind of flirty conversation and felt foolish and tongue-tied. "You're easy to be nice to, and you're so pretty. I bet you have dozens of young men knocking down your door."

She made a face, both accepting and dismissing my

awkward compliment. "Well, now I met you, so maybe there's a happy ending."

I wished she hadn't said that. I didn't much believe in happy endings anymore.

She pulled herself together, as if she knew it was up to her to determine the tenor and direction of our date, if this was what it was. "A girl needs to use her looks to get married," she said matter-of-factly. "That's what men care about. And she needs to do it quick while she's young. Since you were married once, you're a bad risk." She sipped her drink, put it back down, and pushed a few stray hairs away from her face while she searched mine. "Do you make any money being a private detective?" She sounded like the cautious father of a particularly eligible young woman.

This stopped me for a moment. I'd done pretty well as an animator, certainly by her standards. Those days were gone. These days, I scraped to get by. "Not much," I said. Then because she looked disappointed, I told her about the house in Malibu with the pool.

"And you gave that up?"

That stung me. "I didn't give it up. The bastards took it from me." I didn't mean my tone to be sharp but it was.

She ignored my bitterness and spoke like an admonishing schoolmarm. "You could've told them what they wanted to know. What difference did it make? They'd find out anyway."

I took a swallow of beer. Remembering the smug, self-righteous congressional pricks staring down at me from behind their microphones brought a surge of rage I had to fight off. "They already knew. The bastards didn't need me to name names. They wanted to squash me."

Her tone turned sympathetic. "Are you sorry you didn't answer their questions?"

This was something I'd put to rest a while ago. "I regret it happened. A lot of bad came because of it. You could say my life was ruined." I shook off some memories that tried to creep in. "I had no choice. You couldn't live with yourself if you gave in to them."

She pondered that. "I can't imagine if I ever had money I'd give it up for anything."

I understood, I guess. I thought of Eva, Irwin Johnson's widow, and wondered if Elena might take her route.

"I was well-off once; now, I'm broke," I said. "Things being equal, I'd rather be well-off. Still, you might find out someday money isn't the most important thing."

She looked at me like I'd sprouted horns.

I shrugged. "When I was around people who had a lot of money, I didn't like them much. When things went bad, they forgot they ever knew me."

"I can't believe you worked in Hollywood. You're practically a movie star." Elbows on the table, she leaned her chin on her hands. "Don't worry. One day, people will get tired of Red-baiting and you'll get your job back." She'd gotten around to finishing her drink. Even nursing my beer, I'd almost finished my second.

"Everyone should get a chance to start over." She said this as much to herself as to me. "I never meant to hurt anyone. But sometimes you do, and it's done. You can't undo it, so you ask God to forgive you, and you promise you'll do good from then on to make up for it."

Her explanation was the kind a little girl might make. I

wanted to know what it was she needed to start over from and whom she'd hurt, but I didn't ask. I was still figuring her out, not sure what drew me to her. She was timid and vulnerable, and I somehow knew her interest in me was tentative. Like a bird that landed near you, a sudden movement, an unexpected sound, and she'd fly away.

She kissed me lightly on the lips in front of the café, blushed, turned, and began her walk toward home. A couple of blocks later as I crossed Fifty-First Street still starry-eyed, Frank was turning into the garage. His driver's side window was open and he stuck his head out and called to me like I was a longtime pal. I waited for him outside the garage and walked with him toward his apartment.

"You were a big help last night," he said. "You keep that up we'll have to recruit you."

I liked that he could joke about the Party, and I liked the sense of camaraderie he gave off. But I had work to do. "Did you suspect Harold Williams might have been an informer?"

The question didn't bother him as much as I thought it would. Maybe Dr. Carter was right about everyone in the Party suspecting everyone else was a rat. He shook his head. "Harold understood the class struggle in his gut. He got most things I taught him before I finished saying them. He had doubts. Everyone does. The ruling class works overtime to tell Negroes they can't trust Communists, that we're using them for our own aims—"

It didn't take much to get a Red started on a lecture, and it didn't take long for me to get bored with it. I let Frank preach for half a block before I interrupted. "I got all that." I told him what Carter had said.

He spoke sharply. "A couple of Party guys weren't so sure of Harold in the beginning because he thought for himself. He asked questions and didn't fall for easy answers. He got along with anti-union guys, even Forlini's guys. Some comrades expect you just to shut up and follow the line when you're new. He wasn't like that." Frank stopped so he could face me. "The FBI sends rats into the Party all the time."

"Carter said the Party framed Harold because he was an informer." I stretched the truth here, testing the old saw, "if he gets his dander up he might lower his guard."

It didn't work. Frank didn't get angry and he wasn't defensive. "I don't know Dr. Carter. I don't know why he thinks what he thinks. That's not what happened." Frank slowed his steps as we neared his street. "The thing is . . ." His voice lost its energy. "The thing is we weren't sure Harold didn't kill Johnson."

Frank had hinted at this the first time I talked to him and it worried me then, too. "Why not? Do you know something I don't know?"

His stride stiffened as if he'd gotten a jolt from behind. He turned on me. "No. How would I know that?"

"You must have a reason to think Harold killed Johnson."

Something flickered behind his eyes. "Johnson looked down on Harold. Harold was proud. He didn't allow disrespect. The boss hated him and he knew it, so he returned the hate."

"That's it?"

Frank started walking again. The camaraderie gone, he watched his feet until we turned the corner. "We wouldn't have blamed him if he did kill him . . . The Party did what we could. There's injustice everywhere. Look what's happening to Willie McGee. You saw what happened in that farce of a trial at Foley Square."

He was gearing up for another speech, so I cut him off. "Let's say your doubt is unfounded. Harold didn't kill Johnson. Who did?"

He stopped again, folded his arms across his chest, and took a moment. "It could be anybody. I didn't think about that at the time. Maybe that's what *you* do, think about who else might have done it. Even now, I can't think of anybody."

"What about one of your union guys takes matters into his own hands?"

He considered this for a moment and then shook his head.

"What can you tell me about the two drivers who testified at the trial?"

Frank began walking again slowly. "They aren't bad guys. They signed union cards. No one thought they could have done it, if that's what you're asking. They happened to see Harold have an argument with Johnson. The lawyers twisted their words around and made it almost like they saw Harold kill him. The cops made them witnesses even though they didn't want to do it. They'd talk to you if you want; they didn't have any trouble talking to me."

I took a stab in the dark. "A triggerman from the Party?"

Frank shot back. "There's no such thing. That's how Forlini and his crew do business, not us. We organize workers, a mass movement, not individual provocateurs—"

I cut him off. "Okay. Who of Forlini's crew might have taken out the boss?"

His eyes narrowed. "Give me a minute." He looked down Fifty-Fifth Street toward his building and then back at me. "You coming up with me?"

I looked at him.

"I thought you'd want to see Elena."

I stared at him blankly. Was it that obvious? I didn't want to tell him I'd already seen her. My lips still tingled.

He gave me three names. Sheehan, McFarland, and O'Keefe. "These guys aren't regular drivers. They're supposed to be part-time. I don't know if they even do that much. They're muscle for Forlini."

I wrote down the names. "This is the Mob? Where's the Italians?"

His face tightened like he might spit. "Hell's Kitchen punks. They'd slit your throat for the price of a drink. One of them, O'Keefe, was with the goons we met last night."

"How do I find them?"

Frank shook his head. "I don't know. I've never wanted to find them. Ask Fat Tony."

It was getting late, but I walked back to the garage. The hectic comings and goings of the drivers at shift change was over. Fat Tony sat at his desk doping out the trotters again, chomping on a stogie. He wasn't pleased to see me. "I don't want to talk to you. A couple of guys gave me a hard time 'cause I talked to you the last time. I don't need dat."

I looked at my notebook. "Let me guess. Sheehan, McFarland, or O'Keefe?"

Fat Tony's mouth opened and the cigar dropped out. He tried to cover his surprise. "It don't make no difference who dey were. I don't have to talk to you if I don't want." He looked beyond me into the quiet garage and then behind him at the blank wall like they might be coming after him.

He knew about private eyes from the movies, so I figured if I acted like a tough guy—a stance I was working on—he might fall for it. I said out of the side of my mouth, "They can see *me* if they got somethin' to say."

Tony studied my face for a moment to make sure I meant it.

I pushed my luck. "The city's full of two-bit punks. Don't worry about 'em."

Tony shifted his glance again. "I ain't gonna worry about 'em. And I ain't gonna talk to you. Things are getting really voluble around here."

"Volatile," I said. "Were any of those three guys in the garage the night Johnson was murdered?"

"No sir." He shook his head a half dozen times. "No sir. I ain't . . . Forget about it."

"Were you in the garage that night?"

"I said I don't remember and I ain't gonna remember. Find someone else to ask questions to."

"Was Frank DeMarco in the garage that night?"

"There you go. Ask him." Fat Tony gathered his things, such as they were, cigars, the *Daily News*, the *Racing Form*, his hat. He stood. "The relief guy's coming through that door in one minute. Maybe you could leave before he gets here, so I don't look bad again."

CHAPTER SIXTEEN

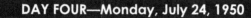

EVENING

When I neared my apartment that evening after another blue plate special at the Greeks on Queens Boulevard—meatloaf again, or more likely, still—two men wearing suits of a better brand than my Robert Hall, though not much better, got out of a grey Chevy sedan parked across the street from my building and came toward me. I knew who they were before they'd taken two steps, and I'd like to say I waited for them calmly and coolly, but I can't. I looked above them for the dark cloud of doom.

"Mr. Mulligan?" the guy in the lead asked. He was younger, slimmer, and spryer than the older and chunkier man, who slouched along behind him showing not much enthusiasm for the encounter. They both wore fedoras, the young guy's black, the older guy's grey with a black band.

I held my hands out in front of me. "Am I under arrest?"

Both agents watched my hands. "No. No. Nothing like that," the older, uninterested man said. "I'm Special Agent Nichols; this is Special Agent Little." He nodded toward the younger man. "We'd like to ask you a few questions."

"Sure. Call my lawyer and set up a meeting. His name is Gil Silver. His number—"

"You don't need a lawyer." Agent Nichols made a

half-hearted effort at a smile. "You're not in trouble. We'd like to ask you about some people you've been talking to."

They took turns—as the neighbors passing by, the nosy Irish, craned their necks—telling me where I'd been and to whom I'd spoken over the past couple of days since I picked up the Harold Williams job from Duke Rogowski. I had no reason to think they'd been following me before I took the job; more likely, someone I'd questioned in the last two days was a snitch.

When they finished their first round of recitations, the younger one asked about Frank DeMarco.

I shook my head. "You know more about him than I do. I just met the man."

"Is Dr. Mortimer Carter a Communist?" the older agent asked.

I glared into his eyes for a long moment. "I lost a career, a house, and a wife and kid because I wouldn't say who was and who wasn't a Communist. Why the fuck would I answer that question now?"

The younger man puffed out his chest. "You have a private investigator's license in the state of New York—"

The older agent turned a hangdog expression toward me. "Don't make trouble for yourself, son. Impeding an investigation won't look good for your—"

"No big deal," I said cheerfully. "I'm not sure this private eye racket is for me anyway, long hours, low pay, everybody telling you lies. You know how it goes."

Their expressions soured. They threw a half dozen more questions at me that I parried almost as well as I had the blows from the goon trying to club me on the picket line the night before. I didn't let on they'd landed a solid punch with the threat against my license.

These guys and the lying bastard they worked for were ruining the lives of a lot of people who hadn't done anything to threaten them or the freedom they pretended to protect. I thought about how they hounded Larry Dennis and a thousand others like him for nothing other than having the common decency to not inform on their friends.

After J. Edgar Hoover's thugs drove off, I went to the Shamrock for a shot of Irish whiskey to stop my hands from shaking.

CHAPTER SEVENTEEN

First thing, I went to my office to update my notes and get my bearings. I had a message from my answering service to call Sol Rosen, which I did. He wanted to talk, so I asked him to come to my office.

He wore a wrinkled suit, probably Robert Hall, took off his hat and put it and the *Daily News* he was carrying on my desk. His gaze was challenging but with that disarming little dance of friendliness I'd noticed the first time I saw him. "I've heard good things about you," he said. He'd talked to Frank DeMarco and knew I'd been on the picket line in Long Island City.

"I hear you're a legend," I told him.

He laughed. "Gil said you were blacklisted." His expression softened with what might be sympathy. And something else, too, that caused me to look away from him, a kind of admiration I didn't think I deserved. "How's the case going?"

"It's not. I'm stuck."

His brow wrinkled. "You know who Dashiell Hammett is?"

I nodded. "He writes detective stories."

"You know he was a private eye before he was a writer?"

I didn't.

He told me Hammett had been president of the Civil

Rights Congress a few years ago and last year had spoken at a dinner to raise money for Harold's defense. I guess he told me this because Hammett had been Red-baited too.

Rosen reminded me of a guy I knew in the cartoonists union who would talk about a bunch of things that had nothing to do with anything before he got around to what you were there to talk about. Sol went on about Joe McCarthy, J. Edgar Hoover, HUAC, The Hollywood Ten, the Smith Act trial, Taft-Hartley and loyalty oaths, and would probably have gone on all day if I hadn't stopped him.

I tapped my desk with my pen enough times for him to take a look. "If I remember right, we were going to talk about Harold Williams."

This almost got him back on track. "Duke walks a tightrope," he said. "I'm one side of the balance bar. Forlini is the other side. President of the United Taxi Drivers is the best job Duke's ever had. If he loses it, he's back to being a working stiff."

Rosen's smile turned into a scowl. "He's developed bourgeois tastes. His wife . . ." He let the thought die. "Duke thinks he can control Forlini. He's wrong. If Forlini and his gang get a foothold in the union, they'll let Duke be president all right, but they'll lead him around by the nose. He won't have any power and neither will the workers."

Sol's scowl deepened. "You know who he works with. They don't care about the workers. They use the unions they control to shake down the bosses."

"Big Al Lucania?"

"Vincent reports to him."

I looked Rosen in the eye. "And what if you win control of the union?"

He pushed himself forward and leaned toward me. "The members will run their union."

I might have looked skeptical, so he decided I needed clarification.

"Let's say you don't buy into the class struggle. You're not waiting for the day the international working class becomes the human race. Yet you believe a working stiff needs an even break." He continued with disarming humility. "The overthrow of capitalism in the US isn't going to happen any day now. It will happen when a large majority of the workers demands it . . . That's a long way off. Maybe not in our lifetime.

"What we do to get there is build a mass movement for socialism. Building democratic unions is the first step. Unions make things better for workers now, and they're the training ground for leaders of the mass movement for socialism in the future."

This was something of a simplification. But I didn't argue. Maybe I should have because he didn't stop there.

"If the workers have a full say in what the union does, the bosses can't buy off one or two corrupt leaders; the bosses have to do what's fair for all the members. In addition, unions only serve as the training ground for the movement for socialism if the workers recognize their union is fighting the class struggle—democratic unionism is class struggle unionism."

I'd have to say his lecture was better than Frank's. But I needed to put on the brakes. So I told him Mortimer Carter said the Party framed Harold for Johnson's murder.

This struck a nerve. He got angry but swallowed the anger. "That's asinine. Mortimer knows better. Harold was a leader.

He didn't ask to be one. He didn't try to be one. He may not even have wanted to be one. Leaders don't grow on trees. When we're organizing a shop, we look for men like him and try to win them over. You can teach strategy and tactics. But to lead other men, you can't teach that."

He sat back and chuckled, not so full of himself after all. "I'm on my soap box. But there's a point to this. When the crisis in the organizing drive comes—and it's coming—the drivers will lose everything if they're beaten—their jobs, the roof over their heads, they won't know where the next meal will come from. With all that at stake, they'll only follow leaders they trust.

"Organizers like me and Frank can come up with strategy and tactics and we can develop leaders. But we aren't leaders. Harold was a leader for the hackies. This made him dangerous. So when the bosses got the chance to put him away, they took it."

I'd been listening like a disciple until he got to here. "I lost you on that last turn," I said. "Put him away?"

Sol spoke patiently. "They framed Harold for killing Johnson because they wanted him out of the way."

"Are you telling me *they*—you don't by any chance know who *they* are?—killed Johnson in order to frame Harold? The bosses killed Johnson?"

Sol was slightly abashed but only slightly. "More likely them than the Party. We've been in hundreds, thousands, of union organizing drives, big and small. When did we kill anyone?" He glared at me. "Never! We don't kill bosses. Look at history. It's the bosses who bring in vigilantes, cops, Pinkertons, militias, every manner of thugs and goons to beat us, kill us."

"This time the boss got killed," I pointed out.

"Killing people is something Forlini does, not something we do."

"So Forlini murdered Irwin Johnson and the bosses framed Harold? I like your line of thinking, but could you point me toward some proof?"

Irritation curled Rosen's lip and wrinkled his brow. "I don't know that Vincent killed Johnson or had him murdered. It's far more likely he did than that the Communist Party did."

We'd gone as far as we were going to go down that road. He didn't know who killed Johnson any more than I did. What he had was propaganda which he should save for the workers.

"Enough of maybe this or maybe that, already," I said, not unkindly. "Let's talk about the lousy job the Party did defending Harold."

"No one did enough or is doing enough." His voice hardened to a deep-throated growl. He seemed to grow larger despite his slight build. You could sense that his easygoing manner was wrapped around a cement core. "The workers should walk off their jobs and shut down the city. But they've been cowed. What do you think this whole Red Scare is for?"

"No marches? No picket lines?"

"There's the vigil at Sing Sing."

"That's not the Party."

"It is," he said quietly. "We have to do things differently on this. Not out in front." His glance shifted away from me. "I'll tell you the truth. The Party's in disarray—key people in jail, others gone underground, clubs and sections disbanded." He folded his hands on my desk. "These aren't the kind of times when we can wave the red banner and expect the workers to follow. What we've got to do is organize, build the labor movement. Fight for democracy and free speech." We were both worn out by the time he finished.

As he was leaving, he picked up his hat and his newspaper. The newspaper was folded open and an inner-page headline caught my eye. I leaned across my desk, grabbed his arm, and yanked the paper out of his hand. The story, with a photo of a subway train and an empty track in front of it, was about a man who'd been killed when he fell off the platform and was hit by a moving train. The man was Larry Dennis. I fell back into my chair in shock.

"You knew him?" Rosen sat back down also.

I reread the story a couple of times, not answering Sol, though I knew he was quietly watching me. For a few moments I sat in a daze. Larry hadn't fallen in front of a train; I was sure of that. Rage began to build in me.

"You can add another one to your list," I told Sol. "They killed him. They hounded him to death, the witch hunters." I told him what had been happening to Larry. "He called me yesterday, and I didn't get back to him . . ." I felt tears—of rage, of shame, of sorrow—behind my eyes and couldn't go on. What was there to say anyway?

"You don't blame yourself." Sol's voice shook with anger. "You blame them, the sons of bitches persecuting him . . . Not even them; the lousy bastards are only doing their jobs. You blame the system—the captains of finance and industry and their lackeys—and you blame the lily-livered liberals who let this inquisition happen. Freedom of speech until it costs them something."

This time, I didn't mind Sol's proselytizing. Conformity and orthodoxy—the refuge of those too weak and too fearful to think for themselves—did in Larry as surely as it had done in the Salem witches.

When Sol left, I walked downtown to Gil's office and called from a pay phone across the street and told him. When he came out we walked a few blocks and sat on a bench in City Hall Park. As I'd suspected, the questions Larry had had for Gil were about his life insurance and what circumstances surrounding his death might get the insurance company off the hook.

"He had a good policy from his job in radio," Gil said. "It was still in effect but wouldn't be for much longer. He couldn't keep up the payments. An accident—especially one that might easily be faked—the insurance company would investigate. Suicide, they wouldn't pay. I told him that."

"You gave him some advice?"

Gil gave me a sour look. "Witnesses saw him stumble. He fought against the fall, cried for help. He tried to claw his way back up from the tracks and almost made it but lost his grip and fell back. I don't see how the insurance company could find evidence to prove it was anything but an accident. No suicide note. No recent effort to put his affairs in order. He was on his way to a lunch he'd set up that morning. The insurance policy was longstanding. He'd told people in recent days he was ready to denounce the Reds he'd known. He'd made an appointment to speak with HUAC investigators."

I sat for a long time after Gil left to go back to his office. If he was as shaken by Larry's death as I was, he covered it well. Not like me, who couldn't cover it at all. Still, time wouldn't slow down for me to come to grips with the misery and misfortune life so cavalierly deals you. Larry, the poor bastard, was an actor to the end—his final performance the most significant. He'd provided for his wife and kids to get along in the cruel world without him.

CHAPTER EIGHTEEN

 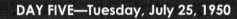
EARLY AFTERNOON

I pulled myself together and headed uptown to the taxi garage to find Fat Tony, determined to get him to talk, picking up a couple of De Nobili five packs from the cigar store on Ninth Avenue as a peace offering. When I got to the garage, the relief guy was still on the job. He told me Fat Tony hadn't shown up for work.

"He's supposed to work day shift this week. First time since I been here, four years, he don't show up. He don't come to the phone at his boarding house neither."

The dispatcher gave me Tony's last name, which was Dukakis, and his address, a three-story limestone row house on Eighty-Second Street closer to Amsterdam than Columbus. The landlady, whose name was Schmidt, said he'd gone on a trip that morning.

"How do you know it was a trip?" I asked, holding my hat in my hand.

"He was carrying a suitcase." A large, tired-looking woman, Mrs. Schmidt took up most of the doorway she stood in. The housedress she wore could reupholster a couch. "Tony's been here four years. He never goes anywhere before."

"No family."

"Work, eat, sleep, and them damn cigars."

"Any friends in the building?"

She got suspicious, so I told her who I was and that I was working on a murder case.

"Mick Mulligan. That's Irish?"

"Irish as Paddy's pig." You'd think no one would have to ask if "Mulligan" was Irish.

Luckily, she, too, listened to *Philip Marlowe*, so I had her attention. Unluckily, she concluded Tony was a suspect who had taken it on the lam. It took a bit to bring her around. Maybe Tony was a suspect, but he wasn't my suspect. Mrs. Schmidt told me he played gin rummy with one of the other boarders, Charley Davis, a bus driver who was at work and would get back around four. I could ask him about Tony. She wouldn't let me see Fat Tony's room and told me he was paid up till the end of the month.

Leaving Mrs. Schmidt, I hailed a cab and went uptown to talk with Victor Young, the head of the Communist Party section in Harlem. The cab driver didn't know Harold and wasn't interested in talking about the union or anything else, so I watched the city out of the cab window, the streets changing from a white world to a Negro world once we got to 125th Street and turned east. We drove past The Hotel Theresa— the Waldorf of Harlem—on one side at the intersection with Seventh Avenue and The Apollo Theater on the other; along both sides of 125th Street were clothing stores, shoe stores, a Liggetts Drug Store, movie theaters—in two- or three-story buildings with offices above them.

I'd known Victor Young as Slim Young during my YCL fellow-traveler days. Growing up in the thirties as a progressive you were hard-pressed not to be a fellow traveler because the Communist Party had its nose stuck into pretty much everything progressive that was happening—including protesting Jim Crow baseball outside Yankee Stadium, which was where I got my start.

Back then, Slim was a cool guy, a bass player in a jazz group that played clubs in Harlem when he might have been expected to be in a high school band. He was a leader of the local branch of the Young Communist League then as he was a leader of the grown-up Communist Party section now. Harlem was the place to be when I was young if you wanted to be hip, and the YCL had great parties in the halcyon days of our youth.

The last time I'd seen Slim he was on the witness stand, testifying for the defense during the Smith Act trial. As the state education coordinator, his job was to tell the jury the Party didn't teach how to violently overthrow the government at Party schools.

To tell the truth, Slim didn't do himself or the defendants any favors when he got a chance to speak. He told the bewildered jury that the Party and the Comintern had erroneously embraced the theoretical possibility of a violent revolution during a period of infantile adventurism and sectarianism known as the Third Period but that this tendency had been corrected back in the 1930s. The prosecutor was so mystified by Slim's presentation that he forgot to object until Slim was most of the way through his discourse on the Third Period. This made little difference because no one—judge, jury, or anyone except perhaps the defendants—knew what Slim was talking about.

The Harlem CP office was on the second floor of a

building on Seventh Avenue above Smalls Paradise, one of Harlem's jazz clubs. As Slim came from behind his desk to shake my hand, I remembered his infectious smile and engaging manner. A large part of his success as an organizer was because he was a likable guy who made anyone he talked to feel at ease.

He was taller than me—and, as you might expect, slimmer. He wore a dark suit, a white shirt, and a maroon tie with white dots. His skin was darker than Harold's or Mortimer Carter's, and he sported a sculpted Van Gogh beard. His eyes were bright and his gaze direct.

When I reminded him we'd met in the old YCL days, he was "tickled pink" (an interesting color for him to choose) to meet up with an old comrade. He spent a few minutes trying to place me but to no avail. Unlike Slim, I'd been decidedly uncool in my radical high school days, so there was little reason he'd have noticed me then or remember me now.

One thing I'd noticed about a lot of the Negro Communists, as opposed to their dour white counterparts, was they were usually upbeat, cheerful, and optimistic. Despite the odds stacked against them—what with discrimination, segregation, and white chauvinism, not to mention the Red-baiting—they managed to have a good time and laugh a lot. When we were young, I'd suspected Slim knew something he wasn't telling me about having fun.

On this day, he was in an upbeat mood too, despite the witch-hunting troubles surrounding him. Even though he didn't remember me, he asked what I'd been up to. I told him a bit about the war and drawing cartoons in Hollywood. But what he really wanted was to tell me what *he'd* been up to.

Which he did after he introduced me to a collection of African masks that pretty much covered one entire wall of his office. The masks were from the Ivory Coast and the Gold Coast, which got him talking about the pan-Africanist movement and Kwame Nkrumah. After he'd installed himself behind his desk and I'd sat down in front of it, he got around to telling me that he'd taken some shrapnel in France in the war and was shipped home for treatment. After a stint at an army hospital near DC, he got a medical discharge and went back to his CP activities—what the Party referred to as mass work and what the Red-baiters called creating "Communist-front" groups. His particular "front group" was The United Negro and Allied Veterans of America.

The UNAVA organized for jobs and voting rights, and against police brutality, job discrimination, and such. Their central issue was terminal leave pay for veterans—this was a lump sum payment from the army due to veterans after discharge. It was an especially big issue for Negroes in the South where—because Jim Crow structure was still alive and well—the local powers-that-be either flat out denied Negro veterans their terminal leave pay or forced them to pay exorbitant fees to cash their terminal leave checks.

What Slim did was build a coalition that included the NAACP and other civil rights groups but also organizations like the National Baptist Conference and the Fraternal Order of Elks, among other respectable groups for middle-class Negroes. The coalition persuaded the Department of Defense to authorize civil rights groups, including the UNAVA, to distribute the terminal pay checks to veterans in the South, thus shutting out the Jim Crow establishment.

After we'd talked for a while longer, he came to understand I'd lost most of the revolutionary fervor of my youth and hadn't followed his path from the YCL into the Communist Party. His relaxed, easy manner tightened up, and he became defensive about the Party's work and positions. Because of Slim's stiffness and formality I became stiff and formal myself, sounding like Gil questioning a hostile witness. And Slim responded like one when I shifted the conversation to Harold Williams and told him about Dr. Carter's accusation.

"Mortimer is correct that white chauvinism continues to plague the Party. But he's wrong that we considered Harold an informer." As Slim said this he stood and began pacing slowly behind his desk, something like a tiger in a cage might pace—with a lot of energy and maybe anger pent up within a sinewy build. Whether he did it on purpose or not, this put more distance between us.

"Our response to Harold's arrest and trial was inadequate. We were concentrating our efforts on the Smith Act trial— which was correct. But we should have mobilized public support for Harold more zealously. In good measure, this resulted from white chauvinism. But we also had to contend with the backward responses of liberals who were afraid to stand up to the anti-democratic movement promoting anti-Communism. Most important, remnants of the non-struggle policies of the Browder era also contributed to a non-struggle approach to the Negro question."

Slim assumed I knew what he was talking about and agreed with him. This was true neither in the first part nor the second part. Though I did know a little bit about what happened with Browder.

Earl Browder—who had led the CPUSA since the 1930s—
ran off the rails, ideologically speaking, in 1944, when he
became overly enamored of the popular front—the Communist International plan to join forces with social democrats
and progressive elements of the ruling class to defeat the
fascists—so much so that toward the end of the war he
declared that the class struggle was no longer operative in the
United States, that the working class in cooperation with
the ruling class would bring about the new and better world
everyone wanted.

To this end, Browder—with the consent of most of the
Party leaders—dissolved the Communist Party and established
the Communist Political Association, which would conduct
itself in the manner of a kind of working-class Rotary Club.

This idea lasted about a year until the central committee
reversed course, ousted Browder, reestablished the Communist
Party, and installed the more class-conscious William Z.
Foster as General Secretary. The Party got back on the
Marxist-Leninist track but created a major schism in doing
so, which brought about resignations and expulsions from
the right—Browder and his followers—and the left—the
would-be sectarians.

I brushed off Slim's snootiness. "Browder was gone by the
time of Harold's trial—"

Slim interrupted me, chomping at the bit. "We recognized
the error of Browderism. Browder and those who continued
with that line were expelled. But some of those tendencies
remained."

I somehow found myself in the midst of an ideological
debate but forged ahead. "My recollection is some of your

comrades were expelled because they argued that the Party line was still too close to Browder's when it came to wishy-washy support for Negro rights."

This stopped him for a moment, but only a moment, and then his pacing took on a new urgency. "Sectarians! Left-wing adventurists!" His accusatory glare suggested I might be one of them. "Browder was wrong to not maintain our independence as the party of the proletariat. The sectarians were wrong to oppose cooperating with liberals willing to work to protect free speech. Lenin said we should exploit differences within the ruling class while continuing to maintain proletarian independence.

"This is what we do. The error of the left-wing adventurists is thinking we can win those free-speech fights by ourselves. We understand the country is run by Wall Street and its lackeys. This doesn't mean we shouldn't work with elements of the ruling class to preserve democracy. Look what happens when we don't."

I'd started off with what I'd thought was a fairly straight-forward comment—an accusation admittedly—and gotten a Marxist-Leninist analysis that would give the Jesuits a run for their money. To top it off, I'd been foolish enough to argue with him. So much for Dr. Carter. I tried another tack.

"Frank DeMarco suspects Harold might have murdered Johnson."

Slim didn't entertain the idea for an instant. "Harold is innocent. He didn't get a fair trial."

I didn't hesitate either. "No one in the Party disagrees?"

A hint of uncertainty, a twitch in his left eye. Luckily, he'd had enough of pacing and sat down again. "Communists have disagreements. We make mistakes. We have erasers on our pencils like everyone else. We discuss disagreements. When we reach a decision, we all support the decision. That's democratic centralism." For a few seconds, I thought he was going to level with me; then his certainty returned.

"If the facts change, our strategy changes. We mounted the Free Harold Williams campaign because an innocent man was sentenced to death for a murder he didn't commit. Harold didn't murder anyone. Neither the Party nor Harold had anything to do with the murder." He weighed what he would say next before he said it. "I'm going to believe you're sincere in your effort to free Harold."

This bullshit got on my nerves. "Why wouldn't I be? That's my job. That's what I'm getting paid to do. No one's paying me to smear the Communist Party. Maybe if I was willing to smear the Party, I wouldn't be on a fucking blacklist."

Slim looked like a horse chewing an apple as he took in what I said. When he finished the apple, his disarming smile returned. "You came for my help and I treat you like you're on the other side." He relaxed, the kind of uneasy relaxing you did in the war when the shells stopped falling . . . for the moment. "That's what's become of us. Like an abused dog, we think everyone's an enemy."

It was easier to talk when he took off the armor. Yet his help, once he decided to give it, wasn't much help. He offered me a theory. I had too many theories already. What I didn't have was information. His theory, to be fair, had as much going for it as Dr. Carter's theory or Sol Rosen's theory. Maybe more. It at least showed some imagination. He laid out for me how the FBI infiltrated any project the Party took on.

"In something like the taxi union organizing campaign, they'd try to enlist some of the drivers with their 'we need your help as a loyal American' line." Here he went off for a good few minutes about how, despite the FBI lies, Communism was as American as cherry pie. When he finally got back on track, his suggestion was that I concentrate on finding the snitch instead of trying to find the killer. "If you can prove Harold was framed, the case against him falls apart."

My thinking on this was that folks should stick to their own line of work and not be all the time telling me how to do my job. I didn't argue but there was reason for skepticism.

"First, how do I know there is a snitch? Next, if there is one, how do I find him? Is there some way snitches look or act that gives them away? Third if there is a snitch and I somehow find him, how do I know he framed Harold?"

The question about how you find a snitch got Slim to scrunch up his face and scratch the back of his head while he looked to the ceiling for inspiration. Finally he frowned and said sadly. "Informers don't give themselves away. All of the rats they paraded out for the Smith Act trial were a complete surprise to us.

"The worst of it is what's happened since the trial. After finding out there were so many turncoats, we were determined to root out any other informants we'd mistakenly recruited or who'd turned on us. The FBI learned about our plan—from the damn snitches probably—and began fabricating evidence against loyal comrades. We started suspecting each other. No one knows who to trust anymore."

When I left Slim, I walked over to Park Avenue. I didn't know what I'd expected from my visit. But I hadn't gotten it.

Maybe I'd wanted a hero's welcome. A powerful guy in the Party would want to join forces with me; we'd become partners; we'd leave no stone unturned. I was like a little kid who went to see the cool kid down the block hoping they'd become friends. The kid is crushed when that didn't happen. That was me. I was back to my lonely crusade . . . What was happening here? I asked myself after a couple of blocks. Was I becoming a crybaby?

With time to kill before Fat Tony's friend got home from work, I took the train downtown and went to my office to make a couple of phone calls and look over my notes. The notes, once again, didn't pull their weight. I needed to find Fat Tony and get out of him what he'd seen and heard the night of Johnson's murder. With luck and a little information, maybe I'd stop running into blank walls.

Meanwhile, for suspects I had the Communist Party thanks to Mortimer Carter, Vincent Forlini and the Mob thanks to Sol Rosen—and a side job tracking down a snitch, compliments of Slim Young. I didn't put much stock in Rosen's trying to shift suspicion from the CP to Vincent Forlini. I'd bet on the wrong horse often enough to know past performance didn't guarantee a future winner.

I didn't put much stake in Carter's hunch that the CP framed Harold either. If I had to pick one, Rosen's notion on the hoods had more going for it than Carter's CP accusation. Of course, Rosen and Carter could both be wrong. Someone other than Communists or gangsters could have killed Johnson. Who that might be I had no idea.

Irwin was a philanderer, said his widow. Lurking about the

sidelines might be any number of scorned lovers, cuckolded husbands, or other revenge seekers, one of whom, with luck, Fat Tony might have seen in the taxi garage the night of the murder. I had no idea what to do about finding Slim's snitch.

I'd believed if I followed my nose, I'd find the truth sooner or later. Now it looked like by the time my nose led me to the killer, Harold would be dead. Much as I distrusted plans, I needed one. I grabbed a pad and a pencil. What I came up with was a list of possible murderers by category: the aforementioned mobsters, Commies, scorned lovers, outraged husbands, former friends and business associates, the FBI (not putting anything past them) or one of their stool pigeons, cabbies other than Reds and mobsters—and the widow. She did keep popping up.

Coming up with this list, rather than setting me off in the right direction, sunk me into a depression bordering on despair. It might take months or even years to look into every aspect of Irwin Johnson's life in the hope of turning up someone he'd pissed off enough to kill him. This wasn't a plan. I had less than two weeks.

Still, plan or no plan, I needed to find out about Irwin's private life. His private secretary, Mrs. Simpkins, was the place to start. Private secretaries were up there with priests in the confessional and bartenders after the second or third round when it came to knowing a man's secrets. When I called the Johnson Transportation Company office to make an appointment, the woman who answered told me Mrs. Simpkins had taken the afternoon off for a doctor's appointment. This was how most of my plans worked out over the years and why I left them alone.

I thought of another place I might find out more about Irwin Johnson. I headed over to the Forty-Second Street Library and consulted the reference desk librarian. She gave me a quick course on indexes and directories and put me to work on the *Readers' Guide to Periodical Literature*, *Who's Who in America*, the *New York Times Index* and a couple of other directories. I was amazed at how many lists of things there were.

I searched the indexes using the name Irwin Johnson and when I didn't find much tried Big Al, Vincent Forlini, and Sol Rosen. Then I tried subject headings—taxi industry, benevolent organizations, gangsters, mob-influenced unions, organized crime, and such. After a while I got cocky and looked up the name Vincent Forlini and the term "murder," Big Al Lucania and the term "extortion," and Aloysius Lucania and mayor. I looked for Irwin under a few topics, like taxi owner, tax cheat, swindler, and found nothing especially interesting. I tried him under philanderer, too, but didn't find a listing for that.

The undertaking at the library kept me busy for a couple of hours. My brain hurt by the time I left to meet Fat Tony's gin rummy partner. What I took away with me were the addresses of a couple of social clubs Irwin belonged to. I might find a friend, an acquaintance, or a bartender who could tell me about his life outside of the taxi industry. Another hope was that Mrs. Simpkins, if and when I got hold of her, might save me some shoe-leather work.

As for Tony, when someone is hiding out, I learned during my private-eye apprenticeship, they either go to a place they've never been before and start over or, surprisingly often, they go to a place known to them. My hope was that Fat Tony was one of the latter.

Tony Dukakis, who for all I knew had been a skinny kid, had grown up in an apartment house on Ditmars Boulevard near the last stop on the BMT in Astoria, where his mother still lived. The neighborhood was called Steinway, after the factory that built pianos there, or maybe after the piano itself. That Tony was from that neighborhood in Astoria I was told by Tony's gin rummy partner. Charley Davis knew a few things about Fat Tony because they'd often talked about old times when they played cards. Since Charley was an easy-going guy, more trusting of his fellow man than Fat Tony, he told me what he knew about his friend, including, unbeknownst to him, Tony's whereabouts.

CHAPTER NINETEEN

EVENING

Ditmars Boulevard was a busy commercial street, not one of the residential streets in the far reaches of Queens where you'd hear a dime drop on the sidewalk from down the block. I found his mother's building, after checking the mailboxes in the lobbies of a half dozen buildings near the BMT stop, and found Dukakis on the second floor. I set up shop in a Greek bakery across the street and ordered a coffee and a slice of a thing called olive oil cake that looked a lot better than it sounded and tasted better than that. If you were named olive oil cake, I figured you'd better taste good.

Cooling my heels for better than an hour gave me too much time to think, and too much coffee made me jittery. I began second-guessing my plan—another problem with plans—which was to watch the building to see if Fat Tony went in or came out. Or if someone else came out I might ask about my army buddy Tony I was trying to look up.

The building and its twin next door were four stories and made out of white brick with fire escapes in front. If the fire escape were in back I might have taken a chance to climb up and take a peek into the apartment. Climbing the fire escape at the front of the building would likely attract an audience.

I took a walk to perhaps find someone at a local store I

could ask about Tony, as this was the kind of neighborhood where people knew one another. I passed on a Woolworth's, got a blank stare when I asked for Tony at a Liggett's drug-store, skipped a department store I never heard of that took up nearly half a block, got a never-heard-of-him at a hardware store, had an orange drink at a Nedick's, struck out at two cigar stores I expected better from, got no at a shoe store, a butcher shop, and two fish markets.

A denizen of Sunnyside, I wasn't used to walking more than a block without coming across a bar. Here, each block had a Greek restaurant of some sort but none had a bar you could belly up to. It wasn't until the third block that I came to the sort of bar I was looking for, where a working man might get a shot and a beer, and a ham sandwich if he was hungry. I ordered a seltzer water and asked the sullen-faced bartender if Tony Dukakis had been in.

He looked at me from the corner of his eye as he backed away. "Fat Tony ain't been around here in years." He gave me one more glance. I took a couple of swallows of my seltzer water, left a dime on the bar, and walked out into the sunlight.

Back at the apartment building, I rang the buzzer for Dukakis on the second floor. When no one answered, I brushed aside my sensible instincts, grabbed the bottom rung of the iron fire escape ladder and hoisted myself up. I climbed quickly to the second floor, headed toward a window, and came face-to-face with Fat Tony, who had opened the window and had one leg on the sill about to climb through it. We stared at each other for a long two seconds until Tony bolted for the front of the apartment and the door.

I dropped from the fire escape quicker than he could get

down the stairs and hit him with a shoulder to the midsection as he came through the front door. He folded up back onto the floor of the vestibule, huffing like a beached whale.

"I'm not who you're running from, Tony." I was huffing myself.

"You're who brought me all this trouble."

It took patience and persistence to get him to talk. At first, sitting on the stairs, leaning his shoulder against the dingy wall a few steps above where I stood, he cowered as though I was going to work him over. I had to convince him I wouldn't tell anyone he talked to me. He gave in when I persuaded him I could get the thugs who threatened him off his back, a bit of a stretcher on my part.

One of the thugs he described was Joe O'Keefe, my pal Scally Cap. Tony wasn't sure about the other guy. "They roughed me up without doing much damage like the bullies in grade school used to do and told me not to talk to you about nothin' or they'd break my legs."

"Did the FBI talk to you?"

Tony's eyes widened. "How'd you know that?"

He tried to get to his feet, so I gently pushed him back down. "FBI agents are following me; they're not after you. Now's when you tell me what you didn't tell me about the night of Johnson's murder. The sooner I get to the bottom of things, the sooner I get those mugs off your back."

I watched the shifting flashes of terror and hope in his eyes as he battled with himself. He didn't trust me. But he trusted being left to his own devices less. The fear was eating him up. I'd been plenty scared myself more than once, so I didn't like pressing him; I put my hand on his shoulder. "You need to level with me, Tony. Were any of those guys—Sheehan, O'Keefe, McFarland—in the garage the night of the murder?"

Tony shook his head, but from worry, not in answer to my question. "They mighta been. When I first got to work, O'Keefe and his pals was leanin' on this new guy about the union and then the Commie guys stepped in. That started some shovin' and shoutin'. I told them all to get out or I'd call the cops."

"Was Frank DeMarco one of the Commie guys?"

Tony gave his head another shake. "Mighta been. I don't remember who was there exceptin' I saw the mugs you asked me about."

Tony's glance darted around the drab and dreary hallway and came to settle on me. Sheehan, he told me, was Mrs. Johnson's driver. This meant he was the cabbie Artie Kaplow had tussled with in her driveway. The other thug, McFarland—big, stocky, mean, missing some teeth, wore a watch cap—I could picture him from the first night I met Scally Cap O'Keefe in front of Grand Central.

"You know who Big Al Lucania is? Vincent Forlini? Were they around that night, the day before, the day after?"

Tony shook his head. "I never saw those guys, ever."

"Anybody else that night? Any strangers? Anybody out of place?"

Tony looked at me for a long time. "I wasn't going to tell you somethin' because I didn't want trouble. Now I got trouble anyway. When you asked me about any broads in the garage that first time, I didn't tell you this. Maybe I didn't think of it then. Maybe I forgot. A broad was around that night, maybe not that night, maybe it was in the afternoon, but a broad was in the garage sometime. I could smell her."

"Smell her?"

"Perfume. When I came into work, I smelled it. I got a good sniffer. It was in the air."

"What did it smell like?"

He looked baffled. "I don't know what it smelled like . . . It smelled like perfume. Didn't you ever smell a broad wearing perfume?"

"Would you recognize it if you smelled it again?"

He shrugged. "I don't know. Perfume smells like perfume."

So much for the good sniffer. "Did you ever catch that scent before or after that night? Mrs. Johnson? Someone else?"

"I don't remember smelling it before but I mighta. Broads wear perfume. Mostly, I smell it because I got a good sniffer, but I don't pay much attention."

Tony asked me if he should lay low or could go back to work. I told him to sit tight for a day or two and I'd get him an answer. That answer would have to come from Gil Silver.

It took a couple of blocks to find a phone booth that had a seat, which I needed since it often took a long time to get Gil on the phone. I found such a booth in a drugstore, bought an egg cream, and set up shop. Gil got to the phone halfway through the egg cream. Before I could tell him what I wanted, he told me to call Duke Rogowski.

He grew impatient listening to Fat Tony's tale of woe, grumbling because he was in a hurry for me to call Duke. Duke was a paying client, unlike Tony or me. He didn't like what I asked him to do either. "Talk to Lenny Volpe. That's the best I can do," he said.

"You're not going to talk to Forlini or Big Al?"

He hung up.

I finished my egg cream and called Duke, who hemmed and hawed before he finally got around to telling me to come to his office the next afternoon. I didn't see how this would help my investigation, so I told him that. He said he was paying me, so I better be there.

Next, I called Len Volpe at the precinct—if he ever went home, it was news to me—and told him what had happened with Fat Tony and who the guys were who put the muscle on him—O'Keefe, Sheehan, and McFarland.

He listened better than Gil did and asked me to hang on while he looked something up. When he got back, he said, "Street crime punks. All three have rap sheets; none have done hard time. Not tough enough for the Irish mobs. They steal lunch money from school kids; shake down mom-and-pop stores in the neighborhood; boost cigarettes and liquor. Word is they pick up work from the Mob—work the Italians don't want. I can have them picked up and lean on them. A few days in the Tombs loosens tongues."

"They work for Vincent Forlini."

A moment of heavy silence. "Forlini's a different story. He's got connections."

I knew about Forlini's connections. What would happen, Volpe said, was twenty minutes after he pulled Forlini into the precinct he'd get a call from downtown that a lawyer was on the way. The best he could do was pick up one of the thugs and run him through the third degree. He'd get back to me.

CHAPTER TWENTY

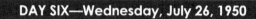

MORNING

In the middle of the night, I woke up with an idea that I wrote down on a pad next to my bed and went back to sleep. The idea still made sense when I read it the next morning, so I went to the scene of the crime, which I should have done earlier. I wore a work shirt with the name Barney above the left breast pocket and a set of overalls, an outfit I'd borrowed more than once from Barney O'Leary, the super in my building, when I needed to snoop around.

Folks by and large trust that a workingman is up to something useful and not something sinister, so they usually don't bother him. Such was the case when I climbed the worn stairs to the offices of Johnson Transportation Company. It was unlikely anyone would recognize me, except Elena. I hoped she'd know enough to not let on. Of course Eva Johnson would recognize me—if I saw her, I'd leave.

I walked quickly past the office, which was behind a wall with one large plate glass window facing the hall. A half dozen or so women, most of them middle age or past it and of varying sizes and shapes, sat at desks a few feet apart from each other with typewriters or adding machines on them. A couple of women looked up, out of boredom I supposed, as I passed the window. They had the numb, trapped expression I'd seen on goldfish in a bowl. I thought I recognized the side of Elena's head, but she was at the back of the room so I wasn't sure.

The hallway continued a good ways past the office toward a fire door at the end of the hall and what I took to be a stairway to the garage that didn't look like it was used much. There were a couple of doors on either side of the hallway, one marked WOMEN, another marked MEN. A couple of doors didn't have signs and I took them to be supply closets. Toward the end of the hallway on the same side as the office was another door. This door had a frosted glass window and a simple lock under the knob that I opened with a skeleton key from my tools of the trade kit.

This was the break room Johnson had staggered out of after he'd been shot. The room was small; a window across from the door—even though it looked out into an alley and a brick wall beyond the alley—gave enough light for me to see what was in the room, which was not what I expected. It wasn't so much a break room as it was a spare bedroom: a full-size daybed against one wall; a small bureau with a mirror above it leaning against the opposite wall next to a free-standing wardrobe; a faded oriental type rug covered most of the floor. A thin grey blanket covered the bed.

The drawers of the bureau were empty, except for the bottom drawer, which held office supplies, a stapler, a scotch tape dispenser, boxes of paper clips and staples, a few rolls of scotch tape, and a half-empty box of Trojan condoms.

A lone white cotton bathrobe hung in the wardrobe. I put my face next to it, sniffed, and caught a faint flowery scent that was vaguely familiar—a scent from my ex-wife? from my mother when I was a child? I thought about taking the robe to Fat Tony to sniff but decided it would be better to bring him to the robe.

Nothing else in the room caught my interest. I thought about various uses for a bedroom in a deserted part of the building and dismissed all of them, except for an obvious one. If I'd had a third leg I'd have kicked myself for not examining the scene of the murder until now. I was mad at everyone I'd talked to, especially Gil Silver, for not telling me that Irwin Johnson was in an off-the-beaten-track break room above his taxi garage on a Friday night—for no explicable reason having to do with taxis—because, in all likelihood, he planned to get laid.

As I passed the window to the offices on my way out, I took a quick glance. This time, Elena, headed from her desk toward a bank of file cabinets, glanced up and saw me. She looked twice, stopped, and stared. I put my finger to my lips and winked. She made a motion with her mouth and might have been telling me to wait. I shook my head and hurried on, taking one last peek at her cute, worried face.

I ate a roast beef sandwich and drank a cup of joe at a lunch counter on Ninth Avenue. Still irritated, I thought to call Gil and give him hell. The sandwich calmed me down, as did a slice of apple pie, so instead of calling Gil, I called Volpe.

"What makes you think someone was with him?" he asked after my rant.

"Someone was with him because he got murdered."

"That doesn't mean he was shacked up with the killer."

"No one told me about the love nest. It wasn't in the transcript. Didn't anyone look into who might have been there?"

Volpe wasn't following my thinking. "We investigated. We

took photographs of the crime scene, collected fingerprints. The whole works. If the investigators found anything that could be evidence, they collected it. We're a police department. What do you think we did?"

"Was the bed used?"

A long silence before he said, "I don't remember. If it had been unmade, I'd have noticed. I'll look at the photos."

I approached my next question cautiously. "Did anyone smell anything?"

Volpe's voice took on a peculiar tone, like one might use with someone you weren't sure was all there. "Smell? . . . Smell what?"

"I'm wondering if anyone smelled perfume?"

"Perfume?"

Was that the sound of his eyebrows going up? I told him about Fat Tony's sniffer.

He was quiet for a moment. "I can take a look through the file, the evidence bags, and reread the reports from the uniforms who responded and the crime scene investigators, see if anything suggests a woman had been in the room that night."

"And the perfume?"

"You can't collect smells."

That wasn't what I meant but I let it go. For my own perverse reasons I didn't tell him about the box of rubbers.

Volpe told me he'd picked up Joe O'Keefe, but Forlini showed up with a lawyer before they could get anything from him. "I'm not through. The beat cops know to keep an eye out. A punk like O'Keefe can't go more than a day or two without breaking a law." The last thing Volpe said was, "Even if you're right and there was a woman, that doesn't mean she killed him."

CHAPTER TWENTY-ONE

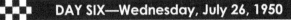
My brain was running a mile a minute, my nose twitching like a beagle's who caught a whiff of a rabbit. I picked up my suit and hat at the dry cleaner, changed clothes at my office, put on my hat, and went calling on a couple of million bucks up in Riverdale. This time a middle-aged maid with the hint of an Irish accent opened the door. She asked me to wait and closed the door.

After a few minutes, Eva Johnson opened the door. "You again." Her eyes twinkled. "What is it this time?"

Before I could answer, she made a come-with-me gesture with a roll of her pretty head and led me to the living room where we'd talked the last time I was there. She sat on a couch and indicated I should sit in the armchair beside the couch. Wearing a brown dress whose long skirt draped over her crossed legs and darker brown high heel shoes, she sat very straight with a kind of sophistication she hadn't shown the last time we met, though her face still reminded me of a child's, with her long eyelashes, blue eyes, delicate features, and timid smile.

"I spoke to my lawyer." She took my measure with a cool glance. "He said I didn't have to talk to you. I don't know why I am ... I guess I'm curious about what you're up to."

What I was up to, if I could figure out how, was grabbing something of hers that smelled of her perfume and taking it to Fat Tony. My mind stayed focused on this maneuver as I told her about the room where women come and go behind the cab company office. I must have seemed distracted because she looked at me curiously.

"Are you all right? . . . Are you tired or not well?" Her solicitousness surprised me.

I told her I was fine. My answer didn't satisfy her. But I carried on. "Do you know the names of any of the women your husband was involved with?"

She answered without hesitation. "No. If a man has enough money to spend, he can find plenty of women to spend it on. I didn't know he'd incorporated his womanizing into his work life. I didn't know about this playroom of his . . ." She grimaced like she'd bitten into a sour grape.

I took her answer with a grain of salt. Still focused on my plan, I got an idea. I worked up a pained expression and asked to use her bathroom. It was off the hallway and she referred to it as a powder room. When I closed the door, I saw I was in luck. A laundry hamper. Sticking my head in, I took a sniff. A flowery scent rose from the clothes in the hamper as soon as I lifted the lid. The smallest thing I could find with the heaviest scent was a flimsy, lacy garment that looked like what my ex-wife called a camisole. Everything else was too bulky or too . . . unmentionable. This lacy garment I stuffed into my suit coat inside pocket.

Eva watched me walk back into the living room with bewildered concern. At first, I'd been distracted because I was plotting my pilfering; now, I was distracted because I felt guilty stealing from her and nervous I'd get caught. The scent of perfume from the camisole seeped out from beneath my jacket.

I pulled myself together and asked about the social clubs Irwin frequented, if she knew any other of his hangouts, the places he might go to pick up women.

"That wasn't how he operated," she said. "Not one-night stands. His approach was to find an innocent and keep her for a few months like a pet hamster. When he tired of her, he'd drop her and go on to the next."

"How do you know that's how he operated? You said you couldn't catch him at it."

"I watched him before he got to me."

Yet Irwin hadn't discarded Eva in favor of a new hamster. I thought to ask why. But she answered before I asked. "I saw his game and I beat him at it. I was young. He was my first. Or I let him believe that. I held back something he wanted and made him work for it. Among other things, he had to agree to a business arrangement."

"The taxi company?"

Her expression grew shrewd. "I'm not a dumb bimbo. Irwin was too full of himself to recognize this at first. Later, he came to suspect I might be smarter than he was."

She moved to the end of the couch, closer to me, took a cigarette from the case on the end table and offered me one. When I leaned forward for a light, my goddamn suit jacket gaped open. First, her nose twitched and then her eyes bugged open. "That scent . . ." She saw as soon as she spoke where it came from.

We stared at each other for a long moment. Some things

you can't explain—and you can't pretend they didn't happen, and a big hole doesn't open up for you to dive into.

"What's that?"

"That?"

"In your jacket." She leaned forward, her face inches from mine, her nose quivering, her lips close enough to kiss. "Did you? . . . Are you? . . ." A strange light glowed in her eyes. She reached inside my jacket and snatched the camisole. Holding it in front of her, she leaned back. We watched it together like it should explain itself. I held the unlit Fatima and waited. Another blown up plan.

Her lips curled into a smile. "You're one of those . . . You're a . . . I never met one before . . . stealing women's underwear." Her tiny smile became a full laugh.

I longed to tell her I wasn't one of those, not a man who . . . but realized I couldn't, so I hung my head and examined the cigarette between my fingers. She held out the lighter and clicked it, her eyes meeting mine as I put the cigarette between my lips.

Closing the lighter she sat back again and crossed her legs, lifting her skirt as she did, holding it aloft for a second or two before letting it flow back over her slim pale thighs.

"You're a handsome enough man." She appraised me with a mocking but not unkind expression. "You should be able to find a woman who'll let you caress her lingerie while she's wearing it."

Her frankness was unsettling. I was already mortified. Usually, I had a quick comeback; this time, I wouldn't even if I sat there all day. I dragged on the cigarette, exhaled, and watched the smoke rise. "I don't know what got into me." I tried to sound humble. Given my situation, it wasn't difficult. "You're beautiful . . . I got carried away."

She stubbed out her half-smoked cigarette and stood. I figured she'd go to the phone to call the cops or maybe Sheehan, her bodyguard. If she was really mad, she might call Big Al, who I'd bet had killed people for lesser offenses than fondling his woman friend's undergarments. Despite the nearness of death, as she stood in front of me an image of Eva Johnson's underwear while she wore it floated in front of me.

She walked toward her front door, telling me without words or gestures it was time to go. I followed. She opened the door and we stood together in the small vestibule. "When this is over, when you've cracked your case . . ." She raised her eyebrows. "That's what you do, isn't it? Crack the case?"

"I guess."

"When it's all done, and you've rested . . . and cleaned up that dirty mind of yours, give me a call. You'd find me more interesting than my camisole." She pointed to a limestone bench next to a flower bed alongside the driveway. "I'll call you a taxi."

Into each life a little rain must fall, I told myself, though the day was clear and sunny. I had the cab take me to the el train on Broadway. At least the subway car wasn't crowded so I could sit while I nursed my wounded pride on the jerking, squeaking ride back to the city to meet Duke Rogowski.

When I got to his office, Duke offered me a beer but I turned it down. He didn't ask me how things were going with the Harold Williams case. He was too wrapped up in whatever was worrying him to look me in the eye. I took a chair in front of his desk and waited.

"I got a problem," he said.

Given that he was waging war against the taxi industry bosses, refereeing a battle between the gangsters and the Commies in his union, and one of his organizers was sitting in a cell on death row, I could see that.

"This has to be private." While he let that sink in, he got up, walked behind me, and closed his office door. I'd never seen the door closed before. He grabbed a beer, dug the church key into it like he would gouge its eyes out, and stood next to the icebox. "I need you to do something . . . You know how to follow someone, right? That's what you private eye guys do, follow someone without them catching on."

I knew how to shadow someone, I told him. "I learned from an old gumshoe who'd been following wayward spouses since the end of the first war, catching husbands with their pants down and wives with their skirts up."

Duke froze and turned such an icy pale I thought he was going to pass out. He took a long swig of beer, finished it in a follow-up swallow, and crushed the beer can with his hands. "I need you to follow Cynthia." He looked at me like I'd stabbed him in the back.

His embarrassment was so profound it not only overwhelmed him, it came after me too, swatting my own lingering embarrassment out of the way, like Joe Louis dispatching a challenger. He couldn't look at me; I couldn't look at him. Some admissions are too shameful for a man to make to another man. The kind of surveillance he wanted wasn't my line of work, I told him when I could get my tongue around some words. "I know a guy who's good at this. It's his specialty."

He didn't want another guy. He wanted me.

"What about Harold? I can't afford to take time away from his case."

"You won't need to. It's only once a day at quitting time for her. When she comes out of the office building where she works, if she crosses Broadway and gets on the bus you're done for the day. If she does something else, you follow her. If you have to miss a day, that's okay."

CHAPTER TWENTY-TWO

EVENING

An hour and a half later, I stood in front of an office building on Broadway at Fifty-Seventh Street where Cynthia Rogowski worked at a small publishing company. You'd think I'd have had enough dealings with glamorous women for one day. But soldiering on, I found a doorway on the downtown side of the office building with a few minutes to spare.

She came out wearing a conservative light grey business suit, a pillbox hat atop her luxurious hair. Pausing for a moment, she glanced up and down the street before walking down Broadway toward me. Not ready for this, I froze for a moment—she was going to pass within a few feet of me. I opened the door to the building I stood in front of and went in.

If she came in behind me, I was a sitting duck. The elevator starter looked at me curiously and came toward me. But at that moment two sets of elevator doors opened within seconds of one another behind him, and a herd of office workers stampeded toward the door to the street. I fell in toward the end of the herd and caught a glimpse of Cynthia's shapely behind swaying gently, headed toward Fifty-Sixth Street. She surprised me again, turning abruptly toward the street and raising her hand to hail a taxi.

I stepped into the street up the block from her, let a couple of cabs go by, one of which stopped for her, and flagged down the next one. I'd gotten part of the license number of her cab but didn't really need it. She was in a Studebaker and you didn't see many of them on the streets. We were off to the races.

The cab driver grumbled, "I ain't supposed to do this," when I told him to follow the Studebaker. He shut up when I told him I was following my wife and I'd give him half a sawbuck on top of the fare. After a few blocks, her cab pulled over to the curb. I had my cab go past her a block. By the time I'd paid the driver, she'd crossed the street and hailed a cab headed uptown. This time I didn't get the license number and she was in a Checker. It took a few minutes before I got across the street and an empty cab came my way. Enough time to lose her.

When I finally got the cab, we headed uptown on Broadway as far as Seventy-Second Street, and then back to Fifty-Ninth Street on Columbus and back uptown on Central Park West. Needles in haystacks have nothing on a woman in a cab during rush hour in the city. I kicked myself a couple of times and called it a day, taking the train back to Sunnyside to regroup.

Over a beer at the Shamrock, I told the bartender I'd had a bad day. The bartender said Eddie Lopat was pitching tonight. Before the ballgame started, I called Gil Silver from the pay phone next to the men's room and told him I needed advice.

"How can I advise you?" Gil asked. "Do I know what happened? You're the gumshoe. You follow leads."

"I don't have any."

"You're whining."

A fitting accusation. What else would a man do who got caught stealing a woman's underwear and then lost the mark he was supposed to be shadowing in the first five minutes of the tail? I didn't tell him any of this. What I told him was I struck out with Len Volpe and needed to know if anyone planned to murder Fat Tony or if the poor bastard could go back to work. He said he'd look into it.

A halfway decent private eye would find something to investigate rather than sitting around nursing his wounds. But sometimes it's best to sit still and let your thoughts catch up with themselves. I drank a couple of beers, ate a couple of pickled pig's feet and a pickled egg, and watched Steady Eddie perplex and bewilder the Tigers with his curve and screwball until I got sleepy. Tomorrow was another day.

No such luck.

Sunnyside was a safe, family neighborhood. You didn't need to watch your back on the street like you would in Hell's Kitchen or some other sections of the city. I watched anyway. I wanted to know who and what was around me, and I took notice of anything out of the ordinary. What was out of the ordinary on this particular night a child could have picked up on. Two black Buick sedans, one behind the other with their motors running, were double parked across the street from my apartment building on Skillman Avenue. I saw them when I came around the corner and did a quick about-face to go back to the Shamrock, but not quick enough. Two bruisers came out of a doorway and jacked me up.

One frisked me. He noted the sap but left it alone. When

he was done, the other one, with his right hand in the side pocket of his suit jacket, nodded toward the Buicks. When we got to the first car, the guy with the gat in his pocket opened the back door and indicated I should get in. No dummy me, I put things together pretty quick. Gil had made the call. Big Al had sent someone to answer my question about Fat Tony's prospects for a longer life. My druthers would have been a phone call. But this was being carried out professionally and efficiently. If I behaved myself, I most likely wouldn't get hurt.

My other choice was to take on the two thugs—an elbow to the solar plexus of the guy with his hand in his pocket, a swift kick to the balls of the other guy, and then a spin to kick the gun out of the hand of the first guy. Right. Or I could stop dreaming and get in the fucking car.

The back seat of the Buick was certainly roomy—big enough you could invite the neighbors in for a drink—and dimly lit by a dome light. A man wearing an expensive-looking dark suit, a sky blue silk tie with a matching handkerchief in his lapel pocket, and a felt hat, kept his gaze straight ahead. As I more or less tumbled into the car, falling back against the plush seat into a sitting position, he began talking.

"This guy you're worried about. Nothin's gonna happen to him. You're da problem, not him. You start somethin' 'cause you think you're doin' one thing. That one thing I can tell you we didn't have nothin' to do with. Things happen you don't know about and you're fucking dose things up wit' your stupid fuckin' around wit' dis other thing.

"You think you're a smart guy tellin' da cops they got it wrong; you'll find the right guy. The cops don't want to get shown up, so this gets them snooping around, too; maybe they find something they ain't supposed to know about. Nobody knows about. You don't even know what you found.

"It don't make no difference who takes the rap for knockin' the guy off. You get what I mean? Let it go. The wrong guy. The right guy. It's over. What you're fucking up is a big deal. You bumbling around gonna cost some guys millions. It ain't me. What do I care? These are guys I work wit'. I can't tell 'em what to do. They do what they want. Nothin' against you except you're stupid and got in the way. Nothin' against the poor bastard gonna get fried up in Sing Sing. He got in the way, too.

"You understand? You and me never talked. My friends wouldn't like it. It ain't up to me to smarten dummies up. I owe somebody somethin' so I do him a favor. You're a young guy. You don't know how things work. So I'm telling you. Find a girl. Go to Atlantic City for a week. You get laid. The thing blows over. The guy dies in the chair. Too bad it works out that way. Maybe it was him. Maybe it wasn't. I told you, not us."

He cocked his head to one side and turned to face me. Maybe he smiled. "*Capisci?*"

I *capiscied*, all right. "I don't want to cause you any trouble, Mr. —"

"No trouble for me, my friend. A lot of trouble for you. My associates, they're busy men. They don't see things my way. They can't be bothered. To them, you're in the way. What can I say? You don't like Atlantic City? Go up to the mountains. Grossinger's. You Jewish? I hear it's nice."

"I'm not Jewish."

He scrutinized my face for the first time. "Italian?"

"Irish."

He grunted and looked away. The car door opened as if by magic. The thug with the gat held it open like a chauffeur. I nodded as I climbed out past him. He didn't so much as blink. I stood on the sidewalk in front of my apartment building watching the Buicks drive away. The message as I understood it was Fat Tony could go back to work. But I should quit work. Or what? This fucking day had to end sometime. I went to bed.

CHAPTER TWENTY-THREE

MORNING

I awoke to a ribbon of sunshine slanting through my bedroom window and a bird chirping on a barren branch of the lone tree I could see from my bedroom. With the dawning of day came the thought that I should forget about trying to prove Harold Williams innocent. Heroes were made of sterner stuff than blacklisted ex-cartoonists turned fledgling private eyes. Then again, if Big Al Lucania wanted me to take Elena for a week in Atlantic City he should have fronted me the dough.

This was bravado on my part. I'd been warned by a dangerous man, speaking for other dangerous men who'd littered vacant lots in Canarsie with the bodies of foolish men who didn't heed their warnings.

Too bad. If I wanted to, I couldn't quit; I needed to pay the rent, put food on the table, pay child support, and with luck one day take Elena out to the ballgame. Heroics had little to do with it. Work wasn't so easy to find when you were on the blacklist. Then, there was that little kid in Brooklyn. What would I tell Franklin?

After breakfast at the Greeks, I took a cab I found parked in front of the restaurant over to Fat Tony's mother's apartment in Astoria to tell him he could go back to work. Once more, I pumped him about the night of the murder and once more got nothing useful. He wasn't overly appreciative that I cleared the way for him either. All he said, was "Thanks. Now can you leave me alone?"

In a light drizzle, I headed into Manhattan to drop in on Walter Bauer, the private eye Eva Johnson hired to get the goods on her husband and whom her husband had bought off. Bauer's office was on Thirty-Eighth Street near Sixth Avenue in one of the few non-loft buildings in the garment district. I climbed the battered stairs to the third floor and found his name on a frosted glass door.

He came out of his office into the shabby waiting room when he heard me open the creaking outside door. The waiting room had a wooden bench against one wall; against the other were two wooden arm chairs that didn't match each other or the bench. No desk for a receptionist.

Not what you'd call dapper, Bauer was in shirtsleeves, wore suspenders over his bulging belly, and had kept his hat on. His thick, stocky build had long before sunk into fat. There were bags under his eyes and his face was pasty, except for red blotches visible beneath the stubble and a bulbous nose that would give Rudolph the reindeer a run for his money. The office reeked of cigar smoke and I smelled whiskey on his breath from halfway across the room. I wondered if this was what life had in store for me down the road, waiting in a barren office like this, stubble on my face and whiskey on my breath, for a live one.

I told him what I was doing.

"He's a fucking Commie. What'd you expect?"

Great! Another disciple of Walter Winchell and Westbrook Pegler.

"I expect he'd get a fair trial for one thing." I thought I'd start with something everyone could agree on.

"That's what Commies always say: 'The guy was framed,' whatever he did. You read about the Commie leaders trial, right? They want to take over the world. Armed revolutions everywhere. They say they don't. But it's right there in their books. They brainwash people. They don't believe in telling the truth. They don't believe in fair trials. Why should they get one?"

I asked myself, "Are you stupid enough to argue with a moron?" It turned out I was. "Let me get this straight. A Communist shouldn't get a fair trial because Communists don't believe in fair trials. Doesn't this mean anti-Communists don't believe in fair trials?"

He took a second or two to ponder this. "You don't get it, do you? You can't believe what they say because they don't believe in truth."

"So my client should be executed whether he's guilty or not?"

"He'd execute you in the blink of an eye."

I'd have better luck talking to a lamppost. "Let's say I'm trying to do a job and need a favor, a professional courtesy."

He blinked a couple of times as if he didn't get what I was saying. It might have been "courtesy" that threw him off. After a moment, he asked, "Who's paying you?"

I didn't think this was something he should ask, but it might have been some kind of shop talk I hadn't learned about yet, so I told him.

"You need some help? I'm available." When I hesitated, he said, "Ask the guy. A union boss, he's got dough."

I began to grasp the values of the man I was dealing with. "Answer a couple of questions; I'll see what I can do."

He grimaced, the harbinger of a snarl. He hadn't taken his eyes off of my face since I'd met him. "There weren't no women."

"His wife thought there were."

"That's why she hired me, to find out. No dames." The muscles in his face tightened, narrowing his eyes and drawing his mouth into a thin line. "What'd she tell you?"

"She said her husband bought you off."

This got his attention. The sinews in his thick neck throbbed and the blotches on his face brightened. "She's full of shit. She didn't like what I found out and didn't want to pay me."

I tried to act toward him with respect as a fellow P.I. It wasn't easy. "I don't care who paid you or what you reported to your client. In the case I'm working, a man's life is at stake. If you could give me the names of people you came across who knew Irwin Johnson, especially women, that might help save my client's life."

His shrewd expression was a marvel to behold, a mix of sidewalk swindler and parish priest. "Ask the guy who's paying you to put me on. I been in this game a long time. I used to be a cop. Nothing against you, but he needs an experienced pro to give you a hand. A professional don't give up his expertise for nothin'. I gotta make a living, too."

Bauer seemed to think his having said this we'd established a partnership. "Come in. Sit down. Have a drink." With a wave of his hand, as if leading us into battle, he headed back into his office.

I felt for the sap in my side coat pocket and wrapped my fingers around it, imagining how it would feel to whack him one on the back of the head as he walked away. But I left while he was bent over his desk, reaching for the bottle I guess, and walked off my anger heading uptown to drop in on Alice Simpkins.

CHAPTER TWENTY-FOUR

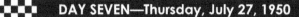

AFTERNOON

Mrs. Simpkins, on the downhill side of middle age, was slim, prim, and officious. With her wire-rimmed glasses, her hair in a tight bun, her nondescript blue dress buttoned up to her throat, she reminded me of central casting's idea of a midwestern small-town librarian. My guess was she hadn't looked or dressed much differently for the last twenty years, come depression, war, feasts, or famines. I knew a disapproving look when one came my way; hers was up there with the best. Telling the truth wasn't going to get me far, so I made up a story and began my pitch.

I was a reporter, I told her, assigned to write a tribute to Irwin Johnson for *Taxi News*. Everyone I'd come across so far told me Mrs. Simpkins was the person I should talk to if I wanted to know about Irwin Johnson.

"Well, I wouldn't say that." She turned from her typewriter, patted the hair bun and folded her hands on the desk. "Please sit down. I'm surprised you're doing a story now after so much time."

She had a point; I should have thought of that. But I'm quick on my feet if nothing else. "It's a remembrance," I said, as if that might make sense. Maybe if she didn't think about it very long it would.

For the next fifteen minutes, Alice—Mrs. Simpkins asked me to call her Alice—gushed over Irwin Johnson: what a smart businessman he was, how caring of his employees, so well thought of in the community. "I'm sure you've been told he was head of the taxi industry war bonds effort for a number of years. He gave speeches to civic organizations and charitable groups all the time and won more good citizen awards than you could shake a stick at."

"Remarkable man," I said. "I've gotten his public side from people I've spoken to. I hoped you might have some personal insights."

A protective shield went up in front of her eyes. "I'm not sure I know what you mean."

Her tone was dangerous, so I softened mine. "His friends. His family. Hobbies. Interests. That sort of thing."

"I don't know if I should talk about his personal life. He was a private man."

My experience with the world of business was limited, but I knew private secretaries knew private things—phone calls from bookies, flowers for dancing girls, angry phone calls from wives, angrier phone calls from other women's husbands. The trick was to get Alice to spill some of this.

"I'm not sure how to put this," I said. "I don't want to write anything that would tarnish Mr. Johnson's reputation. Yet there are those who saw him as a ruthless businessman, and there are the rumors . . ."

"Rumors." She shook her head to ward off the idea. But her antenna went up.

I lowered my voice. "Some say he was quite the ladies' man."

She patted her bun again and frowned. "When he was a

young man, he might have had a wandering eye. Of course, he was popular with the ladies. He was an exceedingly handsome man, and wealthy." The scolding expression ramped up. "Women threw themselves at him."

Not Alice, I suspected. "And Mrs. Johnson . . . ?"

She eyed me warily. "Mr. Johnson was discreet. His private life and his family life were no one else's concern. He kept his private life and his family far distant from his business life."

"So you didn't know Eva Johnson?"

Her jaw went square. Storm clouds gathered. "No one here knew anything about his private life, who he married or even that he was married, until after his death when Mrs. Johnson took over the company. Of course, I knew he had married."

This was interesting. Keep his wife lapped in luxury in her mansion on the hill so he could carry out his extracurricular activities without worrying someone downtown might tip her off. I wondered how much this private secretary knew about his downtown life and if she'd covered for him. Not something I could ask her up front, so I tried a back door. "A lot of women must have been disappointed when he got hitched. Difficult for you to keep the secret under your hat."

She started to answer yes, switched to no, paused, and ended up scowling at me. I was exasperated too. She knew a lot she could tell me, but she wasn't saying it. I must have missed the chapter in the private eye manual on getting a private secretary to spill the beans on her boss.

I tried small talk to get her to let her guard down. That stunt hit a wall in less than a minute. So I asked about his death. She was willing to talk solemnly about that, the tragedy, the ingratitude of the man, a Negro, who Mr. Johnson had taken in off the street and given a job when others wouldn't. "And it wasn't only him that had it in for Mr. Johnson . . ." She caught herself, her forehead wrinkled as if she was surprised by her own words.

"Is there something people don't know about the murder?" *I* was surprised by *my* words. Had I stumbled onto something?

She took a quick glance at the crew of office workers behind her. A half dozen pairs of eyes dropped to their typewriters or adding machines. She lowered her voice. "More went on down in that garage than the police or anyone else knew about . . ." She turned her glance like a spotlight on Elena, who lowered her gaze but not quickly enough. "The murderer may not have acted alone."

Jesus! Just what I needed, another theory. I sensed she was torn between talking or not talking about the murder, so I took a wild shot at trying to get her out of the office and loosen her up with a couple of drinks.

"Mrs. Simpson . . . Alice . . . Mr. Johnson certainly picked the right person for his private secretary, someone whose discretion and loyalty is unquestioned. I have an appointment this afternoon but should be finished by five thirty and I'd like to take you to dinner. We can relax and I believe you can help me paint the portrait of Mr. Johnson that you know he'd want painted."

She frowned. I thought she'd turn my offer down, figuring me for dinner at a hash house. When I suggested the Schrafft's near Columbus Circle, she got a glint in her eye, smiled in spite of herself, and agreed to meet me at 6:00.

After I left the taxi company office, I'd gone barely half a block when a wild-eyed Elena caught up with me. "What were you doing talking to Mrs. Simpkins?" Her voice shook and she glared at me, so I stammered like I did as a kid when my mother caught me with my hand in the cookie jar.

Elena didn't care. "Did she say anything about me?" Her eyes bore into mine. "Did you say anything about me?"

"Easy," I held up my hands. "Neither of us said anything about you. I told her I was a reporter writing a story about Irwin Johnson."

Elena took a deep breath. "What were you doing here yesterday dressed like a bus driver?"

"Not a bus driver, a handyman. I wanted to see where the murder took place. Why all the questions?"

Her eyes were smoldering. "Why haven't you called me? Why did you run away from me yesterday?"

I reached to put my hand on her shoulder. She stiffened.

"Come have a cup of coffee," I said. "You've gotten things mixed up."

She glanced at the garage and then at me. "I can't. I've got to get back to work. Mrs. Simpkins watches me like a hawk."

"Is that what's bothering you, that I'll get you in trouble with her?"

"If she finds out I'm helping you or that I even know you, she surely will fire me." Her lip trembled. "I thought you were going to call me."

"I will," I said.

Her tiny smile touched me. She turned and scampered back to the garage. I was glad she didn't want to get together after work. It would have been tough telling her I was having dinner with Alice Simpkins. I headed to the taxi union hall

on Twenty-Third Street with a couple of questions for Vinny
Forlini.

"You should make an appointment," he said. He sat behind
his desk wearing a grey suit, a felt hat, and a green and yellow
tie that I'd bet would glow in the dark.

This was my day for dealing with pugnacious men. "Why
do you think Harold Williams killed Irwin Johnson?"

Forlini wasn't bothered by my prosecutorial tone. "That's
what the cops said. He was convicted. Read the papers."

"I'm asking about direct knowledge. You saw something?
You know someone who saw something?"

He cocked his head and squinted. "The guy's a Commie."

For damn sure, I wasn't going down that road again. I could
handle this; I listened to *Gangbusters*. "Can you account for
your whereabouts on the night of the murder?"

His eyes exploded open. "What're you talkin' about where
I was? I ain't no fucking suspect. Who the fuck you think
you're talking to? I oughta wring your neck."

"I'm surprised no one asked you before."

"You're asking for trouble pushing me, pal. I thought you
was a smart guy. You wanna bother somebody, bother Rosen.
I told you why Duke hired you."

"Sheehan, McFarland, O'Keefe, those names mean anything to you?"

He flicked his wrist to shoo the question away. "They
sound like Micks. The West Side's full of 'em." He hoisted
himself up in his chair, settled back down, and pushed his
chest out. "I'm gonna tell you once more. There ain't nothin'
to investigate. Go to a movie. Go to a ballgame. Turn in your
timesheet when you're done. Nobody cares the jig gets it, not

even the Reds. What they're doin' it's all for show." He glowered at me. "Now beat it and stay out of my way. I eat punks
like you for lunch."

I wasn't shaking when I left but I did believe him. Maybe
not about lunch. The fact was I didn't expect to get anything
out of talking to him except to let him know I wasn't scared
off by the friendly warning from Big Al. Maybe that was
foolish. I rattled Forlini's cage because sometimes if you pro-
voke a guy like him, a guy who punches before he thinks, you
nudge him into doing something stupid. Of course, that
something stupid could be dumping me into the East River.

CHAPTER TWENTY-FIVE

I took a pass on shadowing Cynthia Rogowski and made my way to Schrafft's and Alice Simpkins. Midway through her second daiquiri, she loosened up. You wouldn't think to look at her she drank like a sailor with a hollow leg. The first thing I wanted to get her going on was "Harold Williams didn't act alone."

"There's more Communists among the drivers . . . I know for a fact." She squinted at me knowingly over the rim of her cocktail glass. I was in for another session of anti-Communist preaching.

"Men from the government came and told Mr. Johnson who the Communists were and to watch out for them. He wanted to fire them all. But the government men told him it was better to keep them on so he could watch them and report on them." She took a healthy slug from her daiquiri. "The leader is the DeMarco fellow." Lowering her voice, she said, "His sister is that hussy you saw in the office."

"Hussy?"

"You must have seen her looking at you . . . She looks at all the men like that. A girl who wears lipstick and eye shadow and those kinds of clothes to the office, you couldn't miss her. She practically hangs out a sign."

Elena—who as far as I could tell dressed like every other office girl her age—had been right about Mrs. Simpkins's opinion of her. I felt like I should object and felt like a heel not straightening Alice out, but I couldn't afford to argue with her if I wanted to get her to talk.

With the patience of a saint and the manners of a prince— and after ordering her a third daiquiri on the QT while she was chattering—I became Alice's confidant. "If I told you everything I knew about Mr. Johnson, your hair would stand on end," she said after moving on to her new daiquiri without missing a beat.

After a light dinner and a glass of wine to chase the dai-quiris and before I poured her into a cab, she gave me the names of a couple of cronies—business associates—Johnson drank martinis with at the 21 Club. More important, perhaps the mother lode, she gave me the names of two women who at one time or another had been regular callers on Johnson's private phone, one who owned a flower shop in Chelsea and another who worked at a club on Fifty-Second Street.

It had been a long day, but I had one more bit of subterfuge lined up. I went back to Walter Bauer's office expecting he wouldn't be there. On my first visit, I noticed—something I do out of habit—the outer door to the building and the door to his office would be as easy to open as a candy wrapper.

For the outer door, I slid the thin blade of my pocket knife from my tools of the trade kit between the door and the door jamb to push the tongue of the lock back far enough from its slot for me to pull the door open. The office door I opened with a skeleton key from the same batch I'd used for the door of Irwin Johnson's pleasure palace.

Most P.I.s keep a running record—a log—of what they come across during an investigation in case they have to testify in court. Judges and juries are more impressed by a contemporaneous account than recalled happenings. P.I.s also keep photographs they take, except if for some reason they pass them along to someone—by selling them to a subject of the photo who buys them off, for example.

I didn't know what I'd find but Bauer struck me as a man who might be careless with his records. I also did what I was doing because I didn't like the way Bauer did business. He was a fraud and that gave all P.I.s a bad name. In my tool kit, I had gloves, a small flashlight, and a miniature spy camera Gil had given me for copying documents on the QT.

I could have tossed the place with no one the wiser, but I wanted Bauer to know his files had been pilfered. And I wanted him to suspect—but not be able to prove—it was me who'd done it. I found his notes from the Irwin Johnson case after a search of the file cabinet; at least he knew the alphabet. The Johnson file was thin and Bauer's handwriting was sloppy enough to be barely readable.

To save time, I photographed the handwritten notes. I'd read enough to discover he'd taken photos. He'd certainly have sold them to Johnson, and Johnson would have been smart enough to demand the negatives as well as the photos. But Johnson might not have been smart enough to know Bauer would keep copies of the prints.

On this, Bauer was too quick for me. Either he hadn't kept copies of the photos he'd sold to Johnson—which I doubted— or he kept them somewhere where I couldn't find them after a thorough search.

What I did find were a couple of keys to a safe deposit box in the file folder. I made an impression of the keys on a bar of soap I also carried in my tools of the trade kit, though this was the first time I'd had occasion to use it. Gil had a locksmith in his stable who could make keys from the impression. But the keys wouldn't be any good to me without a court order to get the bank to open the box. I hoped Gil might pull that off.

It was past my bedtime, but I had one more stop before I slept. Her name was Marcie and she worked at a clip joint on what used to be called Swing Street—Fifty-Second between Fifth and Sixth Avenues—one of the strip clubs that had pushed out the jazz places over past few years. The joint I wanted was in the basement of a brownstone in the middle of the block. It had an awning out front and a flashing neon sign above the stairs.

If you wanted information in such a place, you went to the bartender. If you leveled with him and he understood you were a guy trying to make a buck he might help you out, assuming you knew he needed to make a living, too. Bartenders protect the folks around them from those looking to do them harm—bill collectors after a kitchen worker, a summons server looking for the chef, ex-husbands, angry boyfriends, mashers looking for one of the girls, be she waitress, dancer, or B-girl.

The guy behind the stick this night had a thick neck, a square head, and an Irish mug. His eyes were blue like my father's. He mumbled a greeting that was warmer than I expected and asked what I'd have with a thick brogue that suggested the southwest of Ireland.

"Up Cork," I said.

"Fuck Cork," he said. "Corkonians are all horse thieves."
He laughed easily and peered at me more carefully. "Sure,
you're not from Cork?"

"My father."

"And what brings a decent lad like you into a dump like
this?" He glanced about the barroom, his eyes resting on the
bar flies nearest us who were eavesdropping. "It's all right," he
told them. "They can't fire me. I know too much." The tipplers
looked away.

I drank a beer, chatting with the barman Seamus whenever
he stopped by. A hard-eyed woman with bleached blond hair
and large breasts, wearing a low-cut blouse and leather-like
shorts that had seen their share of rides along the Chisholm
Trail, sidled up beside me and bumped her hip against mine.
"Not now," I said. She pouted but drifted on to the next man
at the bar.

When Seamus brought my second beer, I handed him a
fin. "That's for you." I told him I was a private eye looking
for someone. He stiffened but didn't back away, so I told him
my tale.

He listened, his face impassive.

"Did you know Irwin Johnson?"

He leaned on the bar, his face close to mine and spoke
softly. "Look, Mac." It was Mick, but Mac would do. "In a
joint like this you might see a lot of things, you might know
a lot of people. You want to keep working in a joint like this,
you forget what you see and you don't remember anybody's
name when someone asks. You got me?"

I did. I laid another fin on the bar, "Let's give it a try

anyway. I'm looking for a girl named Marcie. No trouble. Just a couple of questions." This wasn't the honest to God truth. But he probably knew that.

"It's Marcie Taylor you're looking for?" He thought about that for a moment as he watched something no one else could see out in the dimly lit, smoke-filled room. "She's a good girl, she is, but innocent."

He straightened and scanned the room; I did, too, taking in the too loud chatter, hollow laughter, lowdown blues, hungry-eyed men leering at sashaying women in low-cut blouses and leather shorts, not a place that bespoke innocence. "Like a stray, she is, seeing the best in any man who comes through the door and getting the worst." He motioned to my glass with his eyes. "Drink up. You'll have to buy her a few drinks, too. It'll cost you more than the sawbuck. And you can be sure you won't have found your killer."

Marcie was more engaging than I expected her to be. My taste in women didn't run to B-girls who more often than not peddled a bawdiness that was too vulgar for me. Marcie was playful, teasing, coquettish, not bawdy nor sassy, fun, no tricks. No tricks yet; she'd learn them soon enough. I asked her about Irwin Johnson.

She froze. Her jaw dropped. "That's personal. I'm supposed to help you have a good time, not talk personal." She glanced anxiously around us. "How'd you know about Irwin?"

I told her who I was and what I was doing.

Her eyes narrowed. "I can't talk about that here."

"Can I meet you tomorrow—take you to lunch?"

She glanced around her. "Order me a drink or they'll start wondering." She placed her hand lightly on my shoulder and moved a step closer until her hip grazed my thigh. Her eyes met mine, her gaze gentle.

"What should I order you?"

"Anything you want. Seamus knows. It's all tea anyway." Her laugh was a little tinkle and I warmed to her. Relaxed from the beer after a tough day, I liked the pressure of her body against my leg, the glisten of her red lips, the slight scent of something flowery around her. I'd have easily spent an hour or two with her slim fingers stroking my arm, her thigh against mine, her lively blue eyes suggesting fun and frolic, listening to her tinkling laugh as she beat me out of a week's pay.

Two drinks for her and another beer for me, plus the ten for Seamus. This on top of dinner and drinks for Alice Simpkins; I'd put quite a dent in my expense account. Marcie lived in Greenwich Village and said she'd meet me at two the next afternoon in Washington Square Park near the arch on the Fifth Avenue side.

Too much thinking kept me awake a long time that night. I tried reading, but my thoughts kept pulling me away from the story. For whatever reason, I thought about women: the classy one suspected of betrayal I'd been tasked with following; the worldly one who caught me with her underwear and told me to look her up when I finished my case.

Mostly, I thought about Elena running after me down the block when I left Alice Simpkins's office, picturing her trembling lip, the flush of her cheeks, the pleading tone of her voice when she asked why I hadn't called her. I remembered, too, my hands on her waist and her shoulder when we'd almost danced to the "Tennessee Waltz." Could she be as sweet and guileless as she seemed, or had I made her up like a child makes up an imaginary playmate because I needed someone simple and pure and innocent to help me get through the sordid mess I was mired in?

The last thing I thought of before dropping off to sleep was that I almost hadn't paid attention to the flowery scent that floated around Marcie.

CHAPTER TWENTY-SIX

MORNING

As soon as I could get going, I reported to Duke at his office. I wanted to tell him face-to-face what happened. His wife had given me the slip. That was my mistake. It was embarrassing. "The thing is," I told him. "She did it like a pro. She knew she might be followed and took evasive action."

"How would she know that?" Duke's eyelids drooped over his bloodshot eyes; his mouth sagged; he needed a shave. You'd think he was coming off a week-long drunk. "Maybe she saw you."

I shook my head. "I let her get away but I'm not clumsy enough for her to spot me. Did you tell her you were on to her? Give her any reason to think you were suspicious?"

"No. The truth is we get on fine. One time she wasn't home when I expected her to be. It was my poker night, so she didn't think I'd be home till midnight. Somethin' came up. I had to go to a garage on Tenth Avenue. When the meeting was over, it was too late to go to the card game so I went home. Maybe nine o'clock. I'd called her at work around five. She told me she was going home. She wasn't there."

Duke let that one go without much thought. He didn't get suspicious until he caught her in a lie. That time, she told him she was meeting a friend to have dinner. By chance, he ran into the friend on the street and asked where Cynthia was. The friend didn't know what he was talking about. When he asked Cynthia, she said there'd been a mix-up so she had dinner herself at a place near work and went to a movie afterward.

He didn't argue, didn't accuse her. As he spoke, Duke was on edge, glancing every few seconds at the door behind me as if he expected someone to come barging in.

I asked him if he was okay.

He said he was but neither of us believed him.

He didn't ask about Harold Williams but I told him I needed to go over some things.

He glanced at me sharply. "This might not be the best time."

"Should I wait until they execute him?"

Duke bowed into his hands and rubbed his face. "I feel like Job. Do you know about Job?"

I did.

"Sol told me about him. You know all the crap they say about Commies? You ask me, half of it's bullshit. Sol's the only guy I trust in this whole operation. And it's him they want me to get rid of, not Vinnie who keeps patting me on the back looking for a good place to stick the knife in.

"Everything at once," Duke said to an invisible audience. "Some of the garages are restless. They want to strike. Sol's telling me it's time. He's working on a mass meeting in a week, maybe in a couple of days if things keep heating up. Forlini's says if we strike he's gonna hold back his garages. If he does, we'll be a three-legged stool trying to stand on two legs."

Duke was too distracted to think about anything but the looming strike, the union's warring factions, and his wayward wife, so I didn't say anything more about Harold.

Before I left, he gestured for me to lean closer to his desk. "He's complaining about you, you accusing him." He meant Forlini. "He's got guys around him. They're muscle, plain and simple. You know he's protected." He drilled me with a hard stare. "They got pull with the politicos and the cops, with everyone. Big Al goes to meetings when they're appointing judges, for Christ's sake."

Duke rubbed the stubble on his chin. "I shoulda thrown Forlini's ass out years ago. I coulda gotten rid of the bastard when we were starting out. I didn't because I got greedy. He brought garages into the union. I knew he was crooked. I knew he was connected. I figured I could handle him. I didn't trust the Reds either, but I needed them, too." He sat back. "So, we'll see. I got the bosses to deal with. I got the gangsters. I got the Commies. And I got Cynthia." He put the flat of his hand to his forehead. "I'm Job, I tell you."

I didn't tell him about my late-night chat with Big Al. He might have thrown himself out the window—or worse, thrown me out the window. On my way out, I noticed Sol Rosen was in his office, so I ducked in.

He stopped what he was doing, stood, reached out, and shook my hand as if he were ringing the supper bell. He waved me to a chair. Sol was slim and probably average height but seemed taller, smooth shaven, his hair short, his most prominent feature a good-size schnoz. He watched me in an appraising way. "How's it going?"

"I got a dilemma."

He stopped smiling.

"Your guy who's supposed to help me hasn't been much help. Frank DeMarco thinks maybe Harold did kill Johnson."

"Harold was framed because he's dangerous to the ruling class."

"No one told Frank."

Sol's voice hardened. "You misunderstood him. He's saying he doesn't know if Harold's guilty or not because he simply doesn't know. Marxists rely on facts; when you don't have the facts to support your position, you don't pretend you do. You might take the position but you need to be clear you don't have all the facts and the position might change if the facts change."

Sol held up his hand to tell me to wait a moment before saying what I was about to say. Since I wasn't about to say anything, he could have saved his energy.

"Harold trusted Frank. Frank trusted Harold. I know this from experience. When a question came up in our meetings, they almost always came down on the same side. When Frank had something to say, Harold listened and vice versa."

Sol had a convincing manner. I could see why workers listened to him. I had to force myself to take issue. "Suppose the Party had to choose between Frank and Harold?"

Rosen tilted his head like he wasn't sure what he'd heard. "I don't understand."

"If Frank killed Johnson and framed Harold, wouldn't the Party cover for him? I was told he's being groomed for leadership." Another stretcher here—I'd been told this by Elena, not someone privy to the Communist International's master plan.

Rosen didn't bother to ask where I got my information. "Frank kill Johnson? That's ridiculous. How could you—" He caught himself. "Of course . . . Mortimer Carter." He took a deep breath. "Give me one fact—even the tiniest shred of evidence—that suggests Frank is a murderer, or that if he was the Party would cover for him and frame Harold." He waited with exaggerated patience.

He could wait as long as he wanted. I had no intention of giving him any, since I didn't have a scintilla of proof to support what I said, not a morsel, not a crumb.

Maybe he sensed my dilemma. "Vincent's thugs are a thousand times more likely to kill someone than Frank is." His confidence had returned.

"We're not going down that road again," I said. "Accusations don't get us anywhere."

He was polite enough not to point out that was what I'd just done. "You know how gangsters work," he said. "They use the unions they control to lean on the owners. The owners pay them for labor peace. If an owner balks, his business gets hit; people around him get hurt. If he continues to resist they knock him off."

"And that's what happened to Irwin Johnson?"

That bent his nose again. "Forlini and his thugs are getting the bosses in line at the same time they're trying to get the cab drivers in line."

I waited a moment before I said, "I'm told by someone who speaks for the organization that the Mob didn't kill Johnson."

This drew a flicker of surprise in Rosen's steady gaze. "I wouldn't believe this spokesperson if I were you." His tiny smile was mischievous. "If you're taking statements, I can assure you on behalf of the Communist Party Central Committee that we didn't kill Johnson."

When he stood to shake my hand and send me on my way, he said, "Sunday night, Union Square, the largest mass meeting of cab drivers in the city's history. You're invited."

CHAPTER TWENTY-SEVEN

AFTERNOON

So now I'd been told—straight from the horses' mouths, so to speak—by spokesmen for two of the most feared clandestine operations in the city that I could scratch their respective organizations off my list of murder suspects. That was a relief. The only question remaining was: Why should I believe either of them?

Just past midday as I headed downtown to meet Marcie Taylor, it was stinking hot with steam rising from the gutters mixing with the reek of garbage from the cans on the curb and exhaust from the traffic. I walked down Seventh Avenue and across West Fourth Street. Once I got away from Seventh Avenue, the Village was cooler with pleasant scents wafting from the restaurants, bakeries, coffee houses, and Italian delis. The tree-lined streets had a peaceful rhythm you might find on a country lane, a respite from the relentless throbbing of midtown.

As I crossed MacDougal Street I spied Marcie near the Washington Square Arch; she was one minute surveying the goings on in the park, the next minute glancing up Fifth Avenue as if she might make a run for it. From a distance, she could have been an NYU coed, slim, erect, girlish. When I got closer and saw her face without makeup, rosy cheeked and scrubbed, I understood what Seamus meant about innocent. Her manner matched her appearance; she smiled and waved as if I mightn't recognize her.

Like Elena, maybe because of the freshness of youth, she projected a kind of carefree embrace of life; you'd think her too sweet and ingenuous to be questioned about her affair with a married man who'd picked her up at a strip club.

"He lied to me," she said when we were seated on a bench not far from the arch. She spoke with bitterness and disappointment but without any guilt or shame that I could detect.

He'd courted her—her term—with flowers and jewelry and afternoon trips to boutiques on Madison Avenue to buy expensive clothing. She wasn't as easy—her term—as he expected her to be. She wasn't in the market for a sugar daddy and just because her job was to entertain men—in well-lighted spaces where they were told to keep their hands to themselves—no one should think otherwise.

Her gaze was frank and direct. "My job pays three or four times what I made at the dress shop I worked at. People get the wrong idea. I'm an entertainer, like a dancer or a singer."

This private eye business, I was discovering, required a lot of nodding. Since I didn't know what Marcie would tell me, I let her say what she wanted to say and waited to ask questions. She wasn't the first woman to be lied to by a man about his marital status. But to listen to her, you'd think she was.

"He had plans," she said dreamily; then caught herself. "He was a good liar, very smooth. I should have known better." She turned her big blue pools of innocence on me. "My upbringing was proper. I was taught by the nuns. He took advantage of me."

At nearby stone tables, men played chess and checkers wordlessly. Kids roller-skated among couples meandering on the walks through the park. An older woman sitting on a bench near us fed bread crumbs to pigeons. The noise from the city was hushed. The heat wasn't so intense. A breeze ruffled the leaves on the sycamore trees.

Marcie grew up in Woodside, a couple of stops on the IRT from where I now lived in Sunnyside. Her mother died when she was a child and her father disappeared into the city. She was raised by an aunt who she said didn't like her, so she left home when she was sixteen and moved into a women's residence here in the Village, where she still lived. She looked at me when she said, "I thought I'd be a virgin when I got married." Tears glistened and she turned away.

Once you've reached a certain age, a man taking your maidenhood under false pretenses didn't warrant criminal charges; but for a girl like Marcie losing her virginity based on a lie was nevertheless a crime. She'd probably get over it and find a young man who'd love her and marry her knowing she wasn't a virgin. There were a lot of such men but she might not know that yet. Or she might keep knowledge of that particular state of her being away from him, launching her married life on a lie as her own love life had been launched.

Irwin's wooing of Marcie was similar to the way Eva Johnson said he'd approached her. Eva was wise enough in the ways of the world to beat him at his own game. Marcie wasn't. I asked her if she'd told anyone about Irwin. She shook her head.

I asked if she had a boyfriend. She said no. I asked about male friends. I asked specifically about Seamus the bartender, who seemed to have taken a shine to her. My clumsy questions were to find out if she had anyone in her life who might take revenge for her after she'd been violated and betrayed. She didn't or didn't admit that she did. And I didn't judge her to be made of the stuff that would propel her to take revenge on Irwin herself. But you can't tell on a first encounter what someone is made of.

"I thought I loved him." She watched something on the far side of the park. "I didn't know what love was. It wasn't about jewelry and expensive restaurants and nightclubs and trips and fancy hotels. All that's fun and exciting but not what's really important." She looked at me again. "Having someone make you feel special, worship you." She adjusted her mouth into what might be thought of as sensible expression. "It goes to your head, so you don't think it might not be true."

I asked her about Irwin's love nest above the taxi garage. She'd never heard of it. My last question had to do with when she stopped seeing him. A man at the club, she told me, a pal of Irwin's, got mad when she slapped him for groping her. He told her she was a slut going around with a married man. She was shocked. She didn't believe him. Until she asked Irwin and he told her he had a wife. So she stopped seeing him. This was two years ago.

"But what good did that do?" Her pretty face kept asking after the sound of the words died away. "He was tired of me by then anyway and had found another floozy." She caught herself, question marks in her eyes. "Am I a floozy?"

I took her hand. "You got a bad break. You're a sweet girl. You ran into the wrong guy who tricked you." She smiled looking at my hand holding hers. I let go. "You'll meet a nice guy sooner than you think, a guy who won't take advantage of you."

Her smile became a frown but the frown lasted only a couple of seconds. "Maybe you'll come back to the club one day."

I walked Marcie home to a women's residence run by the Salvation Army on Thirteenth Street, and felt like a bum. My chivalrous offer to accompany her to her residence was a ruse. I wanted to know where she lived because I was going to have her shadowed. Gil had a private eye—my former mentor Sid Wise—he borrowed to give me a hand when I needed to be in two places at the same time, which I would later that afternoon since I'd be shadowing Cynthia Rogowski.

Marcie's tale of woe was believable, as was her sincerity. Yet she worked as a B-girl. She called herself an entertainer; others would have said a hustler. And she'd gotten tangled up with a rich man. Despite her disavowal of diamonds, fancy restaurants, and high-class hotels, she hadn't fallen for a truck driver . . . or a cab driver. I didn't think she'd lied to me, but I had to be sure. When I left her, I found a pay phone in a drug store and called Gil's office. I told Effie I needed Sid and gave her Marcie's residence address and the name of the club she worked at.

From there, I went to the flower shop in Chelsea where Alice Simpkins had told me I'd find another of Irwin Johnson's former girlfriends. Her name was Gloria Winthrop, and the shop, Gloria Florist, was on Seventh Avenue in the Twenties around the corner from the flower district. The shop was small, smelled like a funeral parlor, and looked to be a one-woman operation. Gloria smiled prettily from behind a counter as the door chimed behind me. She was closer to Eva's age than Marcie's and had put on her face, as my Aunt Edna used to say; her voice was whiskey and cigarette gravelly.

"Yeh, I knew the asshole." She wore pants and a green smock, and gave the impression it would take a lot to rattle her. She put her hand on her hip and jutted it out, not a bump-and-grind sort of jut, more like a swagger. No daisy-fresh little girl led down the garden path here.

I used the same calling card I used with Alice Simpkins, telling Gloria I was writing an article, a tribute, to Irwin Johnson for *Taxi News*.

She frowned. "Why would anyone write a tribute to him? He swindled investors, cheated the drivers. The other cab companies tried to get the limousine commission to revoke his medallions because he was such a crook."

Gloria was working her way through a box of flowers, slicing off the ends and tying little green stakes maybe two inches long to what was left of the stems. She saw me watching and said, "For arrangements to hold them in place in the vase."

She wanted to know how I'd connected her to Irwin, so I told her I'd been asking a lot of people about him and different people told me about other people and so on.

She didn't press the issue. "Didn't anyone tell you what a jerk he was?" She snipped a couple of flower stems, tied them to the picks, and then answered her own question. "Probably everyone you talked to is glad he's dead. They didn't want to tell you because you might think they killed him."

As long as she brought up the murder, I asked her about Harold Williams.

"I know what I read in the papers." She waved the shears at me. "Like I said, Irwin was a guy every day someone would say, 'Someone should shoot the son of a bitch.' And then someone did and there you are."

She stopped abruptly and looked at the shears, realizing probably she was holding them like a weapon, and put them down. She wiped the debris off the work bench and began making an arrangement. To do this, she laid an assortment of flowers with those little picks attached to their stems out on the bench and slowly picked this one and that one, putting one down, picking up another, and sticking it into a vase, which had a chunk of something at the bottom the picks went into. We both watched the arrangement coming together.

"I wouldn't say I hated him as much as some people did. He's ancient history for me. Looking back, I'm disgusted with myself for believing his lies."

I asked who might hate him more than she did—a mistake.

"His wife for one, I'd think." She glanced up from her work and her eyes popped open. "Why do you want to know that? Must be a helluva tribute you're writing if you want to put down what the people who hated him have to say."

She had me, so I told her the truth.

She accepted that I'd tried to get over on her without complaint. "An innocent man goes to the chair for killing Irwin. Isn't that just like the bastard to fuck someone over— excuse my French—from the grave?"

Gloria intrigued me. I was tempted to ask where she'd gotten the grubstake to open the flower shop but I didn't. It was clear she hadn't gotten off a bus from Iowa anytime recently. One thing she told me that was helpful was that she'd met Big Al Lucania with Johnson.

"Irwin didn't say who he was, just called him Al, but I knew. A charming guy . . . a ladies' man. I could've gone for him. But I figured you do something wrong and get him mad you end up in the East River. Know what I mean?" She chuckled. "There's a story they told about Big Al. Want to hear it?" She chuckled.

"Big Al was dating this young, gorgeous girl. He'd come into this bar with her all the time and then he stopped bringing her. The bartender asked one Big Al's pals what happened to her. He knew better than to ask Big Al. The pal said, 'She died . . . died of gonorrhea.' The bartender said, 'Clap? No one dies of the clap.' The pal said, 'You do if you give it to Big Al.'" Gloria let out a husky, full-throated guffaw a burlesque-show host would be proud of.

She and Irwin had dinner with Big Al and his lady friend at the time, a Rockette. They met a few times over a period of a few months about four years ago, she said. Around that time, Irwin ran into some trouble with investors who thought they were going to be his partners. They owned small cab companies, eight or ten cabs. Irwin wanted their medallions.

"Men like Irwin and Mr. Lucania think attractive women are stupid. They talk to each other like we're not there. So I listened and put things together.

"Irwin swindled the investors out of the medallions. I don't know how he did it. I do know they were furious. Talk about want to kill someone. Irwin found out they actually did want to kill him, that they'd hired someone to do it—maybe someone warned him—so he went to Big Al for help. The price for the help was Irwin made Big Al a partner of some kind in his business."

She'd finished with the flower arrangement, held it up, and showed it me. "What do you think?"

I told her I didn't know anything about flowers but thought it was very nice. She said a person didn't need to know about flowers to find an arrangement beautiful. She wrapped some wax paper around the vase and the flowers, telling me which flower was which and why some kinds of flowers went together and other ones didn't.

When she had the arrangement wrapped, she said, "Mr. Lucania must have stopped protecting him." She thought for a moment. "Or Irwin might have tried to swindle Big Al . . . a bad idea."

She pinned a carnation to my lapel before I left. I offered to pay but she said it was on the house. Maybe I would think of her when I needed to buy flowers.

With some time to kill before Cynthia Rogowski would get out of work, I found a drugstore with a phone booth a couple of blocks up Seventh Avenue from Gloria's Florist and called Len Volpe. The desk sergeant said Volpe was busy and took my number. I gave him the phone booth number, bought a newspaper and an egg cream, and waited at the counter. Ten minutes later the phone in the booth rang.

I told Volpe what Gloria had told me about the men Irwin Johnson swindled and his partnership with Big Al. I asked if there were records of cab company mergers and takeovers at the taxi commission and could he find out the names of the men Irwin swindled. He said he'd try.

I liked Volpe. I trusted him. It would be nice if I could ask him to get me access to Walter Bauer's safe deposit box. But this would mean owning up to a burglary, which—even when done by someone whose intentions are as pure as mine—was a crime in New York, so I didn't mention it.

I dropped another nickel in the slot and called Gil Silver. After a delay, Effie said he was too busy to talk to me. I told her there must be a mistake. "Mr. Silver has standing instructions that I should be put through to him immediately whenever I called."

She laughed lightly. "Nice try, Mick. Try tomorrow. He's in a real snit today."

I got over to a doorway on Broadway at 4:45, a bit too early for Cynthia, so I walked around the block. On the walk, I got to thinking about Duke and Cynthia and how they might have gotten together—lovers from different sides of the tracks.

This figure of speech didn't hold water in New York since a lot of the tracks were underground and the ones above ground for the el trains didn't divide the rich from the poor. The point was they were from different classes—the bourgeoisie and the proletariat, as Marx put it—but no one mentioned class distinctions these days in America, where, the orthodoxy told us, we were one big happy class, those of us not already rich only a couple of good breaks away from a ride on the gravy train.

What I thought about was that at another time and in another place Cynthia could have been my ex-wife and I might have been Duke. Star-crossed lovers. I tried to remember what my married life had been like before things went bad. We were young; Deborah had been twenty-one, fresh out of college, when we met a few weeks after I came home from the war. She was gorgeous and vivacious and talented—one of the few women animators at Disney. Because she was young and glamorous, men often assumed she was a starlet. A mistake they quickly regretted.

Deborah took her inspiration from Katherine Hepburn's movies—a woman who could do anything a man could do, including for Deborah wearing pants to work until she was shown the Disney rule book: women were to wear skirts or dresses. Above all, Deborah was ambitious. Despite her independent streak, she was a company man to the core. She loved her job and idolized Walt Disney, believing absolutely in his benevolence—why did we need a union when Walt was a genius doing such creative things and letting us be part of it?—she paid no attention when I pointed out that we did most of the work and he took all of the credit. When the union called a one-day strike over grievances, I practically had to sit on her to keep her from crossing the picket line.

It wasn't that she was greedy. She'd always had money—her father was a producer—and assumed she always would. She saw herself as an artist and set her sights on becoming a great animator. At the time we met, I had delusions like that myself. I saw us one day creating our own award-winning animated films that folks all over the world would love as much as *Bambi* or *Snow White and the Seven Dwarfs*.

We were young, we were artists, we were in love, we lived in a wonderland. Deborah had a pampered upbringing. Her childhood was idyllic—she sang, she danced, she rode horses, she went to private school, she vacationed in Europe, her family had a maid, a cook, and a gardener, she had a nanny. If she had wanted to, she could have sat back and ate bonbons the rest of her life.

"None of that is important," she told me in dead seriousness. "I have a destiny." She'd gaze at me passionately. "We've found each other. Now it's our destiny."

Well, as it turned out, destiny isn't all it's cracked up to be. For one thing, having a baby hadn't been part of the destiny she'd had in mind. Why she was surprised was beyond me. We were doing the things men and women had been doing together since the dawn of time that led to babies being born.

She was more committed to her art than I was to mine. I didn't see that then. She might have been more talented than I was, too. I didn't see that then either. Nor was she by nature or inclination the helpmate sort. That didn't bother me so much. My iron-willed, take-charge, no-nonsense Irish mother taught me to make my own breakfast, pack my lunch for school, clean my room, and do my laundry.

Deborah and I had a nanny for the baby—paid for by her parents—who also made dinner for us and did a lot of the housework. A new world for me; par for the course for Debbie. While most of the dirty work was taken care of by the nanny, Deborah saw herself as the center of the baby's world, as befitted the mother.

She also wanted—needed?—to be the center of my world, and she didn't like Rebecca taking over first place. Which wasn't exactly what happened, but to someone who had always been the apple of someone's eye, finding the person designated her chief admirer goo-goo eyed over a different apple, even a tiny helpless one, wasn't something to take lying down.

All of this might have worked its way out given a little time.

I loved both of them and was, in my clumsy way, happy to do anything for either of them. Debbie, despite her unwitting self-centeredness, loved both of us also. Her impatience with the chores of motherhood and the whims of an infant were not because of unkindness or lack of love. It wasn't her fault she'd been spoiled her whole life and so expected others to handle the mundane.

We had some rocky moments but we were getting through them with a lot of pouting, too much stomping, tears galore, and a bit of tenderness now and again. When an argument went too far, when I showed myself to be more rough around the edges than she expected and scared her, she'd begin trembling from head to toe and burst into tears. Once that happened, feeling like a bum, I'd relent, I'd surrender, whatever the issue. And she'd find that sweetness at her core that had attracted me to her in the first place. We might have made it.

Then the subpoena arrived via a knock on the door during a chaotic but pleasant supper on a balmy summer night. I stood in the doorway, frozen to the floor, an envelope pressed against my chest, as the US Marshal tipped his hat and backed away.

A sudden memory of Rebecca came back at me on that street corner in New York like a punch in the gut. I stopped and leaned against the granite wall of a building. The memory was of an evening soon after she'd first learned to walk when she turned from her mother as I came in the door, smiled her heartbreaking smile, said something that might have been "Daddy" and toddled a couple of steps toward me. Tears welled behind my eyes.

I peeled myself off the wall and got to a doorway across

the street from Cynthia's office building. Pulling my hat lower over my forehead, I watched her come out, cross the street, and board the bus. A man about my age stood back to let her board first. This particular evening she wore a straight, tight black skirt and I suspected the man found it worth taking a moment to watch the swinging and swaying that went on beneath it as she mounted the steps.

No reason to tail her today, she was headed home, so I watched the bus head uptown with the sinking realization I had no idea what to do next. I'd come to dead stop. An urgency bordering on panic hit me. Harold Williams was going to die in seven days, and I didn't know how to stop it from happening. For a moment, I had the idea I should forget about finding the killer and work on breaking him out of prison. My next idea was to talk to Gil Silver, snit be damned. He got me into this. The least he could do was get a safe deposit box opened for me.

CHAPTER TWENTY-EIGHT

EVENING

I took the subway downtown to Gil's office on Chambers Street. It's harder to dodge a person standing in front of you than a person on a phone call, so I did a soft-shoe around Effie who was packing for home so not guarding Gil's office as attentively as she usually did—and knocked on the door.

When he didn't answer, I opened it and found him at his desk behind a stack of leather-bound law books and binders. Against the wall was a glass-front bookcase with more leather-bound books, and on the walls above the bookcases hung diplomas, certificates, and proclamations along with photos of him with assorted dignitaries, including FDR in one photo and John L. Lewis in another. He'd taken down the one with him and William Z. Foster.

He glanced up with quite a bit of irritation from the book in front of him before reburying his head. After a moment, he glanced up again and closed the book. "You've taken on one of the most obnoxious habits of shamuses, entering without knocking."

"I knocked."

Gil dismissed my qualification with a wave. "Same thing. You're where you're not wanted."

I put the safe-deposit box keys on his desk and started to tell him where I got them.

He stopped me. "I don't want to know your business. You're on retainer and not on my payroll so I don't need to know such things. Without the owner's authorization, one needs a court order to open a safe-deposit box."

"I'll leave it to you to figure out how to get it opened."

"What's in it?"

I told him copies of incriminating photos that Irwin Johnson paid Bauer to destroy.

"You know this?"

"I don't know anything. It's a hunch."

"They're no good to Bauer now. Why would he keep them?"

"He's not so bright so he's still looking for an angle."

Gil grumbled.

I tried to give him a progress report. But he knew it was an excuse to ask his advice. He got paid handsomely for giving advice because he knew what he was talking about. He wasn't inclined to idle chatter. "You don't want advice. You want me to speculate with you about what you should do next. Any bum off the street can do that because no one knows."

Arguing with him was hopeless; I tried anyway. "I tracked down two of Johnson's girlfriends and found out he had a partnership with—"

He'd opened the law book and ducked his head into it; this time, he didn't look up. "I've got a motion due in the morning."

Well, that took care of that. As I stood, he peeked out from behind the book and I could see the worry in his eyes. A man's life was in his hands also.

I took the Third Avenue el uptown and stopped at a joint

in the Forties for a steak at a workingman's price. After dinner, I called Len Volpe from a phone on the wall near the men's room. He had news. One of Johnson's swindled former partners drove a hack out of the Johnson Transportation garage. His names was Ace Jensen. Another one, Adam Sinclair, died a couple of years ago. The third one was gone without a trace.

Before making the trek home, I called my answering service and got a message to call Sid Wise, the shamus shadowing Marcie Taylor. When I did, he told me a man arrived at her building soon after he staked it out. They talked together in the lobby for about twenty minutes. When the man left, Sid followed him to a club on Fifty-Second Street where not long after arriving the guy appeared wearing a blue vest and a blue tie behind the bar. Sid gave me a general description, including him speaking with a mumbly brogue, that pretty much nailed my pal Seamus.

"Exactly what I needed," I told Sid. Often, I'm ashamed of my lack of trust in my fellow man—or woman. After talking with me, Marcie went to her protector. I wasn't surprised Seamus had taken her under his wing. I wasn't really surprised she'd lied when I asked if she'd talked to him about Irwin. Her lying might mean something important. It might not.

I wasn't going home after all. The fact that Seamus Duffy arrived at Marcie Taylor's residence not long after I spoke to her—and probably scared her out of her wits—didn't mean they'd conspired to cover their tracks, though they might have. Seamus might have killed Irwin to avenge the betrayed Marcie. I had no reason to think he did. I had no reason to think he didn't.

Johnson's murder took place more than a year after Irwin

ditched Marcie. Unless something happened more recently to rekindle old hatred, that was a long time after the fact to act on a grudge. The location, the scene of the crime, didn't ring true either. No reason Seamus would meet Johnson in an abandoned office at the taxi garage, especially one designed for hanky-panky. I wouldn't figure Seamus for a killer anyway. But that was partly because I liked the guy. The best thing for my peace of mind was to rule him out. Sometimes, the simplest approach is the best approach. I headed over to Fifty-Second Street.

Seamus watched me expectantly as I settled in at the bar. No smile this time. No cheerful welcome. We both knew why I was there.

"You talked to Marcie, I guess." he said.

"So did you." I ordered a shot of Bushmills with a splash of water.

He froze for a second like a fighter stung with a sharp jab; after a moment he regrouped, grabbed a glass and a bottle, and poured the whiskey into a shot glass in front of me.

"Is it really Bushmills?"

"No." He waited for my questions. When I didn't say anything right away, he leaned closer. "She's a scared girl. She thinks it will be all over the papers about her . . . about her and Johnson." His expression was troubled and in an understated way threatening—or perhaps protective and only threatening if need be.

I asked where he was the night Irwin Johnson was murdered. Since the murder took place more than a year before, I'd have been suspicious if he'd had an answer on the tip of his tongue. He didn't. His face, broad, handsome, and in a peculiar way guileless, registered his reaction: uncertain, quiz-zical, irritated, and then accepting.

"I'd say I was here. I've worked every Friday night for the past five years, except for a couple of nights off in the summers to go to the Catskills. The boss has the schedules for the last couple of years."

I was surprised, but the boss did have schedules going back years. A high-strung but affable and accommodating guy, he said he kept them because the place had been sued more than once. "I keep everything. Someone says they were jackrolled or one of the girls slipped him a mickey. If you can show them who was on the clock that night, who was around, the lawyers like that." He dug through a large metal file cabinet, one of two in his tiny, cramped office up a rickety staircase from the main floor, and found the schedules for April 1949. Seamus was on the schedule for the night shift of the eighteenth, the night of Irwin Johnson's murder. He'd started at 6:00.

I told Seamus the good news and had another whiskey, this one on him. Schedules could be altered, of course. If I wanted to push it, I could check the time cards for that night. But someone could have punched in his time card for him, too. Not much is for certain in this life. Sometimes, even I have to trust in my fellow man when he tells me he didn't do it.

He watched me drink the whiskey. "I didn't like you accus-ing me. I almost took a poke at you. But it came to me you'd be right to ask. I might well have killed the fooker if I'd known what he'd done. I've more than once put a man out of here and on his arse in the gutter out front for a lot less."

CHAPTER TWENTY-NINE

MORNING

Around nine, I called the taxi garage. Fat Tony was back at work and not happy to hear from me but said he'd track down Artie Kaplow—he could reach him at one of the cabstand call boxes—and have him pick me up in Sunnyside. I didn't so much need a cab as I needed to find Ace Jensen. Artie had been driving a hack a long time, so I figured he might know the man and with luck where to find him.

A little over an hour later, Artie tapped the horn on his cab a couple of times beneath my window. He was ready for another adventure, his grin as wide as the grill on his Checker. It was as if Tonto had saddled up to come ride with the Lone Ranger. Artie did know Ace and had a good idea of where to find him.

And we did find him. Jensen was parked in a cabstand in front of Penn Station, the fourth or fifth stand we checked. He struck me as someone with the size and strength to kill you with his bare hands, yet he wasn't at all threatening. With his jet-black hair and sunglasses, he was slick looking in a con man sort of way, too, but he wasn't that either. He carried himself with an air of indifference. Mostly, he was concerned with the afternoon race card at Aqueduct.

"He's a gambler," Artie had told me on the drive into

Manhattan. "Like a junkie to dope, that's him to gambling. If he's flush, he's at the track. If he wins big, he flies to Vegas. When he's broke—which is often—he drives a hack. It's a shame. He's a smart guy. Besides the cab business you're talking about, he owned a trucking company after the war and lost that, too, gambling debts. The bank took his house, and his wife left him."

Talking to Ace was difficult. He held a folded copy of the *Morning Telegraph* in one hand and a pencil in the other hand. He'd circled a number of horses in the first few races but while I was talking to him, he'd get a quizzical look, glance away from me, lean the paper on the roof of the cab, erase one of the circles, and circle a different horse; he was the kind of frantic gambler who's always one step in back of the bet he should have made.

When he did answer a question, he did so without emotion. Unions, he said, were ruining the country; a man needed to stand on his own two feet. Yet his antipathy was colorless, no vehemence, no anger. Same with Johnson's murder. Yeh, Irwin swindled him. He swindled a lot of people, so he was bound to get it one day—said without rancor.

He knew Harold Williams. Williams was okay. "But Negro guys are violent; not a fistfight like you and me when we're mad. You cross them, out comes the knife and they slit your throat."

"Johnson was killed with a gun," I said to keep the record straight. "Do you know anyone who'd want to kill him besides you?"

I'd caught his attention for a moment. He looked up from his scratch sheet for the first time with interest. "The Negro guy didn't kill him?"

"That's what I think."

He shrugged, as if to say, "Who cares what you think?" and waved the scratch sheet at a driver walking past. When the guy stopped, Ace asked about one of his picks. The guy mumbled something and wandered off, so I got in another question, this one about Big Al Lucania.

Once more, Ace didn't flinch. "You think Big Al bumped off Irwin?" He glanced behind me and then behind him over each of his shoulders. "I wouldn't go around saying that if I was you."

I actually hadn't said Big Al bumped off Irwin. But I gathered if Ace knew Big Al—or someone else—bumped Irwin off, he'd keep it to himself. I asked about his partnership with Irwin Johnson and if he knew about Irwin's partnership with Big Al.

He tried to keep his attention on me but his eyes shifted every few seconds back to the scratch sheet. "That's a long story." He put his pencil behind his ear and wagged his *Morning Telegraph* at me, letting me know it was a long story he wasn't going to tell me. "His being partners with Big Al maybe saved his life one time. But you know, you lie down with dogs you wake up with fleas."

What this cryptic proverb was supposed to tell me I never found out because the cab at the front of the line picked up a fare going to Aqueduct, causing a flurry of activity among the drivers. A plan, Artie told me later, was already in place. Ace and another driver jumped into the cab with the bewildered fare. A couple of the other drivers would move their abandoned cabs to a lot behind the station and if the adventurers came home winners would share in the take.

"I sure hope Ace's horse comes in," I said to Artie as we drove away.

He shook his head. "If he won a thousand bucks today, he'd gamble it all away by Tuesday. I seen him do it."

CHAPTER THIRTY

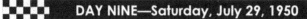

I came to find out later that word got around pretty quickly in the world of hack drivers via dispatchers, cabs drifting around the city, and call boxes at the cabstands. It took the rest of that day and part of the next for me to find this out because for most of that time I was unconscious in a hospital bed in St. Clare's Hospital with a concussion. From a few minutes after leaving Ace and the Penn Station cabstand until I woke up missing most of my senses late the next morning, I was out like a light.

If I were a poetic guy, I'd say when I opened my eyes I'd thought I must be in heaven because an angel appeared next to my bed with cute worry wrinkles on her brow and her pretty brown eyes brimming with tears.

"Elena?"

"You've been hurt," she told me.

I knew that. I also gathered I was in a hospital. I remembered what happened, at least the beginning. "What day is it?" I tried to sit up. "How long have I been here?"

She leaned forward to put her hand on my chest. "Don't jump around, you'll hurt yourself. You've been in the hospital since yesterday; that's all. Today's Sunday. The priest came by to give you communion but you were asleep." She looked into my eyes for a long moment. "I thought he came to give you last rites." She told me I had a concussion, but I wasn't going to die. At least not yet.

I touched my head and felt a bandage across the back.

"You have stitches." She studied my face. "You look younger when you're asleep." After watching me for a minute or two longer, she stood. "I've got to go and help Ma with dinner." She hesitated. "I could stay . . . I could go home with you and take care of you."

Like an idiot, I shook my head, and it felt like I set a bunch of rocks to rolling around inside it. "I can't. I can't stop. I don't have time."

"I knew you'd say that." The brown eyes brimmed again. "You could let this go. Let someone else take over. You aren't getting anywhere anyway . . . Are you?"

I stopped myself before I shook my head again. It was strange. I had little reason to think so, but I felt like I was getting somewhere. "Five days from now I'll know if I get anywhere."

She sat quietly and watched me.

"How did you know I was here?"

"Everyone at the garage was talking about what happened; Frank told me. You're a celebrity. Wait until Mrs. Simpkins finds out she was talking to a private eye." Elena beamed like a naughty child. "Did she tell you anything? I know you talked to her again."

Her cute mug took on a pouting-mouth look of disdain. "She made a snide remark about my looking at you. But I didn't let on I knew you. She thinks she's so smart."

"Do you know about the room behind the office?"

"What do you mean? . . . What room?" You'd think I told her there were Martians in the attic. "Did Mrs. Simpkins tell you about it?"

"No." Again I caught myself before I shook my head. "Would she have known what went on in that room?" I hadn't asked Alice about the room because asking might have blown my cover.

"I don't know what Mrs. Simpkins knows. She acts like she knows everything."

"Would she tell you what she knew about the room if you asked?"

Elena looked worried. "What room? Why would I ask her about it?"

"The break room where Johnson was shot. Do you know what went on in there?"

"I beg your pardon?" Elena stood.

Her reaction confused me. My head hurt and talking was wearing me out. "He used the room . . . to meet women he wanted—" I stumbled; I couldn't find the right words to describe the activity delicately. "He used the room to rendezvous . . . for meeting women he was . . . involved with. Did you know that?"

Her eyes were wide. "How would I know?"

"Did Mrs. Simpkins know what Johnson used the room for? That's what I want you to ask her."

Elena looked away, her shoulders stooped. "I don't think I'd care to ask her about that . . . about his carrying on."

So that was what you called it. "Right, his carrying on. Can you find out if she knew about his carrying on in that back room? Did you know about it?"

Elena sounded shocked. "How would I know about his carrying on?" Her eyes widened again. "I hope I wouldn't think about him carrying on back there."

This conversation would have made my head hurt even if it hadn't been smacked with a tire iron. For that was what had happened. When Ace left for the track, Artie and I had gone a couple of blocks along Thirty-First Street toward the river when a cab cut us off. Cursing a blue streak at the cab blocking his way, Artie pulled up in front of a vacant lot where workers had torn down a walk-up to put up a bigger building, as developers were wont to do all over the city.

At first, I was looking at the building lot, deep in my own thoughts. I'd been thinking about Ace Jensen and if he'd told me everything he knew. When we got to the vacant lot I began thinking about where folks went when the building they were living in got torn down to make room for a bigger building they couldn't afford to live in. Because of all this thinking, which was not far off from daydreaming, I didn't catch on to what was happening until the back door on the driver's side opened and seconds later the back door on the passenger side.

I'd reached toward the man who opened the driver's side door—though I didn't know what I'd have done if I caught hold of him—when I felt a tug from the passenger side. An arm went around my neck, locked under my chin, and dragged me backwards out of the cab. The arm was thick and abrasive against my face. I struggled to get my feet under me, and did for a moment as I tried to twist myself out of the grasp of the arm. But my foot got caught between the well on the back seat floor and the door, twisting my ankle and forcing me down to the curb.

From there, I groped at the arm to get it off my neck. Finally, the arm let go. I gasped for a breath, looked up, and saw a square face with a couple of days' worth of stubble, a mouth with a sick smile around a row of broken and discolored teeth. The head belonged to Moose McFarland, one of the Irish thugs I'd run into before. What I didn't see—I was later told—was a tire iron in his right hand that came down on the back of my head. Lights flashed; a jolt of searing pain, an urge to vomit, and then darkness.

I remembered pieces of what happened next, voices, my bouncing around, a horrible pain in my head—two pains, one inside and one on the outside—later, light shining in my eyes, the buzz of a razor, thick colorless curtains, pale green walls. I remembered being on the flat of my back rolling along a corridor at a pretty good clip, the unceasing horrible headache, my mouth dry as dust, voices murmuring around me, hands touching me gently, or gently in comparison to the arm around my neck.

I might have woken up during the night to hear machines humming, buzzing, beeping or ringing, and to see dim, flickering lights, or I dreamt this, or some of both. People did things to me, lifting my arm, opening my mouth. Now and then I must have thought I should look into what they were doing, thought I should take charge. But I didn't. I lay back and let others do what they would.

When I came back to the present, Elena was watching me tenderly. "You poor man," she said and I thought she would cry. I again turned down her nursemaid offer, so, reluctantly, she left me to go home.

I got out of bed, staggered around the hospital room until I found a wooden locker, not unlike the one in Irwin Johnson's love nest, and pulled out my wrinkled, bloodied, and battered suit. A further search unearthed my unmentionables and my socks in a plastic bag at the bottom of the locker. I'd gotten my pants on and was working my way into my blood-spattered shirt when I heard a sound from the doorway and discovered a grey-haired man in a white lab coat. He wore thick-rimmed glasses and had a stethoscope hanging from his neck.

"Up and at 'em, eh?" he said. "Can't keep a good man down."
This sounded jocular but he wasn't smiling. "Suppose you lie
back down before you fall down? I give you three minutes at
best before you topple."

I started to argue but a wave of dizziness caught me. Luckily, the bed was only a couple of steps away, so I put out a hand,
steadied myself, and sat down on it.

"You're a lucky man. A blow like that should have fractured
your skull." The doctor did smile now. "You must have a hard
head."

"I'm Irish."

He chuckled. "Your brain was rattled; some grey mass
shifted around. You'll have pain for a few days, possibly longer.
We'll give you something for that. You'll have spells of dizziness and nausea. Not much we can do about it. So far not a
lot of bleeding in your brain. We don't want that to increase,
so you don't want to take a chance of falling and hitting your
head. A blow could increase the bleeding and kill you. You
also don't want to be too active because even jostling might
do it."

I told him I appreciated his concern and would certainly
take it easy. But I had work to do.

"Your boss said to tell you to rest for a day or two."

"My boss?"

"Gil Silver. He arranged for your hospitalization." The
doctor waved a hand at our surroundings. "You haven't
noticed, I guess, you're in a private room. He asked me to look
in on you."

"Gil? How did he know?"

The doc shrugged, lifted my eyelids, looked under them,

and said I could go home but I shouldn't do anything else. I'd have liked to follow his instructions but I had a job to do. A few minutes later as I got ready to leave, I felt another wave of dizziness and moved to the bed again to lie down for a minute or two.

An hour or so later, I woke up. I'd wasted some time, but I felt better, not as much fog in my brain. So I headed out. The Eighteenth Precinct was only a few blocks from the hospital. I figured I'd walk over to see what the cops had to say about my run-in with McFarland.

My suit jacket and my shirt were caked with dried blood, so I bought a shirt in the hospital gift shop—it was dark blue and had the name of the hospital, St. Clare's, above the breast pocket. I stuffed my suit coat and bloody shirt in the bag the hospital shirt came in and headed out. My test run didn't go so well as I needed to stop a few times along the way to lean against a building or a mail box to keep Ninth Avenue from spinning.

The good news was the desk sergeant sent for Len Volpe when I asked. Volpe sat me down in a query room and gave me a glass of water and after the water a cup of coffee. I told him what happened but he already knew most of it. Gil had called and clued him in, so he'd read the police report. The report didn't include the name of the guy who assaulted me, so I told him. He asked if I wanted to press charges. I told him McFarland worked for Vincent Forlini.

He watched me sympathetically. "It was a warning." Volpe was right. If Moose wanted to kill me, I'd be dead. It was possible he'd done it out of pure meanness, though this was doubtful. When the Mob wanted to warn you, they might say, "You better watch out," once. After that, it was always painful. And if that "warning" didn't get through to you, it was the vacant lot in Canarsie.

Though I felt guilty about it—because he'd leveled with me—I didn't tell Volpe about the friendly advice from Big Al. The boss man talked to me as a favor to Gil and told me to keep my trap shut about the conversation. So I fingered Vinny Forlini instead. "He's told me a couple of times to drop the investigation into Irwin Johnson's murder. He might be worried I'll find out he killed Johnson."

Volpe's expression was pained, angry, and defeated at the same time. "We can pick up McFarland. We can charge him. No way we can charge Forlini unless McFarland gives him up. And I don't see that happening. Even with McFarland, it's a long shot. Your word against his. He'll have a half dozen people, including his mother and the parish priest, swear he was somewhere else."

"The cab driver, Artie Kaplow, was a witness."

Volpe watched me sympathetically and then rubbed his eyes like you might do if you had headache. "The patrol officers who got the call, they called an ambulance for you. They asked for witnesses. No one came forward. If someone said, 'This is what happened. There's the guy that did it,' they'd have arrested him. If someone said, 'McFarland did it; he went thataway,' they'd have gone after him. No one came forward."

"What about Artie?"

He shifted uncomfortably on his chair, his gaze darting around like he wished he were somewhere else. "They can get to him, too, the cab driver. He's got a family? It's tough to stand up to these guys."

A day ago, one of *these guys* tried to split my head open with a tire iron. Who would want to stand up to them? No one had to tell me about an overwhelming urge to move to the country and plant cabbages. Artie may have thought he was Tonto; I had no illusions about being the Lone Ranger. I was quiet for a moment. Volpe didn't interrupt the silence. "What would you do?" I asked him.

He examined the battered walls of the query room one more time. "What I should say is if you know who committed a crime, of course you should file charges." He sighed. "The sad truth is these guys get away with intimidation, extortion, strong arming, and murder all the time. You tell me why we let them; I haven't figured it out. The syndicate is built into the infrastructure of the society, like rats and cockroaches are built into the infrastructure of the city." He was quiet for a moment before he said, "I don't like what they did to you. I don't like them. Not being able to do something about it makes my blood boil."

The upshot was I wouldn't press charges because they wouldn't stick anyway. Volpe would have an off-the-record talk with Forlini. "I'll tell him if anything happens to you, I'll come after him." He looked me up and down. "You licensed to carry a gun?"

"I am."

"Start carrying it."

Before I left, I asked him to check on Ace Jensen's whereabouts on the night of Johnson's murder. After some thought, I added he might as well check on Gloria Winthrop too. Even though I didn't think her much of a suspect, it was something I should know.

I took a cab home. Not what I'd normally do for that long of a distance but my head hurt, I didn't feel all that steady on my feet, and the doc scared me with his talk about the dangers of my falling. Also, I wouldn't have to be looking over my shoulder so often. I felt dizzy off and on but once I got home, popped a couple of pills, and took a short nap, my headache was only a dull throb, and I could stand without shaking. I took a bath, put on clean clothes, and got out my spare suit. This job was tough on suits; I'd need to make the next big sale at Robert Hall.

CHAPTER THIRTY-TWO

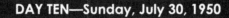

AFTERNOON

Despite a splitting headache, I made my Sunday call to Rebecca. When I asked about her cat, which I always did, she told me the cat was bad. She didn't have much to say beyond that so I never found out what the cat did wrong. She was distracted on the call, more interested in something happening there in her life than in me. I felt her slipping away.

It was the middle of the afternoon when I finished the call but I was too beat to do anything useful, so I popped another pill and lay down on the bed to think things through. The cab driver mass meeting Sol Rosen had told me about was that night. I figured if I rested up and had a bite to eat, I'd feel well enough to head down to Union Square for the brouhaha.

When the doorbell rang, I was somewhere between awake and asleep but alert and wary enough to go down and see who was there rather than buzz the door open. There in the vestibule, wearing the same yellow sundress she'd worn when we'd almost danced to the "Tennessee Waltz," her head tilted, her smile bashful, her eyes searching mine, was Elena. In her hand was a large Mason jar and under her arm a long loaf of bread.

I stared at her. She squirmed like a puppy. "Are you going

to invite me in?" She bowed her head and peeked up at me through her eyelashes. "This is a bold thing for a girl to do. Please don't make me stand here."

I followed the swaying of her hips up the stairs to my apartment, the hem of her yellow-and-white dress brushing against her slim calves.

"Minestrone," she said triumphantly, placing the jar on the counter in my kitchen. "I hope you have a pot to heat it up in."

"Of course, I have a pot." I had two and a frying pan.

She moved in a business-like way in the kitchen, bashfulness gone. "I bet you don't have olive oil."

I didn't.

"Butter will do." She nosed around in the icebox and pulled out the butter dish. Banging around the kitchen like she owned it, she heated up the soup and pulled a couple of chunks of bread from the loaf and buttered them. She then sat down on the second of my two chairs, elbows on the table, chin resting on the backs of her hands, and watched me eat the soup. "You'll feel much better," she said, "and you can nap after your soup."

The soup was the best tasting food I'd had since her mother's dinner the past Sunday, and I made the mistake of asking if her mother made it.

Elena sat back in a huff. "She did not. I made it." She lowered her eyebrows and scowled. "You don't think much of me, do you?"

Chastised, I told her I was amazed anyone so lovely could be a wonderful cook as well. The bashful smile returned.

"I've talked to some of the drivers about the night of the murder and wrote down what they told me in a notebook."

She was back to being business-like. "I had to do it carefully to keep anyone from getting suspicious, so I haven't talked to a lot of drivers yet. But no one's said he was at the garage that night." She pouted. "Frank has something he wants to tell you. He wouldn't tell me so I could tell you. The bum. He has to tell you himself."

I told her I was going to the union rally that night and would look for him.

She thought about that for a moment and said she'd come with me. "I can go and watch. There's nothing wrong with that."

She hadn't talked to Mrs. Simpkins about the room where *the carrying on* might have taken place. "I'll try because you want me to . . . but I don't like it." She stood up and cleared the table. "Time for your nap," she said over her shoulder as she put the leftover soup, bread, and butter in the icebox and the dishes in the sink.

I did as I was told, comforted to hear her puttering around my tiny kitchen as I lay down. My eyes were closed when I felt her standing over me.

"I'm going to lie down beside you," she said matter-of-factly. "And I'm taking off my dress because I don't want it to get wrinkled. And that's the only reason." She said this sternly. "So don't get any ideas."

I caught a glimpse of her silk slip above her dimpled knees and her graceful thighs as she slid into the bed beside me and pulled a light blanket over her legs. Her body, soft and firm, yielding and resistant, pressed gently against mine. When I reached to pull her closer, she turned to face me and placed both her hands on my head like a seer or a mind reader might do, and said, "Close your eyes and go to sleep." The slight pressure of her touch released the pain and I drifted away as you might into a dream.

An hour later when I woke up she was standing beside my bed. I looked into her soft brown eyes gazing back at me with a depth of longing and sadness that took my breath away. I touched her face and she put her hands around mine and began crying. I pulled her down to me and she cried softly against my chest for a moment before she hiccupped herself to a stop and sat up. She'd put her dress back on and now stood and brushed at the front of it. "Look. I went and wrinkled my dress anyway."

CHAPTER THIRTY-THREE

EVENING

Cabs lined both sides of Fourth Avenue and the blocks on the west side of Union Square Park. As we climbed out of the subway Elena held my arm with both hands and pressed it against her chest. I could feel her heart beat. A parade of cabs moved in a caravan along Fourteenth Street, blowing their horns, pulling over here and there, many of them double parking. As we got nearer the park, we could see more cabs stretched out along Broadway and University Place below Fourteenth Street. A sea of brightly colored metal on all sides as far as the eye could see.

"They're going to pull it off," I said.

"I'm so excited." Elena squeezed my arm.

Men poured into the park from all sides, heading toward the stage set up on the pavilion near Seventeenth Street at the northern end. The throng stretched from the stage most of the way to Fifteenth Street and would stretch to Fourteenth Street before the rally was over. The energy was palpable, the mood raucous but jocular, men smiling, pounding the next guy on the back, shaking hands with someone else, shouting to a pal across the way.

Police had gathered on the sidewalk along Union Square East in front of the S. Klein department store; mounted police were spaced along the edges of the park on Union Square West. A few of the mounted cops chatted with the cab drivers standing around them, some of the drivers patting the horses on the nose or the rump.

At a podium on the pavilion, a parade of men spoke one after another, short speeches a minute or two—loud and forceful exhortations. The president of the transport workers union thundered out his support for the cab drivers, followed by leaders of a truckers union local, the garment workers, the furriers, the machinists, and on down the line. Only a small group standing close to the podium listened to them. Everyone else lounged around in pairs or small clusters, laughing and shouting wisecracks to one another.

When Duke got to the podium, the men who'd been loafing on the perimeter pushed forward and the crowd in front of the podium grew larger and more attentive. Elena and I moved closer, too. As we did, I caught sight of a group of men I at first thought were part of the crowd of union men but realized, by the way they carried themselves, that they weren't part of the main group. Unlike the jovial mood of the larger crowd, these guys looked sullen, pugnacious, and menacing. I'd come upon the Forlini faction.

Duke revved up the crowd. His booming voice, his thick-as-mud, tough-guy New York accent, his call for justice thundered across the square: "We deserve the fruits of our labor!" He shouted out a litany of injustices—"low pay," "cheating bosses," "unsafe cabs." After each one, the crowd shouted, "No!"

And then he called out another litany, "Higher pay!" and a roar went up: "Holiday pay!" Duke hollered out each of the demands, and after each one, the crowd took up the chant. At the crescendo, Sol Rosen standing next to Duke, shouted, "Strike!" and the men took up that call, the roar growing and swelling until it reverberated and echoed off the surrounding buildings: "Strike! Strike! Strike!"

Forlini's troops shuffled in place while the crowd chanted. Some of them shouted, but whatever they shouted the fired-up workers drowned out. The "Strike" war cry provoked some pushing and shoving and a couple of fistfights between Forlini's men and a few fired-up cabbies from the larger crowd who stepped up like they'd been waiting for the action.

The melee didn't last long. The mounted cops rode into the fights, and the combatants scattered. Some of the Forlini troops took off toward Fourteenth Street. Surprising to me—and probably to him, too—some of Forlini's group stayed and joined in with the union guys, hollering, "Strike!" along with them.

The cab drivers began marching then. I didn't know where they thought they were going, but someone started off toward Fifteenth Street and everyone followed. The march blocked traffic—which was already tied up for blocks because of all the double-parked cabs—and amid the blaring horns and the shouting a plate glass window in a storefront shattered.

That was enough for the police. The mounted cops came from the far side of the park, across the park, to charge down Fifteenth Street swinging their batons. The cops standing along Union Square East charged into the park with their nightsticks flailing at the cabbies who hadn't joined the march.

Hundreds of cops, who'd been hunkered down in paddy wagons parked out of sight, charged out of the side streets like ants streaming out of an uprooted anthill. They came fast, on the run, swinging their nightsticks. With my head bashed in once already that week, this was exit music for me. I took Elena's hand and we made our escape, heading west between some mounted cops, close enough to bump against the horses' hindquarters, and the emptying paddy wagons.

After a block, we were clear of the tumult and slowed to walk toward the Seventh Avenue subway. At Sixth Avenue, we stopped for a moment to catch our breath.

"We didn't find Frank," Elena said. "But I know where he'll be tomorrow at lunchtime." At a coffee shop on Lexington Avenue, she told me, near one of the taxi relief stands, right about noon.

We started walking again. When we'd gone a half block, Elena, still holding my hand, swung herself around to face me, reached up to put her arms around my neck and crushed herself against me. She laughed and pulled my face to hers and kissed my mouth. And boy what a kiss! It brought stars to my eyes.

An hour later we were in my bed, the yellow dress folded neatly across my one easy chair, Elena in my arms, her lips pressed hard against mine, my head still sore but spinning all the same. We kissed over and over, for long times and short times. I helped her out of her slip and her bra; when I put my fingers under the waistband of her underpants, she put her hand on top of mine, and whispered, "Please don't."

I stopped.

"I'm falling in love with you," she whispered. "I want to be with you more than anything. But I can't do *that*." She brushed my hair with her hand and gently touched the bandage on my head. "I want you so much but I can't . . . I need to know for sure that you love me." She pushed back from me and stroked my face. Her eyes had reddened. "Can you hold me and can we go to sleep?"

When tears slid down her cheeks, I wiped them away with my finger.

"Please don't ask me to explain; I want to be with you. But it has to be perfect. I need to know you love me more than anything."

Instead of telling her I did love her, would always love her, which at the moment I felt to be true, I said, "It's okay." Because she was right. I didn't know if I loved her for sure. I wanted her very much. But I was glad she stopped us—as glad as a man can be who doesn't get laid when he's expecting to.

Elena needed love so badly. What if I was wrong about what I felt for her? It would break her heart—we hardly knew each other . . . I had to sort out my own life; I didn't know what I wanted. And Harold Williams's execution was in four days.

Elena laid her head on my pillow, and I stroked her hair until her eyes closed and her breathing slowed. While she slept, I lay on my back and watched the streetlight streaks on my ceiling as I had on many nights before, remembering another night I lay in bed beside a woman who'd asked me not to touch her. The woman then was my ex-wife. She would be gone the following day, taking our daughter with her.

In the morning, Elena was out of bed and dressed before I opened my eyes. When she saw I was awake, she came and sat on the side of the bed, putting her fingers to my lips. "Hush," she said. "Go back to sleep. I need to go home and get dressed for work. Please, please, don't be mad." She shook her head. I thought tears were coming but she turned away from me so I didn't see. "I don't know," she said. "I just don't know. Everything could be so perfect if only ..." She strangled a cry in her throat and rushed to the door and left.

CHAPTER THIRTY-FOUR

MORNING

I got up an hour or so later and after a cup of joe and a sinker at the Greeks took the train into the city to my office. Elena telling me she kept a notebook on the cab drivers she talked to had reminded me I needed to catch up on my own bookkeeping. I didn't like sacrificing the time but it was important. Gil went nuts if I didn't have contemporaneous notes on any case I worked on. Another thing was you write something down and you don't know it's important when you write it. Later, after you've come across a number of other things, you go back to it and it ties things together for you in a way you wouldn't have been able to do without it.

When I'd brought my notes up to date, I went over them. I didn't see anything tying anything together. I put the file back in the cabinet and went to find out what Frank De Marco had to tell me. I found him where Elena said I would at a coffee shop on Lexington Avenue near a taxi relief stand at Twenty-Seventh Street. He was chowing down at a booth with a couple of other drivers, so I told him I'd wait for him outside.

Frank had heard I'd gotten beaten up, something he would've known by looking at me anyway. When I told him it was one of Forlini's guys who did the job on me, he said, "It could be on account of the union. Payback for helping me with the strike in Long Island City.

"A couple of our organizers got waylaid these last few days. Things are heating up. There's gonna be a strike. We had a big rally last night. You shoulda been there."

"I was there," I said.

He scrutinized my face to see if I was serious and then laughed. "Helluva night. Lots of welts and lumps, a couple of broken arms. But no arrests. The cops knew if they tried to take anyone in there would have been a full-scale riot and the strike would have started right then and there."

I started to tell him Elena had been with me but thought better of it. I didn't want to let on we'd spent the night together.

"Forlini's tellin' the bosses the employers association can negotiate with him and avoid a strike. He and his goons are trying to scare drivers out of walking out." Frank's eyes glistened and gleamed as he talked. "No matter what Forlini does, the strike's gonna come."

He waved his arm as if he were leading the forces of righteousness on to victory. "Somethin' will spark it. A boss'll say somethin'. A guy'll get fired. Maybe someone gets hurt in an accident. One garage will walk out and then another and then: Boom! It's gonna explode." He took a moment to visualize the spectacle—New York City's version of the Bolsheviks storming the Winter Palace.

The country had seen thousands of strikes since the end of the war. The city by itself had hundreds, everybody from tug boat operators to longshoremen and from furriers to bagel bakers had hit the bricks. Taft-Hartley put a damper on a lot of militant strike activity—exactly what it was intended to do—because it outlawed sympathy strikes and secondary boycotts. But workers still struck.

A cab strike would wreak havoc in the city. It would slow me down, too. With luck, they'd hold until I finished my case. I interrupted Frank's reverie. "I heard you wanted to see me."

He shuffled his feet in place for a moment and glanced everywhere around him but at me. "I got to get back to work." He took a quick peek at me. "But now's as good a time as any. Maybe it means something. Maybe it can help Harold. I don't know." He took another look around and then told me he'd seen Eva Johnson in a cab with Mike Sheehan the night of the murder.

"You what!?" I grabbed my head to quiet the pounding. "You waited until now to tell me? Are you crazy?" I calmed myself down. "Let's try this again. What did you see?"

"No. No." He held up his hands to ward me off. "You don't get it. I wasn't holding back on you. I didn't know until now."

What had happened that night, he said, was he picked up a late fare to Idlewild and hung around in the taxi line at the airport to miss the traffic and hopefully pick up a fare and not drive back to the city empty.

"I got back an hour or so after my normal quitting time. As I was pulling up, a cab was pulling away. It was Mike Sheehan. He pretended he didn't see me. That made me think he was up to no good. There was a woman in the back seat. She kinda hid her face when I looked at her. But I saw her anyway. She was somethin' to look at, but I didn't know who she was.

He gestured toward me as if he were presenting his case. "I didn't know what Mrs. Johnson looked like then. The first time I ever I saw her was yesterday at the garage. When I saw her yesterday, I thought I recognized her. Then it hit me. She looked like the lady in the cab that night. And what was she doing at the garage and why was Mike Sheehan with her? I couldn't swear it was her in the cab. But it got me to thinking I should tell you."

He watched me expectantly but kept his trap shut. Almost right away I had doubts. The story was too good to be true. I wanted too much to believe it. Yet it was possible, a possibility I'd considered: Eva to Big Al to Forlini to Sheehan; not Tinker to Evers to Chance but something to consider all the same.

A big problem with Frank's discovery, even if it were true, was that it came from him. If he were called to testify—the sole witness placing the wife of the murder victim and a rival union activist at the scene of the crime—who would believe him? One Communist testifying as to the innocence of another Communist: one lies; the other swears to it.

There was also the nagging doubt I had about Frank that went back to his original lukewarm defense of Harold. Even if he hadn't known the woman he saw the night of the murder was Eva Johnson, he should have told me he saw Sheehan that night—a difficult thing to forget. Also, he knew a woman had called in the tip about the stuff in the trunk of Harold's cab.

I didn't say any of this to him. What I did do was ask him to pick me up at my office later that afternoon. I had a hunch the day for Cynthia stepping out was coming soon. She'd given me the slip once. To keep that from happening again, I wanted a driver I could count on to follow my directions, and I was a bit put out with Artie at the moment.

Frank said he'd pick me up at 4:45 in front of my office building—the floor-tile shop. Despite my deadpan response to his story, I felt a flutter of hope that this might be the big break. My head hurt, so I popped a pain pill before I headed uptown to talk with Len Volpe. I didn't want Frank to know where I was headed, so I let him go and took the next cab that came along.

When I got to the Eighteenth Precinct, Volpe was on his way out. "C'mon," he said. "I'll take you to lunch." When I hesitated, he said, "Nothin' fancy. It's a cop joint."

It was awkward calling him Detective Volpe every time I addressed him. He must have gotten tired of it too. On the way across the street, he cuffed me on the shoulder and told me to call him Len.

The restaurant was a Greek diner—not unlike the one in Sunnyside or a hundred others in the city with dozens of dishes on the menu. I ordered the hot open turkey sandwich. I'd learned somewhere along the way that taking one another to lunch was something cops did, so I felt like I was becoming one of the boys.

I told him what Frank had told me. Before I'd finished, I could sense his skepticism.

"I don't want to be a wet blanket." He fidgeted with his silverware and then lifted and put down his coffee cup a couple of times. "My guess is he made it up." He said this quietly as if he didn't want to hurt my feelings by poking a hole in a story only a half-wit would believe. "Figured he'd throw a monkey wrench into the works, hoping the court would halt the execution while we investigated his claim."

"You wouldn't pick up Sheehan and grill him?"

Volpe shook his head. "You got a guy on one side of this union battle accusing a guy on the other side. Your guy says it's Sheehan. What's Sheehan going to say? 'It wasn't me.'"

"And my guy's a Communist."

We ate in silence for a while.

Frown lines deep in his forehead, his dark eyes darker, Len munched on the dilemma I gave him. There wasn't nearly enough in Frank's accusation to go to his bosses and ask to reopen the investigation. Yet he knew the case was flimsy and that without the Red Scare hanging over the city the homicide investigation would have been more thorough.

"There's not this kind of anti-Communist frenzy in Italy," he said. "It's there but not like it was under Il Duce when the Communist Party was outlawed. There still are anti-Communists and pro-Fascists. But because the Communists played such a major role in the resistance a lot of people support them. They run for office and get elected like Republicans or Democrats here. They were even part of the government right after the war."

I'd spent a year in Rome during the war, so we spent a few minutes talking about Rome, the futility of war, how Italians found good food even in bad times, and how volatile Italian women were in good times and bad. Len had been a university student in Bologna studying to be a priest when his family fled Italy with Mussolini's Black Shirts on their heels.

"We fought," he said. "The seminarians against the student

Fascists. We were doing pretty well against them. Then things turned bad for my father, who taught at the university. The leaders of the university made a deal with the Fascists to keep the university open. The deal was to shut up the anti-Fascists on the faculty; that included my father. He had a cousin here in the city on the police force. He got me a job because I could speak English. There you have it: a New York cop instead of village padre in the Po Valley."

Len and I talked easily, surprising for me with a cop. We had the army in common and I guess that carried over. I told him that was where I'd met Gil Silver.

"When the US got into the war, I enlisted," Len said, "and wound up back in Italy. Because I spoke Italian I got assigned to the Provost Marshal's Office, mostly breaking up bar fights and arresting drunk soldiers. But because I'd been a cop, I got assigned to do homicide investigations by the CID also. When I got discharged, I went back to my job. My benefactor was a captain by then, so I had what they call a rabbi in the department. With him in my corner and my experience in the army, I made detective pretty quick."

Despite Len's dismissal of Frank's story, and my suspicions as well, I didn't want to let it go until the last dog was hung. "There's a dispatcher, Tony Dukakis, the guy I told you was roughed up by the Irish thugs. He was at work the night of the murder. If Sheehan and Eva Johnson were at the garage, he might have seen them."

As we were finishing up, I thought of something and asked if the police had the fingerprints from Irwin Johnson's love nest. I didn't tell him there might be prints from the mystery woman I hoped to find in Bauer's photographs since the only proof of her existence was a robe, a box of rubbers, and Fat Tony's sniffer.

Len reminded me they'd dusted for prints and didn't find any that didn't belong there but said he'd take another look at the file. He also said he'd talk to Fat Tony. "I doubt we'll find anyone to back up DeMarco." He said this with more confidence than I liked.

I found a phone booth at the back of the diner and called the cab company. "I'm not coming to talk to you because I know you don't like that," I told Fat Tony. "But I need you to do something."

He grumbled but didn't say no, so I told him about the room behind the cab company office above the garage. I wanted him to go upstairs and sniff the robe hanging in the wardrobe and maybe take a quick sniff of the bed.

"I don't get it," Tony said. "Why?"

"See if that's the smell from the night of the murder."

"What if someone sees me?"

"What if they do? Tell them you were looking for a men's room. I'll call you later."

He didn't want me to call the garage again, so he gave me his mother's phone number. "I'm staying at her apartment till things blow over." He paused. "No one knows about that . . . except you."

"No one will know from me," I said. "A cop's gonna want to talk to you. It might be better if he calls you at your mother's."

Tony took a moment before he said, "I guess it's okay." After another long pause, he said, "I don't know about you. You bring me nothin' but grief . . . Did you ever get anybody killed?"

"Not so far."

CHAPTER THIRTY-FIVE

"Let's take a ride," I said when Frank picked me up later that afternoon. I told him the address.

After a moment, he asked if I'd looked into what he'd told me about Sheehan and Eva Johnson. I told him I hadn't had time but it was high on my list. "Did you see anyone else at the garage that night?"

He said no.

"For now," I told him, "we're going to follow someone. You ever done this?"

He said he hadn't and asked who I was following. I thought about not telling him but he'd probably know as soon as he saw her anyway, so I told him. This caused more of a reaction than I expected. You'd think it was *his wife* I was tailing. He turned into a sphinx and drove without looking at me the rest of the way.

My hunch on Cynthia was right. She came out of the building, strolled two blocks south on Broadway and hailed a cab. I told Frank to follow the cab but that she'd most likely get out of it in a couple of blocks, cross the street, and flag a cab headed in the opposite direction. I wanted him to make a U-turn before, not after, she pulled her stunt.

After a few blocks, I saw through the cab's back window

that she was moving around like she might be going through her purse to get the money to pay the fare, so when the cab slowed and moved toward the curb, I told Frank this was it.

He pulled to the curb, waited for a break in the traffic, made the U-turn, and pulled to the curb in the next uptown block. I saw her get out of the cab but lost her in the crowd crossing the street when the light changed. I was about to dive out of my cab and go look for her but she stepped into the street to wave down an uptown cab.

Part two was easier but nerve-racking because I didn't know if she might switch to another cab. Unlikely, but my head was foggy from the pills and a dull pain, so I wasn't as sharp as I'd have liked. Frank followed the new cab through Columbus Circle and uptown on Central Park West. As Cynthia's cab approached Tavern on the Green, it slowed. Frank pulled over and we waited. Tavern on the Green was an elegant enough restaurant for a rendezvous. I steeled myself for another assault on my expense account, but her cab moved on, pulling over and dropping her across from the Dakota Building near Seventy-Second Street.

I waited before I got out because she might grab another cab going through the park and I didn't want to be left in the dust again. But she walked into the park on a path away from the transverse road, so I followed her, asking Frank to tag along on Central Park West as best he could. I thought I might be conspicuous in my suit in the park. But enough other men wore suits in the park that I wasn't.

As a matter of fact, the man who approached Cynthia as she sauntered along the walk beside the lake wore a suit, as did the man he'd been sitting with on a bench. Cynthia and the first man walked together alongside the lake heading uptown. A romantic summer evening, you might call it, the sun beginning to sink behind the apartment buildings on Central Park West, boats bobbing on the lake, couples strolling the path, some of them holding hands—but not Cynthia and the man she walked with. I took a seat on a bench and considered what I might be watching.

Before they'd gone very far, the man who'd been sitting on the bench with Cynthia's companion began following them. After a bit, I got up and joined the parade at a good distance. When the couple got near the Museum of Natural History, the second man caught up with them. He shook hands with her and all three talked for a few minutes before beginning to walk again.

At the top end of the lake, near the Seventy-Ninth Street exit, they parted. Cynthia walked on ahead and left the park first, crossing the street and heading west on Eightieth Street. By then I had enough of an idea of what was happening, so I let her go and waited to see what the two men would do. When they left the park, they walked across the street and down a couple of blocks to a dark colored sedan and got in.

Frank had driven up CPW and was waiting a block down from the Seventy-Ninth Street entrance. When I caught up with him, I pointed out the sedan and we followed it downtown until it pulled into a parking garage beneath an office building near City Hall.

"You know what's in that building?" Frank asked when he pulled over. His face was rigid, his teeth clenched. I didn't know but I could guess. He didn't wait for my guess. "The FBI field office." Rage contorted his face so that you'd think he was suffering intense physical pain. "That fucking bitch."

We didn't talk on the drive back to my office. I understood Frank's anger. You'd think Communists had been infiltrated and spied on enough he'd take it in stride. Yet being informed on was a slap in the face; you trusted someone you shouldn't have, so you'd been played for a sap. What this meant for Duke, Sol, and Frank, I had no idea. But it wasn't anything good.

"You don't need to pay me for this," Frank said when he dropped me off. He'd been silent and seething on the trip up to midtown. I didn't feel so great myself—dizzy, nauseous, and my head ached something fierce. The meter read eight dollars and change. I gave Frank a sawbuck.

"You don't have to," he said. "I was doing you a favor."

"You've got a wife and kid . . . and a strike coming up."

He took the dough. "I can't believe that bitch—" He swallowed his anger.

"For now, I need you to keep this to yourself." I explained that I was working for a client and what I found out was confidential.

He said he'd keep it under his hat—although he could guess the client. After another moment, he asked, "You'll look into what I told you?"

I said I would. And I would, sooner than he might think. I picked up a container of coffee and went up to my office. After scribbling a couple of notes, I sat and thought about things—a lot of things, but one thought wouldn't go away. Sometimes if you confront a person unexpectedly with an accusation, they're knocked off their game and they let something slip. On the other hand, they might refute your charge on the spot. It was still early enough for a visit. It wouldn't do to call ahead; I'd have to take a chance she'd be home.

CHAPTER THIRTY-SIX

EVENING

Eva Johnson was in a sour mood when she saw me in her doorway, which was okay. I wasn't in such a great mood myself. She might be a killer and she might not. For the moment, I was betting not.

"This better be important and it better be quick." She held the door and made no move to invite me in.

"There's a rumor I want you to help me put to rest."

"I don't have time to play guessing games." She paused, noticing my bandage. "What happened to your head?"

I told her.

"Well, that's what you get sticking your nose in where it doesn't belong." Her words were harsh but her tone contained a hint of sympathy. "You picked a dangerous business. Maybe you should try a different line of work."

It was too late for that. I wiped my feet on the welcome mat in front of her door, hinting for an invitation. "The rumor is you and your bodyguard were at the taxi garage the night of your husband's murder. All I need is for you to tell me where you were that night. We get someone to verify what you tell me and the rumor goes away."

She closed her eyes tightly and let them spring open. I

thought she'd stomp her foot. Instead she caught herself, a woman accustomed to squelching her anger.

"Who told you that nonsense?"

I shook my head, turned my palms up. "Who knows where rumors come from?"

"I was here."

"And your bodyguard, Mr. Sheehan, was he here with you?"

"Mike Sheehan has been my driver since my husband's death. He wasn't my driver before that and he wasn't my bodyguard then and isn't now. I don't keep track of him. Any other questions? I have an appointment." She stepped back from the door, about to close it.

"Your husband was murdered on a Friday night. His body wasn't discovered until Monday morning. Didn't you miss him?"

"No." She glared at me. I expected the old heave-ho. But she went on. "We'd had a quarrel, and he'd been staying at a hotel." The anger left her eyes and the sharp angles of her face softened into that childlike beauty that had surprised me the first time I saw her. "I told the police this when they came to tell me Irwin had been murdered."

"Did you tell them what the quarrel was about?"

Uncertainty flickered in her eyes. "They didn't ask." She averted her gaze and then quickly looked back at me. "I don't have anything to hide. Irwin found out I'd hired a private detective."

She told me what Irwin said to her and what she said to him, how angry he was, how angry she was, that divorce was in the air, that neither of them threatened violence. He left for a cooling-off period. "I was furious at that crooked detective more than at Irwin," she said.

Her story was plausible. I asked if Bauer, the private eye, had given her any photos of her husband with another woman.

He ears perked up. "That's what he was supposed to do. I told you he didn't." A moment before, she was pushing me out the door. Now she hated to see me go. "You think one of his girlfriends killed him?"

I shrugged.

"You don't really believe the rumor you told me; do you?" Her voice dropped into the seductive murmur she'd pulled on me in the past. "If that cab driver didn't kill Irwin, one of his girlfriends is a better bet for killing him than me. Don't you think?" Her flickering eyelashes kept company with the bewitching murmur.

Regrettably, she was still a better bet than any of Irwin's girlfriends, but I went along. "That's why I asked about the photos."

"Wouldn't he have given them to Irwin? Isn't that what Irwin paid him for?"

I didn't want to mention my nocturnal visit to Bauer's office, so I told her if Bauer was crooked enough to take a bribe he'd be crooked enough to hang on to some prints to try to blackmail Irwin if the opportunity came up. "Even though blackmail is out of the running now, he might not have gotten rid of them. He didn't strike me as someone who straightened up his files all that often."

She closed her eyes for a second. When she opened them, she blinked a few times, reminding me of an adding machine. "If I could get the photos, would that get you off my back?" She watched me expectantly.

"To tell you the truth, Mrs. Johnson, what gets me off your back is finding out your husband's killer isn't you."

She pouted, her pout naughty and provocative.

I had a couple of more questions she most likely wouldn't answer, or would lie about. I asked anyway so I could watch her reaction.

"Did you talk to Big Al Lucania about me?"

She wasn't ready for that one, so she stumbled. "No ... Talk to him? Why would I talk to him about you?" She got her stride back. "You mean tell him about the underwear?"

I was sorry I brought it up. "Have you spoken to the FBI about me?"

This question surprised her but not in the same way. This time it was curiosity. "Are they after you?"

"They keep tabs on a lot of folks these days."

"They talk to Mr. Lucania." As soon as she said it, she knew she shouldn't have. She tried to cover herself. "I don't know what they talk about . . . He talks to a lot of people you wouldn't expect." She was flustered. "You unsettle a person ... Look, I've got to go."

She meant it this time. I hadn't kept the cab that brought me there, so I asked her to call a private car for me and sat down alongside the driveway on my favorite bench to wait. After a few minutes she came out, her face tight with worry. The livery cab was on its way, she said and hesitated, standing forlornly on her bluestone driveway with her mansion-on-the-hill behind her.

"Look," she said. "Something about you I liked from the first time I saw you. I thought you were straight ... and kind. I still do. Can you forget what I said about Big Al and the

FBI? I'm not supposed to talk about anything I see or hear when I'm with him. I made a mistake, a little one maybe. He doesn't like when people make mistakes."

I said I'd forget it. Our eyes held for a long moment, hers brimming with sincerity. That picture of her stayed with me for the cab ride home. Sincerity can be faked too, I told myself.

By the time I woke up and turned on WNEW, the taxi strike was in full swing. To listen to the frenzied tone of the newscaster, you'd think barbarians were sacking the city. "Taxis have been vandalized and set on fire!" "Bands of strikers roam the streets terrorizing the citizens!" "The police are powerless!" "Anarchy reigns!"

The city might be burning but I had my own problems. The first was to report my findings to Duke, and I'd rather another smack on the head from a tire iron than break the news to him that his wife was a rat.

The street in front of the union hall was flooded with parked cabs when I got there, double-parked on both sides of Twenty-Third Street from Eighth Avenue halfway to Seventh Avenue. As soon as I opened the door and started up the stairway to the union hall and Duke's office I could hear the hubbub above me. The union hall was packed. A helluva note. But I couldn't put this off. So I elbowed my way through the ruckus.

He was in his office with Forlini and Sol Rosen. The door was open and he was talking; bellowing was more like it. Rosen and Forlini stood stiffly in front of his desk like two truants in the principal's office. I turned to leave but Duke saw me. His expression changed from tough-guy, I-can-chew-nails to the expression a man must have when he sees a beam falling toward him. "Don't go anywhere," he said to me and turned back to the truants.

The conference went on for a few more minutes. When it was over, Rosen and Forlini bolted out of the office, Rosen in front, steaming ahead like a man whose train was leaving the station. Forlini, who was short and stubby, trotted behind him trying to catch up and talking to the back of his head. They ignored me. I went into Duke's office and closed the door behind me.

Despite being a big, rough-and-tumble guy, Duke had a sincerity about him that made you feel he cared about what was going on with you. He looked at my bandaged head, the bandage only partly covered by my hat.

"You okay? I heard what happened."

"It's something I'd like to ask Brother Forlini about. But I'm okay."

"You'd be wasting your time askin' Forlini about anything." He took a deep breath. His chest expanded; he sat back and folded his arms across his chest. "You got something to tell me."

I told him.

Duke digested what he heard, sometimes nodding, other times pounding the desk with his fist, muttering curses directed at his wife. "A snitch." He unfolded his arms and pushed out his chest. "A snitch, a fucking snitch." He glared at me. "You're lucky I know you're square with me. Anybody else told me that, I'd break him in two."

He asked me for the details a couple of times. They didn't change.

"So there wasn't another guy, right? This was an informer thing, not something else?"

"What I saw was strictly business . . . ratting-out-your-friends business."

"I don't know what the hell she thought she was doing." He lowered his voice. "Don't tell no one about this. Not yet. I'll talk to her. I'll get her straightened out." He looked shame-faced, like a man asking for a handout.

"My report to a client is confidential. Do you want it in writing?"

"No. Nothin' in writing."

I didn't stop to talk to Sol on the way out. He was too wrapped up in the strike. I thought I might pass the time of day with Forlini, but he had a few guys in his office, so I let it go. Duke's response surprised me a bit—finding out the woman who was supposed to love, honor, and obey him got caught spilling her guts to the FBI on him and his fellow workers so the witch hunters could ruin a few more people's lives. This was easier for him to take than if she'd been shacked up with another guy.

If you were me, you had to wonder. My wife left me and took away my kid because I wouldn't rat on my friends. At the time I knew—even though she didn't know it—that if I'd given in and testified as she wanted me to, living with a rat would get to her sooner or later and she'd mistrust and despise me. I wondered what living with someone who ratted on *you* would be like.

I called my answering service from a phone booth at the corner. Seventh Avenue was as quiet as a country road without hordes of taxis streaming downtown. I had two messages.

Eva Johnson left a phone number and Len Volpe wanted me to call. I tried to call Len but he wasn't in. Eva Johnson's phone was busy. When I got out of the subway at Times Square, jostled along by a large and angry crowd of late-for-work straphangers, Forty-Second Street was a disaster area. The intersection in front of the Times Building was blocked with a couple of overturned cabs. Cop cars with their red lights flashing were scattered about like confetti. Mounted police were herding crowds of strikers uptown on Seventh Avenue where there were more overturned cabs. On one block, strikers were fist fighting with the scabs they'd pulled out of the overturned cabs; other strikers were handcuffed, sitting on the curb; everyone else hustled uptown dodging the horses and the billy clubs. The news ticker on the Times Building read: TAXI STRIKE TURNS VIOLENT . . . HUNDREDS ARRESTED . . .

I planned to head over to the taxi garage, hoping to find Frank on the picket line, but first I ducked out of the hubbub into the drugstore next to the Paramount Theater and tried Eva Johnson again.

"Mr. Lucania told me I should stay away from you. You're trouble."

"Then why did you call me?"

"I don't like men telling me what to do." She sounded like Mae West.

"I'm impressed Big Al knows my name."

"You shouldn't be impressed; you should be worried."

"I don't have time to worry. You called me?"

"Yes. But not to confess to anything if that's what you're hoping. Mr. Lucania is angry about the strike."

"I don't have anything to do with the strike."

"He thinks you do."

Great. I wasn't in enough trouble with Big Al because I was stepping on his toes by doing the Harold Williams investigation? I needed him put out about something that wasn't my doing.

"He told me you had a new girlfriend, too . . . I'm jealous."

Not knowing what to say about that, I asked again why she called me.

She'd spoken to Walter Bauer. "He was closemouthed when I asked what he'd found out about my husband and whether he had any photos. He said he could do a search through his files. But he was busy and his time is valuable."

"How valuable?"

"He wanted to know how much his files were worth to me. I told him I was most interested in photos. He said two hundred dollars for photos."

"So he has them. Good work."

"Not all showgirls are dumb." She'd planned to meet Bauer but the taxi strike got in the way. Dealing with him would be tricky since he knew she was now a wealthy widow. I told her to let me know before she met with him. My head hurt and I wanted to take it easy on the pain pills so I bought a tin of aspirin and took a couple with a glass of water from the lunch counter.

When I came out of the drugstore, a knot of drivers had gathered in Duffy Square around a guy making a speech in front of the statue of Father Duffy, so I walked over. The speaker was Sol Rosen. He was exhorting the strikers onward and trying to calm things down at the same time.

"Solidarity!" he shouted. "Solidarity wins the strike. Not

fights. Not burning cabs. The city can't run without you! Stay together! If someone torches a cab, someone beats up a driver, they give the cops reason to attack us. Stay strong! Stay calm! Stay together!"

He said the same thing a few times in different ways and finished up roaring like the MGM lion: "If we stay together, others will join us. The bus drivers will park their buses! The truckers will let their trucks idle! The stitching machines will go quiet! The subways will grind to a halt! The workers of the city will join us and we will win! Solidarity!"

Sol was a powerful speaker. He spoke from his heart, so you believed him. I felt a thrill in my chest that maybe, after all, the workers would stick together and win. What I really wanted to do was lie down and rest my throbbing head. But I left the mayhem around Times Square to the cops and the cabbies and headed uptown to the Johnson Transportation garage.

As I walked up Broadway, every few blocks I'd come across a cab up against the curb with its windshield smashed or a couple of its tires flat. Near Fifty-Second Street, a DeSoto lay on its side, smoldering, smoke curling up from under its hood and leaking out windows. A small crowd had gathered in front of Birdland eager to watch but hesitant to get too close. On the sidewalk next to the burning cab a man watched the fire; he was crying.

Many of the independent owner-drivers were strike breaking. They weren't organized in the way the fleet drivers were, and they had payments to make on their cabs, strike or no strike. Some fleet drivers from the garages Forlini controlled might have been working also but not many.

When I got to the picket line, the garage door was barricaded and things were quiet. Frank had been hauled off by the cops a couple of hours earlier during a battle with the scabs. A guy on the picket line told me the taxi company office had closed up after the melee, so I found a phone booth and called Elena at her apartment. She said she'd meet me at the picket line.

A half hour later, she showed up wearing red pedal pushers and a red-and-white checked blouse with her dark hair in a ponytail, fresh as a daisy and cute as a button, drawing a few whistles. As far as I could tell, most of the drivers didn't recognize her. Not surprising I guess because the garage and the office were in different worlds.

Her expression was solemn despite her flashy clothes, and we did an awkward dance, unsure how to greet each other after our night together. I thought for a moment she might shake hands with me. It was early but she wanted to go to lunch so I took her to the five-and-dime around the corner, where she ordered an egg salad sandwich and a chocolate malted. I had a cup of coffee.

"It was scary this morning," she said. "I'm glad Mrs. Simpkins told us to go home. All everybody in the office was doing was looking out the window anyway."

The drivers picketed in staggered two-hour shifts, a crew of them coming and going every thirty minutes or so. I told Elena this would be a good time to latch onto a few of them and ask questions. She hemmed and hawed. She couldn't talk to strange men on the street; it was unladylike. So I told her we could do it together.

She was okay with that. We stood down the block from

the picket line and snagged likely looking drivers walking by after their picketing shift. We did this for an hour or so and spoke with a dozen or more drivers, finding out nothing that was helpful. Elena was enthusiastic to begin with but soon flagged.

After a few minutes of fidgeting and grouching, she told me she had errands to do. "I don't think I want to be a private detective. It's boring." After a bit of a back-and-forth, she said she'd meet me at the picket line at 4:00 and we could take another shot at questioning the drivers.

"Maybe you can take me somewhere for dinner after that," she said before she walked away. "You're not very good at courting."

I expected a smile but she was still grouching.

CHAPTER THIRTY-EIGHT

AFTERNOON

Without Elena as an attraction, most of the drivers had no interest in stopping to chat so I gave up and walked downtown to Gil Silver's office. He was on the phone, with both phones on the desk blinking from stacked-up calls from a passel of bondsmen and lawyers staked out at police precincts around the city bailing the striking cab drivers out of jail. He was calm and in control but something was bothering him. I thanked him for paying for my hospital stay, which he brushed off.

Before he could brush me off too, I told him Frank DeMarco said he saw Eva Johnson and her driver Mike Sheehan the night of the murder. "I don't think Frank saw what he thinks he saw. It's too pat, too easy. Besides, Eva's willing to help me prove she didn't kill her husband."

I told Gil about the deal with private eye Bauer for the photos. I needed to put the touch on him for the money to pay Bauer, since Duke was too busy with his own problems. "She's hoping the photos will tell me there's a suspect I haven't dug up yet. I hope so, too."

On a normal day, he'd have thrown me out of his office by now. This day, he raised his weary gaze to meet mine. "I suggest you don't spend money until you know what you're getting for it." He took a hundred bucks from a locked drawer in his desk, his walkin' around money—his term for the distasteful practice of paying grifters on the street for information. "He'll settle for that." Gil said he'd get it back from Duke.

"Is Duke going to come up with that much dough in the middle of a strike?"

Gil took off his eyeglasses and rubbed his temples. He looked at the specs like he might smash them instead of putting them back on and glared at me like he might smash me. "The strike's going to settle. Duke's at a negotiating session now. The mayor's office, the governor's office, the fleet owners association, someone from Washington, the powers-that-be want the strike over today. They made Duke a proposition, a sellout deal. If he takes it, the owners association will recognize the union. The union will get a sweetheart contract. Dues money will pour in. He'll have the dough."

When high stakes collective bargaining took place, Gil was most often at the table. I wanted to know why he wasn't at this one.

"Duke asked me when he got the outlines of the offer. Some deals even I can't stomach. He borrowed a lawyer from the labor council." Gil's frown lines deepened. His eyes narrowed to slits behind his glasses. "You know who's at the table with him?" He didn't wait for an answer. "Forlini. You know who's not at the table? Sol Rosen."

"Duke wouldn't do that," I shouted. "Sol is the brains behind the organizing drive. The drivers trust him more than Duke. Nobody trusts Forlini. Duke doesn't trust Forlini."

"That was the linchpin of the deal. Give up Sol and expel the Reds for an industry-wide master contract."

I didn't know why I was so raging mad. It wasn't my strike. But in a way it was. *An injury to one is an injury to all.* "Duke's gonna be sorry." I said. "The drivers won't fall for a bullshit contract. They've got the upper hand. Sol says other unions will go out on sympathy strikes. Workers all over the city will walk out to support the hackies. The owners will have to give in."

Gil looked at me like a wise—and sad—old uncle might. "There won't be a citywide walkout, Mick. Taft-Hartley took care of the sympathy strike. The union leaders who might have said to hell with Taft-Hartley have been banished by the Red-baiters. It's only a matter of time until Sol and everyone like him follows them out the door.

"The piecards that are left have their sweetheart deals, and their soft jobs. They know if they go out on a limb for the cab drivers they'll be called Reds and pushed out of their sine-cures. Duke knows he'll be done for, too, if he doesn't take the deal. The governor will bring in the National Guard to drive the cabs, and the misleaders of labor will stand by and watch. He's taking the agreement to the drivers tonight."

I was still waving the red flag. "The drivers will vote it down."

Gil rolled his eyes. But I wasn't finished.

"Duke's gone around the bend anyway. His wife's a fucking FBI informer and he says to me, 'Don't tell anyone; I'll take care of it.'... like she forgot to pick up the laundry or burned the bacon."

Gil's eyebrows went up. "Cynthia's an informer?"

I told him how I'd followed her to a meeting with her FBI handlers.

He began grilling me. "Who's she informing on?"

"Duke? Sol? I don't know."

His eyes grew larger behind his thick lenses. "Frank DeMarco? . . . Harold?"

"Harold?" My eyes went larger, too.

"There's no telling what she might have seen." He took off the specs and gestured with them. "Suppose they were in on Johnson's murder."

"They? Who?" A lightbulb went on. "The FBI killed Johnson and framed Harold?"

Gil shook his head. "They wouldn't murder Johnson, unless . . ." He placed the glasses on his desk and tented his fingers in front of his chest, something he did when he turned his attention to his own thoughts.

"Even if it's true," he said after a moment. "I don't see how we'd prove it." He said this as if I knew what he was talking about. "Did DeMarco say anything about Cynthia Rogowski asking about the taxi union organizing?" He didn't wait for an answer.

"I'd give odds she did. Frank wouldn't have caught on anyway. Reds are always dumbfounded when someone turns out to be an informer. They never suspect the right person." As an afterthought, he added, "I'll look into things on my end."

I was still a half block behind him. "And what kind of things would those be?"

What he told me in a longwinded, convoluted, on-the-one-hand this, on-the-other-hand that account—with stipulations, provisos, qualifications, and riders—was that the higher echelons of the Mob and the clandestine operations of the federal government had been in cahoots at least since the war.

The gangsters gave the allies a hand in Sicily and did the government other favors, like keeping the dockworkers they controlled from striking during the war. In return, the government pretended it didn't know the hoods on the docks were robbing both the ship owners and the dockworkers. Now the FBI and the Mob had a mutual interest in shutting the Communists out of the labor movement.

Gil led me along in the modulated tone he used that kept juries on the edge of their seats listening to every word. "Let's suppose the FBI has infiltrated the union drive. Because they want to keep getting information, they don't want the informant exposed—this meant they had to look the other way when the hoods knocked off a recalcitrant owner."

This was reasonably close to Slim Young's theory. I waited for a further explanation. Not getting one, I said, "Duke's wife knows who killed Irwin Johnson but she's letting Harold take the rap? And she does this so she wouldn't get exposed as a government informer?"

"I'm not suggesting I know any such thing," Gil said.

"What are you suggesting?"

"You can put two and two together, Mick."

Actually, I couldn't put two and two together when it came to Gil's double-talk. I told him about my nocturnal meeting with Big Al, the man himself, who assured me his enterprise had nothing to do with the murder of Irwin Johnson.

Gil smiled indulgently. "Big Al told you that? . . . Interesting."

"Should I believe him?"

Gil held me with his courtroom accusatory stare. "Do you believe him?"

"I don't know." Given that the man made his living robbing, pillaging, plundering, swindling, raping, and murdering, you could expect he might stretch the truth on occasion.

Gil's voice softened. "I think you'd want to verify what you're told."

When I left, I borrowed the phone on Effie's desk, tried Len Volpe, and got him on the first try.

"We have a problem with DeMarco's story," he told me. "At the time he placed Sheehan at the garage on the night of the murder, Sheehan was stopped at the corner of Bowery and Canal having come off the Manhattan Bridge and run a red light. The time and date are on the citation and the officer who made the stop remembered Sheehan because the guy gave him lip. Otherwise, he wouldn't have ticketed him."

Effie watched me as I hung up. "You look disappointed."

"Don't believe anyone," I advised her.

When I got to the picket line, Frank was back from his stint in the local hoosegow, wisecracking and laughing with a group of drivers gathered around a parked cab. The cab belonged to an owner-operator who supported the strike. I told Frank I needed to talk to him.

He didn't like the idea much and said he was due at the union hall and he'd see me later. He headed toward the subway at Eighth Avenue. I tagged along and told him his story about Mike Sheehan and Eva Johnson at the taxi garage had blown up.

This didn't slow him down; if anything, it speeded him

up. But I kept pace. Frank swore he saw what he saw and said Sheehan was lying. When I asked if the cop who ticketed Sheehan was lying too, he gave up.

"I gotta go," he said. He had a Party club meeting that evening and said he could meet me after the meeting around 8:00 at a coffee shop on Columbus Circle.

I went back to Woolworth's, where I'd had lunch with Elena, for a cup of joe, a glass of water and another couple of aspirin—I was laying off the pain pills to try to keep my head straight—and called Eva Johnson. "I need to see what Bauer has before he gets any dough. And I need time to check on what he shows me." She said we could meet with him together once the taxis started running again.

When I hung up, I got this idea that once Bauer gave us the photos, I'd follow him and when we came to an alley, push him into it, jackroll him, and get the money back. An unscrupulous jerk like him gave private eyes a black eye, so I'd give him one. This was not a thought I dwelled on.

Back at the taxi garage, I grabbed a sign and joined the picket line; after a short time, as tends to happen while picketing, I began chatting with the picketers. By the time I'd asked a couple of the drivers about the night of the murder, everyone in front of the garage knew who I was—the private eye who got his head bashed in—and what I was up to. If anyone knew something and wanted to tell me, they could have. No one did.

Around 4:30, Elena showed up. She'd changed into a black poodle skirt and a white blouse. Her hair, no longer in a pony tail, hung to her shoulders, held in place by black velvet band across her forehead. Despite a sparkling smile, dark circles under her eyes made her look tired and strangely older, not so carefree and girlish.

We stayed on the picket line for an hour making small talk with the drivers, who kept up a stream of bravado, threats against the scabs, stories of crowded subways breaking down, rumors that some bus drivers had parked their buses and others would walk out the next morning.

At the beginning of each new shift of picketers, those arriving shouted and chanted and bucked one another up. After that first wave of enthusiasm wore off, the doldrums set in, and the picketers trudged like battered GIs on the last leg of a long march.

I took Elena to dinner at an Italian restaurant off Eighth Avenue near Columbus Circle. The place was small, maybe a dozen tables, with checkered tablecloths and candles set in chianti bottles. The waiters wore tuxedos (that had a few miles on them), had courtly manners, and spoke with Italian accents.

Elena was charmed. It was, she said, just fancy enough. "If it were later in the evening, after dark, it would be romantic." Her elbows on the table, her chin cupped in her hands, she smiled dreamily. "Do you think we're falling in love?"

I didn't know what I thought. Around us, thousands of cab drivers walked picket lines, demolished cabs, fought knock-down, drag-out brawls with scabs, suffered busted heads, blackened eyes, bloodied noses, and after all that sacrifice were about to get a sell-out contract shoved down their throats.

Weighing on me beyond that, Harold was fated to die in the electric chair in two days. Unless I came up with something soon, I'd be standing in the hallway of a Bed-Stuy walkup, telling Harold's mother and his son that I'd failed and

Franklin's dad would die. How could love be on my mind? Except that whatever went on behind Elena's secret smile bewitched me.

I reached across the table and touched her arm. As I did this, she bent her arm so my hand slipped down to hers. "I don't know how any man wouldn't fall in love with you."

Her secret smile widened and she sat back as smug as the Cheshire cat.

After dinner we walked in the park and talked until it was time for me to meet her brother. She'd sipped her way through two glasses of wine so she prattled on about imaginary futures. One of them took us to Hollywood, where I'd be welcomed back to my job and proclaimed a famous cartoonist. Movie stars would invite us to parties where handsome actors would try to take her away from me, but she couldn't be bothered because she was in love with her wonderful husband and had so many children to take care of.

"So many? I thought you didn't want children."

"Not in the slums." She spoke matter-of-factly. "Hollywood would be different." She swung her hand that was holding mine like a pendulum, like a child might. Then she stopped and turned to face me. Her mood changed as abruptly as if she'd walked into a wall. "That won't happen, will it?" She let go of my hand and turned away again. "You won't take me to Hollywood. You won't love me more than anything. Will you?"

She left me in the dust; I wasn't good at fantasy. "This is all new," I said, "happening so fast . . . My case—"

With her hands on her hips, she glared at me. If she'd had fur, it would have stood up on her back. "Can't you forget about your stupid case? Is it more important than me?"

I stammered, "No," and then "Yes," and then, "You don't understand."

She calmed, so I thought she might have understood after all. Her lashes lowered like veils, which made it look like she was bowing. "You would love me if we had enough time. I know that." She took my hand and we began walking. "But we don't have much time, so you better hurry up and know you love me."

I put my arm around her shoulder and pulled her closer. Her hair smelled faintly of roses. I touched her cheek to gently turn her head toward me and leaned to kiss her. But her expression was so desolate, I stopped.

"I'm going to go home," she said. The desolation was still there. "It's time for you to meet Frank anyway."

I watched her walk away and then sat on a bench while darkness filled up the park. For the time that evening I'd been with Elena, I'd forgotten about the pain in my head. Now it came back with a vengeance. This time I took a pain pill.

CHAPTER THIRTY-NINE

EVENING

Frank DeMarco sat alone in a booth facing the coffee shop door, his hands wrapped around a coffee cup that he squeezed like it might try to get away. His face was that of a man who'd bet everything he had on a horse that was fading in the stretch. His expression didn't improve when he saw me.

I sat down across from him, my back to the door, with faith—a bit shaky—he'd let me know if someone came in gunning for me. I didn't waste words. "You made up the story about seeing Mrs. Johnson the night of the murder thinking you'd help Harold. Why'd you change your mind about letting the chips fall where they may?"

Exposing his lie didn't cause much of a reaction. "I always wanted to help. I didn't know how. I hate that Harold might die. I couldn't stop thinking I needed to do something to stop the execution."

It would be easy to buy his sincerity. But he'd sent me on a wild goose chase, costing me time I could have spent tracking down the real killer. I told him this.

He went back to watching his coffee cup.

I went on to the next item on his list of infractions. "What's the Party going to do about the strike?"

He eyed me cautiously.

I told him what Gil had told me about the settlement but I suspected he already knew. His head bowed closer to the coffee cup.

"Duke's selling us out. We're organizing for the bargaining council meeting tonight. We'll print a special issue of the *Daily Worker* exposing the sellout. Drivers are coming in from Queens and Brooklyn for a rally in Times Square and then we'll march to the bargaining council meeting. Duke's gonna try to ram that contract down the members' throats. We're gonna stop him."

Despite the militant plan and his cocky words, Frank's fiery oratory-of-struggle rang hollow. He was worn down and weary, if not yet beaten. He'd been at it all day and he'd be up all night. He and his comrades would be the last to leave the picket lines.

I clutched my coffee cup the way he clutched his. Someone walking in might think we were about to throw them at each other. We sat like that until he said, "I found out something else about who might've killed Johnson."

This tall tale was harder to swallow than the first one, but I let him finish before I put the kibosh on it. Leaning forward, his arms on the table, he spoke at the volume of a stage whisper. "I know a guy, an independent driver, not in the Party but a solid guy. Back a year or so ago, he was part of a plan to knock off Johnson but he backed out. It looks like the other guys went through with it. They were in a deal with Johnson for counterfeit medallions, and he swindled them. He got the medallions, and they got nothin'. They weren't going to let him get away with it."

"Is your pal willing to identify these guys and send them to the chair?"

Frank looked at me blankly. His earnestness, even now when it was fake, gave him a kind of salt-of the-earth nobility. "He doesn't know who they are. It was all secret. He gave them money. They were going to take care of it."

"Was Harold one of them?"

The blank look became a confused look. "Huh? No. Of course not."

"Is your pal who's telling this story a better liar than you are?"

Frank's eyes closed for a few seconds. When he opened them, he stared at me like he'd been caught robbing a poor box. Yet his story about the medallions was closer to reality than he knew—Johnson had swindled Ace and the other small fleet owners out of their medallions. Close but no cigar.

"I checked out your last harebrained story," I told him. "I'm not biting on this one. You should forget it, too."

He started to argue but I stopped him. "Did Cynthia Rogowski question you about the organizing campaign or the Party? Did she ever talk to Harold?"

Frank's jaw dropped. "What do you mean?" He glanced at the door to the street behind me like he was measuring his escape route. "Look. I got to get to the picket line." He made an effort to stand but something pulled him back. "Why ask me about her?" Not only did he suddenly look guilty, he looked like he'd already been sentenced.

"You tell me."

He squeezed the coffee cup hard enough that his knuckles went white.

"Why does talking about her make you so angry?"

He glared at me. "How do you know? . . . What do you know about her and me?"

Until that moment I hadn't known anything about her and him. But I knew how men react when they're embarrassed and ashamed. I looked across the scarred Formica table top of the harshly lit coffee shop at a man whose life was passing in front of his eyes.

He hit himself in the forehead with the heel of his hand. "I shoulda known." He shrugged, giving up on an argument we weren't having. "I'm an idiot . . . A classy dame like that with a wop cab driver who's lucky to make fifty bucks on the best week?"

This time he punched himself flush on the jaw with the side of his fist, punching twice, three times, each time harder than the last. I grabbed his arm because I was afraid he'd hurt himself. The joint was nearly empty but the few people there—a couple in a booth and a guy at the counter—were staring at us, so he calmed himself and lowered his voice.

"I thought she wanted to know about cab drivers, her husband being Duke and all." His earnestness was back. "That's what she said. She wanted to know about us.

"We met for a drink a couple of times after my shift. She's a good-looking woman, you know? Any guy would have a hard time pushing her away. At first, we'd talk about what it was like driving a hack, twelve-hour day, times you couldn't make a buck, fares treating you like a servant or forgetting you're even there. She listened good, and you could see in her eyes she cared." He picked up his cup as if to take a sip, looked at it like it might tell him something, and then put it back down.

"After a while, she was coming on to me, but not in a bad way like some broads do, like they're hot to trot. This was like she couldn't help it. We couldn't help it. She wasn't happy. She was lonely. I knew what Duke was like."

All this time as he spoke, Frank had stared at his white, greasy-spoon coffee cup or at his hands. He didn't so much as sneak a glance at me. "Duke's okay. But he's a rough guy. Not sensitive about anything. She was fragile; he didn't understand that."

This wasn't Frank DeMarco describing Duke; this was Cynthia describing Duke through Frank. He still hadn't caught on that she'd been doing the thinking for him. "She'd touch my hand, run her fingers over the callouses. She said her life was empty, that she'd made a mistake and didn't know how to undo it. She wished she'd met someone who'd care for who she was, not like Duke who only cared what she looked like."

Then Frank did glance up. His eyes had reddened but his gaze was steely. "I felt sorry for her. But I wasn't going to help her out of her trouble. I have a wife. I love Karen with all my heart. I'd never walk out on her for anyone. No one." He'd gone back to talking to his coffee cup and the battered table. "Someone talks to you like that, builds you up, and it's a gorgeous dame who sits close to you and rubs . . . I told her a lot, too much. Who would have guessed she was a rat?"

He quieted for a moment and then continued, his voice barely above a whisper. "She could use a friend's apartment uptown on Riverside Drive. Jesus, what an apartment. It took up the whole floor. She took me there so we could talk where it would be relaxed and comfortable. And then, one time . . .

"It was just the one time, the sex." Another flash of earnestness in his voice. "I thought I was recruiting her to the Party. I told her a lot of comrades had secret lives, never went public, used false names. There's other uptown broads—women—in the Party, who went to Vassar or Barnard. They want to be with the workers. They want to help."

Something dawned on him. He looked at me like I'd just told him something amazing when I hadn't said a word. "Jesus. I probably would have recruited her into the Party. Like an idiot, I'd bring in one more fucking fink to make up lies about us."

As titillating as Frank's story might be, it wasn't what I was looking for. He didn't get to what Cynthia might have seen or done around the time of Johnson's murder. Could she have known who killed Johnson?

Frank thought this unlikely. She'd known Harold. He didn't know if she'd pumped him for information, too, but didn't think so. But then, he said bitterly, she lied with every breath she took. He had no recollection of her being around the garage the night of the murder or any other time, for that matter. They didn't meet at the garage. She had no reason to go there. And as far as he knew, she didn't know Forlini or have any interest in him or his thugs.

I felt sorry for Frank but sympathizing with him wouldn't help him any. And he wasn't in shape to keep talking. Watching his face, the muscles working like he was chewing shoe leather, I knew he'd break down if he tried to talk much longer, so I didn't press him. I could get to him again later. For now, I wanted to hear Cynthia Rogowski's version of things.

CHAPTER FORTY

EVENING

It was a little after nine when I approached a building on West End Avenue that had a limestone facade and an ornately carved arch around the brass-handled front door. I told the doorman Mrs. Rogowski was expecting me. She wasn't, but I knew Duke wouldn't be home—he'd be downtown making the final arrangements to sell out his members—and figured she'd see me because by now Duke would have told her I'd blown her cover.

I was right, but she asked the doorman to have me wait. The spick-and-span, gleaming marble lobby had a couch and a couple of easy chairs, so I parked myself and wondered if I was waiting for her to put something on or take something off—or perhaps load bullets into her revolver.

"You should be ashamed of yourself," she said when she opened the apartment door. "I can't believe you'd show your face after what you did." She wore what rich women in the movies wear, a dressing gown. Floor length and flowing, silk or satin, elegant but not revealing. She wore lipstick too but if she wore other make-up it wasn't noticeable; she looked and carried herself like a polite woman of the aristocracy engaging with a serf. "I doubt you can do any more to ruin my reputation, so I expect your intentions are honorable. Would you like a drink?"

Surprised, I said yes.

"Canadian Club? Soda?"

I said yes again. My intentions were as honorable as they ever were, and I was fading. The drink might help. I could use a jolt of courage.

She handed me the CC and soda— that I hoped wasn't poisoned—and sat down with hers on a rose patterned couch. I sat on a pastel green upholstered armchair that was more comfortable than the one in the lobby. The room around us might have been on the cover of *Town and Country* magazine. Sipping daintily, she showed neither anger nor embarrassment at my having exposed her as a stooge for the FBI.

"This is about Harold Williams," I told her. "I'm hoping you can help me."

"I hope I can." Her tone was direct, not eager, not blasé. Cynthia Rogowski was an attractive woman, but you wouldn't know it by the way she handled herself, at least this evening, nothing flirtatious, nothing engaging. I was sure she could be charming if she wanted to be. But she wasn't wasting any charm on me.

She was wary. I didn't blame her; I was wary, too. I wanted to know if she knew more about Irwin Johnson's murder than she'd owned up to—as Gil may or may not have hinted at— not a question I could come right out and ask.

"How well did you know Harold?" I was prepared to pretend I believed she ratted on Communists because she was a good citizen and all good citizens should rat on their friends, neighbors, and loved ones if they were suspected of being Reds.

"I reported to the FBI that he was a member of the

Communist Party, as you might have surmised. Harold was a dupe. Communists exploit the legitimate grievances of the Negroes for their own purposes. He was a good man blinded by propaganda." She sipped her drink and I guess thought about how to get through to me. "Are you religious, Mr. Mulligan?"

"I'm Catholic."

"As you believe in God and the infallibility of the Pope, he believes in scientific socialism and the infallibility of Stalin."

"You sound contemptuous of religion as well as Communism."

She took a cigarette from a pack of Viceroys on a coffee table in front of her. I took out a Lucky. We both lit up. "Far from it. I'm Jewish. I respect religion. Communists are deceitful. I suppose, like Duke, you admire their union work. Yet they hide their real motives. For them, Russia is the workers' paradise, so they put Russia's interests over the United States' interests."

Hers was the authorized view: Communists were Russian agents. But what Communists actually believed in was the international working class someday creating a classless society. American Reds didn't so much care about Russia as a nation; they backed what they saw as the first workers state because it was a step forward for the international working class.

I thought for a moment I might straighten out her thinking on this. But I came to my senses. "So you became an informer to battle the evils of Communism?"

"I did it to protect my husband." She took a long puff on her cigarette and slowly let out the smoke. "An FBI agent contacted me at work. He knew a lot about me and more about Duke. He said Duke would be expelled from the CIO and barred from holding office in any labor union in the nation if he continued to be a pawn of the Communists. If I helped expose the Communist plan for the taxi union, I could save Duke's career."

Her piousness got on my nerves. "You're okay with Duke being a pawn of the gangsters?"

She'd been composed, sure of herself, except for nervous puffs on her cigarette, speaking quietly. Now she spoke sharply. "The FBI was going to blacklist Duke for aiding and abetting Communists. They didn't ask me about gangsters. I guess they don't think the gangsters will overthrow the government."

"Sol Rosen is loyal to Duke—"

"He's loyal to Russia first." She punched out her cigarette in the ashtray on the coffee table in front of her. Her eyes reddened. She waved her hand like she might sweep me away. I thought her anger was directed at me, but it was at herself. "It was a devil's bargain; I admit it. Sol doesn't deserve what they're doing to him. I had to protect Duke."

"Did you ask Duke?"

The question jolted her, so she had to gather herself for a moment before she spoke. "I told him protecting the Reds in the union when every other union was expelling them would get him in a lot of trouble. Duke's too stubborn for his own good. Nobody was going to tell him who could or couldn't be in his union. So I did it behind his back." She paused significantly. "Now, he knows. Thanks to you."

"I did my job."

"Your work isn't so clean either."

I didn't defend my oft-maligned occupation. I bent rules, told lies, followed the unobservant and exposed their secrets, manipulated people into telling the truth when they intended to lie, violated people's privacy. Ours was not among the noble professions.

She lit another cigarette. "Okay. You win. I'm a rat. Ask your questions."

I did. Her handlers told her to befriend Frank DeMarco and report on others who might be clandestine members of the Party. She'd spent time with the drivers at cabstands and coffee shops with Frank, some of them Party members who didn't keep it secret around her. She didn't try to hide from me that Frank was her main source. I prodded her carefully about Harold.

"It's sad." She said this unbidden, in such a way that I believed she meant it. "He was the nicest man. He had an infectious laugh and not a bad word to say about anyone behind their back.

"Some of the drivers gave me salacious looks or made crude remarks. Not Harold. He was a gentleman. All of the men I met with Frank besides Harold were white. They had a lot to say about Negroes as a group when Harold wasn't around, none of it nice, but nothing like that when he was there. He's a big man with a soft voice who carried himself with dignity. The drivers didn't know what to make of a Negro who thought he was as good as they were. He didn't hide that he was a Communist, either."

To get to what I wanted to know, I had to come at it side-ways. "Did you run across Vincent Forlini or a couple of thugs he had working for him—Mike Sheehan, Joe O'Keefe, Moose McFarland?"

"I wasn't asked to find out anything about anyone besides the Communists, so I didn't pay much attention to anyone else."

"You knew who they were though. You knew Forlini was a gangster trying to get control of the union. Duke would have told you that much. Your FBI handlers would have known about Forlini and his cronies. Suppose the hoods did something illegal, beat up one of the drivers, say? Would you report that to your handlers?"

My hypothetical didn't get much of a reaction. "I didn't see anything like that. If I did, I guess I would have said something to Agent Anderson." She met my gaze. "My handler."

"What about Irwin Johnson? Did you find anything to report on him?"

"No." She searched my face. A mask dropped over hers. "Why these questions? What are you after?"

"I told you. This is about Harold. You might have seen or heard something that points to someone other than Harold as the killer."

She paused either for a cover up or to search her memory. "I didn't consider the possibility someone other than Harold killed Mr. Johnson . . . Perhaps I should have. Harold wasn't someone you'd think of as a murderer."

At the risk of beating a dead horse, I kept at her. "Duke knew Forlini was a Mob guy. I don't know why you wouldn't know."

Some testiness began to seep out. "I didn't say I didn't know. The union was in danger of being taken over by Communists.

That's what I reported on. That was Agent Anderson's concern."

"He never asked about Mob influence?"

"No."

"Did your handler tell you to ignore what the gangsters did no matter what it was—including criminal activity?"

"I wasn't aware of anyone committing crimes." She looked puzzled. "You're confusing me."

Since it was pretty obvious by now anyway, I said, "I want to know if you kept quiet about who killed Irwin Johnson because your FBI handler didn't want you exposed as an informer."

Not surprisingly, she took umbrage. "That's ridiculous. You can't possibly think the FBI—a government agency—would tell me to keep silent about a murder. And for God's sake, do you think I'd consider letting an innocent man be executed?"

The truth was I thought both things were possible. "I'm leveling with you," I said. "You might have seen something and been told to keep it under your hat. You might not know the full implications of what you saw. Did your handler ask you to keep quiet about something you saw or heard? I'm not accusing you of covering up a murder." This wasn't exactly the truth but it got her off her high horse.

She shook her head but managed to get one last shot in. "No. They didn't. That's something the Communists might do, not the FBI."

Under different circumstance, I'd debate this also. But I had other fish to fry. "Did Frank ever say anything that made you think he had it in for Johnson?"

She took the question in stride, no theatrics this time.

"Him, too? Do you mean did he do or say anything that made me think he killed Mr. Johnson?"

"That's what I'm asking, yes."

"Do you have reason to think so?" Her eyes opened wider.

"I have a reason for asking the question."

"Sol Rosen is his mentor. You might ask him. I never saw anything that made me think that." She stopped to think something through. "He has a temper." She sat up suddenly. "Does Frank know I was . . . what I did . . . ?"

"Yep."

The features of her face twisted; she looked like she'd spit. "You son-of-a-bitch. My husband is paying you."

Little did she know. Poor Duke. He got it from both ends. Not only was his wife a snitch. She'd also done what he feared she might have done. Maybe she did it in the line of duty, a sacrifice to keep her husband's job and keep America free. It wasn't up to me to wise him up on that score. He'd told me to follow her and report. That part of the job was over before I talked to Frank about her. I stood. "The union's paying me. It's not Duke's union. It's the cab drivers' union." I sounded like Sol.

She handed me my hat.

At ten o'clock, I stood on the sidewalk in front of the ornately carved arch and below what might have been gargoyles on the rim of the building's roof. I glanced uptown and then downtown on West End Avenue, not knowing which way to turn in more ways than one. This one wasn't on my job description either, but I wasn't far from a subway stop so I took the Broadway local to Thirty-Fourth Street and walked over to the Manhattan Center and the union bargaining council meeting.

From a block away, I heard an indistinct rumble that turned into the mutterings of large clumps of cab drivers gathered together near the entrance to the hall. A phalanx of cops had assembled across the street from the hall and mounted cops were spaced along Thirty-Fourth Street near the corner of Eighth Avenue, the horses standing as still as statues. I thought the cabbies were outside the hall because they couldn't get into the meeting. But that wasn't the case. Security guards manned the doors but they weren't keeping anyone out. The men outside were waiting for something.

I went past the guards at the door into an auditorium. The main floor was laid out with folding chairs, rows and rows of them, facing a stage with a podium and a few wooden arm chairs on either side of it. Duke was at the podium. A half dozen or so red-faced men bulging out of their suits sat in the armchairs watching him and every few seconds nervously peeking out at the sea of men in the audience.

Duke fielded questions, which were mainly angry harangues. He'd say something and a dozen or more men in the audience would jump up, wave their fists, holler and shout, drowning out him and one another.

When the men weren't hollering at Duke, they were shouting at a group of men on one side of the auditorium near the stage who, arms folded across their chests, faces frozen into scowls, glowered back at them. Sol Rosen stood at the front of the room against a wall on the opposite side from the scowling men. When he got Duke's attention after a half dozen attempts and began to speak, the room quieted and listened. Until someone shouted, "Sit down and shut up, you Commie bastard!" and the hullabaloo started over.

Sol gave up trying to be heard over the tumult and walked to the back of the room, where he leaned against another wall and watched. I sidled up beside him. He had a bandage across his forehead and his left arm was in a sling. He made a slight movement of the injured arm toward me and grimaced.

I pointed to the bandage. "You, too?"

"A run in with a billy club."

After a few minutes of watching what looked like an uprising, he said, "Duke's gonna let them yell for a while and when he's had enough tell them the contract's been approved. Those guys in the front over there." He inclined his head toward the scowling, folded-armed men at the front of the hall who now and again cheered for Duke. "They're longshoremen. Muscle Forlini borrowed from Big Al. Watch."

I watched. The drivers began shouting, "Vote! Vote!" and when Duke tried to shush them, almost all of the drivers in the hall began chanting, "Vote No!"

In the midst of the din, Duke announced—as Sol had said he would—that the contract had been ratified by the executive committee and the executive committee's action already approved by the bargaining council.

With the roar of the hollering, shouting, and menacing drowning Duke out, it took a while for the news to sink in. Word circulated slowly through the auditorium. Someone who'd heard Duke's announcement passed it on to the next guy and so on. A wave of disbelief spread across the room like a brush fire, faces went rigid with shock, until the room grew totally silent, an ominous hush. And then a new roar went up—the cry of men charging into battle.

They charged. The guys who'd been waiting outside poured into the hall. Those closest to the front grabbed their chairs and hurled them toward the ducking, fleeing men who'd been sitting next to the podium. The longshoremen rushed to push back the drivers. Fistfights broke out all over the hall.

As Duke headed for the wings, he turned back for one final glance at his membership, but as soon as he did, he threw his arms in front of his face, bent double, and picked up his pace ahead of one of the cabbies swinging a folding chair like a bat, whacking him on the back of the head and the rear end as he ran.

Sol watched the melee; like me, a bystander. He spoke softly, his tone resigned. "The executive board met behind the stage before the bargaining council meeting. Duke brought in a vice-president from the International, the head of the city labor council, the deputy mayor, and a higher-up from FBI headquarters in Washington.

"The FBI bigwig told the board the Communist Party was using the cab drivers union to infiltrate the taxi industry as part of a plan to control transportation in the city and interfere with the war effort. He said I took my orders from Moscow and provided Fifth Column support for the North Koreans.

"When the FBI guy finished shoveling his bullshit, Duke told the exec committee the FBI had uncovered a plot by me to push Duke out. He'd been betrayed by a trusted lieutenant and needed to take action now to save the union." Sol laughed. "Duke hasn't looked me in the eye since sometime yesterday. The power of the capitalist state was coming down on him and he couldn't take it.

"They told him what would happen if he didn't give in, told him what he'd get if he did give in. He saw the light. He'd met secretly with his guys on the board and had everything lined up before the executive board meeting began. The fix was in. The board voted to expel me and the three other progressives who supported me. When we were out, the guy from the International told Duke and the quislings who were left how they could get around taking the agreement to the bargaining council for a vote.

"Duke began the council meeting with a bunch of double-talk and told the delegates they had to vote to adopt the report of the executive board. He didn't tell them the report included the approval by the executive board of the contract Duke agreed to. The delegates thought it was a formality, so they voted to approve the report. Without knowing they were doing it, they voted to expel me and the others and adopt the sell-out contract Duke negotiated."

"So that's that? The strike is over?"

Sol nodded. "We could keep some, maybe most, of the garages closed. But it would be war. Too many drivers would start driving when they heard we have an agreement. The strike's broken. At least the guys can go back to work; a lousy contract is better than no contract. I've seen it worse—where the strike was broken and the workers were left holding the bag; the scabs took their jobs, and the strikers never did go back to work."

Sol reached in with his good arm and took an official looking envelope out of his inside suit coat pocket. "So yep, the strike is over. And I've got my subpoena, actually a summons. I'm told I've been advocating the violent overthrow of the government and failed to register as the agent of a foreign government."

I left Sol to his broken strike, his exile from his union, his wounds from the picket line, and his looming comeuppance for the US government's idea of subversive activities.

The charge against Sol, like those against the leaders of the Communist Party—advocating the violent overthrow of the government—had nothing to do with something they'd actually done. No stored guns, no militia training in the hills, not even stealing a stop sign or ripping a DO NOT REMOVE tag off of a mattress.

For someone like me, who knew Communists by what they did—mostly trying to make things better for the working stiff—you had to wonder what the witch hunts, the denunciations, the expulsions, and the black lists were designed to put an end to.

Yet the nation had united in its determination to stop the Communists, who, the orthodoxy proclaimed, were biting the hand that fed them by speaking ill of Wall Street and exposing injustice. Here in America we were living high off the hog and if we weren't doing so well at the moment, prosperity was just around the corner. Anyone who didn't buy into this rosy view, we were told, couldn't see straight. That poor folks might struggle to keep a roof over their heads or feed their kids was an unmentionable.

The invisibility of the nation's poor reminded me of something my father had told me about his family in Ireland and his younger brother who didn't grow intellectually like the rest of the brood and somehow stayed a baby in his head as his body grew into childhood and then young manhood. The family was ashamed of the brain-diminished offspring so when anyone came to visit, my father's job as the oldest son was to take his brother Brendan out to the fields behind the house and keep him there until the company left.

This was what *Look* and *Life* and *Time* and the *Saturday Evening Post*, the daily newspapers, and radio and television commentators did with the poor in America, kept them out of sight so they wouldn't ruin the impression we wanted everyone, including ourselves, to have of us.

When I got home, I called my answering service. I didn't often call this late. But things were moving fast, so there was no telling who might have called. Turned out it was Len Volpe. I swear the guy never slept.

"First thing," he said when I called back. "Ace Jenkins is off the hook. He was in Las Vegas the night of the murder. Lots of witnesses. He was quite a celebrity because he managed to win and then lose a couple of grand in the same night. This Gloria Winthrop, the flower lady you asked me about, is another story. What do you know about her?"

I didn't know much and I told him that. He, on the other hand, had a lot to tell me. Gloria Winthrop's first husband died in a boating accident a few years back and left behind a substantial life insurance policy. What piqued Len's interest was that a year after her husband's death she married the man who was with him on the boat when he drowned.

"And the guy who was in the boat when her first husband had the unfortunate accident, they're still married?" I asked.

"Yep. Her fling with Johnson was during her first marriage. She seems to have settled in with husband number two. He's an insurance salesman, was at the time of the fatal boating accident, is one now. They provided alibis for one another for the night of Irwin Johnson's murder."

"Did the second husband by any chance sell the first husband the life insurance policy?"

Len chuckled and said they were looking into that.

Gloria Winthrop was a new wrinkle. I'd felt she was a straight shooter. I thought about that . . . Straight shooter was an interesting characterization to come up with given the circumstances. "Could she have been seeing Johnson at the time of his death? She told me she stopped seeing him years ago."

"She says no. But when you're having an affair you're supposed to say no, right?"

The last thing Len told me—another wrinkle—kept me awake for most of the rest of the night.

He'd questioned Mike Sheehan earlier that day when they picked him up for the picket line fracas, and Sheehan turned the tables on Frank DeMarco. He said another driver saw Frank at the garage the night of the murder. "Same deal as DeMarco's story with a different guy in the driver's seat." Len sighed like a radiator letting off steam. "I don't believe either of them. Still, Sheehan's alibi is rock solid, sorry to say. You might want to find out how solid DeMarco's is."

"Did he tell you the other driver's name?"

"Bob Hastings."

I'd hoped he'd tell me it was O'Keefe or McFarland backing up Sheehan. But no such luck. What Len didn't know and what I didn't tell him was Harold Williams had placed Frank at the garage on the night of the murder too, and then said he was mistaken. Sheehan of course might be lying, and

Hastings, whoever he was, might be lying, too. If they weren't lying, this one was a whopper.

After talking with Len, I lay awake a long time and dozed fitfully when I did sleep. In my saner moments through the long night—unlike the moments when I sat bolt upright staring into the darkness imagining a glowing electric chair—I told myself I was getting closer to knowing who killed Irwin Johnson. But I didn't know who I was getting closer to.

CHAPTER FORTY-ONE

MORNING

When I woke up after a fitful sleep a few minutes after 6:00, I called Artie Kaplow at the home phone number he'd given me what seemed like years ago. I'd mostly forgiven him for his memory lapse after my encounter with Moose McFarland and wanted to catch him before he left for work—if he was going to work. He'd been on strike and might not know it was over. I woke him up. He'd been at the Manhattan Center meeting and was ready to go back to work. I asked how much to hire him for the day. He told me he took home twelve bucks on a good day. I said I'd give him twenty.

At eight o'clock, I was pacing in front of my building when he pulled up. He was resigned to the busted strike. "We took a shot and we lost," he said. "Like the last time we tried striking before the war, same thing, we beat ourselves. Scabs. Selfish bastards gotta get theirs and can't stick together. We got some of the sons-of-bitches, though." He chuckled as he watched me through his rearview mirror. "Don't get me wrong. Nothin' violent. We turned over a couple of cabs." His eyes danced with mischief. "Maybe once or twice we forgot to let the driver out before we flipped them over."

We headed first to my office so I could pick up my gun. I

had a license and a concealed carry permit. The truth was I'd never carried the thing, concealed or otherwise. For some reason—probably because I'd watched so many private eye movies where the shamus packed a rod when it came time for the reckoning with the bad guys—I'd decided during my all but sleepless night I should have a rod with me since things were heating up.

I kept the piece oiled and knew how to use it from my army days. It came with a shoulder holster, but I had trouble remembering how to put the holster on. The snub nose revolver was light enough to carry in my jacket pocket but I already had my sap in one pocket and my tools of the trade kit in the other. Finally, I got the holster on right. The next question was whether the gun should be loaded or unloaded.

Arguments went both ways on this. When the shit hit the fan, I might not have time to load the thing. But if I carried it unloaded, I was less likely to shoot myself or someone else by accident. I finally loaded it so I wouldn't have to carry so many loose bullets in my pockets. I'd take my chances on shooting off one of my toes.

On the way to the Johnson Transportation garage, we drove past burned-out cabs every couple of blocks, grim reminders of yesterday's battle, like the burned-out hulks of tanks and trucks along the road into Paris in '44. The city had moods most days. This day it was solemn. Maybe it was me who brought the mood to the city. But it might also be that the city absorbed and reflected what happened in it. On this day, it knew that a bunch of its citizens had gotten a raw deal, so it was somber.

Fat Tony was in the dispatcher's office, more harried than usual. "They shoulda stayed on strike," he told me. "Fifteen times this morning, someone said I violated the contract. Whadda I know about a contract? I don't know no contract from nothin'. I'm a good mind to quit.

"The union guys want me to fire the guys they say was scabs. The other guys, the scabs, say they're the union now and not to give cabs to the guys who went on strike. Mike Sheehan comes in and he says I have to fire the guys who beat him up.

"What the fuck am I supposed to do? Jesus. I called Mrs. Johnson. She said not to fire anyone and not to listen to Sheehan. She's gonna have someone from the union meet her here this morning to straighten things out."

Lucky for me Tony's thoughts were so tangled up he'd forgotten he wasn't supposed to talk to me. I asked him if he'd sniffed the robe like I asked him to.

He glanced around the tiny office. "It smelled the same as what I remember from the night in the garage." His expression was quizzical. "Does that mean something?"

"When Mrs. Johnson gets here, I want you to get up real close to her and take a good sniff."

His eyes bugged open. "You gotta be shittin' me."

"Tony, you're helping me solve the case."

"Yeh? Well in the movies lots of times the guy helpin' to crack the case gets knocked off and the hotshot private eye walks away. Why don't you sniff her?"

"I will. You sniff, too."

"At the same time?"

"No."

Had I really just had that conversation? I headed toward

the door in the wall at the back of the dispatcher's cubicle that led to the stairway upstairs.

"Where you going?" Tony shouted. "You can't go in there."

"I need to get that robe and I don't want to walk past the office."

"Oh, Jesus . . ." Tony plopped back into his chair like he'd been slugged.

I went through the door and ran up the stairs to the break room, grabbed the robe from the wardrobe, rolled it up into a tight bundle, and headed back down the stairs at full tilt. The fact was I could no longer smell anything on the robe. But it might still be evidence and whoever left it there might remember and come back and get rid of it.

As I opened the door in the wall to Tony's office, I heard voices from the garage and froze. One of the voices I recognized as Eva Johnson's. The other voice I didn't recognize but a quick peek told me it was Forlini. Next to him was my pal Moose McFarland, the goon who whacked me with the tire iron. I closed the door and sat down on a step to think.

I didn't think very long—given the outcome, I might well have spent a few more minutes at it—before deciding to brazen my way through. They'd called Tony over to the far side of the garage, so I waited for them to get engrossed in their conversation and headed out through the garage like I belonged there. This would've worked if Fat Tony hadn't seen me. As far away as I was, I could see his eyes pop open as wide as Barney Google's.

As the others turned to see what set him off, I picked up my pace and made for the door. Someone shouted, "Hey you!" I heard footsteps. I went faster. McFarland caught up with me as

I reached the door of Artie's cab. On an impulse I didn't know I had, I pulled out the gat and stuck it in his ribs. He stopped.

"Face down on the sidewalk. You got two seconds." I pushed the gun harder into his ribs.

He dropped awkwardly, but he got down. I dove into the back seat. Artie put the hammer down, while the door was still open. Moose tried to stand and grab the door at the same time, but it clipped him as he reached for it and the motion of the cab spun him around so he lost his grip. I got the door closed in time to keep it from smashing into a lamp post.

"Where to?" Artie shouted.

I was tempted to say "Kansas," but I took a deep breath. "The West Side Highway. I need to calm down and think."

Artie headed uptown on the West Side Highway alongside the peacefully flowing Hudson, which had flowed north with the incoming tide and south with the outgoing tide for eons before I arrived in the city and would continue for eons after I shuffled off this mortal coil—unless, as the Red Scare folks kept telling everyone, the Russians dropped an A-bomb on the city.

Artie turned off the West Side Highway, which by then had turned into the Henry Hudson Parkway, merged onto the Harlem River Drive at 178th Street headed east to the Triborough Bridge, onto the East River Drive and back downtown alongside the East River. I stopped shaking around Ninety-Sixth Street.

I wasn't an expert on firearms. That wasn't the kind of work I signed up for when I became a P.I. What I did know was you didn't point a gun at someone unless you planned to pull the trigger because more often than not if you didn't use it on the guy you pulled it on, he'd use it on you.

I pulled the gat on Moose not knowing if I'd pull the trigger. I still didn't know. Moose in his split second to think about it decided not to chance that I might. Lucky for me—and him.

By the time I got things sorted out in my head, we were pretty far downtown and it was getting close enough to lunch time. I told Artie I'd buy him a bite to eat at a Ukrainian restaurant I knew on First Avenue. After coming within seconds of killing a man, I needed kielbasa and pierogis.

"I never seen anyone pull a gun on a guy before," Artie said as we waited for our lunch. "That was somethin'. He's the guy that brained you the last time. I'm surprised you didn't plug him."

I didn't like Artie's tone—that he was impressed by my foolish stunt. "It was a mistake," I told him. "For guys like Moose and Forlini, shooting someone is all in a day's work. Now I've got to worry about them coming back at me, and they're a lot better at this shoot 'em up stuff than I am."

To add to the mess I made of things, I'd gummed up my chances with Eva Johnson when I desperately needed her help. All over that stupid robe. It didn't make sense that the robe would be hers anyway. If she'd been waiting there to kill her husband, she wouldn't have been wearing the robe—unless she had a really demented sense of humor.

If the robe was going to be any use, it would be because I found the other woman and could compare scents. To find this mystery woman, I'd need Bauer's photos. And to get the photos, I needed Eva. If I'd turned her against me, I needed to unturn her. This meant going to Riverdale hoping she'd gone home after her visit to the garage and hoping I could figure out a way to explain my dumb stunt.

CHAPTER FORTY-TWO

AFTERNOON

An hour later, the Irish maid answered the door at the Johnson residence and told me stiffly Mrs. Johnson was not at home. She didn't know when the lady of the house would return. Given the upturned nose of this lace-curtain Irish snob, there was no hope of being invited in, so we waited in the driveway, Artie reading a Mickey Spillane book in the front seat, me moping in the back seat trying to figure out what to do next. After about fifteen minutes, a cab nosed into the driveway. I recognized Mike Sheehan's DeSoto. So did Artie, who reached under his seat for his tire iron.

"Let me handle this," I said. I got out and stood a few feet from Artie's cab and said a quick prayer that I wouldn't need to pull my gun again. In the army, I needed to carry a weapon. But since I'd been working as a private eye, either as an apprentice to Sid Wise before I got my license or since I'd gone out on my own, I had never needed a weapon and never carried one.

The thing was if you carry the damn thing the chances were too good you'd end up using it. I didn't know if Sheehan knew about my run-in with Moose. If he did, he might be packing too. Just what I didn't need, a gunfight in a Riverdale driveway.

Luck was with me; Eva leaned over the back of the front seat and spoke to Sheehan for a moment, so he stayed in his cab, his hands with a death grip on the steering wheel, his eyes glued on me, his mouth clamped shut.

She opened the car door herself and stepped out, then stood for a moment, a tiny smile curling her lips. I didn't know what went on with her eyes because she wore sun glasses. She also wore a dark blue suit, pearls around her neck, and a pill-box hat with a tiny veil, the kind of outfit fashionable East Side women might wear.

Sheehan continued to stare at me through the windshield with the expression you'd see on a chained Rottweiler. Eva carried herself like a woman in charge. She and I watched each other for a moment until she bent slightly, tapped on the passenger side window of Sheehan's cab, and waved him away with a flick of her wrist. He looked from her to me and back at her. She flicked her wrist again. He started to slowly pull away and then must have floored it because the lumbering DeSoto leaped forward like it had been kicked in the ass, spit a thousand bluestones out behind it, and disappeared around the bend in the driveway.

"You can dismiss your cab," she said. "I need to change and take care of a few things. We can call a limo when I'm ready."

I let go of my breath. We were going ahead with our plan. "He'll wait. I hired him for the day . . . You've heard from Bauer?"

"We're expected at his office this afternoon. First, I want to hear an explanation for your escapade at the taxi garage." She arched her eyebrows. "A couple of very mean men are really mad at you."

She ushered me into her living room and told the Irish

maid to make tea for us. To me, she said over her shoulder as she strode toward the interior of the house, "You wait here . . . and stay away from my underwear." She smiled over her shoulder too, but not coquettishly; the smile was maternal, a doting mother to a naughty boy.

I didn't have time nor patience for tea. But I couldn't afford to argue with her. It wouldn't take much to piss her off and have her tell me to beat it.

A short while later, she returned to the living room wearing a different outfit, and the maid brought a tea service and set it up on the coffee table in front of the couch. The maid's disapproving glance made clear that tea sets weren't designed for the likes of me. Actually, I was more than conversant with tea in the afternoon, though not from a tea set. My mother and father kept up the custom from the old country; every day around four when my father got home from work, we had tea at the kitchen table. I'd never gotten the hang of balancing a cup on my knee.

Eva was a gracious hostess, another guise she took on easily. "Tell me. What were you doing at the garage and why did you run? You could get yourself killed that way."

She was right. But there were a number of other ways I could get myself killed as well. One of them would be to misplace my trust in a woman of many guises. The gracious and charming hostess Eva had spent the morning with the neither gracious nor charming but decidedly violent Vincent Forlini and Moose McFarland. Not to mention . . .

"How are things with Big Al?" I asked. "I suppose with the union in one back pocket and the Taxi Cab Owners Association in his other back pocket, he's come out ahead."

Eva stiffened; her nose wrinkled with distaste. "The cab drivers received better than they deserved and better than they'd have gotten if the Communists had led the negotiations. They tried to strip the owners of everything they've worked for." She made an unbecoming *harrumph* sound. "I'd like to see how the cab drivers would get along without the taxi owners."

My thinking had things the other way around. "Big Al tell you that? . . . A man who controls both sides of the negotiating table isn't likely to hold himself up." My brain caught up with my mouth then, so I tried to be conciliatory. "Well, the strike's over."

She softened her tone. "I'm glad it's over. It was awful." The outfit she'd changed into was less severe than the one she'd been wearing, this one a light blue number with a full skirt, so she could fling one leg over the other, which she did now quite dramatically. "Why are you all in a huff about the strike? You told me you didn't have anything to do with it . . . You're easily distracted."

I tried to slip a fastball past her. "Did Big Al kill your husband?"

She grimaced. "Are we back to that? Why would he? In terms of Mr. Lucania's overall business interests, Irwin was small potatoes."

"Your husband was a stubborn man. He swindled his business partners. He thought he was tougher than he was. If he tried to swindle Big Al, he'd get more than a rap on the knuckles."

She sipped tea from a delicate porcelain cup before placing the cup gently back on the saucer balanced on her knee. "Well, at least this time you're not accusing me. Am I no longer a suspect?"

"I hope you're not. I'm counting on it."

With a tiny smile and maybe a blush, she considered her tea cup for longer than you'd expect before taking another sip. "If you think Mr. Lucania killed my husband, why do you want the photos from that shady private eye?"

It was a fair question. "I don't know who killed your husband. Mr. Lucania might have killed him. You might have killed him. A woman he misused and misled might have killed him. If that's what happened, the photos might tell us a lot."

"Who's the woman?"

I didn't answer.

"You know who she is, or you think you know. You just don't want to tell me."

Eva was right to think I held some things back from her. She was no dummy but she was wrong on one count. I didn't know who the woman in the photos was. I had suspicions. Some of them I didn't want to think about.

We were quiet on the ride downtown, each grappling with our own thoughts. When we got to Bauer's building, the odor from his office met us in the hallway and accompanied us in. Stale cigar smoke; stale whiskey; stale air from the windowless outer office; and stale Bauer from the inner office. He sat behind his desk, wearing the same suspenders and what looked like the same shirt he wore the last time I saw him but no hat this time. He didn't stand when we entered.

But he did study me for a moment wearing a scowl. I knew he was thinking about the break-in and if it was me. He wanted to say something so badly he clenched his teeth tightly enough to crack them. But he didn't. Neither did I.

"You got the dough?" he said.

I told him I wanted to see the photos first.

His face crumbled. You might think he was going to cry. "Whaddaya mean? What the hell's that? You wanna see the pictures, you pay me. That's it. I ain't showin' you nothin'." He talked tough but his shifty expression didn't back it up. He turned on Eva. "We made a deal. No welching. That ain't right."

"Mrs. Johnson needs to know it's her husband in the photos and that he's in a compromised position with a woman. Otherwise the photos are no good to her. While we don't mistrust you"—I almost choked getting that one out—"not knowing Mr. Johnson all that well, you might have gotten the wrong man."

"I don't make mistakes." Even Bauer had a hard time swallowing that one. But we all let it fly. "Show me the money."

I held out the C-note, pulling it back when he reached for it. He didn't drool but it looked like he did. "That's not enough," he said. But Gil was right. Clearly, it was.

"That's all they're worth," I said.

After a moment of sulking, he very deliberately took a large manila envelope from his desk drawer and beckoned for Eva to come behind him. When she did, he slid a half dozen photos from the envelope onto the desk in front of him, placing them so she could see but not touch them.

She leaned over and looked at them for a long moment. When she straightened up, her eyes clouded with pain but no tears. "It's Irwin. His fat ass on top of a skinny woman."

I gave Bauer the C-note and he handed the envelope to Eva. We headed out—no smiles, no goodbyes, no thank yous—and got as far as the waiting room. I heard something or caught a quick glimpse of someone and sensed danger but it was too late. Moose McFarland and his running partner Joe O'Keefe stood in front of me, O'Keefe holding a small revolver, which I took to be Smith & Wesson .38, a dead ringer for mine, pointed at my midsection.

"Get out of here," O'Keefe said to Eva.

Her eyes searched mine.

"Nice play," I said.

"No." Her eyes were wide and wild.

"I'll take that." O'Keefe grabbed the manila envelope from her hand and pushed her toward the outer door.

"And I'll take that." Moose reached inside my jacket to take my .38. After he grabbed it, he took a short step back and swung, slapping me across the face with it. I went down, blood oozing into my mouth. I felt for my teeth with my tongue and put my hand on my bandaged head to try to protect it.

"You can thank the boss you're not dead, you fuck." Moose's kick caught me square in the chest. I felt a sharp shooting pain and heard my ribs crack. I wasn't out. I was groggy and my mouth hurt like hell. I heard the goons leave and thought: *Why do they want the photos?* I was glad the boss didn't want me dead . . . but not so sure I wasn't about to do something that would change his mind.

Bauer had stayed in his office—my guess would be under his desk—until the coast was clear. He then came to the door of the inner office and bent himself around the door jamb toward me. "You okay?"

On my hands and knees, my mouth full of blood, a stabbing pain in my midsection every time I moved, a new piercing headache—I'd have had to say, if I'd been able to talk, that I was not okay.

"You want me to call someone?"

I tried to shake my head—a mistake; you'd think by then I'd know better—and gurgled out a sound that started out as "men's room" and ended up babble. I struggled to my feet and staggered out the door and along the hallway holding onto the wall until I found it. I spit blood, rinsed my mouth, and pressed a damp paper towel against the gash on my cheek. I felt like a moron for letting Eva take me down the garden path.

Who sent his thugs after me? Why? Eva had talked to Forlini that morning. I didn't know if she'd talked with Big Al. I needed to think . . . This wasn't easy for a man who'd been belted with a tire iron a couple of days back and a few minutes ago smashed in the teeth with a .38.

Moose had said the boss didn't want me dead. At first, I'd assumed he meant Big Al—thinking the Mob boss had taken a shine to me after our brief encounter and decided to spare me despite my transgressions. Now I wasn't so sure. Who knew about the plan besides Eva and me? I'd told Gil. No one else. Artie didn't even know what we were up to.

It was possible Eva had run our plan to get the photos past Big Al and for some reason he wanted the photos, so he'd told Forlini to send the goons. Yet why would he want photos of Johnson and his paramour? This left Forlini. I couldn't think of any reason he'd want the photos either. But Forlini was dumber than Big Al and meaner, so I'd give him the benefit of the doubt. He could have wanted to throw a monkey wrench into my investigation for some reason or no reason.

When I got back to the hallway, a frantic Eva Johnson came running toward me. "I didn't know. I swear I didn't know they'd come here."

"You told Forlini about the photos." I said this with absolute conviction, though I had no idea if it was true.

She withered. Her voice was like a child's. "I didn't mean to. I didn't know he would—"

Maybe she was lying, maybe not. I didn't care. "This is what you're going to do." I grabbed her arms when she reached toward me and squeezed hard just above her wrists. "You know how to reach Big Al?"

She relaxed her arms, not fighting me. "You're hurt. You need a doctor or the hospital. I'll take—"

I spat blood onto the floor. "You're gonna call Big Al and tell him you need to see him right now . . . You're going to beg."

Her eyelids fluttered; her lip quivered. She shook her arms loose from my hold and shrunk back from me. "I can't . . . He won't . . ."

"Beg. Threaten to kill yourself. Tell him you gotta see him now. It's about me. I've gone off my rocker. You can't talk on the phone. Don't let him say no. You got that? He can't say no."

I grabbed her wrist again and pulled her toward Bauer's office. When she stopped, I yanked her arm and she yelped like a pup. I realized I was hurting her and let go. Bauer tried to close the door to his office when he saw us coming, but I got my foot in the way and shoved the door with my shoulder, knocking him back into his office. He stood near his desk, started to say something but thought better of it.

Eva got on the phone. It took some doing to get through to Big Al, but she kept at it, glancing at me every few seconds, her eyes pleading. Once she got to the big guy, she did a good job. Even I who put her up to it thought she was hysterical when she told Big Al over and over she had to see him. It sounded like he agreed without much of a fight.

"I'm to meet him at the downstairs bar at Sardi's in an hour." She held the phone receiver toward me, her face frozen with fear. "What are you going to do?"

Bauer watched us like he'd paid admission. "You were talking to—" He couldn't utter the name. "You're not taking back the dough, right? I did my part fair and square." His voice rose an octave. "You gotta leave me outta this. I didn't know you had anything to do with . . ." Again, he couldn't say the name.

Eva's expression was grim. "He'll kill you . . . He'll kill *us*. When he finds out I tricked him, he'll . . ."

She was right. "Don't-dare-say-his-name" would have to kill me if he didn't return my photos. I didn't tell her this. But she could tell by looking at me.

"I've got to see the photos," I told her. With my brain misfiring on a couple of cylinders, I couldn't hold onto a thought long enough to attach it to the next one. "What did the woman in the picture look like? Did you ever see her before?"

Eva shook her head. "She looked young. Small. Pretty enough, not dazzling. Pale skin. Her eyes were closed. You wouldn't take her for a slut."

"Innocent?" The word caught in my throat.

Eva glowered. "How innocent? She's fucking my husband."

"Can you tell where they are, where the photo was taken?"

Bauer spoke, catching me by surprise. "A hotel on Eighth Avenue. Businessmen in the garment district use it for matinees. I have an arrangement with the manager, so I could take pictures."

"Tell me about the woman."

He snapped his suspenders and shook his head. "Nothin', just the photos. I never tailed her. Only saw her in the hotel."

"What color eyes?"

"Brown, I think. Sad-eyed."

I hustled Eva out of Bauer's office and into Artie's cab. I told him we were going to Sardi's but to drive over by the piers where he could park until it was time for Eva to meet Big Al. I needed to nurse my wounds, get my head on straight. We stopped at a hot dog cart so I could get a soda and take some aspirin and then on to the waterfront in Chelsea. He parked in front of one of the open lots alongside an empty berth.

The river was peaceful, green and brown, rolling rhythmically like a lullaby, flowing south because the tide was going out. I hoped I wouldn't shortly be going out with it.

We walked out along an empty pier. When we got almost to the end, Eva sat on a piling. I stood in front of her and we watched the river. I was sore all over and, no doubt, a sorry mess to look at.

"I don't know if this heist was Big Al's idea," I told her. "I'm betting it wasn't. Forlini's stupid enough to do this on his own. If he did, Big Al might put the kibosh on it if you say pretty please." Did she roll her eyes? She looked skeptical. I pushed on. "The big guy thinks of himself as a diplomat. He stays away from rough stuff when he can. If I thought he'd harm you, I wouldn't ask you to do this."

We both knew this was easy for me to say and that she'd be the one to take the lumps if I was wrong. She was polite enough not say this, yet I had to believe my willingness to throw her to the sharks knocked me down a few pegs in her estimation.

She watched as a cargo ship parked in the pier upriver from us, and then a tug boat escorting an ocean liner down river toward the Narrows and the mighty ocean beyond.

"I don't think he'll hurt me." She sounded calm, not at ease but not jittery, ready for what was coming, resigned maybe. "But it's not like he's going to do what you want because I ask him to." She turned her gaze on me, penetrating like a search-light. "*You* scare me. What are *you* going to do?"

"I'm betting it was Forlini who pulled this stunt and for no good reason." I didn't know if I was talking to her or me. "Big Al might not want to have to clean up a mess Forlini made when he doesn't have to—and there will be a helluva mess if I go after Forlini for the photos; I can guarantee you that."

"And if you're wrong?" She spoke softly; you might say sympathetically. "Is this crusade of yours important enough to die for?"

It was a question I should have given more thought to. I knew who I was up against; I knew what the danger was, and I'd thought about it, but tactically, not whether I should quit rather than get killed.

"I don't like risking my life," I told her. "I don't want to die. I've got a job to do. I might be better off if I hadn't taken it on. But I did take it on, so I've got to do it. This means I have to get my hands on the photographs. I'm sorry you're in this. But it's not a lot of risk for you and you're the only one who can do it."

"You said you didn't know who the woman is. Do you? Is that why you want to see the photos so badly?"

I didn't answer. Something was coming together in my head, not anything I was ready to look in the eye. When the time came I would. I had one more day.

Artie pulled up in front of Sardi's in the dead calm of late afternoon, too late for lunch, too early for the pre-theater cocktail hour. Despite the doldrums, the doorman was on his toes and opened the door of the cab, holding Eva's elbow as she gracefully stepped out.

When he took a look at me, he recoiled like he'd seen a dead rat in the back seat of the cab. Blood had coagulated around the jagged cut on my face and dried on the front of my shirt and the lapels of my suit jacket. The rap in the mouth had opened the cut on my head too, so the bandage was caked with blood and dirt-streaked from the dusty floor in Bauer's office. Every time I moved I got a shooting pain in my ribs to go with my headache; I'm sure my face reflected how I felt, so I looked like I belonged in a gutter in the Bowery instead of on the sidewalk in front of Sardi's.

Undaunted, I grimaced and grunted my way out of the cab and pointed myself toward the entrance. The doorman prepared to bar my way but he didn't need to. Big Al had provided for that. Two goons, gentlemanly looking thugs, came out of

Sardi's. One escorted Eva into the restaurant; the other one stood in front of me and heaved out his chest. I climbed into the front passenger seat of the cab. Artie offered me a cigarette and lit it for me.

"Been a rough day," he observed.

"It has." This time I remembered not to nod. I dragged on the cigarette.

"Nice lady." He gestured with his head toward Sardi's.

This gave me pause. Eva came across as elegant, polite, stunning in looks, down-to-earth in manners. Was she a nice lady? For all I knew, she was sipping a cocktail, planning with Big Al how to get rid of my body.

"You know I got a good look at them mugs that worked you over just now . . ."

"So did I."

Artie kept at it. "I saw them when they went in and when they came out. I mean I could testify if you need me." He shifted uneasily. "The last time, when the cops asked who worked you over, I told them I didn't see the guy. But I knew it was Moose." He studied his cigarette for a moment. "This morning, I felt bad when he came after you. But then you got the drop on him, so I didn't feel so bad. Now he comes and works you over again. I think it's partly my fault. So this time I'll say it was him. It was Moose."

Artie's confession and offer to finger a mobster took some moxie. It's not easy for a working stiff to stand up to professional hoodlums. "If it comes to that, I'll let you know."

Everything was quiet until the lit end of the cigarette burned my fingertips and I jumped.

Artie's forehead wrinkled. "You need to get some rest."

I was doing just that, nodding off again, when Artie roused me. "Here she comes!" It sounded like he saw the cavalry riding toward us. He leaned across the back of the seat to open the door for her. I started to get out to get in the back seat with her but it was too much effort, so I gave up.

I half turned in my seat. "Dapotos. Djuegetem?" Hearing myself, I didn't know what I'd said.

Despite my garbled question, she answered it. "They're coming. You were right. He didn't say it was Forlini's idea to take them. He asked what it was about and if I knew what I was doing. He borrowed the bartender's phone and made a call in which he spoke forcefully, though I didn't hear what he said. When he sat down again, the waiter brought him— brought us both—new drinks. I hadn't hardly touched mine.

"'It was a misunderstanding,' he told me." She sighed deeply. "He talks in riddles, so he might have told me what this misunderstanding was. If he did, I didn't get it. The important thing is he said someone would bring the damn things to my house tonight."

She caught on that something wasn't right with me and leaned forward, studying my face for a moment. I couldn't get my eyes to focus on her while she did this and she noticed that, too. "You don't look so good. I think you're more badly hurt than you think." She addressed Artie. "We should take him to a hospital."

I knew what had happened to me; I'd taken two pain pills earlier instead of the usual one because I'd gotten them mixed up with the aspirin. Now they were catching up with me. I did understand we'd be getting the photos later. And I for damned sure wasn't going to any hospital. When I turned and tried to tell her this, my mouth got itself unhinged and I garbled the words.

I felt her hand on my forehead. She'd reached over from the back seat, so her face was near mine. I got a faint whiff of flowers. Scent? Flowers? My mind short-circuited. I had the robe from the murder scene in Artie's trunk and I had Eva. I steadied myself and said distinctly, "We must spot ap da gardge."

Artie understandably didn't get it. Eva took charge. "We're not stopping anywhere. If you won't go to the hospital, we'll go to my place so you can rest and clean up and wait for the photos."

"Spot apt da gardge."

"Okay." She told Artie to go by the Johnson Transportation garage.

After a number of tries, I got through to Artie that he was to get the robe from the trunk, bring it to Fat Tony and then bring Tony out to the cab. Artie did this and Fat Tony came out, his head drooping like he was being led to his hanging. I gestured toward the back seat. Poor Tony looked bewildered. After a couple of fruitless gestures, I rolled down the window and told him to open the back door. He opened it like he expected Eva to get out. When she didn't, he closed the door and stepped back. I gestured for him to come close to my window. He approached me like you would a steep cliff.

"Scent." I forced myself to enunciate carefully. "Sniff."

His eyes crossed. "I didn't smell nothin' on that robe."

"Smell her," I said. "Is that the smell?" His confusion mounted. "Your fucking sniffer . . . Sniff her! . . . Is that the smell?"

He shook his head. "I coulda told you no; I coulda told you no this morning." He poked his head through my window, pushing my bandaged bloody head out of the way. "I'm sorry, Mrs. Johnson," he said to the back seat. "He's crazy and he latched onto me and I can't get rid of him. He's trying to get me killed."

"That's okay, Tony," she said. "It's not your fault. He's driving us all crazy."

She told Artie to head for Riverdale. I had some thought of arguing, but I'd used up all of my energy on Tony and his sniffer. My eyes closed and I nodded off again before the end of the block.

When we got to Eva's house, she and Artie helped me inside to a guest room, where they helped me out of my clothes so I could take a shower. Eva was calmly efficient, in an odd way motherly, not a guise I'd have picked for her. Handing me a fluffy towel and a pair of silk pajamas, she told me to shower and lie down; she'd wake me when the photos got there.

I did what she told me and awoke sometime later, sore but halfway alert. I was sitting on the edge of the bed in my silk pajamas trying to gather my wits when I heard a gentle knock on the door. Eva had changed clothes again and wore a pastel blue lounging outfit, a robe and matching pants, maybe silk, maybe satin; whatever it was shimmered and flowed gracefully as she moved.

She carried an armload of clothes, a couple of suits and a bunch of other things, as well as a bottle of Mercurochrome and Band-Aids. She tended to the cut on my face and said, "The messenger with the photos will be here soon. These are suits my husband grew out of; that is to say, he became too fat to wear. One of them might fit you more or less. It wouldn't be much baggier than the one you were wearing anyway."

She placed the suits on the bed and waved the other articles of clothing at me, dress shirts, ties, undershirts, and boxer shorts. The boxers were silk like the pajamas, which was nice because I'd grown attached to the pajamas.

She left me to get dressed on my own. The shirt was big in the neck and the suit big in the shoulders. The pants fit hiked up with a belt, and when I put on a tie the outfit looked okay. When I came out into the living room, Artie was seated on the couch in front of a plate of dainty triangle sandwiches, a far cry from our kielbasa and pierogi lunch. He'd put quite a dent in the pile.

"Eat," said Eva. "I made some coffee."

I tried to eat, chewing gingerly. The sandwiches were good and the coffee strong. I didn't have much time to think about what she was up to because I heard a car crunch across the stones of the driveway.

"Thanks for waiting," I told Artie.

"You paid me good," he said as he munched.

My insides were in knots waiting for Eva to answer the door.

CHAPTER FORTY-THREE

EVENING

When I opened the envelope the photos slid out, some onto the coffee table, others onto the floor under the table. My heart raced. My throat was dry as dust. My hands trembled. I chased thoughts out of my head as soon as they tried to come in. I felt rather than saw Artie and Eva watching me. As the photos fell, I caught a glimpse of the young woman's face, soft in repose, eyes closed. I'd seen the face before. I picked up the prints and put them back in the envelope. I didn't need to look again. I didn't want to look again.

The dainty sandwich on the plate in front of me stared back at me. I sipped some coffee, gone cold now, to open my throat. I told myself I should think, not act on impulse. I stood. Artie eyed me suspiciously.

"It's going to be a busy night," I said. "If I give you another twenty, will you stay with me?"

He took a moment before he said, "I'm still on the first twenty. Where to?"

"Back to the taxi garage. Frank DeMarco should finish his shift about now."

Eva stood when I did. "You'll be careful, won't you?" Something that could've been worry flickered in her eyes.

As Artie and I headed down the Henry Hudson Parkway,

twilight was fading into darkness and the flood of traffic was coming toward us out of the city we were heading into. It didn't take us long to get to Hell's Kitchen. Frank had parked his cab and was a half block from the garage walking home when we pulled up alongside him. He turned, blinking with surprise.

I bolted out of the cab while it was still moving. "Where's Elena?" My tone would've told him a lot.

He shrunk back from me in alarm. "I'm not gonna tell you. What're you gonna do to her?"

"It's bad. You know better than anyone how bad."

We gave an anguished and protesting Frank DeMarco a ride to his family's apartment house. He sat in the front seat next to Artie, his face a ghastly white in the intermittent glare of the streetlights. I didn't go upstairs; I couldn't face the family. "Tell Elena to meet me by the pier next to the park. She'll know where I mean."

I left Artie parked on Twelfth Avenue and waited on the walkway alongside a vacant Cunard Lines pier, near the park where Elena and I had walked and talked the day we first met. On that warm, cloudless afternoon, with a breeze from the river fluttering her hair, I could never have seen this day of reckoning coming.

This night, she looked small and slight when she came into view. She wore a sweater over her shoulders, a long black skirt, and a dark kerchief on her head. For the first time I saw in her a reflection of the poverty-ravaged, beaten-down women of lost hope who populated the tenements. She walked slowly, haltingly onto the pier. When she got close to me, she said, "Oh dear, what happened to your face?"

I glared at her. "I know about you and Irwin Johnson."

She didn't move, only her lips. "I knew you'd find out. I'm so ashamed I could die."

"Did you kill Johnson or did Frank?"

She stepped nearer to me. "No. No. It wasn't like that." Her gaze was intense. "Harold Williams shot Irwin." Her eyes burned into mine. "I didn't want to tell you. I didn't want you to know I'd been with Irwin . . . It was a terrible mistake. I was so young, so stupid. I didn't know he had a wife. He said he wanted to marry me. I believed him."

Her story poured out. I didn't interrupt. I rooted for her. I wanted what she told me to be true, though it meant the electric chair for Harold.

"I was in the room behind the office—the room you asked me about. I waited for Irwin there . . . I'd been there before. We'd meet there . . ." Her voice faltered. "Harold found out somehow. He'd been watching me, I guess. He snuck up the back stairs from the garage. It was late. The office was deserted."

She put her hands to her face; her shoulders slumped. "I know what you think of me . . ." Her whole body shook as she spoke, a tremor. Her hands covered her face. I could barely hear her. "You couldn't think any worse of me than I think of me."

She might have waited for me to say something, and I wished I could say something. But I didn't.

She found her voice again. "Whenever I saw Harold, I smiled and said hello. I knew about prejudice against Negroes. Frank told me about the South and lynchings and Jim Crow. I understood it wasn't right. Harold was Frank's friend, a comrade. I wanted Harold to know I cared too, that I was on his side, the Negroes' side.

"He took my being friendly the wrong way. Men think like that. Just because you're nice to them that you . . . But I never thought he would . . . Even when I saw him open the door of that room, I didn't know he was there to . . . he wanted . . ." She stopped. For a moment she lifted her arms as if she would reach for me. Then she dropped them and lowered her head. She spoke to the ground. "I'd already . . ."

She put her hands to her face again. "I'm too ashamed to say . . . I was only wearing a robe that was in the closet. I was mortified. I thought he'd see he was in the wrong place and would leave. But I was so ashamed of his knowing about me and . . . why I was there." She leaned her head back, so that she was staring up into the sky. A sound came from her throat, very softly, not words, a moan, like an animal in hopelessness and pain.

"I thought he'd leave and I'd close the door, so I took a step toward him to do that, to close the door. But he grabbed the robe and pulled it open. He put his hands on me. All over me . . . Everywhere.

"I pushed him and got away from him. Irwin kept a gun in the drawer of a small bureau near the closet. No one used the room. No one went there. Irwin didn't tell me about the gun. I found it one day when I was waiting for him.

"I pushed Harold . . . I kicked him . . . I got free. I remembered the gun, so I went for it. I got it. But I didn't know how it worked. I thought you pulled the trigger and it went off. I pointed it at him. I thought he'd stop. But he kept coming toward me. I was terrified. I pulled the trigger. But the gun didn't shoot.

"He grabbed me around the waist and took it out of my hand. Just then, Irwin opened the door and saw us. Harold let go of me and turned on Irwin. He knew what would happen to him for trying to rape a white woman. And he knew how to work the gun. He shot Irwin."

This wasn't the story I expected. I said the first thing that came into my head. "Why didn't he shoot you?"

Elena hung her head. "I don't know."

"Did he finish what he started? Did he rape you?"

The questions shocked her as if I'd slapped her. "No," she whispered.

"And the gun?"

She froze. Her eyes searched mine. "He took it."

"Who put Johnson's things in the trunk of the cab? Who called the police?"

She was stumped again. "I don't know."

"Yes you do, Elena."

She was trembling from head to foot. "I don't. Irwin staggered out into the hallway. Harold went out after him. I got dressed as fast as I could. I didn't know what he would do. When I came out in the hallway, Irwin was lying there. Harold was gone. I knew Frank was working a double, so he'd have his cab and be home eating dinner at that time. I called him from the office and he came and got me."

I tried to picture what she was telling me. Harold shot Johnson, who staggered out into the hallway and died. Harold had the gun. She was the witness. Why didn't he kill her?

"How did he know you wouldn't call the police?"

"He knew I'd gone to that room to meet Irwin. I knew he killed Irwin. If he didn't say what he knew, I wouldn't say what

I knew. I couldn't stand for anyone to know what I'd done, what I'd been doing. I'd have died first."

I stared at her. She might have thought that. But Harold wouldn't have known she did. I wanted so much to believe her, I could almost overcome my doubts. Almost. "I don't understand why he didn't kill you," I said, as if I were thinking out loud.

She stared back at me. When she spoke, it was in an eerie otherworldly tone. "Of course. It would be fine with you if I'd gotten raped . . . and then murdered along with Irwin. Now you know what I did. You think I'm a whore." She burst into tears, turned, and raced down the pier away from me toward her home.

I called Gil Silver from a phone booth at the end of the pier and told him I needed to see him. Somehow, he knew without my telling him how urgent it was. Artie drove me over to his apartment building and said he'd wait. When I called from the desk in the lobby, Gil said to come up. I asked him to meet me in the lobby. It wasn't a social visit.

We sat on leather chairs across from the doorman's desk and I told him Elena's confession almost word for word.

"I don't believe it," Gil said.

I had a hard time believing her myself but I didn't like that he'd brushed her off so easily. "Why not?"

He started to answer and stopped. He did this, I knew, to get the tone of his voice under control. He wanted to sound patient and sympathetic, which was against his nature. He didn't like to provide answers that were patently obvious, so his first inclination was to be dismissive. Now he sounded almost kindly.

"Why would he leave a witness? If that's not enough, why would he stop—escaping from a murder scene—to put incriminating evidence in his cab? And if you believe he'd do that, for some reason that I can't fathom, who called the police if no one found the victim until Monday morning?"

I was stuck for an answer but gave it a try anyway. "She wasn't going to tell on Harold so he wouldn't tell on her. So why would she call the cops?"

Gil rolled his eyes. His patience had run out.

"I've gone over her story a dozen times in my head. It could have happened the way she said—no evidence says it did, but no evidence says it didn't." I caught myself talking fast, a panicked edge to my voice.

Gil took off his glasses and rubbed his eyes, weary sadness in them—and the sympathy was back. "Think about her story, Mick. You'll see the holes in it. You know what happened. You've cracked your case. Now you need to nail it down. You know who the killer is."

After I'd stood for a few minutes in front of his apartment building arguing with myself, I had Artie drive me to the taxi stand in front of Grand Central. My headache was fierce, so I thought about another pain pill but decided I needed to keep my head clear even if it meant keeping the pain. When he let me off, I gave him two twenties and told him to go home. He said he only wanted one, but I waved him off. That being the case, he said, he'd pick me up in the morning.

I intended to wait for Sam Jones. I was betting that like a lot of hackies he was a creature of habit; if he finished a fare nearby, he'd come to the Grand Central cabstand. Pacing back and forth in front of the terminal gave me a chance to run

Elena's story through my mind a few more times. Each time I reran it, I rushed through the places where it didn't hold water. Each time it got tougher to do.

This evening, after a dozen other cabs had come and gone, Sam pulled up. No crowd waiting. No cab line. He recognized me right off and remembered the night he helped me look for Harold's alibi witnesses, the elusive backroom gamblers.

"You lookin' for them cats again?" he asked as soon as I opened the cab door. "They been around. I saw Smokin' Joe on the street a couple of days ago."

"I have the time and the money tonight, whatever it takes. They don't have to talk to cops or lawyers, only to me."

Sam threw the meter flag. "Might need to grease some palms. Maybe take a double sawbuck or even a half yard if you want to get to one of dem quick."

It was late enough so that the night people were beginning to come out and the joints around San Juan Hill were starting to jump. With an unsaid understanding, I waited in the cab at each place we stopped at while Sam took a look. We'd worked our way almost to Sixty-Fifth Street through a half dozen or more seedy basement gin joints on and off Amsterdam Avenue when Sam came up out of one of them with two aging zoot suiters in tow. For a brief moment, I wondered if either of them was Slasher.

One guy got in the front seat; the other got in the back seat with me. The guy in front did the talking, leaning over the seat; the one in back with me had an easygoing, languid manner and a wide friendly smile. Nothing the least bit sinister or threatening about him, he watched me with great interest, as if he were a rube in the hinterlands and I was a pygmy on display in a sideshow.

The guy in the front seat, Smokin' Joe—not Slasher—asked why I wanted to know about Harold. When I told them what I was doing and said I'd visited Harold in prison, he asked about his well-being with concern as someone would ask after a mutual friend whom he hadn't seen for a while.

It took a while to persuade them that anything they told me would stay with me. I wouldn't tell the police—or as Smokin' Joe put it, The Man.

"I need to know if Harold was with you because someone says he wasn't." I wanted to be straight with them. But I didn't want to name the someone who said Harold was somewhere else, so I worded what I said carefully. The fact was these guys worked the shady side of the street, made their living playing cards and running various hustles outside the mainstream of life. With little or nothing to do with the workaday world, they had to have their wits about them so weren't likely to fall for any evasiveness or equivocating.

Smoking' Joe pondered what I told him and offered a recap. "So Harold beats the rap on what you got already. You don't need us testifyin'. You askin' us so you know for sure in your own mind, nothin' else?"

I said that was the case. This is where the half-yard came in. What with the tips for Seamus and Marcie Taylor, the hundred smackers I gave Bauer, and the fifty bucks to Smokin' Joe and his pal, I was going through money like a drunken sailor.

I went over again the night Harold played cards with them. "It was definitely that Friday night. It couldn't have been Thursday or Saturday?"

The guy in the back seat with me—who was content to do business without giving a name—shook his head a number of times and the guy in the front seat said Harold only played cards for an hour or two on Friday nights. "So he was there Friday night. He never came no other night. Never came no other time, win or lose."

"He got to the game same time as usual; he couldn't have gotten there an hour or half hour late that night?"

"Same as usual," they both said.

"He didn't act any differently, like something was on his mind, like was upset or nervous?"

The answer this time was emphatic head shakes.

I'd gotten what I needed to know, answers I both wanted and didn't want. I asked the same questions a couple of more times in different ways to be sure but the answers didn't change.

"Harold ain't really a gambler," Smokin' Joe said. "He sat in to pass the time while he waited for a meeting up the street that started at nine o'clock." He narrowed his eyes and assessed me. My guess was he considered if he should say what type of meeting—Communist, for example—but decided not to. "Harold didn't drink so the card game was his thing."

I wanted to ask why they didn't come forward for Harold's trial—how they could sit by and let a man die without trying to do something to stop it. Yet that was what they had done, and I couldn't ask why without sounding like I was accusing them—because I would be accusing them.

I said something like this to Sam as we drove away, after the gamblers went back to life in the city's underbelly with solemn farewells and sincere good wishes but no mention of the fifty smackers—greasing the palm not something a person with class would mention.

Maybe because Sam and I had been together for a while that evening, maybe because he was talking into the darkness as much as he was to me, he said, "Them guys, you know, they don't live in the same world as white folks. They don't go to places you go. They don't live places you live. You might be the only white person they talk to this year. Or last year, too.

"You think they don't care about Harold or what be happening to him? They do. They just know what happened to him is white folks' business and don't have nothin' to do with them. They know they went up to a cop and say they was with Harold the night of the murder, the cops'd figure out a way to send them up the river right alongside Harold. They know they couldn't do nothin' to help him. He might as well be in another country."

"Can I believe them?"

"You coulda believed Harold."

CHAPTER FORTY-FOUR

MORNING

True to his word, Artie rang my downstairs doorbell shortly after 8:00 the next morning. I picked up coffee and bagels from the deli on Queens Boulevard and we headed to Manhattan. The time had come to lean on Frank. Artie's years of experience behind the wheel came in handy. We tried a half dozen hack stands before we found his cab parked in front of the Rialto in Times Square. He didn't see me coming when I slid into the back seat or we might have had a car chase through the streets of Manhattan.

When he caught sight of me through his rearview mirror, his eyes widened as if he were watching the Grim Reaper climb into his cab until his expression crumbled into misery and he looked away. A few seconds later, he found his courage and met my gaze in his mirror, this time with the haunting expression of dread you might expect on a man facing his conscience.

"You can throw the meter flag and drive if you'd like," I said. I hated what I had to do; I wasn't cut out to kick a man when he's down. At one time, I'd imagined when a case was about to break I'd feel triumphant, having rebalanced good and evil in a tiny part of the world at least for a moment. Instead, as I got closer to the truth of this one I was being smothered by foreboding.

Frank threw the meter and pulled away from the curb. "I don't have to talk to you. I don't have to incriminate myself." He realized he'd put that the wrong way and tried again. "I don't have to say anything that might be held against me. I got a Constitutional right. It's the Fifth Amendment."

A lot of good the Fifth Amendment did his comrades when they held the Constitution up in front of its supposed defenders at the Smith Act trial. "It's a sad sorry mess," I said. "Elena told me a story last night that broke my heart. What I'll hear today will be worse."

Frank drove a couple of blocks before he started talking. "Life dealt Elena a dirty deal. She'd have been better off if she'd been born homely as a mule. Being pretty has been a curse for her whole life. When she was little, she was so cute, people would stop us in the street to tell her how sweet and pretty she was."

Driving was good for Frank. Slipping from lane to lane, slowing, speeding up, stopping, starting, he became part of the cab, part of the flow of traffic. It was as if behind the wheel in the crush of the city's traffic he'd become whole.

"It didn't do her any good, being pretty. It didn't put food on the table or find us an apartment that had heat. But it spoiled her all the same. It gave her airs and let her dream she wouldn't end up stuck in the slums like the rest of us, that she wouldn't spend her life in a stitching shop and a tenement.

"She didn't see that the beaten and battered women of the slums once had been pretty girls like her. But their prettiness faded and being poor wore them down, and they never did get out of this life of misery."

Frank half-turned to look at me over the back of the driver's seat. "Don't get me wrong. Even with her airs and her dreams,

Elena was a good kid. She was good to Ma, did good in school, was as prim and proper as the child of a country squire.

"She was kind and sweet to everyone, too sweet. Grown men gave her things, dolls, candy, toys; they paid attention to her, hugged her, pawed her, bounced her on their laps."

We'd stopped at a light when he'd turned to look at me over the seat. His face was gaunt; his expression hollow. I didn't say anything. The light changed and he turned back to the street.

"She was my little sister; she followed me like a lamb, so I had to watch out for her, and I did. You couldn't count the black eyes and bloody noses I got from dragging her away from some guy in the neighborhood mauling her. Then she grew up and she wanted fancier clothes than the other girls, nicer shoes, saving up to get her hair done, wearing make-up. She wasn't the least bit boy crazy and she didn't have a bunch of girl friends to giggle with. But she got better and better at getting things from boys and from men.

"She started to see if she played her cards right, she could use being pretty to get a rich husband and a way out of the slums. Her and I saw life differently. I wanted to build a workers' movement and make life better for everyone—what we say, 'rising with your class, not from it.'

"I'd give her books to read. But she'd rather read romance books and fashion magazines. She understood what I was talking about. She wasn't selfish; she wanted a better life for Ma and me, for everyone. But she wanted her better life now. She set her sights on going after a rich man and she didn't know what she was doing. She didn't know she'd be a sitting duck for a rich man to use her for what he wanted and then throw her away like an old shoe."

We were quiet as he drove the city streets while the meter clicked away. The question I needed to ask was the first one I'd asked Elena the night before. But I held back. Frank had driven over to the far west side in the Fifties, into Hell's Kitchen, like a chicken heading home to roost.

We were stopped in traffic on Tenth Avenue and I watched a stickball game on the side street—remembering Franklin and a stickball game in Brooklyn what seemed like ages ago—a dozen grimy hellions running, shouting when a kid hit the ball; regrouping when the ball was caught, settling down, the pitcher throwing the ball again, the batter hitting it again; all hell breaking loose again. Until the ball went between two parked cars and everything stopped. The crew gathered, both teams, around and between the cars looking down. The spaldeen had gone down the sewer grate. The game was over.

"You knew she was having an affair with Irwin Johnson?"

"No." Frank stared straight ahead, holding the steering wheel in death grip. "I'd have stopped it if I knew. I'd have stopped if I had to ki—" He caught himself and gagged on the rest of the words.

"Are you going to stick with the story Elena told me last night, that Harold tried to rape her and shot Johnson when he discovered them?"

Frank's shoulders tightened; he hunched over the steering wheel. His face reflected in the rearview mirror was drawn into a ghastly grimace. He had a wife and child. I had no idea what he could do or say to get Elena out of this . . . to get himself out of this.

"Is Elena at work?"

He didn't answer. And then he did. "You're going to finish her, you know. You're going to ruin our lives."

Frank didn't tell me anything else. He wouldn't talk about what happened to Irwin Johnson; nor would he admit to knowing anything about the night of the murder, or say where he was or where Elena was. He did tell me Elena hadn't gone to work and dropped me a few doors from his family's apartment building.

This time I did go upstairs. She wasn't at home. Her mother—her face furrowed and careworn; her eyes black with despair—said Elena went out walking. A mother's eyes begged me to tell her what trouble had come to her child. She knew I knew what it was and that it was terrible.

Artie had followed Frank's cab on a doomed procession through the west side streets. Some men develop an unshakeable loyalty to their fellow man. Maybe it was the war that did it. Maybe it was innate. Frank's loyalty to his cause, his loyalty to his sister. Artie's loyalty to me whom he hardly knew.

Now he drove me slowly through the teeming slums of Hell's Kitchen. It had been hot all week and would be another scorcher, already in the high eighties before noon. The stench from the garbage cans along the curbs was as thick as fog. Men in undershirts and women in house dresses sat on stoops. On one block, firemen had opened a hydrant and a swarm of barefoot, bedraggled, half-dressed kids danced in the shower.

I found Elena in DeWitt Clinton Park, the haven from the city's rush and roar by the Hudson where we first talked. She sat on a bench, a small, forlorn figure, across from the statue of the World War I soldier. If she saw me coming toward her, she gave no sign. I sat down beside her.

"My father was in that war," she said as we both looked at the statue rather than at one another, "the first war. I didn't know that he was until after he left us. Ma said what happened to him in the war was why he was a drunk."

At the far end of the park, an ocean liner was parked in a slip, its engine rumbling softly, smoke billowing from its smoke stack. Elena turned to look that way, so I did, too.

"I knew you wouldn't fall in love with me if you knew what I'd done . . . if you knew my past. A girl doesn't get to make mistakes like that."

I tried to meet her gaze but she wouldn't look at me.

Her voice was shrill. "You knowing that happened . . . my doing that . . . ruined everything." She turned to me, the girlishness gone from her face. "Do you love me?"

"My heart is breaking if that's what you're asking." I heard the choked, haggard sound of my own voice as if it belonged to a wretched despairing stranger.

She stood and began walking. I followed and caught up. We walked along a path beneath a canopy of sycamore trees toward Twelfth Avenue, the passenger ship terminal, the ocean liner, and the river. Ornamental iron railings lined both sides of the walk. No one was around.

"I wanted you to love me more than anything. If you did, you would understand I made a terrible mistake, but you'd forgive me." She stared straight ahead as she spoke.

I didn't know if she meant the mistake was her affair with Irwin Johnson or killing Harold. "Maybe I am in love with you," I said. "It doesn't help. It makes it worse." Once more I didn't recognize the hoarse rasping of my own voice.

She faced me, her eyes alive with hope. "We could go

away . . . to Hollywood. You could . . ." She studied my face and what she saw stopped her. She began walking again, watching her feet as she walked. "You'll turn me in?"

"I have to."

"No you don't. If you loved me, loved me more than anything, you'd let me go; you'd take me away."

She talked like we were living in a romance novel where everything turns out happily in the end, where true love overcomes all. Ours wasn't a romance; it was a tragedy.

I heard my own voice again as if it were separate from me, disembodied. "I won't let a man die for something he didn't do."

"But you'll let me die? You'll send me to the electric chair?"

We'd reached a secluded section of the park near Twelfth Avenue, the walk meandering under a grove of trees. I looked down. Elena had a snub-nosed revolver in her hand. "I shot a man to death. I could do it again. The second time wouldn't make any difference."

I stared at the gun and thought I might die, but I wasn't afraid. It wasn't that I thought she wouldn't pull the trigger or that I thought I could disarm her. What went through my mind was her killing me was one possible outcome of where we'd gotten to. Harold might die in the electric chair; Elena might go to jail for the rest of her life; I might die today in the park. At that moment, none of the outcomes seemed better than any of the others. She began walking slowly, her head bowed, the snub-nose at her side.

"You might love me. That's not enough. Sometimes a man loves a woman so much he'll do anything for her."

"Loves her enough to kill for her? To let an innocent man die for something she did?"

She stopped; her voice rose. "Yes. You don't know him. You know me. What happens to him anyway if he goes free? He'll drive a stupid taxi and get married and have kids and be poor and live in the slums and be miserable and who knows maybe he'll turn into a drunk or get fed up and kill his wife or someone else."

She put the gun back into the pocketbook that hung over her shoulder and stopped in front of me. She took both my hands in hers. "I love you. I loved you since the first day I saw you. I would make you so happy. Irwin tricked me. He took advantage of me. He ruined me. That's what rich people do. I should have listened to Frank. So what if I killed Irwin? He was a horrible man." Her eyes had gone wild and desperate. She squeezed my hands pulling them toward her, trying to put my arms around her.

"I could make up for what I did. You could help me. Letting that man die would be a terrible thing. But we had to do it. We did it because we had to be together. We loved one another more than anything. We'll make up for what we did. We'll do good for everybody. We'll make up for the bad we did."

She made one more effort to get my arms around her, pulling on them and pushing her body against mine. When I held back, she dropped her arms and began walking away from me slowly toward the fence at the end of the park. I watched her walk. I should have taken the gun. I knew I should have but the moment passed. And then it was too late. She bent forward. I thought she was crying. I thought I'd tell her I'd stick with her; she wouldn't be sentenced to death; she'd get out of prison someday; I'd wait for her. I saw a quick glint of sunlight on metal near her hand and lunged for her but too late. She put the gun in her mouth and pulled the trigger.

CHAPTER FORTY-FIVE

MIDAFTERNOON

The first cops on the scene—at first two, but soon a half dozen, and then more—weren't sure but maybe Elena hadn't killed herself; maybe I'd killed her. If they'd given me a lie detector test at the scene, I'd have failed it because I believed I did kill her. When the cops weren't throwing questions, I sat on a bench with my face in my hands. Artie sat on the bench with me for a while and then went back to sit in his cab.

He'd been waiting on Twelfth Avenue and heard the shot, or maybe he saw what happened and flagged down a police car. He came running behind the cops roaring into the park. Frank arrived soon after the cops or maybe it wasn't soon. I had no idea of passing time.

A couple of cops stood alongside Frank while he sat on a bench not far from me and sobbed, his shoulders slumped and shuddering, his face between his hands. He'd looked at me when he first got to the park but from a distance, yet not so far away that I couldn't see the hatred in his eyes. After that, he didn't look at me. The uniformed cops kept everyone away from Elena's body and kept an eye on the witnesses, which was me and no one else.

I asked one of the cops about Len Volpe. He was surprised

I knew Len's name and said the homicide team would get there soon and take over. He didn't know if it would be Len.

"Could you let Detective Volpe know I'm asking for him?"

The cop wasn't sure he could do this. Officers on the scene didn't get to decide which detective they called. He didn't think suspects got to make requests either. Whatever happened, Volpe turned up not long after I'd asked the cop about him. He sat down on the bench beside me where Artie had been sitting.

"She confessed to you?" He rubbed his chin and watched the crime scene crew do its work; without looking at me, he said, "I don't know if that's enough to charge her with the Johnson murder before tomorrow."

My heart stopped. The trees and shrubs and lawn wavered in front of my eyes. "I'm going to pass out." Volpe grabbed me and steadied me. I took a couple of deep breaths. "Harold's execution is tomorrow."

Volpe's face reflected this grim knowledge. "If she gets charged isn't up to me. It's the DA's office. They might not go out on a limb to stop an execution with what I have."

I grabbed his lapels and said, "You've got to—" I shouldn't have. I knew better. Putting your hands on a cop is something you can't ever do. Volpe, from instinct, grabbed my wrists; a uniformed cop got his arm around my neck from the side, pulled me off the bench, and pushed me face down onto the ground. Another cop knelt on my back and they pulled my arms up behind me, mashing my damaged face into the macadam walkway as they wrestled my wrists into bracelets. I didn't resist.

Volpe bellowed at them to stop, so they stopped and took

off the cuffs, the guy kneeling on my back giving me one more good push with his knee—like the junkyard dog getting in one more bite—crushing my cracked ribs with such a shot of pain I gave out a yowl you could have heard in Brooklyn.

I needed Artie after all. When I left the park, he was sitting behind the steering wheel in his cab like an old hound waiting for a command. I had to find Gil Silver, a search that took us to his office, the courthouse at Foley Square, from there to the federal courthouse in Brooklyn. I caught up with him at lunch with a couple of other lawyers at a Syrian restaurant on Atlantic Avenue. I didn't have to say anything. He put down his utensils, pushed himself away from the table, and walked with me outside. I told him what happened and what Volpe said.

"The brother," Gil said. "Take me to him."

This wasn't how it was supposed to work. Folks came to Gil; he didn't go to them. Artie drove us to the tenement that housed the DeMarco family. When we pulled up outside, Gil said, "Wait here," and went in. Close to an hour later he came out. Artie drove us to his office. Gil didn't say anything and I didn't ask.

"He signed an affidavit," Gil said when we got to his office. He held out a legal pad. "Write out what you told me earlier that she said." I sat at Effie's desk and wrote. Before I got too far, he came out of his office and said, "Leave out any speculation you might have about the brother at the crime scene. You didn't see him there, did you?"

I finished my affidavit. Gil grabbed it and headed to the district attorney's office; from there, with an ADA in tow, he gathered up the criminal court judge who presided over

Harold's trial, and dragged them both over to the Court of Appeals. I was still in his office waiting—along with Artie who for reasons of his own wouldn't leave me, even though I told him there was nothing we could do but wait. Around 11:00, Gil called and told me to go home. Nothing more would happen tonight.

After the call, Artie drove me home, stopping at a liquor store on Queens Boulevard so I could buy a bottle of Irish whiskey. I tried to give him another twenty when he dropped me off. But he shook his head. We said goodbye. Artie was one of the good guys who understood that sometimes it's better to not say anything. I sat at my kitchen table and drank a bottle of whiskey and smoked a pack of cigarettes until the sky darkened and much later began to lighten again beyond the fire escape outside my kitchen window.

CHAPTER FORTY-SIX

AND LATER

Around 10:00 Gil called to tell me the governor had issued a stay of execution. He'd struck out in court but still had a few strings to pull. I didn't ask how he did it. He wouldn't have told me anyway.

Soon after, Duke Rogowski sent me a check for $1,000, paying for more days than I worked and covering all of my expenses. He included an invitation to a homecoming party for Harold at the new union headquarters but I didn't go. I also had an invitation to Franklin Williams's birthday a few days after that, which I did go to. The bandage was gone, my face had healed, my ribs only hurt when I laughed.

The birthday party turned out to be an unofficial welcome home party for Harold as well. I'd guess every family on the block showed up. The kids were playing a modified stickball game as Harold watched, stopping now and again to shake hands with a well-wisher.

His smile grew wider when I approached him. "I'm happy you came along. Look at all this . . . I didn't expect this kind of ruckus." We surveyed the festivities in front of us. Folks from grandparents to toddlers meandered back and forth across the street in front of his mother's building, everyone stepping aside, waving good-naturedly when the infrequent car nosed its way through the crowd.

Rickety makeshift tables on either side of the street overflowed with every kind of food you could imagine—fried chicken, ham, fried fish, ribs and barbecue, macaroni and cheese, baked beans, hush puppies, cornbread, collard greens, and salads. A grill cooked hot dogs for the kids. Music blared from a record player set up in a first-floor apartment window.

After another moment Harold laughed and said, "I come across kinfolk today I never knew I had." We stood beside each other awkwardly for a couple of minutes. I'm not much for small talk and I guessed neither was Harold. I asked how old Franklin was, and he told me ten. And I asked if he'd gone back to work or if he'd rest up for a while.

"Back to work. The struggle don't wait," he said, and then quietly, "They tell me it was you saved my life." His dark eyes met mine. "You know there ain't words to thank a body for something like that."

This wasn't what I wanted to talk about. I didn't feel any triumph, nothing to crow about. I was glad Harold was alive but I wasn't glad Elena was dead. You'd think when you got the justice you were aiming for, it would turn out better than that. "It wasn't just me," I said for something to say, "I did my job."

Franklin came up to bat then. I nodded toward him. "He was the boss. Him and your mom. They let me know if I didn't get this right or there'd be hell to pay."

Harold laughed. "Ma says you saved Franklin's life, too. You and Artie, who I didn't hardly know." He pointed me toward the front of the apartment building, where Artie sat at a small card table that had at least six plates of food set down in front of him along with a couple of cans of Rheingold. Harold's mother hovered over him along with a group of admiring neighbors.

Sol Rosen and a few other white folks probably from the Party were shaking hands with the neighbors nearby. Not surprisingly, I didn't see Duke or Forlini. Nor did I see Frank DeMarco. I wondered how that would turn out. What Harold would say to Frank. What Frank would say to him. No one besides me—and Gil—knew the whole story, and probably no one would. I wasn't surprised Gil didn't show up. He never socialized with his clients.

A few weeks after the party, Gil called to tell me he was appearing in court the next morning with Sol Rosen for sentencing on his Smith Act conviction and asked if I wanted to be there. So I went. The sentence was three years but Sol tried to give a speech and wouldn't stop when the judge ordered him to stop, so the judge tacked on an extra year for contempt.

The speech, I'd say, would have connected with everyone in the courtroom; but he didn't get to say it. Yet in light of what happened over the next few years, he wasn't far off base. I got a copy of the speech from Gil before it disappeared from history.

The exchange with the judge went like this:

Sol: Your Honor, I'd like to make a statement.

Judge: No. You've said more than enough already.

Sol's lawyer, Gil Silver: I object.

Judge: Overruled.

Sol: Your Honor, I want to warn the American people. The

real danger is not from the so-called Red Menace but from the anti-democratic crusade to silence any speech that is not given the stamp of approval by the Chamber of Commerce, the National Manufactures Association, and the American Legion . . .

He had a lot more to say, but about then, the US marshals got a gag in his mouth and some handcuffs on him and dragged him out of the courtroom.

The government had subpoenaed Frank DeMarco too, Gil told me. But the Party told Frank not to testify and sent him underground. By then, the Party had given up the free speech fight and determined it needed an underground organization if it was to survive. Frank left his wife and baby behind in Hell's Kitchen with his mother and disappeared. Word had it he went to Mexico.

I paid the back rent on my office from the grand I'd gotten from Duke, put a hundred dollars in a savings account I kept for my daughter, and gave the Franciscans twenty bucks to say a special Mass for Elena. The rest of the money I got from Duke I sent to Frank's wife with the Mass card.

ACKNOWLEGMENTS TK